W9-AAV-360

SHINING SEA

FRUITVILLE PUBLIC LIBRARY
100 COBURN ROAD
SARASOTA, FL. 34240

MIMI CROSS

SHINING SEA

FRUITVILLE PUBLIC LIBRARY
100 COBURN ROAD
SARASOTA, FL. 34240

3 1969 02395 7698

This is a work of fiction. Names, characters, organizations, places, events, and incidents are either products of the author's imagination or are used fictitiously.

Text copyright © 2016 Mimi Cross
All rights reserved.

No part of this book may be reproduced, or stored in a retrieval system, or transmitted in any form or by any means, electronic, mechanical, photocopying, recording, or otherwise, without express written permission of the publisher.

Published by Skyscape
www.apub.com

Amazon, the Amazon logo, and Skyscape are trademarks of Amazon.com, Inc., or its affiliates.

Lyrics from "Alive" written by Pete Yorn © 2006 reproduced with kind permission of the artist. All rights reserved.

ISBN-13: 9781503935532
ISBN-10: 1503935531

Book design by Shasti O'Leary-Soudant

Printed in the United States of America

To my parents.
Thank you for a lifetime of sun and sand
and swimming in the sea.

I to the world am like a drop of water
That in the ocean seeks another drop,
Who, falling there to find his fellow forth,
Unseen, inquisitive, confounds himself.

—*William Shakespeare*

Your senses are sacred thresholds.

—*John O'Donohue*

GOODBYE

Tuneless humming is coming from the bedroom next to mine. I've always been the better singer, no secret. Even before I could talk, I sang. To me, singing feels like . . . flying.

As a little kid I sang in the church choir, later on in the choruses at school, and about six months ago I started writing songs—not that I'd call myself a songwriter yet. My first gig was last week, down in the Mission District. Standing on the spotlit stage of the black box performance space, I played one long set—twelve tunes total—while hipsters watched with crossed arms.

Performing in front of an audience is a good way to tell if your songs are finished.

Or not.

The song I'm trying to capture now definitely falls into the *not* category.

I give the guitar a soft strum—a ghost of a chord slips out. Playing the haunting notes a little louder, I listen for the melody. It'll come, eventually, but we're leaving any minute.

Not just leaving . . . moving.

"Do you know," I whisper sing, *"where lost things go?"*

In the next room Lilah falls silent. The lyrics tangle in my throat.

My fingers fumble, then jerk—playing a rhythmic pattern atop a single minor chord: one and *two*, one and *two*. Words tumble out of me.

"Saint Anthony, can you come around? There's something lost, and it can't be found."

Saint Anthony—is he the one?

A quick Google search on the laptop perched at the end of my bed tells me he is. Saint Anthony is invoked as the finder of lost things. Pulling my guitar closer, I play the line over and over.

"Arion? You up there?"

Dad. After shoving the laptop into my backpack, I shut the guitar in its case and head into the hall. Hands full, I stand in my sister's doorway.

She doesn't see me.

Even as thin as she is, even with the ever-present dark shadows beneath her eyes, Lilah is beautiful. Her features are regular and in proportion. Mine . . . are slightly exaggerated. Nose longer, lips fuller. Now, without music to distract me, the tears I'd vowed not to cry fill my eyes. Brown eyes. On a good day, they're hazel. Maybe.

There's no mistaking the color of my sister's eyes. Bright blue. Her hair is black and shiny, cut straight across her forehead and blunt at her shoulders in a way that has always made me think of Cleopatra, but especially since the accident, when she became a mystery to me. Lilah no longer tells me her every thought. She can't.

My sister blinks her bellflower eyes now, and for a split second—seems to focus on me.

But the illusion vanishes just as quickly. I swallow around the lump in my throat, wondering for the millionth time if she has any idea what's going on.

Her bed is up against the window. In the distance—over a nearly invisible San Francisco Bay—the Golden Gate Bridge hovers in fog. Sitting down beside her on the bed, I lay a hand on one of her legs—feel bones, atrophied muscles. A raw feeling spreads through me, like a dull blade is scraping the underside of my skin.

"So . . . guess it's time for goodbye." I take a deep breath in, let it out slowly—which doesn't help at all. "I'll see you in Rock Hook Harbor. Dad's one-horse hometown . . . Sounds happening, huh?" My attempt at lightheartedness fails completely. The words drop like bricks.

Leaning in, I kiss her cheek.

She turns away, as if looking toward the ghostly water. Or, *is* she looking at the water? Or just staring blankly?

I so want it to be the former. The doctors say it's the latter.

In my chest, a hairline fissure I've fused together with lyrics and chords pops open.

"I love you," I choke out.

She doesn't answer. Of course she doesn't.

Biting down hard on my lip, I stand up, trying not to feel like I'm leaving my best friend stranded. But I am. She is. Stranded. She's *been* stranded, for a year.

Swiping at my eyes, I take a few steps down the hall—then turn suddenly into my parents' room, which is mostly Mom's room now. Dad spends the nights he's here on the living room couch, where, after dinner—usually something complicated he's cooked up involving lots of pots and pans—he falls asleep with the TV on. Blue screen to white noise; maybe the sound helps him. Music works better for me. Or, it used to. I used to lie in bed at night and sing. Lately, all I want to do is sleep.

Like the rest of the house, my parents' bedroom is crowded with canvases. Filled with slashes of color and geometric shapes, each painting has the name "Cici" scrawled in large letters down in the right-hand corner. Mom's pictures pulse with unfamiliar energy, and my nostrils flare at the scent of paint fumes as I move a half-finished piece—an abstract portrait of a girl, I think—that's leaning up against the glass door. Slipping out onto the balcony, I clutch the cold railing and eye a moldering stack of *Psychology Today* magazines. Therapy is Mom's religion.

A pair of paint-splattered jeans hangs off a chair. A handful of paintbrushes soak in a bucket. There's no sign of Dad.

My parents are like a couple of unmoored boats. Drifting. One of the few things they agreed on this past year? The accident was Dad's fault. A pretty stupid conclusion, really, considering he hadn't even been on the boat. But he's a ship's captain. Lilah and I inherited our love of the water from him.

Water. I hate it now. Because of the water, I'm on this balcony almost every day, drawn out here as if for a long-standing appointment, some prearranged meeting between me and my broken heart. I cry here; sometimes I yell. Sometimes I write, and one day, I nearly threw my guitar over the railing.

Splintered wood, snapped strings, I'm interested in broken things.

The circling song lyrics fade at the sound of Mom's strained voice.

"Arion, have you finished saying goodbye to Delilah? Your dad's ready to go."

I stay another second, then scoop up a stray guitar pick from the terracotta tiles and head inside, not paying any attention to the paintings now, just intent on leaving before I get any more upset.

But then I'm passing Lilah's room—and I see it.

The slim black notebook I've searched for probably a hundred times over the past year.

Oh, I've *seen* the palm-size Moleskine with its curled cover, seen it clutched in Lilah's fist, watched as she whisked the small black book beneath her quilt, or shoved it between her sheets. I just haven't been able to get my hands on it, and I've wanted to, desperately.

So many times I've seen her slip the notebook between the oversize pages of the art books that Mom insists on bringing home from the library. She'll hug the book close then—her treasure safe inside—but she'll never actually look at the glossy pages. Not like she looks at that notebook. She looks at that black book like it's the only thing she recognizes.

It's definitely some kind of diary. Not that I ever see her writing in it, not since *before*. But she's always got it on her.

Only, she doesn't have it on her now.

Now, there it is, on the floor next to her bed. And Lilah, there she is, still looking but not looking out the window. Transfixed, it would seem, by the gray bay. As I watch, she lifts one hand, bringing her fingertips to the glass—as if there's something out there she wants to touch.

It's kind of amazing how I do it, how I steal her most precious possession without breaking my stride. How I silently sweep into the room and, bending low, snatch it up—then keep on walking like nothing's happened. Like I'm ten-year-old Lilah herself, that time at the rock and gem shop down near the beach, trying on one sterling silver ring, then another. I'll never forget it, how she smiled at the shopkeeper—maybe even said thank you—then practically skipped out the door, still wearing at least one of the rings. Once outside, she tossed a half-dozen more rings onto the pebbles that served as the shop's front yard, so that she could retrieve them that night when the gem shop was closed, so that *we* could retrieve them.

Eight-year-old me, I'd held the flashlight for her. She'd given me one of the rings as my reward, but only one.

I feel bad taking the book; if I could read it and leave it, I would. But there's no time. Through the hall window I can see Dad standing down in the driveway by the old green Jeep Cherokee, the car that will be mine once we get to Maine.

So I slide the notebook into the pocket of my backpack where it burns a hole so big I think it will surely fall out—pages fluttering like fiery wings—and slap the floor with a sound so sharp, Lilah will shudder to life. She'll spring up and shout at me, her old self at last.

But nothing like this happens.

Leaving Lilah. Taking the notebook. My skin ripples with guilt. But we have to go on ahead. School's starting in a few weeks, plus Dad's new job—they won't hold it any longer.

And really, I have to take the book. I need to know what happened.

Out in the driveway, I crane my neck, trying to see if Lilah's still at the window.

"Hold on," Mom shouts from the house, "I almost forgot!"

Time seems suspended as Dad and I wait by the car, the limbo of the long ride already upon us . . .

Mom reappears holding a square box wrapped in gold paper and a purple ribbon. Balanced on top is a fat cupcake with pink frosting.

"Happy birthday, Arion." Her flinty blue eyes soften. She hands me the awkward duo and gives me an equally awkward hug. "From both of us."

Dad smiles, shakes his head. "Seventeen." He's always been a man of few words.

"Thanks, Mom. Dad." Swallowing hard, I climb into the car with the gifts on my lap. Mom pecks Dad on the cheek, and he gets behind the wheel. As we pull away, she blows me a kiss.

Twisting in my seat, I wave—then look up at the second story.

No Lilah.

My chest hurts so much—I actually glance down. But there's nothing except a smear of pink icing on my shirt, where I'd leaned into the cupcake.

We'll fly back close to Thanksgiving, when Lilah is scheduled for the operation that my parents have finally decided is her best bet: a surgical procedure to implant a device in her brain.

It's not as sci-fi as it sounds. The battery-operated device is kind of like a pacemaker, only for your brain instead of your heart. This kind of surgery is used to treat a variety of disabling neurological symptoms, although I think whoever came up with DBS—deep brain stimulation—was thinking of people with Alzheimer's or Parkinson's, not, well, whatever's wrong with Lilah. Her case is—entirely different.

I'm not going to pretend: I'm scared. But the plan is, we'll all be together in Maine by Christmas, so that's what I'm trying to focus on.

I'll miss Lilah. Mom too. But I'm glad to be leaving San Francisco. My life here . . . is on hold—except for my music. The rest is a waiting game.

We've all been waiting for Lilah to find what she lost. As if she can look for it.

VIEW

Breathtaking.

That's the only way to describe the vast, endless view from Rock Hook Lighthouse.

None of the wonders, none of the famous landmarks we saw on our trip across the country compare to this view, not even our stop in Wyoming, where we hiked at the base of the Tetons, stunning snow-capped mountains that made something shift inside of me.

Unfortunately, the night we arrived here, the silver-edged mountains that the full moon conjured out of the dark sea made my chest tighten in terror. The crashing waves just kept coming, watery walls with sharp crests that shattered into fountains of moonlit sea spray as they hit the breakwater below the lighthouse.

That was nearly three weeks ago, and since then? Pretty much all I've done here at the light station is play guitar. Inside.

But today it's almost like I've been pulled out here, like I just suddenly *have* to climb the gazillion steps to the cast-iron gallery deck of the black-and-white-striped tower.

Now, nearly two hundred feet up in the air—

The mournful shriek of a seagull startles me, and I almost drop the heavy binoculars—the birthday present from my parents. Like I need a better view of the water.

With its slanting drizzle, this afternoon looks like every other. I'd used the weather as an excuse to stay inside, but now, dampness beads on my clothes, my hair, my skin, and I barely feel it as I lean against the slick railing with its ornate iron bars. The Atlantic heaves below me. The closely spaced bars are meant to ensure safety—only I don't *feel* safe. I close my eyes. Can't seem to bring myself to go back inside despite my discomfort.

Lilah. She hadn't been safe. Not on that boat. And maybe . . . not on land either. Even before the accident, something was going on with her. I know that now, because of the notebook, because of its contents, which are both disturbing and deeply disappointing.

I wanted more. Wanted an answer, some way to fix things, to help her. But the notebook didn't tell me anything, not really, despite its obvious importance to Lilah. She'd held it compulsively in her grip for the last year or kept it hidden away, but she'd *written* in it too, obsessively, in those couple of days before the accident. That's why I wanted it so badly.

I remember the way she bent over it, like she couldn't get close enough, like she didn't want anyone to see what she was writing, writing, writing . . .

Turns out, she'd written obsessively because she *was* obsessed. Obsessed with some guy she'd met here, on Rock Hook. It had to be here, because where else? The airport? The plane? Even Lilah couldn't fall in love that fast. But a week? No problem.

Not that she wrote anything about love. The book's first entry, if you can call it that, is a string of complaints. Verbal eye rolling, basically, about having to go to Maine at all, let alone for an entire week with nothing to do while Dad did whatever he was doing. Visiting the harbor, seeing old friends—it's clear from what she wrote that Lilah had no idea that Dad was looking for work. I don't remember if I knew or not. I was at music camp at Sonoma State that week, a program my sister wouldn't lower herself to attend.

Mom was part of a group exhibit downtown, so she didn't go on the trip either. It was just Lilah and Dad, gone and then back, Lilah with her new appendage, the black Moleskine.

Lilah was never into journaling—that's me. But it makes sense that she might have wanted to keep a record of her trip, although more likely she was just bored. What's bizarre is that after the eye-rolling entry, there's only one more entry, and then Lilah's *handwriting changes.* It's definitely still her writing, but the words are much smaller, like she wanted to save space, wanted to fit as much as she could on each page.

And she did, she packed every page, filled each one with that new cramped writing.

But she only wrote one line. Wrote it over and over again.

I am waiting.

She traced each word multiple times, so that every letter became darkly impressed upon the page. The words look etched, carved almost. In places, her pen actually pierced the paper.

I remember thinking how strange it was, the way she hunched over that notebook after she got back. She wouldn't tell me what she was writing, just laughed when I asked. She wrote feverishly, usually in the afternoon, and then at night? She went out. Snuck out. She was almost eighteen, but still. I threatened to tell Mom and Dad. She said if I did, she'd never speak to me again.

It was only a few days later, a few short days after she returned from Maine, that Lilah—

Stepping away from the railing, I begin to hum under my breath. The wind gusts, and my hair flies up around my face. I pace the ridged metal deck, circling around the tower, trying to distract myself by considering the choice of activities on "the Hook." That's what locals call this long, rocky spit of land. It feels more like an island—the ocean's everywhere. At the end of every street, the view out every window.

A few short days after she returned from Maine. That's when it happened. She went out on that boat—it could just as easily have been me. The water—it could have been me. Sucked beneath the sea.

Wishing my fearful imaginings were as easily changed as a radio station, I start to sing now.

I've worked hard at this "game," playing it when I need to, ever since I—ever since Lilah nearly drowned—

Hands trembling violently, I move back to the railing. Hold it tightly.

Aquaphobia. That's what Mom says I have, but Dr. Harrison says there's nothing abnormal about my fear. He says it's a reaction. A result of . . . Lilah's traumatic experience. That it'll fade over time. But did Dr. Harrison figure this into the mix? Living in a lighthouse—is it supposed to help?

I lift the binoculars back to my eyes—but look away from the water.

Comprised of the lighthouse, the keeper's house, and one small outbuilding, the light station is about twenty minutes south of the harbor—the center of life here on Rock Hook Peninsula. The compound sits at the edge of a parcel of land designated to become a park, and next July, Rock Hook National Seashore will officially open to the general public. Tourists will invade the beach, trample the woods, and leave litter in their wake, ruining the wild beauty that stretches away to the south. And yes, it *is* beautiful. Even with the water all around. For now, it's untouched, a wilderness. Breathing in the fine rain and salty mist, I scan the dunes and bluffs leading from the beach up to the woods.

The forest is sparse where it starts, then the hilly terrain becomes dense with undergrowth and trees. As the incline steepens, the land begins to show again, becoming mostly barren. Sheer granite rock faces stretch up, up, up—until finally, with rugged shrubs and tall trees clinging to the top, the park's most dramatic feature emerges, thrusting itself from the earth and jutting into the sky: Rock Hook Cliff.

The huge ridge goes on and on, dipping and climbing out of sight, leading eventually to the end of the peninsula. It looks like the end of the world.

Sunlight streams through a break in the clouds. I notice my arms are tiring from holding up the binoculars. I've gotten out of shape in the last year—I need serious exercise. Hiking might work, although I'll probably be wiped by the time I finish taking a walk in these woods. My gaze sweeps the miles of primeval forest, made up largely of pine and birch trees. I'll be totally fried before I even set foot on the hills that lead up to the craggy cliff.

Squinting, I manage to pick out what looks like a trail, then follow it with the binoculars until it vanishes into the green growth. Cloud-dappled sunlight hits the next beach over. Half-hidden by high dunes, the white strip of sand appears similar to the long, curving cove the lighthouse overlooks, but there's been so much fog and rain since we arrived—sea, sky, and sand blending, horizon invisible—I haven't had a chance to study the land below in such detail before.

Between the two beaches there's a big jetty, similar to the seawall in front of the lighthouse. I imagine a giant tossing the black boulders . . .

I adjust the binoculars. Now I can make out part of a shingled house, weathered to the soft shade of driftwood. I can't see more. The tall sand dunes below the bluffs loom over the empty beach, blocking the rest.

A flash of movement catches my eye. A figure, coming from behind one of the bluffs near the house that's stayed stubbornly just out of view. A boy. A man? Whatever, some guy, maybe a little older than me.

Tall, he carries a surfboard under one arm, heading toward the water with long strides. The way he walks, the way he holds himself is so . . . different. He moves in a way that's flowing, almost . . . liquid. His shoulder-length hair is an unusual shade of gold, the color of late-day sun striking the sand. The wind whips the strands around his face where they shimmer.

He's wearing nothing but a pair of black board shorts.

What is he, crazy? The water must be freezing.

The clouds change direction, swallowing the sun, turning the afternoon a deeper shade of gray. The ocean darkens in response, reflecting the steel sky, whitecaps standing out in sharp relief. Today's low temperature has to be a record for the last day of August, even in Maine.

Closing one eye, I focus on the boy's face. His jaw is set. Determined. He must be insane and—even at this distance—easily the most beautiful person I've ever seen.

A weird ache settles in my chest as I stare through the binoculars, watching the surfer catch wave after wave, riding each one to its curling end, before turning and paddling back out to catch the next. He surfs with uncanny intuition, like he's one of the waves.

Finally, he rides the board into impossibly shallow water, and, perfectly poised, casually steps off. In one quick crouching movement he scoops the surfboard under his arm. Then he straightens and looks up. He looks up, at *me*.

Goosebumps race along my arms and I drop the binoculars—they smack me in the stomach like a fist, the edge of the plastic cord slicing at the skin on the back of my neck. Grabbing them up again, I bring them to my eyes—

He's still staring up at me, head slightly tilted to one side now, as if he's listening to something.

Maybe he's not a boy.

Lilah's voice in my head: her seventeen-going-on-twenty-five voice from before the accident. I shiver. Lilah. She'd always been right about everything.

Oh God, Ari. You're so easy. What else *could he be? Trust me, once you know one . . .*

And then I hear something else, something like . . . music. Flutes, or pipes, or chanting voices—I can't tell. The distant music tugs at me somehow . . .

Still, I keep the binoculars trained on the boy. Maybe he isn't looking at me—he can't possibly see me from there. Maybe he's staring at the sky, or a bird, anything besides me. Feeling like a complete idiot, I slowly raise my arm—and wave anyway.

Continuing to look up, he gives a brief nod.

I freeze at the railing.

The wind begins to howl, and again, I hear the far-off music. Together the two create a primitive, atonal composition, music that the boy seems to move to as he pivots with aqueous grace—

And glides out of my line of vision, disappearing behind the dunes.

MISSING

Red cowboy boots clanging on the iron stairs of the tower, I descend around and down. At the bottom I pull open the heavy arched door that leads into the vestibule house, an upturned rectangle of granite blocks nearly four stories high that forms the base of Rock Hook Lighthouse and surrounds the cylindrical tower. The stone building juts out in front where it faces the sea. I trace my fingertips along the damp walls of the vaulted hallway, my footsteps echoing eerily. *Who was that boy?*

Lifting and lowering my arms, I imagine my shadow play isn't created by the dim light of bulbs caged in wire but from flickering Gothic torches . . .

Opening the thick wooden door to the outside—I stare in surprise. The drizzle has turned to a deluge.

Through the sheets of rain and the tops of the gnarled pines that surround it, I can just make out the roofline of the keeper's cottage nestled partway down the bluff.

When I'd first seen the tiny cottage I knew life there would be way too crowded. Mom heard the measurements of the rooms and groaned, and even to me, with my five-foot-four bird-boned build, the house felt claustrophobic.

The first time I climbed the lighthouse and stepped out onto the deck, my feelings had been just the opposite. I'd felt as if I were inside my own spacious—and private—cloud.

That's when I got the brilliant idea that my bedroom should be in the lighthouse. Not actually *in* the lighthouse; technically the room I chose is in the vestibule house, at the top of the great granite rectangle. But since the spiral stairway inside the lighthouse tower is the only way to get there, it *feels* as if my bedroom is in the lighthouse.

I consider turning around and climbing the winding stairs—only partway this time—and going to my room. Instead I hurry through the pouring rain along the path and down the cement steps, using my hands as an ineffectual shield against the water.

A light glows yellow in the picture window of the keeper's cottage and, as usual, the door is unlocked. I step into the little foyer, then down the narrow hall to the tiny living room. Empty. *Hmm.* Dad's usually here at dinnertime, but he isn't in the miniature kitchen either.

The restored wood-shingled cape with its low ceilings and small doorways sits crooked on the uneven granite-topped bluffs, and as the ocean crashes against the seawall out beyond the white curve of Crescent Beach and thunder shudders across the sky, I have to remind myself that the cottage has been here since the late 1700s. It isn't about to wash away.

Still, I jump when the phone rings.

"Hello?" Dial tone. Yet somehow the ringing continues. No cell towers on Rock Hook, so I rule that out; besides, my cell is up in my room, probably dead at the bottom of my backpack.

The front door opens with a *whoosh*—

Dripping wet, Dad rushes across the room to grab a receiver buried in a nest of tangled USB cords, wires, and hard drives on his desk—the Coast Guard radio. He flips a switch, and static fills the room along with an unfamiliar voice.

"George? Is that you?"

"Skip here," Dad corrects. Dad's nickname suits him better than "George" or "Dad," but "Captain Rush" fits him best. Even now, the look he casts toward the window and the sea beyond is one of longing.

"Right. Skip. It's Wagner. Henry Wagner, Coast Guard."

"Hank! I wasn't expecting to hear this contraption ring. Great to hear your voice."

No surprise that Dad knows the man on the other end of the line; he grew up in this place and still has lots of friends here: fishermen, lobstermen, people who work at the marine labs. When the light station became available just as my parents were desperate for a fresh start, I took it as some sort of sign. I realize now that Dad's boating buddies must have rigged things for us. Maybe he'd been talking to them about his troubles with Mom.

The radio buzzes.

"Hank?" The interference grows louder, and Mr. Wagner's voice becomes unintelligible. "Hank, what can I do for you? Besides get a new radio installed out here."

Dad had slipped easily into his role of lighthouse keeper. He knows all about weather, wind, and water—although it probably wouldn't matter if he didn't. All of the lighthouses in the United States are automated now. The only real responsibility we have is to contact the Coast Guard if we see a boat in distress.

Mr. Wagner's voice suddenly comes through clear again, sounding tense. "I'm not sure if there's anything anyone can do, especially with this unexpected weather. We're looking for a boat up from Portland. One of our boys picked up an SOS signal not too long ago. Thinks the Portland boat sent it from your neck of the woods."

"*Thinks* they sent it?" Dad grimaces. "Didn't the vessel identify itself?"

"The signal was garbled. I'm betting the boat doesn't have the best equipment. It's a rental, small fishing boat, out of Bay Place. You know how they are."

"Sloppy."

"Yup. They've got two other boats out in this soup, both on their way in, but the *Lucky* is unaccounted for. She was up around the end of the peninsula when she signaled."

"Damn. Then what? She disappeared off your screen?"

"Right. And there's another problem. You remember our old friends at Bay Place? True to form, the paperwork is slipshod too."

"Nothing new. What are you saying, Hank?"

"Well, we're not sure who's on that boat. Bay Place said they rented it to a teenager. Didn't look like a fisherman. When the boat left the dock, three more boys were aboard."

Dad winces. He peers at the sky through the rain-streaked window. "Looks like it's clearing here, but this one's tricky. May be a two-faced storm. What's your radar say?"

"I've got the same. Clearing for now. Looks like we're in for more later."

"What do you think? Meet in twenty?"

"Skip, that's not necessary—"

"Yeah, well, if that boat's up around the tip—" Dad's voice falters, and I know what he's thinking. He's thinking: *teenagers.* He's thinking: *Lilah.*

"Hang on, Hank." Dad turns to me. "Ari?"

I shake my head. "Nothing. Sorry."

"Arion's been here all afternoon, Hank. She hasn't seen anything."

"No, I thought that would be the case. They were closer to the—"

"Right, to the end of the peninsula. Be there shortly." The crepitating static of the radio dies abruptly as Dad sets the receiver down with a *crack.* He tries to smile. Fails. "You heard, Water Dog."

I cringe at the old nickname.

"Gotta go." He hesitates. "There's leftovers in the fridge."

"Okay. Be—" My throat feels thick. "Be careful."

"Don't worry, I will be." He heads into the kitchen, emerging a few minutes later with a cooler and a first-aid kit. "There's chocolate in the breadbox," he says. Then he's gone.

Chocolate. The two of us joke that it's the most important of the food groups. We even used to talk about getting a chocolate Lab. "A puppy to match your hair," he used to tease. "But who'll walk it up the hills? You don't need a water dog, Arion—you *are* a water dog."

And I was. Mom and Dad couldn't keep me off his boats, or away from the local pool or beach when school was out. When I turned twelve, there were scuba lessons, and in seventh grade, junior surf team. I swore that someday I'd surf under the Golden Gate Bridge, even though the waves are notoriously dangerous, but after Lilah's accident, I vowed never to surf again. I won't swim or sail—won't set foot on Dad's boats; my heart pounds just thinking about it. He can't even get me to go for a beach walk.

Anxiety crawls in the pit of my stomach where dinner should be. Maybe music will help.

I head outside and up to my room, about as far away from the water as I can get.

But once I'm in the tower, I pass the door to the bedroom almost unaware, continuing up the spiral stairs as if pulled, stopping in the watch room only long enough to grab the binoculars from the floor.

Clouds race on the wind through the deep-purple dusk as I step out onto the gallery deck, feeling disoriented—and strangely expectant. Gripping the binoculars, I search the rough sea for a lone boat . . .

Like this afternoon, I can't seem to stop looking, and soon it grows dark, the night sky becoming a starless black field.

Glittering lights spark in the water of the neighboring cove—as if that's where the stars are tonight—until the tops of the breakers flicker and glow.

Bioluminescence. Must be. Caused by fish, squid, or krill.

But the brilliant gold—that isn't any kind of sea life.

It tops a shadowy boy, surfing shadowy waves.

MIRROR

On the first day of school I walk into homeroom chanting a silent mantra—*this is not my real life, this is not my real life*—just in case Rock Hook Harbor High sucks.

The first person I notice is a boy at the back of the room. Not only is he sitting alone while most of the students mill around in small groups or pairs, he's somehow solitary. Sitting back in his chair with his head lowered, shaggy black hair nearly covering his eyes—which are focused on the small paperback book in his hands—he looks like he's trying to hide. He also looks . . . familiar. I'm not sure if this is the reason I can't tear my gaze from his face. It's bruised along one side, and sculpted, almost delicate, although the strong-looking shoulders and muscled arms beneath his white T-shirt are not. His eyelashes are so long they cast shadows on his cheekbones, and below the hollow of his cheeks a hint of darkness runs along his jaw, setting off the full bow of his mouth, a curved crescent lifting a little at the corners now—

Our eyes meet—*sadness, loneliness. Like looking in a mirror.*

The impression is unnerving, then suddenly gone, as if a sheer curtain has dropped, so that I find myself staring into startlingly light-gray eyes, their only expression one of amusement. The slight curve of the boy's lips grows into a grin.

Hurriedly making my way to an empty chair, I sit down, shaken and embarrassed.

"Jeez," someone behind me snickers. "Just ask for her number."

Glancing over my shoulder I watch a girl with long dark hair slide behind the boy. Her coloring—fair skin, blue eyes—and something about the way she moves remind me of Lilah.

His grin gone now, the boy pulls his chair in, making room for her to pass. But even with the extra space, she manages to bump up against him as she heads toward the next chair over in order to retrieve a purse that's nearly large enough to be mistaken for a slumping student.

Then she sidles back toward the boy, stopping directly in front of him. "She might actually answer her phone, unlike some people I know."

"You don't know me," the black-haired boy says, voice low.

She swings the big bag to one side and leans down to whisper something in his ear—

He tips his chair back, putting distance between them, muttering something I can't hear.

She gives a dry laugh. "I'm sure you'd like to."

"Actually, no. I wouldn't."

At the desk next to mine a pretty girl with an auburn braid and orange-rimmed glasses says something in a soft voice. It takes me a moment to realize she's speaking to me.

"Sorry, what did you say?"

"I said, you're new, aren't you? I'm Mary." She smiles. "Mary Garrahy."

I force myself to smile in return. "Arion Rush."

"Can I see your schedule?"

"Sure." I hand over the crumpled piece of paper I've been having difficulty deciphering.

"Hey." The girl with the long dark hair parks herself on the edge of Mary's desk.

"What's up?" Mary asks.

The girl lifts her chin. "New Girl should give Logan her phone number. He totally needs to get—" She stops and runs her eyes over me, then they go lazy, her cool, appraising gaze becoming apathetic. "You know what? Bet he asks you for it himself. Just—don't hold your breath waiting for him to call. No charge for the advice."

Before I can say anything, the girl hops off the desk and heads out of the room, her large bag catching on the door, causing it to rattle in her wake.

Mary and I look after her for second, then at each other, before we burst out laughing.

"What was *that* about?" I ask.

"*That* was about Alyssa. So sorry I didn't get to introduce you."

"Why do I feel like that's a good thing?" I muse, smiling for real now.

"Because it is. Not that I can save you from her for long, but no one should have to deal with Alyssa Saffer on their first day." Mary hands back the schedule. "It's almost exactly the same as mine."

The bell rings and the room bursts into motion just as an older man in a jacket and tie hurries through the doorway. "Everyone's here, Mr. A," Mary tells him as she stands. The man—presumably our homeroom teacher—thanks her several times. She replies that it's no problem, then says to me, "Come on," and starts for the door.

Relieved, I follow. My sense of direction defies description.

THE THING CALLED LOVE

Friday, I pull into the crowded lot at school and find a space. Almost through week two at Rock Hook Harbor High, and things are actually going pretty well.

But not for the *Lucky*, which . . . wasn't so lucky.

The night Dad went out to look for the missing boat, I'd gotten ready for bed, then huddled under a blanket on the living room couch, waiting. Dad came in after midnight, tired and discouraged. He didn't even scold me for being up late, only shook his head and said good night. I stayed on the couch, tossing and turning, unable to sleep.

Last night, just over two weeks since the *Lucky* vanished from Coast Guard radar screens, Dad went out again. Two divers had discovered a small fishing vessel and contacted the Coast Guard. The boat had been anchored—in a way—tethered by a thick chain to a nearly impossible-to-reach rocky outcropping close to the end of the peninsula. The boat was the *Lucky*.

She'd been sunk.

"Makes no sense," Dad said this morning at breakfast, his voice filled with defeat. "A dozen fist-size holes, pierced right through the bottom of the boat."

There'd been no trace of the four boys, but their identities were known now. Teenagers, kids a year older than me, the boys had been on a road trip, a long weekend before going off to college. Two days after the boat disappeared, relatives from out of state traced the boys, all no-shows by then at their respective schools, to Portland. The police connected their disappearance to the boat rental from Bay Place.

Rap, rap! The sharp knock on my window makes me jump, my hands reflexively balling into fists. I'd barely registered the battered white pickup truck that rolled into the spot next to mine. Now as I turn, I see its owner, who flashes a wide grin, and opens my door.

"Miss Rush. Allow me." Logan Delaine, the boy from the back of homeroom, stands with one hand on the door, the other outstretched, as if we have an understanding that he'll take my backpack and escort me into the building. His mocking smile is dazzling.

"Logan, tone it down, will you?" Squinting, I hold my hand, visor style, to my forehead. "You look like a toothpaste commercial."

The truth is, besides his smile—and his comedic efforts, which Mary said are strictly for my benefit—there's nothing light about Logan Delaine. I unbuckle my seat belt.

"Fight club?" I ask, gesturing to the cut at the edge of his slightly swollen lower lip.

"You're funny."

"Seriously, what happened?"

"Unfinished business."

"With who?"

He gives me a long look, and I feel the beginnings of a flush spread across my cheeks. Not wanting him to notice, I move quickly now, ignoring his proffered hand and slinging my pack over my shoulder as I get out of the car.

"Fine," I say. "Forget I asked."

"Wait." He closes his eyes briefly. "My brother. The unfinished business—it's his."

"Oh. I'm—sorry."

I've heard about Logan's brother. You can't live in Rock Hook Harbor and not hear about Nick Delaine. The water that sustains so many in this area—had drowned him.

Was it a freak current? A riptide? I don't know. Don't want to know. Ever.

"No worries," Logan says. "C'mon. If we're late Mary'll give us hell." He grins.

As we walk, Logan bends his body nearly double, as if his own backpack weighs a ton. "Hey, how come you never offer to carry *my* backpack?" he huffs.

Distracted, I don't respond. *Nick Delaine. The* Lucky. *A dozen fist-size holes . . .*

"Planet Earth to Airyhead. Wake up." Logan nudges me, and I become aware of the crowds entering the school, the number of people staring at us: the new girl and the hunchback of Notre-Dame. Embarrassed, I yank the hem of his T-shirt.

He straightens his tall frame and shrugs. "Whatever."

When we get to homeroom it's more of the same. He bows low, ushering me into the room. And although I can't help laughing, his faux chivalrous gesture attracts enough attention that it makes me uncomfortable. But once again, he doesn't seem to care about the looks and whispers.

"He doesn't care about anything—except maybe you." That's what Mary told me last night on the phone.

I told her, "That's pretty heavy considering Logan and I have only known each other a couple of weeks."

"Maybe," she replied. "But I still think it's a good thing. It's like . . . he's coming back to life or something. Losing his brother . . . that changed him. I just—I want him to change back."

At that point, I said I knew exactly what she meant, and told her about Lilah.

"I am so sorry," she responded. "I heard something, about an accident. People talk, you know? But I didn't know the details. I'm really sorry."

Neither of us mentioned the strange parallel with Logan and me. Maybe because it's not really a parallel at all: my sister is alive. Still—the water. It hurt us both. I can't help but wonder if he hates it like I do. Can't help but wonder—if he's afraid.

The morning passes quickly, and when lunchtime comes I sit down in my usual seat next to Mary at a table near the back door of the cafeteria that leads out to the patio.

"Finally, girrrl time," she growls with a sneer.

I laugh. We're far from riot girls. Like me, Mary's focused on school. Unlike me, she has a boyfriend, Kevin Eaton. She has friends, but Kevin—a tall, serious guy who wants to be a doctor—is her priority. His lunch is next period, though, so Mary and I have eaten together every day since the first day of school.

The three Kevins in our little group love to rib Mary, asking her over and over if she's sure she's chosen the right one. She and *her* Kevin plan on getting married when they graduate. Not my idea of a good time, but I'm not about to criticize my new best friend. My *other* new best friend, I correct as I look up and see Logan leaning against the window of the radio station.

The station is housed in one corner of the cafeteria and run by students, and apparently Logan Delaine puts together a pretty good playlist. Two younger girls are gazing up worshipfully as they chatter at him—although the color in their cheeks suggests they may have something other than music on their minds. He nods at them but grins at me. He crooks a finger, but I shake my head.

Time to ask Mary about the suicidal surfer. I'm pretty sure he doesn't go to RHHH, because I haven't seen him, and I realize now, I've been looking. Scanning the hallways, the faces—I can't stop thinking about him.

To be so consumed with someone I've never met—I'm worried Mary will think I'm a freak, which is why I haven't said anything yet. But I'm hard up enough now for info about Mr. Black Board Shorts to reveal my obsessive-compulsive tendencies to her.

Something has kept me from asking Logan.

I turn to Mary, but she's already watching me with a certain amount of glee. It appears she's been following the silent exchange between Logan and me.

"Oh yeah," she says. "I like it. Man, he is *staring* at you."

"That's just those ghost eyes of his, how they look." I lay my head down on my arms.

"Oh right, like Logan looks at everyone the way he looks at you."

"He does," I mumble.

"Not. Come on, I've seen you two talking on the front steps after school. Every day, I might add. Why don't you go out with him? He's hot, his family's nice, and plus, his dad's a cop."

"Mary, please." The table smells like cleanser. I sit up.

"Hey, you never know when you might need the law on your side." She gives a sly laugh.

"Um, I really can't think about that kind of thing right now." I've never had a boyfriend, never really dated anyone. Actually, I *could* think about it, only, not with Logan. "Mary, there's a cove, over near the lighthouse—"

She cuts me off. "What kind of 'thing'? The law? Or *The Thing Called Love*?"

We both start laughing. *The Thing Called Love* is one of my favorite old movies. It's about a bunch of songwriters trying to make it in Nashville. Dad bought the DVD, but I claimed it. I told Mary about the film one day so she watched it. Now she loves it too. And she loves music, the one serious interest I have now that all water-related activities are banned from my things-I-want-to-do-when-I-grow-up list.

Someday, I want to go to Nashville to hear music and write songs, like in the movie. Mom and Dad took a trip to Nashville once. Inexplicably, Dad came home with the red cowboy boots. They were two sizes too big for me. When they finally fit, I started wearing them. I wanted to remind my parents there'd been a time when they'd gotten along, sort of. The boots are broken in now and feel like slippers. When I first showed up at RHHH, they definitely got a few looks.

Mary wants to hear my songs, and I told her she can—at my next gig, which will have to be in Portland, because Rock Hook Harbor doesn't have a music scene. Somehow, I'm pretty sure the mainland doesn't either. Kids around here drive all the way to Portland just to go dancing.

Lilah and I used to blast music in her room and dance.

Music. It saved my life when she nearly lost hers . . .

One of the Kevins shouts as he passes by, jerking me back to the moment. Mary's leaning in across the table, gesturing for me to do the same.

Without waiting to hear what she has to say, I blurt, "Mary, this is going to sound stupid, but there's this guy. I saw him surfing at the beach next to the lighthouse—"

"Hate to break up your girl *thang*, but it's time for class."

Logan. Hard to believe I hadn't seen him coming.

"Oh yeah, *girl* thing." Mary grabs my hand.

"Mind if I watch?" Logan slides onto the bench, the side of his body pressing against mine. The bell shrills and the noise in the cafeteria doubles.

I shove my shoulder hard against his—and get up. Mary stands too now. She's headed to gym, the only period besides her art class and my music theory class that we don't have together. Walking backward, she blows a stream of kisses at me for Logan's benefit.

He arches one dark brow.

I say, "In your dreams, Delaine."

"*My* dreams?" Laughing, he stands and takes my hand. "Hey, don't blame me for Mary's perverted ideas. Just—remember to include me in them." He laces his fingers with mine.

And even though I'm not sure where his joking ends and he begins, the way our fingers are entwined—feels good.

But after we walk across the cafeteria together and out into the crowded hall, I ease my hand out of his. Because . . . the school feels stuffy. The weather is humid and my hair is doing its puffy frizzy thing. Plus my ears are ringing. Not ringing, really, but—I don't know.

Pushing my hair back irritably, I'm twisting it into a knot when a group of boys passes by, one of them jostling me—

Logan grabs the kid who bumped me, slams him up against a locker. "Watch it, idiot."

The boy's eyes go wide.

Before I can protest—the boy's shoulder had barely brushed mine—Logan releases him and starts walking. Almost reluctantly, I follow, catching up with him only when he slows, as if he's suddenly remembering that we'd been going down the hall together.

"Sorry," he mutters, "but I swear—some of these guys . . . It's like they're part of a different species or something."

LIBRARY CARDS

The Rock Hook Harbor public library doesn't have that library book smell. It smells more like the inside of a guitar. Wooden beams cross high ceilings, and tall windows show the surrounding woods, making it a soothing place to study, a better place to daydream.

Whether I do those things here or in my room, each day by late afternoon I'm up on the lighthouse deck, searching for that lone surfer. So far the only sign of life I've seen is a flock of seagulls.

Maybe the surfer was just visiting. Maybe he's a tourist. That would be a drag. I might never see him again.

School, however, is not a drag, not like San Francisco, and I'm glad.

For most of last year I stayed home from school, unable to deal with Lilah not being there, unable to handle the continual questions from friends, classmates, teachers. My assignments were sent home along with Lilah's. Mine were sent back completed.

Worse, though, was toward the end of the year, when I went back to school full time. At that point, people must have decided there was no hope for Lilah—or maybe they just didn't want to keep asking questions that had no answers. Abruptly, the inquiries stopped.

It was then that I turned invisible.

No one knows what to say to the girl whose sister is gone but not gone.

Here, I'm definitely *not* invisible. In fact—not to be paranoid, but—sometimes it feels like someone's . . . watching me. And sometimes, somebody is. I get that. I see Logan looking at me, or I catch some other boy at school—some boy I don't know—checking me out from across the cafeteria. But that's not it. I mean, *watching* watching. Like, a creepy kind of watching.

I don't get that feeling when I'm busy, when I'm writing a song, or caught up in classes, so that's good. Rock Hook Harbor High is a magnet school specializing in marine technology and science, and Early Oceanography has actually started to draw me in. The class meets three times a week, and we have to log an additional six hours every other week in the lab—or out in the field. I'm sticking to the lab, because in this case, "field" means water.

Thanks to contributions from the Ocean Zone Institute, the labs at RHHH are extremely well equipped. OZI is the largest private nonprofit oceanographic institution in the world, with main offices in Portland and a satellite facility in Rock Hook that employs half the town. It has a vested interest in supporting the school.

Yesterday in the lab I was looking at slides of water samples through a microscope. Fascinated, I watched as miniscule creatures swam to and fro. Obviously a few drops of water can't hurt me, and a powerful lens—it provides a window into another world.

"It's amazing how the ocean holds so many life-forms we can't see with the naked eye," I said to Mary. She stifled a giggle and looked sideways at Logan.

"She said *naked*," he obligingly shouted, causing everyone to stop and stare.

"Mary, you shouldn't encourage him. Logan—you're not even *in* this class."

"Oh, but he should be," Mary said, leaning her head on Logan's shoulder.

I must have looked skeptical, because Logan said, "Don't act so surprised, Rush. Mary loves me, just like every other woman who's ever met me. Except you."

"Yeah, well, you guys have been friends since, what? Preschool? Maybe you're an acquired taste."

"Hey, you just let me know if you want a t—"

"Delaine!" bellowed Mr. Kraig. "What are you doing in this sacred space I call my classroom?"

"Leaving," Logan replied, giving us a little wave. He grabbed the edges of two lab tables and vaulted over a chair, stopping only to pick up a book that slipped from his back pocket—I confess I craned my neck to read the title but the book was upside down—before heading out the door.

Smiling at the memory of Logan in midair, at the fact that he's always got a book on him, I look around, like I think I'll see him or something. But of course he's not here—I'd totally know if he were. No, the library is practically empty. Quiet. And yet . . . I've got that feeling, that weird watched feeling.

I push aside a book about lighthouses. Open one on marine biology.

When I was ten, Dad was hired to captain a large research vessel. He was going to be gone for an entire month. Before he left, we spent the weekend on the boat with the group of scientists, professors, and grad students who were preparing to study the complex waves of a particular inlet in Turkey. Listening to their conversations, I desperately wanted to understand everything they were talking about. Over the weekend I became a mascot of sorts and decided I wanted to study oceanography.

Here in Maine the ocean is my front yard, but handling slides of salt water in the lab is the closest I've been to the sea . . .

When I first started seeing Dr. Harrison, he said I was suffering from depression. I didn't want to go on medication, and he was fine with that. He told me that if I paid attention, I'd be able see a bout of depression coming, and then I could handle it appropriately.

That made sense to me; Nick Drake wrote a song calling depression the "black-eyed dog," which definitely sounds like something you can see coming.

But Dr. Harrison also warned that "an episode" might be preceded by a loop of obsessive thinking, and that's the thing that still trips me up sometimes. He said what I need to do is break the loop—because the loop can work like a lasso, and anxiety and depression can swing it like a couple of cowboys and catch me if I'm not careful. I'm careful, but . . . guess I'm not always quick.

Another thing Dr. Harrison said was, *"Having a social life without your sister is going to be a big change."* Which is why when Logan asks me over to his house, or out to the movies, I say no. Mary told me I should go out with him, that she loves him. *"Like a little brother, of course."* She'd laughed. *"But still. You should go."*

At home I'd always been Lilah's little sister. Everyone wanted to be friends with Lilah Rush. Piano prodigy, precocious child, gifted young woman. *"Oh, isn't she the one who—"*

After the accident, the phone at our house literally stopped ringing.

I run my hands over my face. *What about him?* is all I can think now. The boy that Lilah met here; did he ever call her? How am I going to find him?

If I could just go back, ask her again—*What are you writing? Can I see it?* I'd snatch the book from her hands when she laughed, run off and read it and *insist* she tell me the boy's name—because even though Lilah's accident took place off San Francisco, I can't shake the feeling that he was involved. I close my eyes. I'm so, so angry.

Lilah. The anger turns to heaviness, as if I'm weighted down everywhere.

But the reality is, she said no, so I didn't grab the book away, I just—backed down. Lilah's way or no way, that's how it was with us. I was—*I am*—just her little sister.

Although here in Maine . . . nobody knows that. Here on Rock Hook, I'm not anyone's little sister. I'm not anyone's anything, and somehow that makes me feel . . . hopeful. About what, I have no idea, because after the accident, hope makes me suspicious, gives me the sensation of being on one of those floating docks, where your feet tell your brain that you're standing on solid ground, but your body senses movement.

Thinking of the surfer, tourist or not, gives me that same hopeful feeling for some reason. But that little bit of optimism is like an atrophied muscle. It needs exercise, fresh air. Sunshine.

Despite the fact that I arrived at the library early due to the half day at school, the leaden sky outside the expanse of windows makes it feel like five o'clock. No sunshine here, although now I sense a strange change in the light. But the clouds aren't clearing, despite the wind that pushes the pines, the wind that sounds . . . musical.

The back of my neck prickles.

Someone is standing in the stacks to the left of me.

I twist in my chair—

Surf's up.

The boy from the beach faces the tall bookshelves, his profile toward me. His shoulder-length hair creates a shimmering shield of gold, hiding his face as he concentrates on—what? Reading the title of a book? How long can that take?

I have a strange urge to stand up, to go to him and push aside the curtain of hair, as though seeing his face is of some kind of crucial importance. Luckily I can't move.

He seems frozen too, or lost in thought; he's holding his hand on the spine of one large book, like he's trying to absorb the information through osmosis.

Clearing my throat, I say, "You might actually have to open it." My voice sounds loud, startling in the silence of the library. "The book, I mean."

He turns—

And walks away.

Whoa—so rude. Besides, that was funny, right? Or had it sounded sarcastic? Critical? No, that comment had definitely been funny. Lilah would be cracking up if she were here—and still herself. She'd be teasing me now. I can almost hear her: *Were you trying to hit on that guy?*

But no, I wasn't trying to hit on Mr. Black Board Shorts. I just want to know who he is. Not that he's wearing the trunks today. I looked at every inch of him. Now, behind closed eyes, I play the image like a video: jeans faded to the palest blue, broad shoulders under a black cotton surf shirt—the old-school kind with a band of tropical flowers across the chest.

But fine. I snap my eyes open. Whatever. I don't need to know who he is—he's obviously a jerk. What I need—is to go outside and get some air. I gather my things.

But then, I go over to the shelves where *he* had stood.

I pull out one volume, then another—

Yoga?

Huh.

Sliding out the biggest book—the one he'd held his hand over—I'm surprised to discover it's mostly about yogic breathing techniques. Pranayama.

Deciding to check it out, I head toward the front desk, arms straining to carry what's become a wobbly tower—

A rush of heat warms my cheeks.

The fact that I can recognize him from behind, that the tall, broad-shouldered frame standing before the counter is already so familiar, is disturbing, makes me feel . . . kind of stalkery. Stalkerish?

I turn around, wanting to move away before he notices me, only to find a line forming behind me. I turn back, and hearing the librarian thank him, step forward—

At the same time he steps backward.

The sound of our bodies colliding is practically audible, we hit so hard. My books avalanche, my nose presses into his back—and I can't help it. I inhale. I take a deep breath in—

That comes out almost immediately as a sigh.

A microsecond passes. Then he turns to me, a look of horror on his face, as if my sigh heralds some kind of terrible event. And before I can even make out the color of his flashing eyes—blue? Green?—he's gone.

The bang of the books hitting the floor echoing in my ears, I stare out the double doors.

Somebody sniggers.

Another voice says, "Can you move it along, Miss? There's a line."

Fingers clutching one last book that threatens to join the rest down by my toes, I look around and see Pete Hill and Bobby Farley, guys from school who hang out with the Kevins.

"Oh. Hey. A little help here?" I ask.

Pete fakes a groan as he heaves the giant volume onto the counter.

"Yoga." Bobby nods sagely. "That explains a lot." He gathers a few of the books.

"*Working in the Wet Field: A Handbook for Aspiring Marine Biologists*," he reads aloud. Pete chuckles as Bobby puts an arm around my shoulders and says, "You know—I'm into that stuff."

Removing his arm from around me, I give him a bland smile, nothing like the gorgeous grin on the face of the boy from the beach, who's driving past the glass doors of the library at an unthinkable speed in a midnight-blue Mercedes. My head seems to turn of its own accord, eyes following the car.

"Seriously." Bobby waves a hand in front of my face. "We should study together."

Unable to stop seeing the boy's stunning smile, I blink at Bobby uncomprehendingly.

"Hey, Farley, I'm out. You coming?" Pete strides over to the doors, pushes one open.

"In a sec." Bobby holds up a book—the last of the ones that had fallen—as if it's an incentive, or maybe a hostage. "So what do you think? You, me—a few books, a few beers."

"Pardon me," a woman with black-rimmed glasses says from behind the counter. "May I please have your library card?"

"Ah—" Reaching for the book, I shake my head. "No. Thanks."

With a shrug, Bobby relinquishes the book. "Your loss." He follows Pete out.

"No?" The woman behind the counter folds her lips into a sober line.

"Oh—sorry, here." The librarian looks dubious as I hand over my card but returns it a moment later with a prim nod. She watches as I carry my awkward armful away.

Outside on the steps Pete and Bobby are talking with Alyssa. Despite the fact that she must not be able to breathe in those jeans, she looks great as usual. She gives me a wave that somehow uses her entire body, but I hardly see it. *That guy. His eyes. The way he smelled, like—*

"Arion! Hold up."

Reluctantly, I turn. Pete. He's stayed on the steps and I'm already halfway across the parking lot, so he's pretty much shouting across the space between us.

"Hey, what did you say to Bo Summers? He looked pretty freaked out."

Bo Summers.

A long eternity of a second goes by. Nobody else seems to notice the time warp.

"You don't seem like a scary chick," Pete continues. "Not to me, anyway." He grins and takes a cigarette out of the crumpled pack in his top pocket. He lights it, and waits.

Smoke of any kind grosses me out, but in this moment, Pete's cigarette is my savior.

"Pete, that thing in your mouth? You might want to watch it." Barely balancing my books on one hip, I pull on a pair of sunglasses I don't need. "It's on fire."

Bobby laughs. Alyssa tosses her hair and says to Pete, "When was Bo here?"

So Alyssa knows him. Makes total sense. Alyssa's a transplanted New Yorker, same as Mom; maybe that's why, despite her attention addiction, I find her interesting. But her big blue eyes—which ignore the line between polite eye contact and rude staring—always have some guy in their sights. Of course she knows Bo.

I head for the Jeep, lifting one hand high after hearing a couple of goodbyes behind me. Stomach flip-flopping, I get in and drive all the way to the lighthouse—with no music.

On our trip cross-country Dad had a hard time with the fact that I couldn't drive without the radio blasting. Today, I don't listen to anything, and feel like I could drive around the world.

My mystery man has a name.

CENTRIPETAL

At the loud *pop* my head whips around—

But there's nothing to see. Backfire, that's what the noise was, the Jeep acting up again. Dad's truck—which is big and blue and has the words **Park Ranger** stenciled on the sides—isn't in the driveway, so I'll have to tell him later. Fingers crossed he can take care of it.

The earthy smell of damp stone permeates the vaulted hallway of the vestibule house. Closing the heavy inner door behind me, I start the spiraling climb, realizing as I heft the load of books that no one in the group back at the library had been carrying any. That explains the attention I've been receiving from the guys at school. They just don't have enough homework.

The kids at Blaine, Rock Hook's private high school, probably get a ton of homework. Graduates of Blaine tend to go to Ivy League colleges. Although as excellent as Blaine supposedly is, its science program doesn't hold a candle to the marine biology and oceanography classes at RHHH, thanks to the generosity of the Ocean Zone Institute—

Bo *Summers*. Bet that's why he's such a snob. Professor Julian Summers—his dad, I'm guessing—is the founder of OZI. The man's practically a celebrity.

The sun's breaking through the clouds as I drop the books on my desk. Would Bo Summers finally be out surfing again? I refuse to succumb. No deck, no binoculars. The guy's stuck up. At least now I know why.

In the green-tiled bathroom that was fashioned out of an old storeroom during the lighthouse renovation, I wash my hands and braid my hair. Then I head back down the stairs. The sound of my boots ringing on the metal steps reminds me that I probably have better shoes for hiking than Dad's souvenirs from Nashville, but I don't turn back.

The trailhead is just past the sandy lot earmarked for visitor parking at the edge of the woods, and the path is already groomed in expectation of the tourists who'll arrive next summer. Not a happy thought. They'll ruin this place.

But as I start up the wooded trail, it isn't the park that's on my mind. It's the library. On either side of the library steps, nestled among the purplish sea grasses and Rugosa roses, I'd seen a small boulder with a modest bronze plaque.

DONATED BY PROFESSOR JULIAN SUMMERS

THIS LIBRARY IS OPEN TO ALL TO ENJOY.

Surprised that two years of Latin made any impression, I recall the other words etched on the plaque: **HOMO SUM, HUMANI NIHIL A ME ALIENUM PUTO.**

Google will know what that means.

About to turn around, I stop short. It's idiotic to spend another minute thinking about anything I saw at the library, including ridiculously handsome boys and obscure Latin phrases. I need exercise.

The path splits off—or has it divided twice now? No matter, my irritation evaporates as I press on, the smooth bottoms of my boots slipping occasionally on the carpet of fragrant pine needles. The sound of waves crashing in the distance floats through the forest along with the water's salty scent, and rays of sunshine poke through the branches overhead.

The path grows steeper, the trail winding through the woods, the crashing of the waves far below me now. I gasp out snatches of a song I've been working on.

The path forks again. Becomes harder to follow. Breathing deeply, I push through an overgrown tunnel of green, trip on a tree root, get a face full of spiderwebs, and—

"Amazing." The sound of my voice is snatched away by the wind that blows across the vast expanse of the granite plateau. The view of Rock Hook Cliff from the lighthouse had been misleading. The park is bigger than I thought, but the cliff? It's *much* bigger. This summit is only the beginning of the long spine of a ridge that stretches away into forever.

The huge, sunlit cliff top has woods on three sides. The fourth opens out into thin air. I start across what's basically a flat field of stone dotted with sparse green plants and tiny purple flowers. As I walk toward the cliff edge, the wind cuts through my jeans, and I wrap my arms around myself. Looking up at the last of the clouds scudding across the blue sky, I wish Lilah were here. She'd love this.

Or maybe not. The rocky land juts into the ocean, isolated, like her. Lilah eats, she sleeps. She showers on her own—dresses herself. Or she doesn't. Some days, she doesn't do anything but lie in her bed. Sit by her window. She won't answer questions, can't seem to hold a conversation. Doesn't respond to anything—except for that black book.

And now I've got it. *Guilt.*

That scraped feeling, as if my nerve endings are uncovered, spreads through me. The surgery, will it work?

Looking down at the pale patches of lichen and dark-green smudges of moss spotting the granite, I skirt the end post of a low wooden fence—

And find myself at the threshold of another world.

The ocean booms below me like a reprimanding voice, its waters extending endlessly. My ears begin to ring; no, the sound is more like humming, more like *music.* Coiling melodies shiver my skin.

Something crosses the sky overhead, throwing a dark shadow onto the plateau.

I think of looking up, maybe even start to—then feel the lightest touch, like silk, against my cheek.

I pitch forward—

And then,

I'm flying.

SPEED

It's not true what they say.

Your life doesn't flash before your eyes.

My mind is blank. Still.

But my body moves fast, plummeting through space with desperate speed—

I squeeze my eyes shut.

The wind roars past my ears.

SKIN

In the next instant I'm shocked to find I'm not alone.

Two arms, strong as stone, encircle me and draw me close against a smooth, bare chest that's definitely *not* stone. The scent of salty skin surrounds me, along with the smell of springtime, at night. Something slaps against my back, against my hips, and the backs of my legs. Viscous satin blankets me, slick and wet against the side of my face that isn't pressed against skin.

Things might not be okay.

We smash into the waves.

SHATTER

The steel embrace that holds me so tightly shields me from the worst of the impact—

But the force of it knocks the breath from my lungs and pulls our bodies apart.

Hands reach for me, fingertips slipping over my skin—

And then the protective grasp is gone, and except for a shattering sadness, I'm alone.

Alone—

Underwater.

IMMERSION

I can't breathe.

I must be dead. Definitely. Dead.

Sinking endlessly through the sea, I open my eyes. The world is water.

But I can still see the surface—

And beyond that—

The sky.

What am I looking at?

White wings—a giant bird. Spiraling high above me, close to the place I'd fallen from.

But—*did* I fall? Yes. No.

Whose voice is singing?

The wings—I've never seen wings like that. So big and white . . . It must be a sea hawk, an osprey. An eagle. Not an albatross, they're not from here . . . *I'm not from here . . .*

The water darkens, turning a deeper shade of black. *I'm dead.*

No. *Drowning.* But not drowned. Not yet. I kick. The weight of the water, the weight of my body—it's too much. Clothes. Boots. Dragging me down. *Lilah, is this how it was for you?*

Now I hear my mother's voice competing with the rushing sound of the water.

An angel.

At the sound of her voice, I close my eyes. No longer propelled by the force of the impact, I sink slowly, the sadness crushing me in a way the water can't—from the inside.

But Mom's voice, it comes again. *Arion, look up—look up!*

Even now, sure that I'm on the brink of death, I don't believe that's what I'm seeing, don't believe that those are an angel's wings, carving great circles in the sky so far above the water.

Haunting melodies swirl around me, as if the sea itself has a voice . . .

Then all at once a song so stunning *fills* me, I no longer care that I'm drowning.

The song soars inside me like a meteor, bathes me in a shower of shooting stars. A fluid counterpoint to my devastating sadness, the music escalates in beauty until it *replaces* the sadness.

My lungs are begging for air, but it doesn't matter, not anymore, not while the song courses through my veins.

Then, I feel the presence.

With a huge effort against what feels like an intense desire for sleep, I open my eyes.

His hair washes around his face, late-afternoon sunlight mingling with dark seawater.

Bo Summers pulls me up, up, up—from the subaqueous depths, until we break through the surface of the sea. I claw at the air, gulp it.

I don't know how he does it, how he holds me afloat in the rough water as I cough and struggle. I'm dizzy and disoriented—oh right, I'm dead. Trying to move my head, I can't lift it. Further proof.

He brings his hand to the base of my skull, his spread fingers forming a support, turning me toward him. As I focus on his face, the breath I've just caught nearly leaves me. His pupils are ringed with flames, two suns, surrounded by green—no, blue—a shifting combination of the two. The colors move, like the ocean.

Even with me in his arms, he swims effortlessly, hauling me through the breakers. I assume he's taking me to land, but his eyes—I'd let him take me anywhere.

My inner clock is broken, the concept of time nonexistent. The cliff, the fall, the sea; suddenly I'm lying on the sand, peering through wet lashes, studying him as he leans over me.

"Arion, are you all right?" His voice is a whisper of concern, his voice—is music. Only a handful of words, entwining with the wind and waves, but my ears catch them, toss them to my swaying senses. Music. *How is it possible?*

Gazing into his eyes, oceans of color shot through with sunlight, it's like I'm at the top of the cliff again, beginning to fall, and this time I want to, want to sink into the strange sea of him.

Still, after another moment of staring into those eyes, something—some instinct—takes over, and I try to look away. I can't.

The droplets on his lashes catch the light. Water drips from his skin onto mine—

A strong *pulling* sensation washes over me—a spasm almost. I gasp in surprise.

At the sound of my sharp breath, Bo's dark-gold brows draw down. His hands, on either side of my face, press against me urgently as the fire in his oceanic eyes flares.

"Why, you're holding your breath," he mutters. He gives a short laugh and stands. He looks down at me for a moment, then turns, taking several steps away from me.

My clothes heavy with salt water, I struggle to sit up, wanting so badly to follow him. But I have no strength.

I know, though, what will give it to me. His voice.

Will he say my name again? How does he even know it? How did he catch me in his arms?

Supported on my elbows, half lying on the sand, I begin to grow cold, unsure. *Had that been his voice?* The goosebumps that cover me now, are they from the sound of it? Or from the chill sinking into my bones? His voice is a song so familiar, I know it by heart. At the same time, it's new, and so different from anything I've ever heard. *I have to hear it again.*

As I noisily release the breath I have indeed been holding, he spins around and springs toward me—almost animal-like—then stops, still several feet away, in a low crouch.

"How do you know my name?" I manage to sputter, trying once more to sit up.

He watches me for a moment with his sea eyes. Then he says, "You're the girl who lives in the lighthouse. And apparently"—his lips twitch—"you don't have the best sense of direction."

His voice. Honeyed sound.

My own voice scrapes out through chattering teeth. "H-how? How did you—" But I'm shaking uncontrollably and the words break apart.

Bo stands, reaches for my hands—and the bizarre pulling sensation streams through me, growing stronger as he helps me to my feet. He must feel it too; abruptly he steps back, his arms dropping to his sides. Then he snatches something up from the sand.

"Here," he says. "Put this on."

He's wearing the black surf trunks and must be cold too, but it seems weird that he has a *coat* here on the beach. Now I notice more clothing scattered on the sand.

He watches as I wrestle with the heavy cotton bomber jacket, seemingly unwilling to help as I struggle to stick wet arms into soft sleeves. Then, as if realizing I can't accomplish this task without his assistance, he does help. I stop shivering as he moves closer. Carefully, he does up the zipper. An easy feeling comes over me. Without actually deciding to—

I lean against him.

He goes absolutely still, his fingers at the top of the zipper, his knuckles grazing my throat.

"Say something," I whisper. "Please."

For a moment he just stares down at me, stares especially, it seems, at my mouth. Then he backs away—one step, two.

"Wait—" My chattering teeth start up like a motor. "I—I want to know how you caught me. In your arms."

"I didn't 'catch' you. I dragged you. Out of a tide pool. Over there." He's speaking in clipped tones now, but still his hushed voice fascinates me, the way it resonates in his chest, the way it's somehow like warm spring air moving through thigh-high grasses in some wild, deserted place . . . He gestures to the water's edge. I take a quick look—then swing my gaze back to his face. His eyes hold mine, the swirling blue green, the glint of gold, hypnotic.

I'm about to tell him not to be ridiculous, that there aren't any tide pools where he's just pointed—

When my head nods forward.

"We have to get you home," he says.

But I've never felt more at home than in the moment he was speaking. "Please—" I begin.

All at once I stagger, nearly falling, my eyes closing. I want to take a nap in the worst way.

He scoops me up in his arms. I start to protest—but my head drops against his shoulder.

The skin of his neck smells of the ocean, of sunbaked pine needles, of something delicious I can't name. All at once I want more than sleep, I want—

But I don't know what I want, because the music . . . the music . . .

Mysterious melodies delicately entwine with barely there harmonies to create a web of dreamy sound. The music slips inside of me. His murmured words make no sense yet speak to every cell in my body. Pleasure washes over me, the coldness of the beach seeping away.

A question filters down through the music. "Arion, can you bring your thumb and your little finger together? Can you touch your thumb to your pinkie?"

What? "Sleep now," I say thickly. Then, words slurring, I try to explain where I live.

"I know where you live," sings the beautiful voice.

A sensation of weightlessness . . . of strong arms enfolding me, legs somehow twined around mine . . . a dream of wind in my hair . . .

Behind closed eyes I sense shadows crossing my face then receding, again, and again. Darkness. Then light. Dark. Light.

His words come as if from a distance now, tumbling over me. *"Cold skin. Cotton clothes. Inadequate. This is Maine. You're unprepared. Outdoor activity. Life. Save. Emergency. Why? The cliff. Why?"*

He sings my name. My breath comes slower. We move faster. This boy who isn't a boy, I want to see him—

I can't open my eyes.

FALSE FRONT

My bed. I'm in it. *How?* A thousand sharp needles prick the underside of my skin. Blankets falling away, head pounding, I sit up. Start to swing my legs over the side of the bed—

Then suddenly stop.

Voices. Voices just loud enough to echo slightly off the bricks of the tower out in the hall.

"Bo, you should go." A voice like Bo's only different. Deeper. But just as musical.

"No, *you* should go. You're the one who can't handle—"

"Save it—this isn't about me. So she's what's got you revved, yeah? A girl who's—"

"Like you said, this isn't about you. It doesn't concern you, J."

"Oh, but it does. And if you were thinking straight, you'd be concerned too—"

"I don't have to be. I'm not you, Jordan."

"Obviously. Check it out—you're shaking. Good thing I got here when I did."

"Not a good thing. I don't follow you everywhere, what the hell, J?"

There's a long silence. I realize I'm holding my breath.

Then the voice that isn't Bo's, the low voice that makes me want to lie back down for some reason, to close my eyes, and surrender to sleep, says, "Will she remember?"

"No. Not most of it, not—no. Maybe. I don't know!" Bo is clearly angry, but his voice is still beautiful. *A storm at sea.* "I've never done—this."

"Oh, I'm well aware of that." The speaker pairs this comment with a derisive snort of laughter. "But you did—"

"Yes! I already told you. It was instinctive. Like being on autopilot."

"That—is why I'm worried. You need to be *in control*."

"I am in control."

"Yeah, now maybe. What about the father?"

"What about him? It helped that she was basically in the beginning stage of hypothermia, if I hadn't had her up against me— Hold on. Doesn't that count as control? And what about now? She's behind that door, alive. I'm standing in this hallway, with you. In control."

"Bo, don't you get it? If you'd fucked up this close to home—"

I don't hear what comes next. I'm too busy examining my pants—I'm wearing *yoga* pants.

Earlier, I wasn't.

I had jeans on earlier. I know I did. I was wearing jeans when—

When I fell from the cliff.

I let out a small involuntary sound.

The speaker breaks off. My head snaps up. I stare at the door. A long moment passes.

Now all I hear is a soft ringing in my ears. They've gone. Bo, and whoever was out in the hall with him. Their conversation made no sense, but the questions racing through my mind are just as incomprehensible.

Had I really fallen? Had Bo actually caught me? And these pants—who dressed me?

Whoever it was, they must have undressed me first.

Frantically, I look around. Wet clothes hang from the top of the bathroom door, from the doorknob. An empty glass and a bowl with a spoon sit on the bedside table. I jump up—

Bad idea. Head swimming, I cautiously sit back down on the edge of the bed. My feet are stuffed into wooly socks, and I'm wearing three shirts. No underwear. No bra.

There's a knock on the door. I slip back under the covers.

"Arion?" The door opens— Dad eases into the room. When he sees that I'm awake his shoulders seem to straighten. "How are you feeling, sweetie?"

"Fine." And I am, as long as I don't move. Ignoring the mug in Dad's hand—not that he'll let me do that for long—I make another attempt to get out of bed.

"Whoa, just a minute, young lady, you're not going anywhere, not until you drink this."

My head throbs, but I manage to roll my eyes. He can command a crew, but with his family, Dad's usually a complete pushover. Love for him surges through me, and something catches in my throat as I imagine my body spinning through space. *How much does he know?*

He hands me the hot mug and I lean back. "So, um, how did . . . I'm a little tired." I look up at him hopefully.

His face pales as he concludes that I have no idea what happened—which is mostly true.

"Bo Summers showed up at the house, carrying you. You were soaking wet. He said the two of you had been horsing around, that you'd fallen into one of the tide pools."

"How long have I been asleep?" I ask casually, wanting to erase the worry on his face.

He tries to make his voice equally casual. "About a day and a half."

"*A day and a half?* I have to get down to school!" I have two tests today, but more importantly, I need to find out about Bo Summers. Mary must know—

"Ari." Dad watches me carefully. "It's Sunday."

"Oh." I relax against the pillows—then tense. I'd lost both Friday *and* Saturday night? Not like I had big plans, but—*scary*. Taking a sip of the broth, I try to calm down, try to hide just how freaked out I am. "Dad, this chicken broth is, like, gourmet. Did you put in lemons?"

"Glad you like it. And yes, it's got lemons. But don't think I'll give you the recipe."

"Way to go with the reverse psychology. Did you learn that from Mom?" He laughs, and I'm relieved, wanting things to get back to normal. But suddenly images assail me: churning water, oceanic eyes, immense white wings. Not the normal I'm looking for.

"Dad? Did you say a day and a half?" He nods, his smile vanishing. I force one of my own. "Who's the stylist?" Like a game show hostess I sweep one hand down the length of my body.

"Oh, ah—I picked out your clothes." He rearranges the empty dishes on the bedside table.

"Nice choices," I say, waiting for the rest.

"The doctor was the one who actually dressed you."

"Doctor?"

"Old Doc Watson. Local guy."

I duck my head. Dad knows how much I hate hospitals. He hates them too. We'd spent entirely too much time at UCSF Medical Center with Lilah. "Thank you," I whisper.

"And don't worry. He kept things private. Used your top sheet here, kept you covered up. He said you were in the early stages of hypothermia, and Bo said that made sense, that you'd gotten cold, too cold. You had all the symptoms, you were talking some strange talk."

"Can you touch your thumb to your pinkie?" Now I remember where I'd heard those words before: scuba diving lessons. I was thirteen, then fourteen . . . I'd loved those classes. Lilah's accident had changed my feelings, but the memories remain. Scuba safety. If you can't touch your thumb to your little finger, you're on the way to hypothermia. I shudder.

"This far north, the water can be deceptive," Dad says. "Cool one day, frigid the next."

Deceptive. Right. Instinctively I keep quiet about the fact that I hadn't seen any tidal pools, let alone fallen into one.

"Bo seems to know everything there is to know about hypothermia," Dad says. "Impressive. Although I don't know why he wasn't worried about his own body temperature, kid only had on a bathing suit." He shakes his head. "Anyway, I offered to lend him some clothes, get him a towel. His only concern was for you. I got busy making soup and forgot all about the fact that he was wearing next to nothing. Guess his brother brought him something dry."

"His brother?"

"His older brother stopped by. Twice. Very concerned about you. And Bo. Never met him before. He was here when Doc said you'd be okay. He seemed as relieved as I was. I've met their dad, of course. Nice guy. Smart as hell."

So the other person in the hall had been Bo's brother. That doesn't help me understand their weird conversation any better. But does it really matter? *People die from hypothermia.* I shove the thought away. I'm fine. Only frustrated at not being able to remember the doctor, or how I got home. Bo, I remember. And the—the wings. They aren't something I'll forget, ever.

"I've never seen Bo at school, do you know if he goes to Blaine?" A chill runs through me despite the hot mug in my hand. *What kind of person can do what he did?*

"Professor Summers homeschools his kids. Although I'm not sure how that works out. He travels a lot. His wife passed on soon after the birth of their youngest boy . . . I don't know the details."

"Oh. That's sad."

"It is."

"Do the Summers use the cove next door? I think I saw Bo surfing over there."

For just a second Dad's face looks like it did the night he'd come home after seeing what was left of the *Lucky*. Then his expression clears and he says, "They live there."

"They *live* there? You mean they live in the park too? But—that cove looks so wild."

"Like I said, the professor travels quite a bit. Sometimes he takes his family with him, but yes, that's their home. And it *is* wild. In fact, I don't want you going over there."

"What? Why not?"

Dad picks up the dishes and gazes out the south-facing window. "Summers Cove. That's what folks have always called that stretch of land. Summers have owned it forever. But it doesn't really belong to the family anymore. The government is taking over this end of the peninsula in the name of your favorite project, Rock Hook National Seashore." I make a face.

"The state of Maine wants to make the national seashore part of Pine Park, over on the mainland. I'm not sure how that'll fly; the Summers used to own that land as well. I believe the adjoining land still belongs to them, so they may still have some say. They've got a lease now at the Cove, which means they can live there as long as they want. Looks like they're going to stay, though I don't know why they'd want to, after—" He breaks off abruptly.

"After what?"

"Nothing. Forget it. Look, next summer their land will open to the public, just like this place. But for you"—Dad comes close to scowling—"Summers Cove is closed."

"Dad, you can't just—"

"I can. The professor's a good man; don't get me wrong. He created the Clean Ocean Zone, and that protects the waters all along the coast . . ." Dad's train of thought seems to pull out of the station. "But I still don't want you over there."

I give a mumbled response that could be construed as a yes or a no, then watch Dad mentally slap his forehead as he remembers he's talking to his teenage daughter.

"Arion. *If* you ever go over there, be careful, okay? And don't go by yourself."

"Aye, aye, Captain Rush." I salute him. *Bo lives there. How dangerous can it be?*

Balancing the dishes, Dad returns the salute. Then he picks up a pile of newspapers stacked on the overstuffed armchair I'd insisted we drag up here, an armchair being an essential factor of the getting-lost-in-a-good-book equation. The blanket from the living room hangs off one side.

"Dad?" I nod toward the chair. "Aren't you a little old for babysitting?"

He stops in the doorway. "Aren't you?" We both laugh, but his chuckle is off. Embarrassed. "I didn't want to leave you by yourself, sweetie, I admit. I stood watch for a while. Sat here talking with Bo, actually, had a nice chat. Read the paper."

Bo Summers, *in my room.*

"Front's coming in." Dad continues standing in the doorway, as if he has more to say but hasn't decided if he wants to say it. Today's talk is already the longest we've had in years.

Finally, he confesses, "Bo and I sat here for quite a while on Friday night. It got late. I started to doze off. I'd been up since four. At some point, when I nearly rolled out of the chair, he told me to go to bed." Dad looks apologetic. "I was worn out. He said he'd stay, make sure you were all right."

I try to imagine what it must be like for Dad, starting a new job, a new life, with a seventeen-year-old daughter in tow, worrying about his other daughter's health, waiting for his wife. It must be hard, but he loves me, and love shows on his face as his words come faster now.

"He's a responsible boy, bringing you home like that, making sure you were okay. Said he wanted to stay whether I slept in the chair or down at the house. I couldn't say no—and I *tried* to. He said he wouldn't dream of leaving. Kept saying something about this being his fault."

His fault? Goosebumps spring up along my arms.

"I didn't let him stay in *here*, of course. You two barely know each other, is that right? He said he met you at the library."

The library. He remembers. The odd conversation I *just* heard between him and his brother is already fading, but Bo remembers our humiliating non-meeting at the library. Great.

"So I told him to stay as long as he liked, and I put your dressing table chair out in the hall. He left for a bit yesterday, last night he came back, saying all the same things, insisting he wanted to stay, that he *had* to stay." Dad looks impressed. Again. "Early this morning he was wide awake. Told me to go get some breakfast. So I did. And I made more broth. He stayed until I came back. Passed him on the stairs. You were alone for about one minute.

"He's quite a guy. Actually thanked me for letting him sit in that cold hall all night long, on a straight-backed chair. You must have made quite an impression on him." Dad gives me a little smile, then shuts the door.

Another shiver passes through me, a series of shivers. I need a hot bath.

Afterward, I examine my cowboy boots—still wet, probably ruined—then open the door to the hall. The antique ladder-back is still out there. The chair doesn't exactly match the dressing table, but Mom had painted both with climbing vines that hid curling words, phrases like, "Know thyself," and "Art fills the void," and given me the two as a pair.

Trying to imagine the tall surfer sitting there, keeping watch while I slept, I sway just a little on my feet. *Two nights.*

You could knock me over with a feather.

BEACH WALK

Carrying *Maine Lighthouses* under one arm, I finally leave the bedroom, intending to take the big book of photographs down to the cottage. Compared to the companionable clang of hard-bottomed boots, my sneakers are nearly soundless on the metal stairway.

Nearly soundless, unlike Bo's footsteps—and his brother's—which, I realize now, had been *completely* soundless. I heard them talking in the hall but never heard them leave. Not like that's important, but it feels like another hole in my memories. I've lost an entire weekend.

But once I'm outside, inhaling one balmy breath of salt air after another, I remember enough to know that all I want to do is forget Friday afternoon—when I'd been unable to catch my breath—forever. I just want to curl up on the couch, near Dad.

Only, when I get down to the cottage, I have an almost physical craving to stay outside. Sitting down on the landing, I lean against the front door and open the library book. On page fourteen, Rock Hook Lighthouse juts up into a stormy sky.

Rock Hook Light is 208 feet tall, almost as tall as the tallest lighthouse in the country, but that's nothing. The Pharos, when it had existed in 330 BC, had stood 450 feet high.

Tourists destroyed the Pharos. They were referred to as invaders back then. Okay, so it was earthquakes, but tourists could have done it, if there'd been any around . . .

The book slides from my lap. Had I dozed off? I blink—

An image of enormous wings flares in front of my eyes like a flash from a camera.

Standing quickly, I nearly stumble as I start down the steps to Crescent Beach.

I'd vowed not to come down here, but it's like I'm being pulled. Leaving the book behind, I tear off my sneakers and plunge one foot, then the other into the cool sand.

The relief is immediate. *This is where I belong.* The sound of the surf, the slightly feral smell of the sea, the ocean itself—although too close for comfort—all say, *You're home.*

Music became my life over the last year, but music isn't something you can touch, not like the sand I scoop up now. Letting it fall through my fingers, a thousand aches seem to fall with it, leaking from a heart that music sutured but didn't heal. The music brought flashes of joy, but this—the sun, the sea . . . this is what I love.

But—the water. It scares me to be so close to the water. And yet I feel like I *need* to be.

I begin humming a melody, a song I've been working on, and try to imagine that fear is something I can simply walk away from. Lifting my face to the sun, I walk south.

The waves slide up— *Shh* . . . spreading glassy transparency over the sand before slipping back to the sea. Gulls plummet from an almost piercing-blue sky, diving down into the dark water.

Soon, the giant black jetty is just up ahead. It sprawls from the bottom of the bluffs down to the water and into the waves, which . . . makes no sense at all.

The breakwater in front of Crescent Beach was built parallel to the beach in order to protect it, and to protect the bluff that the lighthouse stands on. This jetty is *perpendicular* to the beach. It's basically a towering wall. A wall big enough to hide something behind.

Like, maybe, the fact that you aren't the same as other people.

Even though I'm thinking about him, I startle as Bo appears at the top of the rocks. Still, I only hesitate for a second.

"Come down," I call to him, beckoning with a hand that's suddenly trembling.

He stands motionless, as if considering. Then all at once he's climbing down the rocks, his movements like falling water. What would have cost me at least ten minutes and a twisted ankle takes him two seconds. Before I've even taken another breath, he's standing next to me.

I'm not sure why, but I take a step back.

He gives a short laugh. "Smart. So why aren't you smart enough to stay away from here?"

"What the—" I scowl. "Whatever. In case you're interested, I came to thank you."

"Oh, I'm interested. My brother, apparently, thinks I'm very interested. How much of our conversation did you hear?"

"How did you know—"

The sharp look he gives me now is enough to make me catch my breath. At the sound, a thin smile appears on his handsome face.

Confused, I simply glare at him. Then I stammer, "Enough. I heard enough to know that I have no idea what you were talking about." And I don't.

Impulsively, I shut my eyes, pretending Bo isn't the most gorgeous guy I've ever seen. When I open them, I make sure to look *past* him, to the bluffs. If this is how the conversation is going to go, I'd better cut to the chase.

"Why did you lie about the tide pool?"

"Tide pool?"

His voice is all innocence, and so melodic—my eyes shift involuntarily back to his face.

"Y-you know what I mean; you said I 'fell into a tide pool.' You told me, and my dad."

"Would you prefer he knew the truth? Because I can—"

"No!" Briefly I imagine what Dad would do if he knew I'd fallen from Rock Hook Cliff. "No, actually, now that I think it through." Our eyes catch, and I try to look away, try to remember the questions that seemed so urgent just a minute ago, but I can't do either.

Then he drops his gaze, and my head clears. Quickly I say, "But *I* would like to know the truth."

"Oh, would you? Well. The truth is, you should go home."

"Fine, I'll go home. And you can go—"

"To hell?" Bo looks amused. "I probably will. If not for my sinful thoughts, then for my rude behavior." With a lithe movement, he sits and begins cupping handfuls of sand—releasing the grains slowly over the tops of my feet. "You're welcome."

He sounds slightly chagrined. I look down at the top of his golden head, not sure what to think, but finally decide to sit down.

The sand on my right foot slips off.

"You should be more careful," he says, covering my foot back up.

"Maybe if I knew exactly what I needed to be careful of . . ." I begin adding to the hill of sand.

"But that's the problem, isn't it? There's nothing *exact* about building a sandcastle."

The blond hairs on his forearms glint in the sunlight. He has long fingers, the hands of a musician. Remembering how he'd held me in his arms, warmth spreads through me. It's embarrassing to be so physically drawn to him, someone I hardly know.

The three buttons at the neck of his shirt are undone, showing his collarbone, the hollow at the base of his throat. I examine his thick gold lashes. Lowered, they hide his eyes.

"There are no blueprints," he says, shaping the tower that rests on my feet. "Nothing but constantly shifting sand—and imagination.

Shovels should be banned, I think, because hands"—he smooths the base of the castle, his fingers brushing my ankle—"are far more articulate."

The brief touch sends me drifting somehow, so that I have the sensation of floating . . . on my back . . . in a warm bath, or . . . or . . .

"Friday," I say. The word is an unsteady thing. "When I fell. How did you catch me?"

"Water, of course, is the third ingredient." He bends over my feet. "Sand, imagination, and water. Some people would put water first on the list." He lifts his gaze until we're eye to eye. "Not you."

It feels like—I'm slipping into the sea. "How?" I demand faintly. "How did you do it?"

"How did I do *what*?" A hint of a smile plays on his lips.

I tear my gaze from his. "You know what—you just said it. You admitted you lied to my dad. So, how? How did you drop out of the sky and into the water just in time to save my life?"

In an instant Bo is on his feet. "I did *not* drop out of the sky." His voice is rough with anger.

"You did—I saw you."

His eyes are on fire. Blue flames, green, a shimmer of gold. "Go home, Arion."

A thrill speeds through me. On his lips, my name is a song.

"I just wanted to say thanks—"

"You said it." The three terse words cut through the salt air, and before the sound of them has time to fade, Bo disappears behind the black wall of the jetty.

ECHO

Dr. Harrison joked once that all musicians have OCD tendencies. Ha-ha.

Bo. *What is he?*

During dinner with Dad, and later, while I'm doing homework, that question—and a million others about Bo—slices through my thoughts like a swimmer's strokes through water, again and again.

Listening to the new song I'd managed to download before the nearly nonexistent Internet connection dropped, I write to Mom, telling her I've met the most beautiful boy—then hit "Delete." After starting over and writing about school, I hesitate. But Dad wouldn't have told Mom about my fall; he's smarter than that. Closing the note with *x*'s and *o*'s for Lilah, I shut down the computer. The email will have to go tomorrow, from the library.

But thoughts of Mom won't go so easily, even though, in a way, she herself has been gone longer than Lilah has. And I'll probably never know why. She'd blame it on her art.

Tonight, I wish I could talk to her, about Bo, about my walk. But she hardly ever picks up her phone, and even if she did, we wouldn't really *talk*. We'd just exchange trivia.

After getting out my guitar, I open a notebook filled with lyrics and bad poems, and turn to a blank page. I pick up a pen, then put it down. Straighten a stack of paperbacks. Line up a handful of guitar picks. Focusing on small things can save you. I learned that even before Lilah's accident. Learned to focus on the small things. When you look at something small for a long time—it opens. Then you can see a long ways.

Usually when I'm looking at that long view, I see words, find songs, and something's clarified. But sometimes, I just see the past. I see Mom. Loving me. But I can't *feel* it. It's like having a photo of something but not the thing itself.

As if the love she gives me now is an echo, and the original sound is gone.

Mom used to joke, *"I loved you until you started talking back."* But I hadn't talked back, Lilah had, and Mom still loves her more. Why do adults joke about things that aren't funny?

Playing around with a bunch of different chords, I settle on a minor one, of course. Next, my fingers land on the strings and form another chord, but not one I recognize. The combination of notes is—different. Dissonant. *Don't think. Just play.*

"To tell the truth," I whisper sing, *"I'm not okay."*

"Thank you for asking, and now will you stay? Or smile politely and just walk away."

I have no idea where this is going, but the next verse comes out as if it's already written.

"To tell the truth, I'm sure I look fine. You can't see what's hidden with the naked eye, it's like trying to find something blue in the sky."

My voice shoots into my upper register—

"Gently—pick me up carefully . . .

Gently—hold me. Rock me . . .

Gently like she—used to do."

Scrambling to write the words down, the bridge bursts from the center of my body and up through my throat. I can almost hear the drums: a broken roll on the snare, a hesitant kick on a bass drum that *just* makes it to the downbeat on time. An ascending bass line that sends the next section soaring— Tears start rolling down my cheeks, but I must be feeling better, because depression is debilitating. You can't write a song if you're wasting away. You wouldn't want to. Grief, that's fuel, but the "depressed artist" thing? It's a myth.

"Myth!" I shout. Then I shout it again, listening carefully—although not, I realize with a start, for an echo, but—for an answer.

Don't know why I'm surprised when none comes.

SUNSET

"Ready for this?" Mary asks. Of course, she's the first one here.

"Not really." I stroke one of the hot-pink petals on the one last flower that clings to a Rugosa rosebush at the back of the lighthouse. Late-afternoon light edges the petal with gold.

"Don't worry. I told you. You won't have to do anything. The guys will dig the fire pit, my Kevin's bringing food, and Pete said—"

"He'll bring beer."

"How did you guess? And your contribution?" Mary holds up a bag of marshmallows.

So far, though I've been invited to a bunch of parties, I've only been to two, both at Mary's house. Each time I ended up wedged between a couple of Kevins.

But today is different. Today the party is here.

"We really should've waited until tomorrow night," I say.

"True," Mary agrees. "It's not like this is going to help anyone's test scores."

For students concentrating on marine sciences, school will have a slightly later than usual start tomorrow. Not so we can sleep late "'cause we're gonna be partying half the night," like Pete claims, but to give us time to make it over to Seal Cove, a public beach on the west side of the peninsula. The longest and supposedly prettiest beach on the Hook, it's also the site for the infamous rules-and-regulations exam.

Listing a bunch of rules and filling in blanks won't be a problem. It's the hands-on part I'm worried about. Tomorrow at nine a.m., I'll be on a boat, *in the water*.

As much as I want to embrace the beach, want to walk at the ocean's edge, the idea of actually *being on a boat*, of actually being *in* the water, terrifies me.

"You're still stressed, aren't you?" Mary says. "But not about the party." I nod, and she gives me a sympathetic look. "You'll be fine tomorrow; it'll be like riding a bike."

"Yeah . . . if you saw the hills in my old neighborhood, you might not think that was such a good comparison." But tomorrow's test isn't the only thing bugging me. Earlier this week I asked Mary about Summers Cove and told her how Dad had said not to go there. I was going to ask her about Bo too, but she got this weird look on her face. Then she said she had to go and hurried off to PE. Maybe now is a better time.

"Mary, when I asked you about Summers Cove—"

"Here comes Alyssa," Mary interrupts. A 1960s yellow Mustang convertible skids to a stop in front of us, spraying stones.

"And Pete and Bobby," we both say at the same time.

"Jinx." I start to laugh, then stop, a second late in hearing the weight Mary's given the word. Her eyes hold a warning. *She really doesn't want to talk about Summers Cove.*

Would it make a difference if I told her what happened to me over there?

Wet lashes catching light, water dripping from his skin onto mine—

"I didn't 'catch' you. I dragged you. Out of a tide pool."

Lies, all lies.

But even so, I can't possibly tell Mary. Not about any of it.

"Niiice," Pete says, climbing out of Alyssa's car. Bobby gives a low whistle.

"It'll be *awesome* when this place opens for real next summer; it's so much closer than Seal Cove." Alyssa points to the lighthouse. "Can we go up?"

"Um, yeah, sure." It had to happen sooner or later, might as well get it over with.

By the time we come down from the tower, Alyssa is my best friend. "Hey, I'm driving the mantrap to Portland pretty soon. I need new winter clothes. You guys want to go?"

"It could happen," Mary says. "You in, Ari?"

"Maybe." I'm betting Alyssa approaches shopping like an extreme sport, but I wouldn't mind checking out some clubs.

A van drives up, and some kids I recognize from school pile out with blankets and coolers. As the crowd heads toward the steps, Logan's white pickup rolls in. He takes his time walking over to where I stand waiting at the top of the stairs.

"Who invited them?" He jerks a thumb toward the group on the beach below.

I roll my eyes. "Come on, before Pete drinks all the beer. He brought Shipyard, and Geary's. Not that I care, but you might."

"Damn right I do." We make our way down the steps. "But promise me something?"

"Sure," I say, not really paying attention, "anything you want." We walk across the sand.

"Anything?"

"Wait, what am I promising?"

"Too late. But don't worry, I won't ask you for anything you don't want to give." Logan's light eyes glint in the sun, and I notice, not for the first time, that he has ridiculously long eyelashes. "And I'll start with something easy, like a beach walk."

I'm off the hook for a reply—Dad arrives carrying two platters laden with lobster rolls. He puts the trays down on one of the coolers, and he and Logan shake hands.

"Young Mr. Delaine. Pleasure. How are your folks?" I'd forgotten Dad knows the Delaines, but it makes sense since he knows everyone on the peninsula.

"Doing well. They want you to come over and cook for them this weekend." Dad's face lights up, and Logan shoots me a wide grin that says, *See? I'm totally charming.*

"This weekend ought to be fine."

"I'll tell them." Logan takes my hand. "I'd love to continue talking to you, Captain Rush, but I promised Arion I'd go for a walk with her."

I start to object, but Dad runs right over me. "Great idea. Going to be a fine sunset. I'm going inside myself, Classic Regatta's on. I'll leave you kids to your walk and your bonfire business." He eyes our clasped hands, and leaves.

"Oh, you promised *me*, huh?" I laugh and yank my hand out of Logan's.

"What? A promise is a promise. I make it to you, you make it to me, same difference."

"Okay . . ." I look at him sideways, feeling like I'm missing something. "Guess a walk is a good deal. I mean, you could have asked me to write your Existentialism papers."

"That comes later." We start walking, and he slips one hand beneath my hair, his warm fingertips finding the back of my neck. I shiver under his touch and pull away, landing a punch on his arm. Swiftly he catches my hand, murmurs, "Resistance is futile. You know that, right?"

"I'll keep it in mind." I laugh, but my cheeks are hot. "Move over, will you?" I reclaim my hand as we change places, so he's walking next to the water instead of me.

Washed in shades of pink and streaked with purple, the sky curves above us like the inside of a seashell. After about fifteen minutes, we sit down on the sand at the end of the beach.

A few weeks of friendship with Logan feels like so much longer. He's always seemed familiar, and we've gotten tight, fast. But the closer we've gotten to the jetty separating Crescent Beach from Summers Cove, the quieter he's become. This silent side of him is new to me.

One afternoon, when we'd hung out on the front steps of the school, Lilah's story had slipped from my lips. Not her story, really, no one knows that, but her *condition*. Logan listened without interruption, as if he knew it wasn't easy for me to talk about her. It probably wasn't easy to hear about her either, but he'd been there for me. I need to step up.

"Do you want to talk about it?" I ask.

"Talk about what?"

"The thing that makes us alike."

A beat goes by. Then he turns to me. The sinking sun shines directly into his light-gray eyes, illuminating them. "I do," he says. "Because it's you." We gaze at each other for a long moment. "You know about my brother, right?"

"Some. I'm sorry, Logan. So sorry."

He shakes his head. "Nick and me—" Grief and anger vie for control of his voice. Anger wins, and he begins to spit the words out. "We were best friends. We were, like, glued together when we were little. We had our own rooms, but at night, one of us would sneak—or get this, sleepwalk—into the other's room. Sometimes I'd wake up on the floor in his room, or when I'd get up in the morning, he'd be at the end of my bed. Nothing could keep us apart.

"I remember one night, I was about eight, and I got out of bed to get a drink. The room was dark and I stepped right on him. He was on the floor next to my bed. He didn't even wake up. The next day, though, when I told him about it, he was mad. That was the first time he punched me. He did way worse when we were older. And then, everything became about him."

"What do you mean?"

"I mean he went to that private school on the mainland, the one that's close to the west side. Where the peninsula connects. Blaine. You've seen it."

"Sure. Pretty place. Prestigious too, right?"

"Pretentious is more like it."

"All right . . ."

"Not all right. I blame that place for everything." Logan's tone turns sarcastic. "'Nick Delaine the brain,' 'the brain at Blaine.' Nothing would have changed if he hadn't gone there. He wouldn't have started acting like he was better than everyone. Better than me. He became someone else, some big-deal preppie boy. As if we'd come from that kind of family."

Logan's lips compress into a frown, making his wide smile hard to imagine. Behind him, crimson streaks cut the sky.

"The last couple years we drifted apart," he continues. "We fought all the time. *He* fought—loved to fight—about everything. We became . . . enemies."

"That's harsh." I lay a tentative hand on his back.

"Yeah, it was bad." His voice grows quiet. "And . . . there was Beth."

"Who's Beth?" I move my hand in slow circles.

"His girlfriend." He shakes his head. "Supposedly. Beth was so into him going to Blaine. Her family couldn't afford it. Then she got a scholarship, like Nick. Still, she didn't go."

"Why not?"

Logan's pale gaze seems to search my face for a moment, then he turns away. "She wanted to stay at Rock Hook High."

But I'd caught the hesitation.

Sliding my hand off his back, I study Logan's profile. I hadn't heard anything about Nick's girlfriend. She must have graduated, because—

Suddenly Logan scowls toward the jetty.

"What?" I ask. But then I follow his gaze—

My stomach dips.

Bo Summers is climbing—more like flowing—down over the rocks.

He walks toward us now, the rays of the setting sun at his back, glorious in the glowing light.

CLOSER

"Hi." Bo manages to make the one small word sound musical.

I stand up as if yanked by a string. "Hi."

Logan remains sitting.

Bo gives a curt nod, extending a hand down toward him. "Hey," he says, in the same dulcet tone. But Logan only glares at Bo's hand briefly, before looking back toward the ocean.

It's as if someone's turned up the sound of the surf.

Bo lets his hand drop to his side, his expression thoughtful.

"Logan—" I hesitate, then ask, "Do you know Bo?"

But what I really want to say is, *What's up with you two?*

Logan's short laugh is humorless. "Everyone knows him."

Shifting my weight from one foot to the other I look back and forth between the boys. The three days since I've seen Bo feel like three weeks, and I'm desperate to talk to him. Alone.

Abruptly Logan stands. "I'm going back," he says, ignoring Bo completely. "You should come."

"Um. Okay." I tuck my lower lip between my teeth. Don't move.

Logan crosses his arms and looks at me steadily, as if taking my measure. "Fine. Stay. But—" Worry creases his brow, then he glances at

Bo and his eyes harden. "Don't do anything stupid. That would include, but isn't limited to, swimming."

My mouth goes dry. *I don't swim,* I almost shout. "Since when is it your job to tell me what to do?" Logan gives another short laugh, then heads down the beach.

Mad at myself, I spin toward Bo. "What the hell was that about?"

He arches one dark-gold brow. My tone is all wrong. Clearly there's something between him and Logan, but Bo isn't the one who's been rude, for once.

"Can you hang out?" He gestures to the sand.

At the sound of his voice I automatically plop back down on the beach, immediately wishing I'd been more graceful as he melts down to the ground in one fluid motion.

Turning toward the water I ask, "Why did Logan ignore you?"

"Surely you have other, more interesting questions." A smirk colors his voice.

My head swivels—I can't help it. "Questions for *you*? The guy who literally appeared out of thin air and saved my life?" He frowns at that, but I hurry on. "Oh no, I don't have any questions. It's perfectly normal to pretend the water temperature is eighty degrees, when it's more like forty. Nope, no questions, not when I know that cold-water surfing is tough enough, *with* the right gear. Do you even own a wetsuit?

"Because from what I've heard, you're an *expert* on hypothermia." My heart begins to race. The way Bo risked his life to save me, the way he nonchalantly surfed in such cold, rough water the day I first saw him, is suddenly beyond upsetting. It doesn't matter that we don't know each other—*I care*. The reason why I care is a mystery, but I do. "And what about the other hazards of surfing in this area? Like a tidal swing of, oh, say, twenty feet? Or riptides?"

"*You* surf?" Bo runs his eyes over me.

"Oh, you have questions too? Great, let's swap. I don't see my dad anywhere, so maybe you'll tell me how you managed to break my fall from Rock Hook Cliff *and* pull me out of the ocean *and* carry me to the lighthouse." My words seem to bounce off his calm demeanor.

"Like I told you, I helped you out of a *tide pool.* Helped you home. End of story."

"More like, beginning of story." About to call him a liar, I stop, drawn into the depths of his oceanic eyes. *Heat* from those eyes wafts toward me, I swear, and the chiming in my ears—nearly constant these last few days—grows louder, more lovely, until it becomes impossible to ask the most important question of all: *What about the wings?*

"You say you fell from the cliff, but . . . people don't just fall, do they?" he says quietly.

But thinking about the fall is a bit like reliving it, and all at once my emotions threaten to overwhelm me. Swallowing hard, I fight back tears.

"Are you—" His eyes narrow as he studies my face. "Are you going to cry?"

"No!" I shut my eyes. "No, I'm not going to cry."

"Hey," he says softly. "I have an idea. Why don't we start over? Just, start again."

Blinking, I open my eyes and look straight into his. I hardly know him, it's just, when he held me in his arms that day . . . but he's right. Do-over. I nod.

"Hi." I hold out my hand. "I'm Arion Rush."

"Hey. I'm—"

Our hands come together, and the pull—the pull is like some kind of bizarre sideways gravity. Seawater washes over my toes, the tide is on its way in. Some instinct tells me to move back, but I can't—I can't move.

"Closer, I want you closer."

His voice. All at once his mellifluous voice is everything, the impetus behind my smile, the ache in my chest. His voice is *everywhere*, in the sudden curl and crest of the waves, in the thrum of my pulse—*but not in my ears*. He'd spoken—but he hadn't. The world tilts. My confusion grows, my clothes seeming to chafe against my skin, even as his velvet voice lulls me.

"I need you . . ."

I hear him—*feel* him—but his lips aren't moving! His lips are still. His lips . . .

I lean in—

He drops my hand and leaps to his feet, his eyes riveted on my mouth.

Gasping at the abruptness and fluidity of his movement, I bring my hand up. "What is it?" I whisper through the cage of my fingers.

He turns away, the movement sharp. "This isn't a good idea," he says over his shoulder. Ragged music seems to surround him—angular melodies roll off of him.

Words are impossible. *Music, I want music.* I want to hear his voice again, want to hear it whispering inside my mind, the way I did just a moment ago.

But he's walking away. I can't let him. Not again.

"What about my answers?"

He stops short. "You mean your questions." He shakes his head. "I can't do this."

"Do what? Be friends?"

A dry laugh escapes his lips. "*Friends.* Being friends would be a very bad idea. Trust me, I'm not what you need." He scales the jetty with an aqueous movement, looking almost unreal as he stands on the rocks with the cobalt sky behind him, his light hair a nimbus.

"But maybe *I'm* what *you* need," I say impulsively. "And how can I trust you when—"

"Unfortunately, you're exactly what I need. And that is *not* a good thing."

"I don't understand. Why?" My voice is so full of pleading I want to kick myself, but I go on anyway. "Why isn't it a good thing?"

"Because—" He pauses, looking down at me, his face half in shadow now, his expression unreadable. "It's a very *dangerous* thing."

TARRADIDDLE

"Arion!"

I whirl around. At the same moment, the sun slips from the sky.

Alyssa is coming down the dusky beach with Pete and Bobby.

With a sort of desperateness I spin back—

Bo is gone.

A sound of frustration slips from between my lips. "He moves like magic," I mutter.

"What did you say?" Alyssa asks as she arrives at my side.

"Nothing," I answer quickly. But I can't meet her gaze.

"Party girl, where've you been?" Pete says.

"Yeah, everyone's like, where's Arion? Isn't this her shindig?" Bobby adds.

"Really? Sorry. Didn't mean to be gone so long—"

Pete shoves Bobby. "Bob's just goofing on you, but if you want any food . . ."

"What were you and Bo Summers talking about?" Alyssa demands.

What can I possibly tell her? That Bo saved my life but doesn't want to be my friend? No, I can't talk about him, no way. But . . . I bet she can.

Linking my arm through hers, I start walking. "Bo's kind of cute, don't you think?" I ask in a low voice, so the boys won't hear as they walk behind us.

"*Kind of?* Kind of, if you're blind. He's gorgeous." Alyssa lifts her chin, as if positioning herself as the expert in this area. "So what were you guys talking about?"

"Not much. I asked him about the waves."

"You asked him about *the waves*?" She gives a little snort.

"I did consider asking him if he snacked on magnets."

She laughs. Point for me.

"You think he's a hottie, don't you?" she says, tossing her dark hair. "Trust me, he's a snob. He won't ask you out. He doesn't go out with anyone."

"Sounds like you know him well." I file away the info. *He doesn't go out with anyone.*

"I do. Well, I—we—haven't ever . . . Everyone knows him," she finishes irritably.

Huh. *Didn't I just hear that?*

People have dragged logs they found stacked up against the bottom of the bluffs over to the fire pit, where they're being used for benches and backrests. I sit on the sand and hold out my hands to the flames. Alyssa veers over to the opposite side, sitting down between Sarah Hisano—a girl with long, enviably straight peacock-blue hair and narrow, fiercely beautiful kohl-rimmed eyes—and a guy I vaguely recognize from English class. Mary's Kevin seems to be in charge of the cooking. She's handing out paper plates.

Looks like Logan left, which makes me a total jerk. *Damn.* Hugging my knees to my chest, I stare into the fire.

Mary appears next to me with her pile of plates. "Don't worry, he'll be fine. He's handled way worse." Kevin's close behind her with a platter of hamburgers.

I've handled worse too. I've just never hurt a friend through sheer idiocy. "Not hungry."

She pushes a plate at me, and Kevin slides a burger onto it. "Eat," she says. "Seriously, whatever happened between you guys down the beach? He can take it."

A few people start talking about tomorrow's test. The exam is a sort of triathlon. Three boats, three skill sets. We have to pass in order to place into Advanced Oceanography next semester and continue on in marine sciences senior year.

I wish I could lie to myself. Pretend I'm not afraid. But if I play my mental "changing radio stations" game now, my fears might bust out on the boats, create chaos for me. I have to at least own it. I'm scared shitless.

The fire's suddenly too hot—its flames shooting up into the night. I lean back, glancing at the sky. There's no moon tonight, and as the clouds move in on the wind, the stars wink out, one by one, as if the darkness is slowly smothering them. Not a welcome thought, but it comes unbidden, as do Lilah's written words.

I am waiting.

I look around the circle at the people I know, the few that I don't. How will I find the boy she met here on Rock Hook? Or maybe he's not a boy at all; maybe she met a man. *Oh, Lilah.*

Blink; flash. The long narrow beam of the lighthouse reaches out over the black beach toward the waves and my thoughts shift back to Bo. Is he watching the beacon tonight from Summers Cove?

As if my thoughts have moved through the misty salt air, the guy sitting next to Alyssa says, "I wonder who's looking at the light tonight. I mean, who's this lighthouse *for* anymore?"

Alyssa inches closer to him—she's definitely giving him the eye. "It's for us, for our personal entertainment."

Sarah of the blue hair shuffles the layers of bracelets she wears on both arms.

"I've always wondered why Rock Hook Lighthouse is here," she says. "This isn't exactly the most dangerous place. When was the last time a boat wrecked anywhere near Rock Hook?"

The question hangs in the air for a second before the breeze takes it—

And blows it toward the shadows, one of which answers.

"Three weeks ago."

Separating himself from the night, Logan steps forward, his expression tenebrous in the firelight. Obviously this isn't the time to ask if he's still pissed at me.

"It was a fishing boat," he says, addressing the crowd. "Up from Portland."

"What are you talking about, Logan?" Mary's tone is skeptical.

"The mayor tried to hush it up, tried to keep the media from covering the story. I'd say he was pretty successful."

Logan's answer hits me hard. *No one knows the story of the four missing boys?*

"Be serious," Mary says. "How can the mayor keep the papers from printing a story like that? Why would he? And what exactly happened to this boat?"

"The 'why' is easy," Logan says. "Think about it. What happens next summer?"

"That's crazy," Mary replies. "The mayor wouldn't try to keep a story out of the papers because he's afraid of losing tourist dollars. Besides, I don't think one accident will keep vacationers away from Rock Hook National Seashore when it finally opens."

"Funny," Logan muses, "how some people, like the mayor, want to share Rock Hook with as many people as possible, as many tourists as this place will hold, no matter what kind of secrets they have to keep. While other people want the crowds to stay *away* from Rock Hook, no matter what kind of secrets *they have* to keep." He scowls, looking around the circle, as if trying to determine who belongs in which camp.

The group bursts into conversation. "Secrets? What's he talking about?"

"When Rock Hook becomes another tourist trap . . ."

"The mayor? I'll ask my mom, she'll know."

"You haven't given us any details about this mysterious accident," Mary says to Logan, and everyone looks at her now. "Was anybody hurt? Obviously none of us heard about it—maybe you've got it wrong. Rock Hook Harbor is a small town. People get bored. Rumors fly."

"Ha—who could possibly get bored around here?" Alyssa says, jostling Sarah.

Sarah, her hair shoved behind her shoulders now so that she's rendered nearly invisible against the night in her black outfit, pushes back. Alyssa makes the most of it, falling into the boy next to her.

"You know what I mean," Mary continues. "'The one that got away,' that kind of thing. Probably just another Big Fish story, Logan, probably nothing."

"Mary, four guys gone missing is not *nothing*." He looks across the fire at me. "They only found their boat, just their boat—with a bunch of holes in it. That's something. Something bad. Someone *murdered* those kids."

I look away, heart hammering as I squeeze two cool handfuls of sand. *Am I really the only one here besides Logan who knows about the* Lucky*?*

Two boys sitting next to me begin whispering to each other. "He's paranoid," says one.

"Yeah," says the other. "This sounds like one of his conspiracy theories."

"Right, like when his brother—"

I glare at the boys and they stop, but I feel bad for Logan. I want to defend him, to tell everyone that he's right: someone *did* sink the *Lucky*. But Dad asked me not to talk about it. He said the Coast Guard didn't have all the facts, and that folks around here didn't need to get upset all over again. At the time, I didn't know what he meant. I didn't know—he was talking about Logan's brother.

"It happened at Devil's Claw," Logan says suddenly. Everybody stops talking. The sound of crashing waves echoes off the bluffs. "And Sarah," Logan looks down at her, "to answer your question, that's why the lighthouse is *here*. The end of the Hook, where the lighthouse was supposed to have been built, where it was needed the most, is such a hazard they couldn't put the light station there. No one can build anything at the tip of the peninsula."

"That's true," Pete says. "It's like bizarro world out there. The tides are weird. The waves are gnarly. Plus it's rocky as hell. Even with modern nav systems, boats still use the lighthouse to steer clear of the tip of Rock Hook, 'cause even the best equipment fails at Devil's Claw."

"If the guys who built Rock Hook Light, Standard Smith and his partner—" Logan stops for a second, then continues, "the rest of his party, if they'd succeeded in constructing the lighthouse at Devil's Claw, it would be totally lost to the sea by now instead of simply missing its . . . twin, the second tower." He pauses again, and I think he's finished with the disturbing history lesson. But then he goes on, talking about how Smith vanished, disappeared without a trace. And finally he says, "All you have to do is dig. You'll find a whole lot of strange stories about Devil's Claw and the rest of the coast along this part of Maine. There are more drownings, more unexplained boating accidents around here than any other place on the entire East Coast."

"The water can be treacherous around here for sure," Mary says. "But ever since OZI got together with the state to help regulate usage and protect certain areas, keeping boats *out* of those areas, things have changed. This part of the coast—"

"Riiight, we have the Clean Ocean Zone now, to *protect* the *coast*." Logan's voice oozes sarcasm. "Bet you and Arion's new boyfriend could have a nice chat about what a good job OZI's doing with that." Logan turns and walks away, leaving for real this time.

Part of me wants to run after him, to apologize for earlier. Another part of me wants to run after him so I can kill him.

"So there *is* something going on between you and Bo," Alyssa huffs. "I knew it."

I'm thinking I'll have to grab one of the shovels the boys used to build the fire pit to dig my way out of this when Bobby unknowingly helps me out, announcing that he's hitting the road. Mary gives me a hand as well.

"Arion, do you have a copy of O'Keefe's requirements for the term paper?" *Go,* she mouths.

"Sure—I'll get it." Grabbing Dad's trays, I run toward the steps.

Behind me people start gathering belongings, dumping ice out of coolers. They'll be a while, but Mary catches up with me at the bottom of the stairs.

"Hey, do you have something to tell me about Bo Summers?" she asks.

"Do you know him?"

"Everyone knows him."

I stare at her. "We need to talk."

"We do. But first, go after Logan, will you?"

Our eyes lock. Either Mary's more concerned about Logan than she let on, or she's become more concerned after hearing what he said at the bonfire.

"I'll make sure he's okay. Don't worry."

I give her a quick hug, then race up the steps.

QUESTIONS

By the time I reach the top of the stairs, Logan's backing down the driveway.

"Hey," I shout, trotting alongside the truck. The night can't end this way, all dark mysteries and implied accusations. "Logan, wait!"

He stops and rolls down his window the rest of the way. "Wait, what?"

"Just *wait.*" I lean against the driver's side door, trying to catch my breath. "Bo Summers—you know he's not my boyfriend."

Logan mutters something that might be, *Not yet.*

"Oh, come on. And what was that about, at the bonfire?"

"You knew about the fishing boat, Arion?" Feeling caught, I nod. "From your dad?"

"Yes." I try unsuccessfully to read the complicated expression on Logan's face.

"You didn't find out from Summers?"

I look at him quizzically. "No. Bo and I—" The anger in his eyes catches me up short. "Logan, I'm sorry, about earlier. I should have walked back with you, I just . . ."

Logan leans back in his seat. "You just, what?"

"I just—nothing." What am I supposed to say? *I just wanted to talk to Bo for a second. He's my neighbor.* Lame. How about, *I just—am so attracted to Bo Summers I'd blow off even my best friend so I could hold his mysterious hand for less than a minute.* Great. "I'm sorry," I repeat.

"Hmm. Whatever."

Shifting the empty trays, I ask, "Are you still picking me up tomorrow? For the exam?"

"Of course. What's with your car again?" Logan sounds suspicious, like he thinks maybe the Jeep is fine, that I just want a ride because I need my hand held, which I do.

"It's being cranky. I'll tell you about it in the morning."

"Okay. Pick you up around eight thirty."

"Thanks." Getting through the test might be hard, but at least I'd be there. "Good night."

"Sleep tight."

A faint version of his smile appears and I feel my shoulders relax. Stepping back from the truck, I watch as the red taillights disappear into darkness.

The relief I feel at seeing even part of Logan's wide grin is no surprise. Tonight I discovered just how much I care about him.

Even if I don't understand half of what he says.

The wind gusts around me. Balancing the trays, I reach up for my hood—then let my hand fall.

How had Logan found out about the *Lucky*?

Maybe more importantly, why did he think I'd learned about the boat from Bo?

The group from the beach straggle up the steps and begin their goodbyes. "Is everything cool with Logan?" Mary asks.

"Why, is Delaine pissed or something?" Kevin laughs. "'Cause that'd be different."

Mary had warned me that her Kevin wasn't a big fan of Logan; now she winks at me.

I grin. "Everything's fine. How about with you guys?"

Swaying slightly, Kevin twines his arms around Mary and buries his face in her neck.

"Um—ooh." Mary starts to giggle. "We're good. But we're gonna go now."

"Yeah, that might be best." I laugh.

She pushes Kevin toward the passenger side of his parents' Prius, then turns and waves.

In another minute, the car vanishes down the drive and I'm left alone with the wind, wishing I'd asked her, *Why does Logan hate Bo so much?*

REGISTRATION

From this vantage point on the peninsula, Wabanaki Bay (Forfeit Bay, the locals call it down here where it's widest) looks just like the ocean. In fact, except for the outlines of a few distant islands between here and the mainland—which, although we face it, is invisible—it's identical.

"Anyway, my dad's taking it in . . ." My voice fades as I finish telling Logan the Jeep saga and stare at the rough waters of the Bay. Even though just below us the curve of the land shelters Seal Cove and its waters are clear and calm, I have no desire to leave the sanctuary of Logan's parked truck.

He probably knows car trouble isn't the real reason I chattered incessantly for the entire ride. Still, he hooks his hands behind his head and leans back, playing along.

"How long have you had the Jeep?"

"Forever. I learned to drive on that thing."

"And that was when? Yesterday?"

"Ha-ha. Probably way before *you* learned to drive. Not that you're a bad driver."

"Gee, thanks. So you'll *let me* continue to be your chauffeur?"

"Hmm. I don't know. Don't want you to work too hard."

"I wouldn't have to work too hard. You never go anywhere."

I start to laugh, but he's right. And he's laughing too, as he reaches over and tucks a strand of hair behind my ear. Suddenly he seems so close. As if my senses are on zoom, I smell his shirt—clean laundry—and notice the shine of his hair, the shape of his lips.

"I *could* drive you crazy," he says now, his voice soft, resonating low in his chest in a way I haven't heard before. "If you wanted."

I look down at my hands. *If you wanted.* Do I want?

He turns to look out over the water, his hand dropping from my hair. I steal a glance at his shadowed jawline, the hollows beneath his cheekbones, his impossibly long lashes. But he's a friend—*and* a total flirt. At least he's honest. Or maybe he's playing. How can I tell?

Lilah told me most guys lie about what they really want. I hadn't known what she meant at the time, but now I picture Bobby asking me if I want to "study." I'm beginning to get it.

As I follow Logan's gaze, the water catches my eyes, won't let go. Still, I'm hyperaware of his body across the bench seat of the truck's cab. Maybe I'm the liar.

But my palms aren't lying, they're sweating, and it's not Logan's offer that's making them so damp. Leaving the truck—suddenly it seems like a very bad idea. Surreptitiously, I wipe my hands on my jeans.

"Ari." Logan lifts his right arm so it lies along the back of the seat and gestures with his other hand. We look at each other for a moment, then I slide over and curl against him. He wraps both arms around me. "You'll be fine," he whispers into my hair.

Trapped sunlight fills the truck. If we don't make a move soon, we'll be late. My thin sweater is clinging to me, damp like my hands. Logan slowly takes his arms from around me as I strip it off. Draping the sweater over the seat, I notice that he's staring at the cove now as fixed as I'd been staring just a few minutes ago.

"It's time," he says without taking his eyes off the water.

"Mm. Thanks for telling me." Sweat beads along my hairline. I wipe it away with the back of my hand. Still, he doesn't open his door. I don't open mine.

When I asked him questions about the exam on the way over, he'd answered easily, so why is he so hesitant—

A flame of intuition blazes through my body.

Last night as we'd walked down the beach, Logan had grown quiet. I'd mostly carried the conversation. But by the time we sat down near the jetty, he'd gone completely silent. Then we'd talked about his brother.

Nick Delaine had drowned, and now I know where. Not this cove, but *a* cove.

Summers Cove.

That's why Mary didn't want to talk about Summers Cove, why Dad warned me away.

Logan wouldn't say hi to Bo, wouldn't shake his hand. My pulse pounds at my temples.

We open our doors at the exact same second. Our feet come down with an identical crunch on the broken clamshells that fill the parking lot, sun-bleached white as bones. Together we walk toward the water. My legs are shaking.

A crowd of kids is gathered around the teachers from the marine sciences department. Mr. Kraig is gesturing to the three boats moored in the quiet cove. We've spent hours over the last couple of weeks studying the boats, working in makeshift classroom labs that served to simulate the vessels as best they could. Today we're supposed to be ready to experience the real thing and be tested on what we've learned.

This is a test of the emergency broadcast system. This is only a test.

I stare at the first boat, a Colgate 26 daysailer, a standard boat used by the Navy to teach basic sailing skills. The second boat is bigger, a forty-three-foot fishing boat. Donated by one of the local families, it's been refurbished with the latest navigational gear. We'll focus on the equipment once we're aboard. The wooden fishing boat is a troller, the kind I've been on a million times with Dad. That doesn't make me feel any better.

There are five dinghies, three with oars, two with outboards, waiting to ferry us out to the boats. Floating in the pale-green shallows, the dinghies look small and insubstantial.

A girl from lab hands out orange life jackets as I look at the last of the large boats, a forty-foot fiberglass motorboat. It's an Alliaura Marine Jeantot Euphorie power catamaran. The name sounds like poetry, but that's the only good thing about the boat, about any of the boats. Twenty feet wide, the gleaming white vessel is crammed with state-of-the-art navigational gear and can hold over thirty people. Nearly new, it must have cost hundreds of thousands of dollars. It doesn't take a rocket scientist to figure out where the catamaran came from, or the daysailer. OZI.

The scene is nothing less than picturesque, a postcard. *Miss you. Wish you were here.* The backside of the granite cliffs tapers gently down toward the water. Softly swaying pines and puffy white clouds complete the idyllic setting. My stomach is acid.

"You can do this." Logan reaches for me, his palms warm and dry against the clammy skin of my upper arms. The warmth of his hands makes me realize how cold I am.

"My sweater." Is that my voice so far away? "I left it in your car."

"I'll get it." As he jogs off, Mary approaches.

"Arion, you're super pale. Do you feel okay?" Mutely, I gaze at the water. She squeezes my hand. "I'll go make sure we're in the same group."

"Your sweater, if that's what it is." Logan reappears next to me with the limp cardigan. "Here, take this too." He gives me a faded blue sweatshirt.

Fingers fumbling, I take the heavy shirt, put it on over the sweater. "Thanks, Logan."

"Sure thing," he says. Then he purses his lips, looks at the sweatshirt. It's thick and soft. The lettering across the chest reads, **Blaine.** "Go ahead and keep it," he says.

Before I can thank him, he ruffles my hair and turns away, heading over to the registration table. Mary gives me a little nudge, and, lifting the two anchors that are my feet, I tuck both hands into the kangaroo pocket of the sweatshirt and follow.

SWIM TEST

The morning actually passes. Mary stays by me the whole time.

At noon everyone gets a break. Seniors wearing name tags with the word **Mentor** written in thick black letters bring out coolers filled with sodas and brown-bag lunches from the deli in town.

Immensely grateful to be back on land, I stretch out on a sunbaked rock. All around me other students are doing the same. Mary comes over with a sandwich, Logan with a soda. But after being out on two boats and two dinghies—the dinghies scared me the most for some reason—I feel like any food that goes down is going to come back up. No lunch for me.

"Check out our girl Alyssa," Pete says, as he and Bobby join us on the rocks.

Alyssa's wearing a bikini and standing in the water with Bonfire Boy, who's rubbing sunblock on her back. Sarah is trying to talk her into taking a plunge.

"She ought to go in now, while it's still her choice," Bobby says. "Have your suit on?" he asks me. I shake my head vigorously. Rumor has it that quite a few people go swimming on rules-and-regs day, some voluntarily, some not. The mentors determine who gets tossed. I pray it won't be me.

The lunch break isn't nearly long enough, and soon it's time for the last segment of the exam. Mary and I wait for a free dinghy to take us out to the Euphorie.

"You made it, Ari," she says as we climb into one of the little boats. A senior I don't know gives the dinghy a shove, then hops in after us, manning the motor. "Almost done."

"Done?" We hit a small swell and I glare at the boy, grabbing the sides of the boat. "That's one way to put it." We draw up alongside the catamaran. "Later we'll pay homage to the wind gods for taking a vacation day, make a sacrifice or something." Mary looks at me like I have two heads. "Seriously, check it out. No wind. We can't possibly sail anywhere." She laughs, and the next hour passes in an almost pleasant blur.

But then the boat becomes crowded. The office made a mistake on the master schedule, and everyone's running behind. By midafternoon, my forehead is home to a dull headache, and a lot of the girls are complaining about the heat, lifting their hair off their necks to catch a nonexistent breeze. I'm hot too, and thirsty, but at the same time, I'm nearly as cold as I was this morning. Goosebumps crawl along my arms, even though my skin is sticky with sweat.

Stranded on the deck of the catamaran, I idly watch the action back on the beach. People are shedding layers and shoes. Two boys kick water on a group of girls. And finally, the seniors go after Alyssa. Her screams travel out over the water as I squint into the glare of the sun, eyeing a dinghy that's drawing up to the daysailer across the cove, this one empty of passengers, and powered by oars and a golden-haired boy—

The Euphorie lurches beneath my feet, and the mundane sounds of the day are subsumed in the low roaring that fills my ears. I stare at the back of the boy, at the long muscles of his tanned arms. *What is he doing here?*

He turns the boat now, angling it until it disappears around the other side of the daysailer, but just before it does, I think he looks my way—think he sees me. A bead of moisture rolls down between my shoulder blades. The edges of objects turn bright, and the day takes on an unreal sheen. He's out of sight now, but irrationally, I'm still trying to get another glimpse of him, looking in vain across the water.

I keep on glancing over at the daysailer, even as my teammates try to involve me, handing me a piece of paper, and then a pencil, a clipboard. I have no idea what they're for.

The clouds hover way up in the sky, still and cottony . . . Then, they start moving.

No. *I* start moving.

I'm going ashore.

The idea seems to come from somewhere else.

"Wait!" someone shouts.

The word is a buzzing insect in my ear as I hit the cold water with a splash—

My head goes under and immediately comes back up, the temperature of the water bringing me sharply to my senses. *What am I doing?*

Even though the water is shoulder height, I don't get the chance to stand.

As soon as my feet touch the sandy bottom, somebody grabs my legs—

And pulls me under.

Holding my breath, I kick, trying to understand—

A pair of iron arms lock around my waist—hold me down.

The water turns opaque with foam as I thrash frantically, I can't see—

I kick wildly, lungs bursting. Salt water seeps between my lips . . .

Water, water, everywhere . . .

The roaring in my ears becomes a gong. Pressure builds inside my head.

Water rushes down my throat—

And reality

S h i f t s.

I'm in San Francisco, clutching at Lilah—

Who's lying on her bed—unconscious?

No! I scream. *I won't leave. I'll never leave her!*

People try to calm me. Mom, Dad, a doctor. Somebody puts a hand on my arm. I throw it off. *Why was she on that boat? Dad took the charter today. He had a boatload of tourists!* Babbling, crying, I go on about the tourists. Lilah wasn't supposed to be on an oceangoing fishing boat! *A swordfishing boat!* One mistake on a boat like that can cost your life.

Another second, a flood of memories—

And I remember it *all.*

My heels hit the sandy bottom, the hold on my waist releases—

And two strong arms sweep me off my feet. Heat. Skin. My body held against—

As my head clears the surface I gasp, the sound of my breathing jagged and raw as I fight for air. I have the strange sensation of watching myself in an old film—like a weird kind of déjà vu. I see each separate frame. I see Bo Summers, lifting me—out of the water.

MENTOR

Bo carries me up the beach and sets me down on one of the rocks, which is exactly what I want—for him to put me down. And yet, as soon as our bodies are no longer touching, I—I—

Gagging and coughing, I sputter, "Where did you come from?" But inside my head I'm screaming, *Why did you let me go? Hold me—hold me!* My heart pounds with fear, adrenaline. "What are you *doing* here?" I demand.

"What are *you* doing? Since when is a swim test part of the rules-and-regulations exam?" The water has painted his golden hair black. His smile is the Devil's.

"What do you know about the exam?" I practically shout. "You don't even *go* to the high school." Shaking, disoriented, I look down at my wet clothes. My gaze continues to travel downward to the sand, and I wish I could vanish into one of the small holes there. Maybe I can be reincarnated as a ghost crab—the tiny translucent creature can disappear from sight almost instantly. That would be perfect, because despite my absolute terror, I'm embarrassed.

Taking a deep breath in, I lift my gaze, my eyes drawn to the bright blue of Bo's swim trunks. Just above his left thigh, a white, rectangular tag is stuck to his soaking suit. The label is identical to the ones all the seniors wear. *Mentor.* I release my breath with a disbelieving huff.

Bo's eyes move to my mouth. His smile vanishes.

A group of students forms around us. Mary makes her way through the crowd.

"It's okay—she's all right. She just wanted to get off the boat. Back up, people."

Logan pushes through the wall of bodies. "Bikini or one-piece?" His tone is joking, his eyes, furious. Even in my bedraggled state I can see that his hands are shaking. Clenching them tight now, he yells for Pete to get a towel.

Mr. Kraig hurries over. "Catch of the day, Mr. Summers!"

Glaring at Bo, I unbuckle my life jacket with trembling fingers. Sure, he'd pulled me out of the water, but the bastard had pulled me under first. What a sick joke.

"Are you all right, Miss Rush?" Mr. Kraig asks.

"I'm fine, really." But everyone seems to be too close, too loud. "I was just . . . hot."

Snickers rise from the back of the crowd. Bo smirks before turning to the teacher.

"Mr. Kraig, great to see you. Good thing you got in touch last night; you were right, short of hands today." He looks around. "Seal Cove, perfect weather, I'm surprised you couldn't get more seniors here on a day like this."

"I know, I know." Mr. Kraig shakes his head. "So many kids just don't *get* community service. They're missing out today, though, for sure." He waves a hand at the clear blue sky.

Bo continues to smooth-talk the teacher like nothing's happened, his gaze sweeping over me occasionally. He waves an arm at Pete, who's appeared with an armload of towels. Pete tosses a towel—Bo deftly catches it.

Logan takes a step closer to me. Glowering at Bo, he says, "Thanks, cabana boy, I'll take it from here." He holds out a hand for the towel.

"Sorry," Bo says lightly, cutting in front of Logan. His arms encircle me as he wraps the towel around my shoulders.

"Yeah, you will be," Logan mutters from behind him.

Let me sink to the bottom of the ocean next time, I fume inwardly as I scowl up at Bo, who gives the towel a little tug so that it tightens around me, and draws me closer to him at the same time. I make a small startled sound and his lips curve, his blue-green gaze holding mine for just a second, before he steps back and instructs Mary to help me out of my wet clothes.

"There's a T-shirt and trunks in my car if she doesn't have anything dry." He points to the red Jeep Wrangler with mud-splattered tires I noticed driving into the lot a lifetime ago.

"That's okay," Alyssa purrs, coming up behind him. "I've got an entire wardrobe in the back of the Mustang, because, you never know."

Is she actually batting her eyelashes? But she's also looking down at her hands, not quite as bold as usual. Maybe that's why Bo doesn't seem to notice her. He melts into the crowd, which is starting to disperse, everyone probably deciding I either jumped into the water for kicks or was clumsy and fell in.

Logan stands with his hands fisted looking like he's about to say something, or maybe hit someone, until Mary passes the drenched Blaine sweatshirt to him and gives him a little push.

"She needs to change, Logan."

He turns and strides angrily toward the water. Throwing the soaking sweatshirt on the sand, he strips down to his swim trunks and dives in. Mary sighs. "The Delaine temper. He likes to say it's his hot Latino blood, but I don't know."

"Plus 'Delaine' is Irish," I say with a wobbly laugh. Angry as I am, anxiety is still creeping through me like a feral cat.

"Guess he gets a double dose," she says softly, still watching Logan.

Alyssa grabs my hand and drags me over to the Mustang. She hadn't been exaggerating. The backseat is stacked with what looks like the remains of several shopping trips.

"Normally I'd never lend my clothes." She puts the top of the convertible up. "But since it's you." Her curling smile is saccharine. "Change in the back. I do it all the time."

Bet you do. A few minutes later I emerge swathed in layers, and Mary oohs enthusiastically over the fuzzy apricot-colored sweater that covers the two shirts I've borrowed. Alyssa just scowls and looks down at the jeans I've chosen. They're several sizes too big. Who knew? She rolls her eyes and walks away.

An almost inaudible melody sounds near my ear. I whirl around.

"Do you need a ride?" Bo asks. The song fades into the light breeze, and I shiver despite the extra clothes. "Because Mr. Kraig said it's fine for you to leave."

Is this his way of trying to make up for his bizarre stunt? Lifting a hand to my eyes I look out over the water. Logan's just climbing aboard the daysailer. He hadn't taken a dinghy and, instead, had swum all the way out to the boats. He'll be at least an hour.

"Sure. I'll take a ride." We walk across the shell-strewn parking lot to the red Jeep.

Bo opens the door for me, eyeing my multiple layers. "Guess we don't need the heater."

"Yes," I say, climbing inside, "we do."

He starts the car and the air warms up fast, but I swear some of the heat is coming from him. And as shaken as I am, I feel something else as well, that fairly unused mental muscle. *Hope.* What, exactly, is it doing here? Why now, when my memory is bursting with Lilah's harrowing story? The story I'd shut away, the story that I'll never know completely, because Lilah can't tell it.

"Other than the contusions, there's no damage."

One of the police officers actually said that to my mother. *No damage.*

Oh, Lilah! I was supposed to go with you to the café!

"Her brain's not injured," the neurologist said. "It's simply doing what it needs to do. Protecting her. It's in a different mode, a primitive one, supporting only the necessary functions. In the process of blocking out one ghastly night, she's barred everything. No, we can't say if she'll speak again."

Did I meet the doctor? Did he come to our house? No, but I heard my mother convey his pronouncement, heard my father's fist strike their bedroom wall.

The silence inside the warm car is suddenly nerve racking—I can't get my thoughts in order.

Bo. I have a million questions for him. I just can't seem to *think straight.*

Finally, I say something, just to crack the quiet.

"Community service?"

A million questions, and in my confusion I ask one that's meaningless.

"Yeah, my father's big on that kind of thing."

"Oh." I've never done anything in service of another person in my life, unless fetching and carrying for Lilah counts, which it doesn't. She's family. And I bet if anybody had ever talked to *her* about service, she would have said, *Serve yourself, and first too.*

Now, she can't say anything. She was wounded in a manner so grievous her mind has hidden away, leaving her literally speechless. And this disconnect—some days it seems to affect her body as well. She doesn't move for hours, just sits by her window, seeing but not seeing. Her muscles—her very being—wasting away.

"The trauma," the psychiatrist said, "most likely set in the moment she went over the side."

Yes, but—what happened *before* that? Why was she even on that boat?

The police officer shook his head. "We're not positive, but we have our theories."

Only, their "theories" were bullshit. Lilah wouldn't run away from home, she wouldn't steal a boat! I remember now, the way I shouted at Mom. *You don't know her!*

But did I know her? When Lilah came back from the trip to Maine, she was—different. She was curt to me. Cold. Although Lilah had always been cool, even when she took me on her adventures.

But her *new* adventures, they lasted all night. I had no idea where she went, what she did. I only knew she'd sneak in around dawn—

And write in that book when she thought no one was looking.

Lilah. She always told me everything, even things I didn't want to hear, didn't want to know. I was part of everything she did, even when I didn't want to be. I was her audience. Sometimes more.

And then, she was gone.

She left the house in the morning to go to the café with the red geraniums out front where we liked to eat pastries on special occasions—only she never got there.

And she never came home.

That evening, Mom reported her missing. And then there was that long dark night.

I'd stayed behind with a summer cold—*I should have been with her.*

Later that same night, when Dad discovered one of the boats had been stolen, he tried to put things together.

"I've known the men on those docks for years—I know my crews! There's not a man among them who would do something like this. Take a boat. Take my daughter! But who else had access? A theft like this—it's impossible!"

From the start my father knew the two things were related—even before our lives turned nightmarish. Even before it became clear: Lilah wasn't the only one missing.

There were two men—fishermen. We learned later they'd vanished as well that night.

My father raged at my mother—I'd never seen him get so angry before, nobody had. His easy way was part of the reason his crews loved their captain. Their captain . . .

"You're a ship's captain!" Mom screamed those words over and over again, as if it made a difference, as if he had control. Dad was captain, like all of us, only of his own ship.

It's almost hot inside the car by now, but I'm shivering as I lean my head back against the seat, close my eyes—

And I see him.

Not Bo; another boy. I see his flayed jeans, his T-shirt so worn you could easily watch his muscles move beneath it. And I had watched—

Just as suddenly, the image spins away, replaced by the faces of the two fishermen—

I *knew* them. They worked for Dad.

Their families came forward around the same time Lilah was found. But they—were never found.

A baseball cap—the image jars me now. A baseball cap over dark hair—I think it's dark, or maybe just wet. Younger than the fishermen who disappeared, I think, but—his face, I can't see it, it's hidden by the brim of the baseball cap. Did I ever see his face?

He was there, and then not there. Down on the docks. A stranger—I thought.

But Lilah—the way she bounced on her toes with excitement. The shine on her the day she disappeared—I remember it now. That shimmer—was it for him?

And why is he a blur, when the rest of my memories are suddenly so clear?

I am waiting.

She could have met him here in Maine, just like I imagined—it's possible. He could have traveled to San Francisco to see her. Boys. They fell hard for Lilah—she *made* them fall hard. She could have bewitched him. He could have flown out to see her. Moved out. It's possible.

But not probable. Some guy from the docks, some fisherman? Not probable.

"I knew it would happen!" Mom cried to Dad. "Your damn docks—those men! Out for weeks at a time, months even, with nothing to look at but the sea. My Delilah . . ."

I put my pillow over my head that night, and so many others, not wanting to hear, not wanting to be there. I wanted to disappear, but I couldn't.

So I forgot.

A distress signal from the ship came in—one of several the Coast Guard received once the storm hit—but by then it was too late, too late for Lilah, and too late for the two men, who must have been washed over the side.

A dinghy—they found her in a dinghy. Bruises on her shoulders and her wrists and her ribs—she couldn't have managed to climb in herself. Someone cared enough to help her.

Or maybe someone just didn't want to be a murderer.

No one knew who sent the Mayday call. Thank God, the Coast Guard heard it.

What I heard was my parents—fighting. I heard the doctors, and I heard the police. I heard everyone trying to piece together a patchwork picture of twenty-four terrible hours.

Then I shut it all out.

So that up until today, the only things I'd allowed myself to know for sure, were that my sister had almost been killed, when a boat was lost, on a day that started out as deceptively beautiful as this one.

And one more thing.

I hate water.

SALT

"Hmm?" My ears are ringing. Distant chimes. Fading, getting louder—I can't tell.

"I said—we're here."

We're here, and I know everything, as much as I can know. I look out the window at the back of the lighthouse. "How did we—?"

"You crashed out. Think you were dreaming."

"No." I rub at my face. "Remembering." And the pain of that remembering is sharp, so sharp it clears my head.

"It looked a lot like sleeping to me." Bo's voice is a reticent song. He taps a rhythmic pattern on the steering wheel now, and I remember how his hands had felt on me as he carried me from the water, and last week, the way his fingers slipped over my skin.

"Bo, I know that when I fell from the cliff, you caught me in your arms. And you already confessed that you lied to my dad, so you and I both know, you didn't help me out of any tide pool."

"I did." He turns toward me. I look into the seas of his eyes. He says, "I found you by the pools. You'd obviously slipped and fallen. You were halfway in, halfway out—"

"Fine. Maybe someday you'll trust me enough to tell me what really happened. If we, I don't know . . . Sometime in the future."

"The future," he says softly. Then he scowls. "Why can't you just believe me?" He runs his hands over his face, and from behind his fingers I think I hear him say, *"Don't make me convince you."* The hair slowly rises along my arms.

But when he drops his hands to his lap, the smirk he'd been wearing when he carried me out of the water today is back. "Maybe you should reconsider your footwear."

I follow his gaze down to my feet, which are back in my boots. During the exam, I'd gone barefoot, something I'm sure to lose points for. "Got something against cowboy boots?"

"Not at all. They're great. For cowboys. Not so great for hiking maybe."

Lifting my legs, I brace my feet against the dash. "Red's my favorite color."

"Not mine. Too bright." His lips twist. "Too wild. Like your imagination."

"*Red* is the color of your Jeep. You like it, admit it." *Admit everything, while you're at it.*

But he doesn't. He only says, "So what about today? What happened?"

"You tell me. You were right there." *And if you didn't drag me under . . .* "Bo, listen—"

"Oh, I'm listening," he says. "I've *been* listening."

"What's that supposed to mean?" Our eyes catch— My thoughts begin to blur.

I try to focus on my anger, thinking of what a fool I'd looked like today, how it had been his fault. But the anger isn't enough to hold back my confusion, or my tears.

He held me down, under the water.

Bo continues to stare at me, then slowly, he reaches over and with one finger traces a tear down my cheek. Then he draws his hand back just as slowly, studying his fingertip—

Before he puts it in his mouth.

"What are you do—"

"It's salt," he muses. "It really *is* salt water."

"Riiight, so?"

"So, that's fascinating." The golden late-day suns at the centers of his blue-green eyes seem to pull at me, and all at once, it doesn't matter that he just tasted my tears in a strangely scientific manner, doesn't matter that he lied to me, ran from me. Again, he brings his nearly scalding fingertip to my face, runs it down my cheek. Leaning into his touch, my blood buzzes in my veins as, this time, his finger stops at the corner of my mouth. He traces the line of my lower lip and his eyes darken. I close my own eyes, feeling his hands slide to my shoulders. Even through three layers his touch is so warm, evokes something in me so intense, I gasp—

He draws back so fast my eyes fly open—

Spots of color top his cheekbones, and his hands grip the wheel. "I've got to go," he says in a low voice edged with something akin to violence. His eyes are oceans—on fire.

My fingers fumble for the door handle. I leap out of the car—the urge to run coursing through me. *What just happened?* Opening my mouth to say goodbye—goodbye doesn't come out. "Was it supposed to be funny," I ask, voice hitching, "when you pulled me under today?"

A small, derisive sound escapes his lips. Then he says, "Arion," and gives that brief nod, just before he reaches over—and shuts the door.

I watch him drive off. *He scares me.* But . . . it seems like I can still hear his voice, saying my name. The way he'd said it . . . didn't sound anything like goodbye.

Waves of wondering swell inside of me, rising so high, they breach the walls of logic, the reasonable part of the construct that is my brain.

What would kissing him be like?

Just the *thought* of kissing him—it gives me this feeling, like the time I walked across the Golden Gate Bridge and stopped in the middle to look over the edge. My stomach went *swoop* and my vision turned sharp. But it wasn't like I was afraid I might fall. More like, I was afraid I'd jump.

TIMING

The aroma of something spicy meets me at the front door of the keeper's cottage.

"Sweetie, how'd it go?" Dad turns from the stove—the source of the savory smell. He's got a spoon in his hand, and now he takes a taste from it.

It can't be easy for him to maintain such a neutral attitude. He must've been trying to contain his worry all day.

"Good, Dad, um—fine." The white lie weaves itself. "I'll tell you about it in a minute, I have to phone Mary really quick."

"Your timing's perfect, as usual." One of our running jokes is that some people—me—come into the kitchen in time to eat but never in time to cook. "I'm making gumbo."

"Yum. Be right back." In the living room, I find the cordless under a pile of papers.

From the kitchen Dad says, "Logan rang. Said he wanted to drop by tonight, say hi. I told him to come on over." Dad peeks around the corner, wondering if he's gone too far, but I nod, not surprised that Logan wants to come by. He'd been totally freaked this afternoon—his pallid, panic-stricken face and trembling hands had said as much—but not only about me. Just like I'd been pulled under, it was a good bet that he'd gone under too, in a way. My "mishap" had probably served to trigger his worst memories.

In the middle of dialing, I stop for a second. I'd left Seal Cove with Bo; that can't have made Logan too happy either.

"Arion!" Mary picks up on the first ring. "How *are* you?"

"Fine. The hottest bath ever fixed me right up. But, um, we need to talk."

"Yeah, we do. Did you do that on purpose today, or what?"

"I'm not really sure."

"Okaaay . . . well . . . you had me worried for a sec, I couldn't figure out what was going on. Couldn't tell if that was your idea of a good time, or if you were freaking out because of the test. Not the test itself, but, you know, the fact that you had to deal with . . . the water."

I cup the phone, wishing I had my cell and could go outside, but forget that. The Hook is basically a dead zone. "Mary, you were watching, right? When I went into the water?"

"I was," she says slowly. "It was weird. It seemed like you were doing fine, but then . . ."

"Then what?" My fingers grip the phone.

"You got a strange look on your face and held your hands over your ears. Then all of a sudden you swung one leg over the side of the boat, then the other, and you were gone. You honestly don't remember? I would have grabbed you, but I couldn't quite believe what you were doing." Her voice holds a question.

"I was hot," I say quickly. "I just wanted to get off the boat." I'm glad Mary isn't next to me, can't see my face. *Why don't I remember?*

"You made a serious splash before you went under. Then you popped up, went under, thrashed around for a minute. You kicked up a total froth. It was impossible to see if you were having fun, or what. At least ten people were ready to jump in, though, just so you know."

Thrashed around for a minute. Because someone was holding me down.

"Ari? You still there?"

I swallow hard. "Yes."

"Logan was on the beach. He started running toward the water."

"Logan." I say his name dully, thinking of the fear I must have caused him.

"But even before he got his feet wet, Bo had you—one of the Summers kids is usually there on rules-and-regs day—and he hauled you out of the water before anyone could say boo."

"I remember. He carried me out. So . . . he wouldn't have pulled me under. Right?"

"Nooo . . . I mean, why would he? Seriously, what makes you ask that?"

"Nothing, it's just . . . nothing. I don't know why I said that. Brain's a little waterlogged, I guess." I scramble to change the direction of the conversation, but I still want answers. "Did you guys think I was drowning or something?"

"No, not at all." Mary laughs. "It wasn't like that." More quietly she says, "I think Logan was the only one who was really worried, and I was kind of concerned, because I knew how stressed you were. But everyone else just thought you were acting wacky. "'*There's always one or two,*'" Mary says, imitating Mr. Kraig's boisterous voice flawlessly. "*Always someone who thinks that just 'cause we're at the beach, just 'cause we're on the boats, it's summertime.*'"

I try to laugh, but my mind is back at Seal Cove analyzing the afternoon like a slide in Mr. Kraig's lab. *No one knows that somebody pulled me under.*

"Mary, what do you mean, one of the Summers kids is usually at rules-and-regs day? And what about Bo? You said you know him."

"I know him to say hi to, that's about it. And yeah, usually one of the Summers kids is at the test—maybe to check up on OZI's investment? I mean, those boats aren't cheap. I heard Bo's big brother was there a couple of years ago. He's a little spooky."

I still have a million questions about Bo, about his family, but a *clink, clinking* comes from the kitchen now; Dad putting out plates, my job. The conversation hasn't been so quick after all.

"Hey, I've got to go. I was just hot today, you know? Didn't mean to worry you. The sun was brutal. Do we live in Maine or Florida? Seriously, what does 'Down East' mean, anyway?"

"Good one. But yeah, you didn't eat or drink anything at lunch, plus today was superhot. You may have even had heatstroke. Still, next time you want to go swimming? Wait for me. Not that I would have gone in today, but"—she gives a little snicker—"Logan would probably go with you anytime. Or maybe"—she pauses for dramatic effect—"you'd prefer swimming with Bo."

Ha. That would be at least an hour-long conversation.

Dad appears in the doorway. I hold one finger up, and he turns back to the kitchen.

"I'm sure you're going to find me a boyfriend, Mary, but not tonight. Dad cooked up one of his famous southern seafood recipes, so I've got to go eat."

"Wait! I need details, about your *ride home*." Mary's voice is heavy with innuendo.

"You've been hanging out with Logan too long, you know that? But okay. Details. Bo drove me home. He dropped me off. The end." Unfortunately.

"Really? He seemed pret-ty attentive at Seal Cove . . ."

"Trust me, he's not interested."

Or he would have kissed me.

TABLE TALK

"So it went well today. Good to hear," Dad says as we sit down to eat. "Maybe you'll come out on one of the boats soon. There are some real beauties down at the marina."

Glad my mouth is crammed with spicy gumbo, I nod. I do not want to talk boats.

"Sounds like you and Mary have really hit it off."

Another mouthful. Another nod.

Looking down at his plate like he's more interested in his food than my friends, he asks, "How about Logan? You two becoming buddies?" *Ah, the money shot.*

"Yes, Dad, we're becoming *friends*." I spear a piece of crabmeat. Dad knows my privacy policy. And obviously, as I saw last night, he knows Logan. Although I'm pretty sure he's never witnessed Logan's ravening grins and sidelong glances.

"Logan's folks took a real shine to you. 'Course, I don't blame them."

"Dad, come on, they don't even know me."

"Yes, they do. You all met here at the cottage, remember?"

One night when I came down to get my laundry Logan's parents were in the living room with Dad. The three of them were on the couch, talking in hushed tones. They were facing the empty fireplace, their backs to me. They didn't notice when I slipped into the house.

"One of the worst things about losing Nick is what it's done to Logan." Mrs. Delaine's words carried into the kitchen.

"She's right," Mr. Delaine agreed. "Logan was always a joker, a happy kid. Not so much anymore. Nick, well, he had a temper on him. He wasn't so easy to handle."

"Liam!"

"It's true, Anita. I miss him as much as you do, but Nick had an edge to him."

"And I've sensed that same anger coming from Logan—ever since Nick died. But I don't know what to do for him. I miss Logan's laughter—" She started to cry.

Then I sneezed, and Dad told me to come into the living room where he introduced me.

"I do remember," I say to Dad now. "We talked for, like, two seconds."

"It was longer than that, Ari."

He was right. It had been longer. And I'd given Mrs. Delaine a hug. She'd seemed so full of . . . hurt. She didn't hide it behind a smile and two fists, the way Logan did.

"Dessert?" Dad holds up a strainer full of fresh blueberries.

"Thanks. And your gumbo was awesome. When are you going to open a restaurant?"

"Soon as you learn to cook." He spoons berries into two bowls.

And it hits me. "Dad, I have a great idea."

"What is it, Water Dog?" he asks warily.

"Well, since you have a cooking compulsion . . . can we have a few people for dinner?"

"You want to have people for dinner? That doesn't sound very appetizing."

"Ha-ha. You know what I mean. Not people *for* dinner, invite a few people *over* for dinner. Like Professor Summers and his family. You can make your paella."

"Oh, can I?" His eyes twinkle. "Glad I have your permission. Love you, sweetie."

"I love you too. So what do you think?"

"Well, I think it's true, I think you might love me a little, but I'm guessing that you're thinking about someone else right now." Uh-oh. The teasing. I'm such an easy target, no wonder Logan won't let up. "The Summers *family*, you say? Or *one particular* Summers?"

I laugh but won't give him the satisfaction of telling him he's right.

"So . . . no go for Logan?"

"Dad!"

"Okay. Giving up. It's just—Logan's a good kid. And, you're probably better off trying to see Bo on your own. Don't know when Professor Summers will be back in town, but I've already invited him over, twice. Wanted to thank him for making the restoration possible."

"Oh. I didn't know." I take my dishes to the sink. My face is probably matchy-matchy with the bright bits of lobster shell littering the counter.

"Sorry, sweetie. The word is, they rarely accept an invitation. My guess? Professor Summers is a busy man, so he doesn't socialize much. His dad was the same way, kept to himself. How about some more berries?"

"No, thanks." I'm not hiding my disappointment very well, and finally Dad is kind enough to leave me alone with it. He goes into the living room and turns on the TV.

Bo may be on the fast track to becoming my personal lifeguard, but apparently that doesn't include getting to know him.

Outside the kitchen window the waves hit the breakwater with a *shush* . . . and Venus is bright against the darkening sky. It would be beautiful up on the deck. *Fine. Bo, who?*

"I'm going up," I holler, heading out the door.

"Okay, good night. Oh, hey, what about Logan? I mean as far as tonight."

"Um, right." Logan. A guy who actually wants to be around me, a guy who doesn't run away every time we talk. And, bonus, Logan isn't someone who'll make the hair on my arms stand up—except maybe in a good way. "Will you tell him I'm up on the deck?"

STARGAZER

"She's got a place inside

It's like the night sky.

You keep on giving her the moon and the stars

But you can't fill her up and you don't know why—"

Hearing the door opening, I quickly put my guitar in its case and lean back against the bricks of the lighthouse.

"Hey." Logan throws himself unceremoniously down on the deck, so close to me I can smell his shampoo. "Can you play that thing?" He nods toward the guitar case.

"Not really," I fib. Play for Logan right now? No way. "What's up?"

"Nothing's up with me, but what about you? What the hell were you doing today?"

"Today?" Denial seems the easiest route. "What do you mean?"

"Oh, c'mon! The rules-and-regs exam isn't a 'swim test' as your *friend* put it—the one you *left* with, I noticed—so what were you doing? Besides giving me a heart attack."

"I guess . . ." I hug my knees into my chest. Half a minute ticks by.

"You were saying?"

"I don't know." I try to remember what Mary said, try to make my voice even like hers. "I didn't eat, didn't drink anything. I guess I was just—hot."

I have no clue what I was doing, but trust me, no one's more freaked out about it than I am.

Logan takes a deep breath—then seems to change his mind about something. "Hot, huh?" His smile flickers and spreads. "Tell me more about that." He slings his arm around my shoulders, like, no big deal.

I make a face at him, but nervous laughter bubbles out of me. His shampoo actually smells really good. Kind of minty.

"It's getting chilly, right?" I say this like it's an excuse for his arm being around me.

He draws me closer, pulling me against his black leather jacket, and looks up at the stars.

"You know . . . I was really worried about you today."

"I know. Mary told me. I'm sorry." The sound of the surf hitting the breakwater carries up to us and we fall quiet, listening. Turning my head slightly, I look at Logan's familiar features. *Stargazer.* The stargazer lily is bold, dramatic—

"What is it?" he asks, obviously sensing that I'm staring at him.

"Um—nothing."

"Nothing."

"Well, it's just—you have really long eyelashes."

"So I've been told." He squints up at the sky. "You can probably imagine—I give a wicked butterfly kiss."

I swallow, not moving.

He turns toward me, nudging me forward, his arm sliding from my shoulders to my waist. My stomach goes *swoop* as he bends his face toward mine, and I feel his breath warm on my lips, his hair brushing my cheeks—

Suddenly the ringing—louder than ever—invades the night. I leap to my feet.

"Can you hear that? That ringing?"

"No . . ." Logan stands and joins me at the railing—worry creasing his brow.

"Look! Logan, what—who is that?" But even as I point toward Summers Cove, I know.

He's bodysurfing. Expertly catching the next wave, he rides it in, then steps out of the water and picks up a shadow—which turns out to be a surfboard.

Bo Summers. Surfing by starlight. He heads back into the waves.

"Let me grab the binoculars," I say eagerly.

"Yeah, okay." Logan follows me into the watch room. "Actually, I'm gonna get going."

"Oh. All right." *I'm an idiot. Like Logan wants to watch Bo surf?* "Wait. Maybe—do you want to do something over the weekend? How about I give you a ring?"

"Sure." He heads for the stairs. "But I'll only say yes if you get down on one knee."

"You're so funny," I shout after him as he disappears down the dark spiral. I almost follow him then, thinking maybe I'll ask if he wants to stay just a while longer, listen to music, or—something. But even as I'm thinking this, I step out onto the deck and hold the binoculars up—

Just in time to see Bo leave the beach.

How long had he been out there? Who does that anyway? Surfs at night, in Maine water.

I wish more than anything that Lilah was here. Her voice in my head—had been right.

Bo isn't just a boy. He's proved it again and again.

But then, Lilah, what is he?

Anxiously, I listen for her voice.

But it's gone.

PHANTASM

After slipping into the white cotton pajamas that Mom gave me before I left San Francisco, I lie down on the bed, white emptying into white . . .

Emptying into night . . .

I wake in a sweat, sitting upright, legs dangling over the edge of the bed, feet just above the floor. Adrenaline pumps through me, along with pulsing music—*music?* Even as I strain to hear it, the driving music dies, disappears like Alice down the rabbit hole.

A dream. It was just a dream. Trying to remember it now, I close my eyes—and seem to hear the creak and sigh of the pines. A path, that's all I can remember, a path of sand and dirt—

Beneath my back.

A chill runs through me, and I snap my eyes open—

I'd been on my back, and this boy, this man, was leaning over me, his wet hair dripping water on my neck, the side of my face. This beautiful boy with—

Wings.

It seems I've dreamed of Icarus—with a strangely familiar face. Although I can't picture it now, can just see his hair, gleaming wetly.

I pull my own hair back now. Wrap it around itself in a loose knot. Draw my knees into my chest.

From the water below the cliff I saw something with enormous wings, circling. It hadn't been a bird, and I don't believe in angels, although when I saw those wings so high up in the sky . . .

Bo. He's certainly not an angel, but he's done things I can't understand, things that *prove* he's not just—human.

The dream . . . but there's nothing else to discover. It was only a dream. Still my mind struggles to make a connection.

A vibrant streak of orange appears in the still-dark early-morning sky, running along the horizon like a tongue of fire . . .

At the bonfire Logan talked about Standard Smith and his colleagues. He talked about how Smith had lost his life trying to build the lighthouse at Devil's Claw—

Smith's partner. Of course. The partner in Smith's venture was *Summers*, Bo's grandfather—great-grandfather? Whatever. Dad said the Summers' land had belonged to them forever.

So what? I rock gently back and forth.

Professor Summers is a science rock star. Plus, Dad told me the entire family excels at scuba diving and sailing. Bo's an amazing swimmer. He surfs.

Big deal. He swims. He surfs.

It's no use. All I really know about Bo is that water is his thing, and that he's dragged me out of it twice now. If it weren't for him I'd probably be dead, because—

Hypothermia kills.

And yet. When Bo helped me out of the icy water below the cliff, he showed no signs of hypothermia, or even exertion. He held me against his bare chest, and his skin was warm. Obviously I lived. I'm alive. But Bo, with his ocean eyes, their black pupils eclipsing aureate suns, is even more alive. He thrums with energy.

There's something recalcitrant about that energy, but I don't care; I want to know him, to know everything about him. Those eyes . . . Not many people looked directly into Bo's eyes when they spoke to him yesterday at Seal Cove. *Nobody—except me.*

The Ocean Zone Institute has a cluster of research laboratories in Portland. It also has a huge archival facility. In fact—OZI's collection of texts relating to aquatic life is the largest in the world. The Institute is open to the public for certain lectures and exhibitions, but there's no online access to its resources. To view material *at* the Institute, you need to be approved. RHHH students are preapproved. Could there be a better place to find out about Bo?

But. I have no way of getting to Portland. I shut my eyes, trying to think.

The dream—I need to write it down. To write what I remember, at least, then maybe more will come. I cross the cool floor, then take a seat at the desk and open my notebook.

But nothing shows up on the page. No details. No revelations.

Only now—I remember the music, the forceful rhythm of the bass-heavy melody I swore was playing when I woke up. I remember it so clearly now, it's almost as if I can still hear it. Almost as if, somewhere, it continues to play.

Softly, I begin to hum, and after a few minutes, a curling melody begins to wend its way inside of me, an aphotic song, slipping to the tip of my tongue . . .

I reach for my guitar.

RESEARCH

"Drive to Portland to do *research*?" Alyssa is obviously appalled.

"No, huh? Okay, well, do you know where Mary is? I tried her at home, tried her cell—"

"She's having some kind of drama with Kevin. We're getting together later, though. In fact, our plans are right up your brainiac alley."

"Really. What are you guys doing?"

"Study session."

Maybe my ear thing is getting worse. "What?"

"Study. Session." There isn't a chance to voice my disbelief before she says, "Mary and I'll be by to get you at one," and hangs up.

But that afternoon when she picks me up, Alyssa says, "Mary texted. She can't make it."

"Hey, Arion. Do you know what's up with her and Kevin?" Sarah is slouched in the backseat. I do a double take. Her hair is no longer peacock blue. It's purple—although the roots are black, and gleaming, which makes me wonder why she covers its naturally dark luster.

"Ah—no. Who are we listening to?"

"What, did you and your BFF take a vow of silence?" Alyssa scoffs.

She's annoyed, apparently, that Mary and I have a connection that doesn't include her.

"No, it's just that—their relationship is their relationship, you know? So what's playing?"

Sarah launches into a scathing critique, and she's right: the band actually does suck. But they're worth talking about to change the subject. I reach over to turn up the volume. Sarah groans. Alyssa grins.

We drive toward town, and I let their girl talk roll over me. Guys, clothes—clothes, guys. As a contribution to the conversation, I mention my sweater deficit, though what I really need is answers. Then Sarah—whose all-black-all-the-time look doesn't create the impression that she's some kind of artist or goth girl or nihilist but actually makes her look kind of witchy—basically reads my mind.

"So why is Bo Summers hanging around you if there's nothing going on with you guys? I saw him at the library last week. He was, like, lurking in the stacks by your table."

"Huh. Didn't notice. I was probably working on that paper for O'Keefe's class. Did you finish reading *The Return of the Native* yet?"

Alyssa snorts. "That's not the native Sarah's talking about."

They've probably already micro-analyzed every detail of Sarah's story. Of course she's wrong. Bo had definitely not been waiting for me to talk to him. Alyssa plainly agrees.

"That family is totally antisocial. I doubt Bo was interested in anyone noticing him."

"Your opinion may be slightly biased," Sarah says. "Not everyone lives to party."

"The people who matter do," Alyssa contends.

"So what'd you say to Mr. Model Man?" Sarah asks. "He bolted like he'd seen a ghost."

"And Pete told me, you mistook Bo for the book drop." Alyssa sniggers. "That you showered him with fine literature. Way to get a guy's attention, Arion. But there must be more. What were you two really talking about on the beach? Tell us, what did you *do* for that boy?"

"I didn't *do* anything."

"Oh, come on," Alyssa says. "How about the rules-and-regs test yesterday? *That* was convenient. You practically jumped into his arms!"

"He was there doing community service," I mutter, putting on my sunglasses.

"Yeah, well, he can service me anytime." Alyssa cackles. Sarah laughs.

And finally, I start laughing too, realizing that they don't have a clue about my obsession with Bo. They're only teasing. And they're both right. The idea of me with Bo *is* laughable.

"Of course I know someone who'd never *dream* of running away from you," Alyssa says. "He's tall, dark, and handsome—and pissed off at the world. Except when you're around. Though I hear his temper's nothing compared to the short fuse his brother had. Guesses?"

Luckily, as she asks this, Alyssa turns into a driveway and parks.

Surprisingly, we aren't at the library but at a house nearby. Still—the timing's good.

"Can we even fit another person back there?" I ask, twisting around to gesture to the pile of clothes that tower over Sarah.

I stop midturn.

Sarah is sitting still as stone. The hair on the back of my neck stands up.

In a heartbeat the atmosphere in the car changes completely. It's like we're on a sailboat, and the wind has died, leaving us in irons.

"Sorry, Sarah, didn't mean to bring him up." Alyssa starts digging through her purse.

"Yeah, no, it's okay. I've got to get over it. I can't get upset every time I hear his name."

"You know about Logan's brother, right?" Alyssa asks me. I nod. "Well, Sarah had a thing for him."

"But it never went anywhere," Sarah blurts, "because he had Beth—Beth, who never loved him. The messed up thing was, Nick *knew* she had feelings for Logan. But he wouldn't let her go. She could have made Logan happy. Instead? She made Nick miserable."

So that's what Logan left out of his story. Beth was in love with him.

"Maybe she could still make Logan happy," I suggest.

Alyssa looks at me like I have a contagious disease. "Uh, except—she's dead?"

A nasty chill goes through me.

"She drowned," Alyssa says. "With Nick."

"I came to Rock Hook in August," she continues. "A year before you, Arion. When school started, it was like a bomb had dropped or something. The flag was at half-mast for months. It was totally dismal. Sarah was—well, just look at her. She's still wearing black."

"Ha-ha." Sarah kicks the back of Alyssa's seat. To me she says, "It's cool that Logan likes you. He needs someone. Losing Nick had to be like losing his right hand or something."

Or his heart. Lilah's face flickers in my mind's eye like a pale flame. But Lilah is alive, while Nick . . . And yet, Logan's always trying to make *me* feel better.

"That's probably why he's drawn to me," I say. "I get it. Get him."

"Please—I know about your sister," Alyssa says. "Shocker, right? Not really. You must have noticed that Rock Hook Harbor isn't exactly a teeming metropolis; we all, unfortunately, know each other's business. But it's not *about* your sister—Logan's into *you*."

The generosity of Alyssa's comment surprises me, but before I can think of what to say, she goes on. "I've seen the way he looks at you. He walks you to class, follows you to lab—after school he's always on the front steps waiting for you, puppy-dog style. It's pretty obvious you're more to him than just some girl who has"—she stumbles over the words—"a sibling with problems." She cracks her door as if she can't wait to escape the conversation.

Sarah shuffles her bracelets. “If only Beth had *told* Nick how she felt about Logan—”

“He would have killed her!” Alyssa says. “Some people think he did.”

“Jeez, Alyssa. You didn’t even know him!”

“But I know all about him. And Foster Care Girl. Her parents—guardians, whatever—are alkies who came here on vacation and decided to stay. Old news. Nick’s the star of the tragedy, the one everybody still talks about, another hot, hot-tempered Delaine. She and Nick had something sick, that’s what I heard. No wonder she wanted out.”

This is definitely beyond me. “Why would you stay with a guy if you didn’t want to?”

Alyssa shrugs. “Maybe she liked it rough, who knows. And he was rough, that’s what I heard. Caught it from his dad. Mr. Delaine used to hit Nick. Beat him. Not Logan, just Nick.”

It’s hard to picture Mr. Delaine hitting anyone. Then again, I’ve only met him once.

Alyssa looks out at the house in front of us. “Let’s go,” she says. “We need to lighten up.” She hops out of the car. In just about the same second, the front door of the house opens.

Pete Hill and Bobby Farley step out onto the porch.

“I hope you guys have beer!” Sarah pushes her way out of the backseat.

Closing my eyes, I let my head drop back. A Saturday-morning study session? Right. Not only do I *not* want to spend the day partying, I need to get to Portland. Somehow.

“What’s wrong?” Sarah leans in the window.

“Um—” *Think.* “I don’t feel so well.”

“That sucks. What is it? Headache? Stomachache?”

“Both.” I try my best to look pathetic.

“Hey, Al, wait up. Arion doesn’t feel good.”

"Don't call me that," Alyssa snaps. She comes back over to the car. "Problem?"

"I think I'm sick, or—going to get sick."

"*Don't* puke in my car."

"Do you think you could drive me home?"

Alyssa purses her lips. Then she turns toward the house. "Hey, Pete, can Sarah borrow your car to take Arion home?"

Borrow a car. Great idea.

"I'm not planning on driving," Pete says with a grin, lifting a beer as if in a toast. Then holding his cigarette between his lips, he reaches into a pocket with his free hand, and, squinting against the smoke, tosses over a set of keys.

ART

Back at the light station, I hurry down to the keeper's cottage to look for another set of keys—Dad's. He's on a fishing trip and won't be back until later. His truck is here because his buddies picked him up from the breakwater, something that freaks me out. The seawall isn't a dock; one wrong move could ruin a boat. People could get hurt. Dad said not to worry, that no sane person would tie up to the seawall unless the tide was just right.

Keys in hand, a note is the next logical step. Dad definitely won't be happy about me using the park service truck, but then again, if I can get home before him, he won't even *see* the note. In the morning, I'll tell him I took the truck. It'll be too late for him to be angry.

Too late.

I glance at the kitchen clock. *Damn.* By the time I get there? OZI will be closed.

Where else can I find information about the Summers? I've already looked online . . .

Where I haven't looked is at the Wayside, the ancient museum down past the harbor.

Hi Dad,

I borrowed your truck. Hope that's okay. Going downtown to do research. Be back by dinnertime. Thanks!

Love, Ari

But then I realize—my backpack is in Alyssa's car. Am I willing to risk driving without a license?

A half hour later I park in front of a rambling three-story Victorian, the museum's current home. The house sits on a large lot well back from the street. The gingerbread trim needs painting, and the fanciful turrets lean with age, but it's easy to see, like its overgrown gardens, the house had been elegant once.

Although most are shuttered or abandoned now, the neighboring houses, also on sizable lots, must have been lovely once too. Part of a long-ago seaside resort for the wealthy.

A banner flies from the white pillars of the museum's expansive front porch. It has a conch shell painted at one end, a sailboat at the other. The words in between read: **SHELLS & SWELLS, JUNE 1–SEPTEMBER 24**. Today is the last day.

At OZI there'd be millions of papers to search through, but here, really, what do I think I'll find? And at either place, where do I start? *Hi! The Summers family has been in this area forever, right? Do you have any personal information on them?*

Feeling like an idiot, I head inside. If nothing else, museums are perfect places for procrastinating.

The grand entrance foyer is dark save the glow from a large computer monitor that's probably the only thing from the twenty-first century for blocks around. Centered on an antique desk, the computer competes for space with piles of papers and stacks of exhibit catalogs.

"Hello?" The word echoes off the parquet floor and freshly painted gallery-gray walls. The museum is obviously preparing for its next exhibit, yet no one is around. At least a dozen doorways line the high-ceilinged hall stretching before me. "Anybody here?"

In the first two rooms, oil paintings of flesh-colored seashells take up entire walls. It looks like Georgia O'Keeffe decided to paint a shell collection and Julian Schnabel advised her on the size of the pieces. Schnabel is one of Mom's favorite artists, made famous by his huge paintings set with smashed plates. I prefer his films.

Nautical scenes by Maine artists fill the next two rooms, but the following rooms are in transition. Now I look into a room where Neptune slash Poseidon is depicted with a trident and a flowing beard that becomes one with the water. Numerous watercolors show Aphrodite standing on a seashell. Looking at the last picture of the "Cyprian," as Homer referred to her, I recall a piece of trivia I learned writing an eighth-grade paper on Ancient Greece. The Greeks considered Aphrodite both Greek *and* foreign. How exactly does that work?

The Wayside is great, but it's for tourists, not someone looking for answers to questions that don't make sense to begin with. Despite that, I continue on to the next room.

Endless shorelines, oceans reaching toward distant horizons . . . The walls are crowded with portraits of the sea and its surroundings. As I peruse the paintings, one thing becomes very clear—whether the land at the ocean's edge is comprised of woods or raw cliffs, or whether it appears tame and civilized by villages or cities, buildings balanced on pilings black with creosote or steel girders offering false security—*this is a watery world.*

And water doesn't give up its secrets.

Water—only takes.

Heaving a sigh, I turn to go, nearly tripping over a sign by the door, which informs me:

This room houses the museum's permanent collection. Photography is strictly—

My sharp inhalation is loud as a slap.

A large oil sits on an easel at the front of a nearby roped-off alcove. In the picture, a darkly handsome man rises partway out of white-capped waves. He appears to be in pursuit of two women with terror-filled eyes who are running across rocks at the edge of the sea. But their flight is futile. A second man stands in front of them, a serpentine appendage splitting through the tangle of kelp draping his hips.

The silvery scales are painted so that they appear to be spreading upward—nearly reaching the young man's waist, and also scattering down one leg. It's as if the shimmering taillike limb is in the process of growing, of stretching toward the horrified girls.

The terrifying mermaids vibrate with energy—

In fourth grade, a redheaded boy named Scott told me he loved me, then punched me in the stomach. The shock is the same now—worse. I can barely breathe.

Bo is a mermaid.

As insane as it sounds, it has to be true! Not that Bo shares the creatures' dark beauty—but he shares their *aliveness*. And—I stare at the eyes now, the creatures' sea eyes—*their eyes*.

Tearing my gaze from the painting I peer into the dark recesses of the alcove, then duck under the velvet rope. Paintings similar to the one at the mouth of the deep niche fill the small space. Variations of the men—the creatures—loom and leer from the walls. *Beauty is a beast.*

Strikingly sensual, the images of the mermen cling to my imagination—or perhaps I cling to them—as I almost knock over the stanchions in my hurry to get back to the entrance of the museum.

A girl with cropped hair is sitting at the computer now. My words spill over her.

"Excuse me, can you tell me about the—the really intense oil paintings—"

"Oh!" The girl startles. "I didn't know anyone was here. We're closed, actually. We close at two on Saturdays." She blinks up at me. "How did you get in?"

"The door was open. Please. I need to know, the paintings—"

"The mermaids? Everyone asks about them. They were donated years ago—"

"So you think they're mermaids?" My tone is urgent, accusatory.

"Well, yeah. Aren't they?"

"Yes. I guess. I don't know. They're . . ."

"Scary, right? The tails?"

"Tail" is a ridiculously insufficient term to describe the distortion. "Who donated them?"

"You look really pale—are you okay? Do you want some water or something?"

"No, I don't want any *water*," I nearly shout. "Where did the paintings come from?"

The girl cringes. "Professor Julian Summers, founder of OZI. They're the oldest things in this place. They should be in Portland, in a climate-controlled facility, but . . ."

Her words fade as she peers up at me, probably wondering what my problem is.

I just stare dumbly at her for a moment. Then I thank her. And go.

Outside, twilight paints the streets of Rock Hook purple—the sky, periwinkle.

Was I really inside that long?

Long enough to learn the truth about Bo.

Blue shadows cast by a tall stand of pines behind the Wayside shift and stretch—darkening fingers following me to the truck. Unable to shake the feeling that I'm being watched, I shove the key into the ignition.

My thoughts turn over, along with the engine.

But unlike the engine, they won't catch.
Mermaids don't fly.
Yes, but they swim.
But then—
What about the wings?

NETHERWORLD

The park service truck doesn't have anything more than a radio. Trying to ease my anxiety as I drive through the Victorians, their faded colors ashen in the half-light, I sing along with the only decent song I can find—which happens to be about an angel—and get spectacularly lost.

I end up on the coast road—driving in the wrong direction, of course. The dying light tells me that. Specter-like rays thrust themselves out from behind lead-colored clouds, heavy-looking masses that appear as though they'd do damage if for some reason they fell. In another moment, they take over the sky.

The road narrows, becoming a winding passage between sea and stony outcroppings. There's no good place to turn around.

Finally, I make a left onto a road that runs east–west and drive through a silent neighborhood lined with rickety fishing shacks and weather-beaten cottages. The small houses give way to cleared lots where scrubby dune grass and new pines are trying their best to reclaim the land.

The northern end of the peninsula is home to the now-closed canneries, and though I haven't made it that far, I must be close, must have missed Smith Street, which runs—albeit crookedly—the entire length of the long neck of land that is Rock Hook.

The air inside the cab grows scented with wetlands, the odor slightly sulfurous. I'm probably close to the bay. Which means I've gone too far west. Above the sound of a sudden gust of wind, I swear I hear music. Less than a minute later, the back road I'm on dead-ends.

In front of me a row of shadowy cabins crouches in the darkness. Opposite the cabins is a two-story building. Long and boxlike, the obviously new structure has been painted a shiny black, with cyber-yellow trim. Bar? Restaurant? No sign to tell me.

Though it's early, the large pine-ringed parking lot is crowded with cars, and now the door of the boxy building opens. Music spills out into the evening, along with several black-clad boys with guitars.

The music is indie. Alternative. Dreampop. Whatever you call it—it's good. And it's *live*. Maybe I've just found a place to play.

Right now, though, I don't have the time or the desire to go inside. I have no idea where I am, and I need to get the truck back. I'll check it out online.

Following the road back toward the ocean, I figure sooner or later I'll run smack into Smith Street. I half expect to hear Lilah's voice, making fun of my "direction impediment" as she used to call it. Although after yesterday . . . I've finally allowed myself to recall everything I know about her accident—and maybe that will make a difference. Maybe I won't hear the voice anymore—*her* voice, her dark advice, the twists of sarcasm. I miss Lilah horribly, but I don't want her voice in my head. I want mine. Turning up the radio, I press the "Seek" button.

Many minutes later, after finally turning onto Smith Street, I let out a sigh of relief as I pass the intersection where the causeway meets the peninsula. The radio goes berserk all of a sudden—I shut it off with a snap, but as soon as the sound fades to silence, my eyelids begin to grow heavy. It's not late, yet I'm so tired . . . *Only twenty more minutes—stay awake.*

Streaks of purple run alongside the white lines of the road as it dips down—the ocean rolling on my left. Not much between the sea and me . . . just a strip of granite . . . My thoughts wander dreamily. *I'd like to watch the waves for a while* . . . A sweet sound seems to surround me, and I long for the music of Bo's voice . . .

Then, I hear it. Or, I think I do—

Something white streaks in front of the windshield. I sit up straighter.

There it is again. A whirl of motion—

Bam! I almost let go of the wheel as the truck rocks sideways—

Kshh! The driver's side window shatters. The seat belt grinds into my hips as my body arcs toward the passenger side. Dark woods loom on my right as I stamp on the brakes—

Unintentionally sending the truck into a sickening spin.

The truck slides fast toward the side of the road where the surf slams against the rocks so hard it shoots up into the air. Frantically I spin the wheel, jamming my foot on the brakes again and again. The truck bucks but continues sliding out of control. Still skidding, it turns, hood pointed straight at the water. Waves rear up in front of me—in another second I'll be in the sea—

The front tires hit the rough along the edge of the road. I squeeze my eyes closed—

The truck judders to a stop.

My torso whips back and forth— A sharp pain travels up my neck.

My eyes fly open to the strangest sight:

The ocean is receding.

No.

The truck—is going backward. Is being *pulled* backward, slowly, by—something.

The engine whines in protest—

I scream—

Then it's just me, screaming, as the truck comes to stillness, sitting sideways in the center of Smith Street.

Out of nowhere Bo appears at my window. "Arion, can you hear me?"

The scream dies in my throat.

The glass gone, Bo reaches through and touches my face. *Warmth.* I look down at my hands where they lie locked together in my lap, fingers intertwined in some kind of complicated prayer.

"Are you okay?" he asks as he opens my door. "Slide over."

Unclasping the seat belt, I do what he says. "How did you—?"

The engine is still running. Bo begins to drive.

"You st-stopped the truck. *How?*" Fingers shaking, I try to fasten the passenger-side seat belt.

"Brakes, Arion. You hit the brakes."

Right. I *did* hit the brakes, over and over, but . . . My neck aches. So does my head.

"How do you feel? Do you want me to take you to the hospital?"

"No!" Hospitals. The funereal smell of too many flowers. *Lilah.* "I hate hospitals. No."

"Okay." Bo glances at me. "No hospitals."

Finally I get the belt buckled. "What happened? Bo, I wish you'd—"

He begins to sing softly.

I wish nothing.

The sea of his song . . . sends me somewhere else . . . I drift . . .

In some kind of netherworld, I listen to him sing. Wind, water, longing . . . love. The lyrics are like poetry. His voice slides up into his falsetto range, then drops down, becoming an urgent whisper. The low notes are dark, and rough, the breath at the back of his throat raw and sensual. Desire, craving, control . . . death. I don't move, wonder if I even can. The smell of crushed grass mingles with the scent of the sea. The conclusions I reached today are crazy and—*Oh, the truck!*

I open my eyes. We're between the lighthouse and the small outbuilding. My limbs feel weighty, loose. I'm stretched out on the damp grass. My head is in Bo's lap.

He stops singing and draws his hand back from where it rests close to my face. "We should get you inside. You'll probably feel the whiplash tomorrow, but I think you're okay. I wouldn't have let you sleep if I thought you had a concussion."

Sleep? Is that where I've been?

His light hair hangs down around his face. I want to touch it.

"You might want to go see a doctor tomorrow, but you didn't hit your head or anything."

Or anything. Right, I didn't hit *anything. Why didn't I hit anything?*

"Bo—"

"Look, before you start with the questions . . ."

But I *am* looking. Looking at his lips. Staring, actually. I reach up—

He dumps me off his lap unceremoniously and stands. "Are you going to keep ogling me like that? Because, really"—he glances toward the sky—"it's not attractive."

"I-I'm not interested in *attracting* you," I manage to get out, climbing to my feet.

"Oh no? Well, that's too bad."

Scowling with confusion, I start around the side of the lighthouse. Bo follows me, watching as I struggle with my key, and then with the door, which feels impossibly heavy. Finally, he reaches around me, opening the door easily, holding it as I walk through. Looking up into his shadowed face, my thoughts tangle, but at least I have *one* answer now. It just doesn't make sense. Because mermaids don't fly—everyone knows that.

But I can't deny I saw the wings again tonight.

And Bo had been right there.

PROMISE

The wire cages of the bulbs lighting the vaulted granite corridor throw spiderweb shadows on the walls, making the passage between the inner door and the outer door of the lighthouse seem more like a tunnel than a hallway. I've only just stepped inside when, as if we're both swimmers in the same still body of water, I feel the ripple of Bo's movement as he turns to go.

"Good night, Arion." He releases the door.

I catch it—stomach in a knot—hold it open. "Wait." I don't plan to say the word; it just pops out, followed by, "Don't go." My hands are trembling. Physically, I'm not hurt, not really. But mentally? A tough attitude about hospitals and an interest in kissing Bo only go so far.

He gives a slight nod. We stand on either side of the threshold.

"So what happened tonight?" he asks. "Did you fall asleep? Looks like your tires kicked up a rock."

"I—I don't know." But I do know. I was attacked. Someone deliberately tried to run me off the road. Some*thing*. In a shaky voice I say, "You . . . were there."

He hesitates. "My brothers and I were driving by. Your truck had its front wheels in the rough at the edge of the road. When I saw that it was still running, that you were okay, I told them to go. What were you doing up near the north end?"

Nothing makes sense. Totally tongue-tied, I shake my head.

Bo gives a low laugh. "Third time's a charm, is it?" He shifts his weight, his stance changing almost imperceptibly. Shadows fall across his face. He's taken my silence to mean something other than the fact that my voice is simply unavailable.

But his story doesn't ring true—and something else is bothering me. "How did you know I was up by the northern end of the peninsula?"

"You mentioned it, in the truck." His blue-green gaze is unblinking, *insistent.* "You're still shaken. I should go."

"How—how will you get home?"

He looks pointedly down at the beach. "We're neighbors, you know."

"Yes, I've figured out that much." And more, and I need to say so. But instead I watch as the lighthouse casts its intermittent illumination across the sea. *Blink; flash.* Light. Then dark. We both watch as the beam creates a path on the waves that leads straight to us—or straight away—before it disappears. *Light. Dark.*

"Thanks for helping me out tonight." My body sways a little—as if the invisible water surrounding us has suddenly become deeper. Before it can close over my head and render me speechless, I say, "I want to know you."

"I understand, but—"

"But that would require you to actually hang around. With me." *And not run off when things get weird.*

"Arion, I can't just 'hang around.' There are things—" His angular jaw tenses.

This confuses me, but not so much that I don't know what's coming, and I don't want to hear it. "Stop, okay? Look, I get that you're allergic to questions, but what if I found the answers on my own? Would you tell me if I was right?"

His lips curve. "That sounds suspiciously like a question."

Standing there, I feel the pull of him, an energetic thing, like when you rub your palms together over and over then hold them facing each other. A current runs between your hands. But this isn't just energy—isn't even attraction. It's something more . . . *necessary.*

My heart kicks. Am I afraid? Definitely. But it doesn't matter, because the strongest of my raveled feelings is no mystery.

That doesn't mean, though, that I can just blurt out what suddenly seems like a wild accusation. So I simply start talking. I speak into the silence that pools between us, telling him I want to play down in Portland, that I need to practice more first, that I'm not writing enough.

"I want you to play for me." The tone of his voice is low and . . . complicated.

"Sure. But not—"

"Not now, no. You're probably tired. Sorry, I should leave." But he doesn't look sorry, he looks . . . intense. And I don't want him to leave. His elegant cheekbones, the straight line of his nose—he's so incredible looking.

He's also not human. I take a deep breath—

Bo looks at my mouth—then bites his lip.

Is he thinking of kissing me? My pulse jumps, and I let my breath out slowly—

A look of pure irritation crosses Bo's face.

No. The almost kiss we shared is going to remain just that. Yet—the current holds steady.

The lighthouse beam sweeps out over the waves, creating a sparkling path that's visible one minute, invisible the next.

I point to the light dancing on the water. "I wish I could play that. Wish I could sing it."

That glimmer on the ocean—whether it's from the lighthouse lens, or the moon, from the early-morning sun, or the long reaching light of late afternoon—it makes life seem full of possibility, yet at the same time hollow, with wanting. Bo's eyes hold that kind of light, and when he looks at me I feel just that way. "It's like . . . promise, that shine on the water."

"Promises," he says, and his tone in no way matches mine. There's a hard edge to his voice now, even though he's speaking quietly. "There are always two sides to them. They can be fulfilled—or broken."

I hadn't meant that kind of promise, and his response isn't exactly encouraging, but I know what he means, and despite the misunderstanding, the current continues to travel between us, as if we're aligned in a myriad of other ways. But the connection—it's disturbing somehow, like the black reaches of the sea, and also as mesmerizing as its continual curling waves. And as much as I don't want to, I need to step into this unseen stream now. Need to tell him—I know what he is. But first I'll make him promise—the kind of promise he was thinking of. A vow.

I take a deep breath. He shudders.

"Will you promise me something?"

"Probably not." But he doesn't look away.

"Try, okay? Promise, that no matter how idiotic I sound, you'll tell me the truth. And promise that whatever I say, you'll still be my friend." My face heats. Friend, right. *I'm a liar.*

And at the thought—something in me freezes.

A liar. That's not me—that's Lilah.

A memory spins out now, plays itself at the back of my mind like a movie, showing a brick apartment building in a decaying neighborhood . . . an artist friend of Mom's . . .

"Playground," Lilah said, tugging me to the door. "In the backyard." And then we were outside, walking. And Mom, she was still inside—I guess. But I didn't care. I had Lilah.

To me, at only four or five, the walk lasted forever, but in reality, the grubby playground had probably been only a few blocks from the apartment building. Either way, it certainly wasn't in the backyard.

A rusted metal jungle gym . . . "Swing!" I said, pointing.

"Seesaw." She scowled, yanking on my arm, twisting it, until nausea crawled up my throat. *Seesaw.* The kind they don't make anymore, because they're too dangerous.

Up high, down low, up high, down low. Having fun but afraid I'd fall, I alternately giggled and squealed. My feet pressed the earth. Earth—sky. Earth—sky. Up high—

Lilah slung her leg over the wooden plank and stepped off. I slammed down on the packed dirt. *No air.* Lilah laughed like it was wildly funny—me rolling in the dust in my favorite red dress, afraid I was dying, though I didn't know what that meant.

And that's when the feeling came. The raw, scraped feeling under my skin, down in my belly. As if her betrayal had gutted me.

Then Mom was there—out of the blue. Seemed Lilah had betrayed her too, because she was angry, so upset; she barely gave me a glance, although she helped me up from the ground.

It happened again, and again. The small hurts, the bigger ones.

As we got older, her games grew more twisted . . .

"Kiss him," Lilah commanded, before she drank from a bottle of something nasty that I'd refused. "Go. On. *Kiss him.*"

"No!" I'd shouted. But Lilah caught my jacket, pushed me toward him.

"Use your tongue," she said, laughing. And he did. Her boyfriend.

How old was I? Barely twelve.

Then the accident happened, and the raw feeling became a permanent part of my life, a part of me. *But Bo doesn't know about that.*

Light from some source I can't discern glints through the deep-gold fringe of Bo's eyelashes now as he tips his head back, like he wants to see me from a different angle.

But I can't focus on him—my head feels fuzzy, crowded with images of my sister. I grope toward one thin thought that's blowing loose inside me somewhere, luffing like a sail set too close to the wind.

And finally I grasp it, and understand. I *was* right—I *am* right. She met someone here, and she *did* fall in love. It *can* happen that fast, in a day, or a week.

It's the same way I'm falling for Bo: Fast, and hard, and stupidly. Messily. It makes sense now—there's *someone.* A boy—a boy I need to find.

"Bo—" I begin, but my knees buckle—

And then I feel one of his hands sliding across my back, one of his arms catching behind my knees—

The night air's cool against my cheeks as he swings me up into his arms—cool and soothing compared to the heat I feel emanating from him.

I imagine I feel his lips as well, against my hair, but I can't keep my eyes open, can't see his face as he murmurs, "The best promise I can give to you—is that I'll stay away. But I'm not sure I can promise that."

The outside door closes behind us.

I hear the inner door open—

And then, there's only silence.

INTRUDER

In the morning I wake curled in a tight ball, like I'm steeling myself for a blow. As if this isn't alarming enough, I hear music—someone singing. Not in my head—like music from some fading dream—and not an earworm either, a song from the radio that even in sleep I can't shake. No, it's more like a deep voice, backed with a thrash metal riff.

Sitting up in bed, head swiveling, I look around the room—

But there's no one here—of course there's no one here.

Bo. He must have brought me up to my room, although I have no memory of it. I touch my head. But there's no pain, just a little stiffness in my neck and upper back.

And obviously Bo's not here now, and no one's singing anything, let alone some pumped-up hardcore song with shifting time signatures. *So what the hell was that?* I shut my eyes—

Gleaming wet hair—

Then quickly open them. It was a dream. That's all. Another dream. I remember more details this time—but the boy, he was different. Not a different boy, but—I'd watched his hips swivel and shudder, tearing through the sea tangle at his pelvis. Watched his body contort, as the silver-scaled appendage emerged from his lower torso, the end splitting into two fins edged with gossamer membrane making prisms of the light. It was as if the sharp-edged glass of the lighthouse lens had come to life—then the coiling reptilian limb had snaked around my waist. And all the while the music: a throbbing bass line ribboning through my rib cage.

Quickly I get up and cross to the bathroom, peeling off the clothes I fell asleep in. The pale-green tiles make me think of murky water.

The window is open and I lean my hands on the sill, looking out—

Something slick sticks to my fingers. A piece of seaweed—all the way up here. I start to slide the window closed, wondering how—

A gust of cool air blows my hair around my face, and I lose my grip—

The window slams shut, and I jump back—

But I don't take my eyes off of it, realizing—

I don't remember opening it.

Although I must have. Last night is a bit of blur, that's all, because of what happened. Maybe Bo opened the window. He brought me up here, definitely. And then he left. He wouldn't have stayed—I know that for a fact. And even though I can't shake the feeling that someone's been here? There's certainly no one here now.

But there is an envelope, tucked partway under the door. A slip of paper lies next to it.

Ari,

Are you okay? What happened to the window of the park service truck? I'm not thrilled you borrowed it. It's state property. Call the marina, they'll find me.

Love, Your Dad

P.S. Mary phoned.

I'd beaten Dad home easily but had totally forgotten to get rid of the note I'd left for him. Not that it matters, with the driver's side window of the truck broken and all.

The letter is from Mom. As I'm about to open it, a wave of nausea hits me. I hurry back to the bathroom, trying to remember if I ate anything weird—

My nausea is suddenly arrested.

There's water on the bathroom floor.

I'd seen it a minute ago—a small puddle beneath the window. But from this angle, I see more now—more water, glistening on the floor. Drips and drops that form a wet, weaving trail from the bathroom, across the bedroom—

To my bed.

I bring my hands to my mouth. This is—this can't be what it looks like.

Walking back to the bed now, I don't even have to touch the sheets to tell that they're wet. Just in one spot, as if someone had been sitting on the edge of my bed.

While I was sleeping.

I hurry back to the bathroom, grab a towel, and wrap it around my naked body. I wash my face at the sink, look in the mirror. My skin is pale, my hair hangs limply—I need a shower. No, I need . . . I need . . . But I can't seem to finish the thought, can really only hold one thought, one face, in my mind. The two of us not seeing each other—that's not an answer, that's a cop-out. And if he's really some kind of—some kind of different . . . type of person than I am, then . . . then . . .

But there is no then. There's only now. I need to see him.

I throw on jeans and a sweater. Down in the kitchen of the keeper's house—I can't eat. Taking a few deep breaths, I try to calm down.

Okay, a calm person is logical. Responsible. She, for example, calls her dad.

But the harbormaster can't find Dad and he puts me on hold.

After several long minutes in which I'm forced to listen to elevator music, he comes back on the line. "Captain Rush has a charter. He'll be back tonight."

Good, because as soon as we actually talk? I'm grounded.

After leaving a message at the marina, I grab a pen. I'll write another note just in case Dad gets home early. But then I frown down at the blank page. If I tell the truth, I'll get more than grounded. Dad will overnight me to Dr. Harrison.

Bo's idea about what happened suddenly seems like a good one.

Dear Dad,

I'm fine. I'm really sorry about the window. A rock from the road hit it pretty hard. I'll pay for it out of my allowance. Sorry again.

Love, Ari

Done. If he gets home before me, Dad will see the note.

But of course he won't see the truck.

Because I'm taking it.

PURSUIT

Whizzing through the rain, the plastic wrap I've duct-taped to the window flapping rhythmically, I don't see one other car on the road. Rock Hook may be a peninsula, but it feels like an island—a deserted island.

After half an hour, I veer off the main road and onto a dirt road. Soon, I turn again, heading southeast on what's nothing more than a narrow trail. Branches scrape the side of the truck as I head deeper into the wet woods.

Devil's Claw. Everyone knows the Summers have a house out there, maybe not at the end proper, but somewhere in the woods—not that there's any guarantee Bo will be there. But none of the cars I've seen him driving were at Summers Cove. I checked down the overgrown private road first. I couldn't see the house from where I was, but I could see the drive, and there weren't any cars. Besides, Bo's got to know I won't let this go—what exactly happened last night? And Summers Cove is too close if he wants to avoid me today.

Like he said, we're neighbors.

Devil's Claw. Wabanaki Wilderness is the official name, and US wilderness areas don't usually allow motorized vehicles, but—the truck jounces over a series of bumps—I'm in a park service vehicle, and I've already driven up this way once, with Dad.

I stop in front of an old cabin surrounded by evergreens. We didn't go beyond this point, the day we drove out here. The sign on the side of the building is worn, but I manage to make out a few dates. The area will be closed for the season in less than a week, the end of September. Under the dates are warnings so faded they're illegible.

A clipboard with a pen hangs from the wooden counter below a shuttered window.

Sure enough, Bo's name is there along with today's date.

A few yards in front of me a rusted gate blocks the road. I push it open, then climb back into the truck and drive past it. I stop again and jump out, closing the gate behind me.

The trees tower over the truck as I continue driving. I'm trying to concentrate on my surroundings, but mostly, I'm thinking about Bo. I feel almost feverish with the desire to talk to him—I just want to talk. To hear how I managed to miss our goodbye last night, and to tell him he doesn't have to shut me out. I can keep his secret.

I hit a series of ruts in the road and feel a hot flush of anxiety.

He was there when I nearly drove off the road. What does that say?

Nothing. It doesn't say anything. It's a coincidence, that's all.

Then who tried to run me off the road?

I try to calm myself by looking at the land, the rocky peaks reaching up through the tree line stretching toward the sky. It's beautiful—and untouched. I shiver a little. Tell myself it's from the damp of the day.

At last I reach the top of a granite outcropping—

And there's no place else to go. I've passed barely there side roads, possible hiking trails. But this truly seems to be the end of the main road.

I get out of the truck and begin hiking down what to me is a nearly nonexistent trail. The only reason I know to follow it is because of the bent branches at the top, low-lying bushes that have recently been disturbed. Hiking downward over the steeply slanted ground, I imagine Bo moving fluidly over the mossy rocks and tree roots, intensity radiating from him.

I'm having trouble with the slippery soles of my boots and try to keep my attention on my feet, rather than the fact that inside every one of my shivers a needle of heat is burning.

The trees shield me from the rain for most of the hike, which, like the drive, probably takes three-quarters of an hour. At the end of it I discover—

Logan is wrong. Someone *has* built at Devil's Claw.

I thought the house would be a cabin, would be like the ranger station in the woods.

It's not.

The rocky site of the bunker-like house is shockingly close to the ocean. The hard look of the concrete walls makes the house appear armored, yet the way the structure seems to cling to the rocks makes it seem organic as well, and . . . barnacle-like.

When I reach the unassuming door, I stop. But I've already berated myself for coming, already pictured the various responses my showing up unannounced might elicit. At this point, I don't care. Nothing surpasses my need to see Bo.

I knock. No one answers. I knock again, then again, thinking of Dr. Harrison now, of what he'd say about obsession, about triggers and loops.

I imagine how I'd tell him, *The hike was good exercise.* And, *It's just this one time.*

One last volley of knocking and I give up, heading around the side of the house, peering in through a large window. The L-shaped floor plan is compact. Efficient, like a boat. The concave wood ceiling gives an embracing sense of shelter, but everything else is open. The main rooms have no partitions between them, so there's a flowing feeling.

Nothing interrupts the view of the sea, and the sea—I realize now that I'm observing the way the house hangs out over the water—

Is all around me.

"What are you doing here?"

I quickly turn toward him. "Looking for you." His board shorts, the bare skin of his chest, shoulders, and arms, stream water as if he's just climbed out of the sea.

"You found me. Now what?"

"Now—we talk."

Bo doesn't say anything right away, just pushes his wet hair back from his face. The pewter light of the rain-soaked sky hits his ocean eyes. Finally, he nods. "Okay. Come on."

Once inside, Bo stands in front of the huge wall of a window that faces the ocean. The rain is falling harder now, in dense gray sheets. His wet shorts drip water on the slate floor.

He gestures to the low couches.

I sit.

"Are you hungry? Do you want something to drink?" He walks past me and grabs a black T-shirt from a hook by the door.

"No. Thanks." My tongue is in a knot. Eating or drinking would definitely present a problem. "I want to ask you something."

"Some*thing*? Singular?" His lips curve. He pulls the shirt over his head.

I ignore the attitude. "Your dad—he founded OZI, right? So—" *So an oceanographic institute is the perfect place for a merman—I know what you are.*

God, I can't say that.

Bo is watching me closely. "I'm sure you knew that," he says. When I don't reply, he sighs. "My father is in India right now; perhaps you didn't know that. My mother—is dead."

"I—I know. I'm sorry."

Bo looks at me skeptically. "I like your father," he says suddenly. "We had a few good conversations. While you were sleeping," he adds drily.

"Ha. That must have been after you hauled me out of that *tide pool.*"

His gaze flickers, lands on my lips. "Good guess. And *your* mother—where is she?"

"Home, with my sister. I mean—at our old house, the one my parents are trying to sell, in San Francisco."

"Right. I suppose I could ask you about your sister now, or you could ask me about mine—yes, I have a sister, and two brothers. But I'm guessing we've both made enough small talk to pass as civilized if anyone was listening, and since nobody is, tell me why you're really here."

I'm not ready, it's just—I can feel the words forming themselves on the tip of my tongue. It's like I'm eating a piece of saltwater taffy, and he's got one end, and is pulling. I feel a small surge of anger at this . . . coercion, though that doesn't make any sense, so maybe it's frustration that forces the words from my lips.

"Why are you pretending?" My tone is sharper than I'd intended.

"Why are you?"

And he's right, I am—I'm pretending. Pretending I'm brave. Pretending I know what I'm doing. Pretending there's only one reason why I'm here.

His expression changes now to one of amusement. Condescension.

He doesn't think I can figure him out. Figure out his secret.

"I'm not sure what happened last night—"

"You are, though. You had a shock. It caught up with you. I helped you to your room."

"That's all?"

And there it is, that hesitation. But it's so brief, as soon as he starts talking, I think I must have imagined it.

"That's all," he says.

"Maybe—maybe as far as last night goes. But there's more, and you know it. You move like water. And you're homeschooled, or, you were. I think it's so you didn't have to deal, with regular people. You sing like . . . an angel. Although I'm not sure if that's part of it."

"It?"

"Bo, you kept me from drowning, easy for you, because you can swim, and surf, in super cold water, frigid waves." I pause, remembering the way he held me in his arms, the feel of his body. I imagine it now beneath his soft-looking T-shirt, a V-neck that's fitted to his shoulders and clings damply across his chest. My stomach dips—

And I'm lost.

"Ah," he says softly. "Now we're getting somewhere." He comes closer to the couch, looking down at me with those eyes.

So what if he's a gorgeous guy who moves like an athlete? So what if he's a strong swimmer, has an amazing voice, was homeschooled? My loaded guns are beginning to feel like they're filled with nothing but air. My brain stalls.

Air. What is it about air?

"A fairly flattering list of facts about me can't bring a girl like you any satisfaction, not unless it's brought you to some sort of a conclusion. Answers—that's what you like, am I right? I prefer questions. Still, it might be entertaining to hear what you're thinking, beautiful."

In his mouth the word "beautiful" is the shimmer of light on water, a dangling promise.

It feels like I have no choice but to reach for it.

"You're a mermaid," I say at last, looking up at him. "A merman."

SECRETS

Bo bursts out laughing, and I might be embarrassed, that he's laughing at me, except that I'm too busy being mortified. Along with the metaphorical reaching, I've actually stretched my hands out—my fingers spreading over the tops of his thighs.

He looks down at my hands—his eyes glittering, his laughter dying abruptly—watching as I quickly bring them to my lap. He swallows a smile.

"Siren. That's the correct term. Have you ever read Kafka?"

"Some."

He begins to recite, as if reading a poem. "*Now the Sirens have a still more fatal weapon than their song, namely their silence. And though admittedly such a thing never happened, it is still conceivable that someone might possibly have escaped from their singing; but from their silence certainly never.*

"My father insists we spend our lives in silence, in order to remain undiscovered. But my brother Jordan and I don't completely agree. The two of us have been . . . exploring our options.

"Jordan has been 'exploring' a little longer than I have. He tells me that soon, you won't be able to live without my Song. He says that will be a problem, for both of us."

His words baffle me. "I—I want to spend time with you."

"Of course you do. But at some point, your self-preservation will kick in. You'll want to go, and you *will* go—possibly running and screaming—once you understand what I am."

"What I understand is—you saved my life." *I always knew you were more than a boy.*

"But I could *take* your life as easily as I saved it."

"Why would you? You wouldn't hurt me—that doesn't make sense." I thought I understood what was between us, at least in part, but now . . .

Sitting up straighter I repeat, "You wouldn't hurt me."

"I might," he says. "Even though I don't want to. I told you, I've been listening to you."

Listening to me? I'm desperate to know more, but I'm too confused to formulate a question at this point, and too . . . too . . . I can't stop looking at his lips. Energy pulsates in the space between us. Does he feel it? I wish he would sit down, I wish—

He says, "Once you know more—"

"So tell me," I say impatiently.

"We change, Arion." He watches me intently as he says the next words. "Change our forms."

"But you just said—Fine. Do I get to see your fish tail?"

His laugh has an edge to it. "Afraid not, seeing as I don't have one." He touches my hands, both of which I'm appalled to find, have somehow made their way back to the tops of his thighs. With a start, I jerk them away—

He presses them in place. Goosebumps rise on the skin beneath my shirt.

"There's something else you may want to consider." His eyes drill down into mine.

I nod in acquiescence, but I don't really want to know anything—not anymore. I just want . . . *him*. A wave of desire rises and falls in me, like a sort of sensual seasickness.

"Sirens need the breath of living creatures to survive. Do you understand?"

What I understand—I slide my hands to his hips, draw him toward me, the front of my body brushing the front of his as I stand up now.

"Arion, do you hear what I'm saying? Living creatures. We *take* their breath."

Breath: the essence of life.

He's taller than me, but it doesn't matter. I already know our bodies will fit perfectly together. I shake my head a little—but it's like I can't control my own thoughts.

"Breath," he says again. My own breath is growing shallow. But—

Breath.

Oxygen. Nitrogen. Carbon monoxide.

Air.

Then, I get it. Every time I've gasped in his presence or released my breath. Each time I'd inhaled deeply, then exhaled slowly. I begin to see the pattern.

When he'd helped me out of the water, when he'd appeared at the window of the truck. There'd been more than just an expression of concern on his face, more than a worried look in his eyes. There'd been a look of lust, of *hunger*. I'd thought he wanted *me*.

Whenever I'd been close to him and expelled a breath, he'd seemed irritated, horrified even, but he wasn't horrified by me. No, he was horrified at the idea of *what he might do to me*, and now I am too.

Suddenly his gaze—so steady and level just a second ago—travels down over my body. Then he looks back to my face and stares—positively stares—at my mouth.

"I'd wanted to keep this from you, but . . ." He gives a small shrug. Then he says something else, only I don't actually hear what he says, don't hear the words, because the sound of his voice is like an instrument now, emitting notes that strain against their very edges, bending and extending beyond expected tonal parameters to become something strange. The music seems to reach for me.

"Arion, listen. If you stay *still*, there may be a way for both of us to get what we want." Bo brings one hand up to the neckline of my shirt, and I do—I go still as he runs a finger along my collarbone. But alarm bells riot in my head. *Sirens—they use their voices.* Listening is a very bad idea. Staying still is a close second. I take a step back. Effort.

He says my name now, his voice an orchestra playing with the utmost precision. My eyes flutter closed, and I fight against the exquisite beauty of the sound of him. Glowing colors—sunrises, sunsets—bloom in the darkness.

"Arion, try to understand, I *have* to. But maybe—maybe with you, it can be different. You're able to look me in the eye, and your *voice* . . . maybe I can take . . . just a small amount."

"A small amount," I echo. I can't seem to say more.

His voice is soft, hypnotic. "I tried, I really did. Tried to warn you."

"I—I need to leave—"

"You need to *stay*." It's mesmerizing, the way his voice rings with the beauty of bells, ancient pealing chimes, calling people to prayer, to their god. The idea of people willingly giving their lives for what they believe in suddenly seems so understandable, so right.

Siren. The word comes to me from a great distance. Bo is no myth, but how is it possible that he's a Siren? They're the stuff of imagination. Artists of all kinds through the ages have conjured them from their own linings. What maker could bring those imaginings to life? Had Sirens been created the same way as the rest of the world? Made of atoms and molecules, flesh and bone, sound and vision? What other way is there?

Slowly, like I'm coming awake from a dream, I manage to open my eyes. Bo starts, as if in surprise—then whispers my name. I waver, feeling the way a mirage looks, quivering in the shimmering field of his heat. His voice, no louder than before, becomes achingly seductive. My torso seems to float up out of my hips, my head drifting among the clouds of a night sky, stars swirling at the edges of my sight . . .

It feels like I'm moving against a strong current as I make my way to the door, where I cling to the frame for a hundred years before stumbling outside, searching for the path that brought me here.

Behind me I imagine Bo's stride. Measured, even . . .

My misguided sense of direction takes me straight to the sea—*the last place I want to be.*

Then he's next to me, with his light hair and golden skin—like he's been kissed by the sun. Envy shoots through me, but *who envies the sun?* I'm gone. Wanting to touch him so badly I feel I might scream, I breathe in his scent—sea, and sky, and everything I've ever wanted.

A trick! My mind insists, *Run!* My legs are water. My brain commands, *Go!* My body won't obey. My heart abandons me—and beats for him. I'm stranded between two worlds. Bo's eyes swirl with color. Sky blue, sea green. "Don't make me force you, Arion." But his voice communicates the strength of the sea. It's like the ocean, knocking against me. Any minute, I'll fall. Go under. "Then again, I don't hear you saying no." He reaches for me, his fingers sliding down my arms until his hands reach mine, his grip tight, tight, *tight* as a lock. Fear courses through me—

But alongside the fear, desire swells now, as it did inside the house. In an instant I'm undone, nothing but rhythm, nothing but chant. *Kiss me, please kiss me—*

He lets go.

The cold sea breeze snaps at my face, whips my hair. The Siren spell is broken.

"Jordan's right," Bo says, turning away. "It's not possible. I can't be alone with you."

SNARL

The hike back up to the truck is arduous. I can't tell how long it takes—time is something foreign. Even though the rain's stopped, the woods are dark as night.

Bo doesn't look at me once.

Finally we reach the top of the trail where I parked the truck. Bo insists on driving, and I don't object. I feel drained. I ask him where his car is. In return, he says something about the weather. I don't pursue the issue.

The woods blur by as we cut across the peninsula, the dirt road mostly mud now. Bo shifts the gears roughly. My stomach writhes. The silence between us is deafening.

I keep fiddling with the seat-belt strap where it crosses my chest. It feels too tight, then too loose. Not realizing at first that I'm even doing it, I begin to sing softly, trying to soothe myself.

There's a barely perceptible shift in Bo's attention from the road, to me. I sense it. I look over at him and on his lips—the lips I know now I can never kiss—is the ghost of a smile.

And that frightens me.

Because there's nothing funny about what happened this afternoon.

As we pull down the pebbled drive to the lighthouse, steel-colored clouds scud across the sky, revealing robin's egg blue beneath. The wind has changed direction.

Bo. As afraid of him as I am, the idea of not seeing him again scares me more. *How can I want to get away from him so much in one minute and want so badly to be near him in the next?*

What is this, is also that. Words from the Bhagavad Gita, paraphrased. I came across the concept in the yoga book that Bo had seemed so strangely fascinated with at the library. But can I accept his duality? Bo saved my life, but . . . where does he get the life-sustaining breath he needs?

The question isn't where—it's who. *Who does he get it from, and* how *does he get it?*

Not that he's giving me a choice. I should be glad this is the end of our friendship. I'm not. Bo, on the other hand, looks serene in the late-afternoon light as he parks the truck.

Now he opens the door and gets out. I do the same. The vehicle looms like a blockade between us.

Then Bo says, "Come here."

"What is it?" I walk around and meet him by the back of the truck.

"It's this." He brings his lips to my cheek, keeping them there for such a long second—I have time to hear his unsteady breathing before he draws back. "Goodbye, Arion." He turns away. His hands are clenched, two fists.

Finality hangs in the salt air. But even as my heart sinks to the bottom of the sea, his kiss burns on my cheek, claiming something in me the same way the rising tides are claiming the edges of the land everywhere. That he did this, connected us even as he left, is slightly sick on his part, I think.

So why does it make me smile?

I watch his receding figure. And then he's gone. A minute ticks by, maybe more. Either way, Bo's out of sight when I hear a car coming up the drive. In an odd sensory illusion—the kind of thing you experience when, say, there's a warm humid day in the fall, and just for the briefest moment you think it's spring going into summer, instead of autumn going into winter—I think it's Bo coming back. But of course it isn't; he was on foot. And yet I'm still hoping it's him somehow, even as the white pickup truck rolls to a stop, and Logan gets out.

"That smile's not for me, is it?"

"What's up?" I ask, purposely ignoring his comment.

"Nothing really. Just wondering what you've been up to all weekend. Looks like you've made a miraculous recovery. Since Friday, I mean."

"I was fine on Friday; you were here Friday night. Remember?" I tilt my head to one side, blinking rapidly, implying that he doesn't have a brain. He rewards my acting efforts with a laugh, then unexpectedly, he hugs me.

It's not a careful hug, not the kind of hug two friends might exchange. It's a hug that brings the fronts of our bodies together.

"Um—"

"Let's go for a walk," he murmurs in my ear just before he releases me.

"I—I can't. I have to eat something." My stomach growls as if to back me up.

"Okay, so let's go out to dinner."

"I really can't. I've been out all day, and I need to talk to my dad." Not that I want to.

"Doesn't look like he's home." Logan gestures to the empty driveway. Then he says, "Oh yeah—got something for you."

He reaches into his truck—and comes up with my backpack.

"Hey, thanks." I shoulder the pack. "How'd you get it?"

"Ran into your friend."

"*My* friend? You mean Alyssa?"

"Mm hmm. I mentioned that I was going to head over here today, check up on you. She told me she had your backpack."

"I'm so glad you got it. Thanks again."

"Yeah, well, you *should* thank me."

"Why, because you actually had to talk to her?"

"That, and, you know. She wanted—Ah. Whatever." Logan looks away.

"Yeah, I bet she wanted whatever." Picturing Alyssa with her waterfall of gleaming black hair and big blue eyes I say, "I hope you didn't give it to her."

But I should know by now that teasing Logan is an unwinnable game.

"Why?" He lifts his chin a little. "You want it?" His tone implies that I've not so cleverly worked my way into a corner he's intimately familiar with.

"Anyway," I say lightly. "I need to go."

"You do, huh?" Logan smirks. Then he scowls a little. "Need to go see Summers? That is who I saw walking out on Smith Street, isn't it? Walking from here?"

With a pang of guilt I remember how I told Logan I'd call him this weekend.

"Come on," I say. "I can take a short beach walk."

He makes some comment about not wanting to twist my arm. We head down the stairs.

Flinching, I step onto the sand, but my beach boycott really is over. Will my fear of the water continue to haunt me? I'm not sure, but soon Logan has me laughing like the gulls, and I'm not thinking about anything but his "close encounters," as he puts it, with the teachers and administrators at school. His stories are hilarious. He has to be exaggerating.

But then, as the sun slips down the sky and the air grows cooler, Logan abruptly changes the subject.

"So what's with you and Summers anyway?"

Hearing him say Bo's last name makes my stomach twist. "Nothing," I say flatly.

"Something." The evening light sets off Logan's startling eyes, and his skin seems even darker against the background of white sand dunes that stretch away behind him, reaching toward the bluffs. "Thought you were going to get in touch over the weekend."

"I was—I would have, but . . ." I tell him how I'd somehow spent hours at the museum, and for a split second, consider telling him how someone had tried to run me off the road. But remembering his reaction on Friday, when he thought I was in danger, I cut the story short.

"Hours, huh? How come you didn't ask me to keep you company?"

"No reason, really." I look down at my feet, white skin on white sand.

"Okay. I get it."

"Hey. Don't be like that. Sorry we didn't connect, but things got a little crazy—"

"Does Summers have anything to do with the 'craziness'? As in, he's crazy about you? 'Cause I gotta tell you, I don't think that's a good thing. Nick—" Logan kicks at the sand.

"Believe me, Bo Summers is not crazy about me. What were you going to say? About Nick?"

But Logan just shakes his head.

Fine with me. I don't want to talk to him about Bo, though I would like to know what Logan has *against* him. Does he really believe Bo had something to do with Nick's death?

The memory of Bo's words whispers insidiously in my ear: *"Sirens need the breath of living creatures."* No. No way. Anxiety gnaws at my stomach—which is empty.

"How about I take you up on that offer? To go to dinner."

Blink; flash. Logan's smile against the darkening sky is a beam from the lighthouse.

"Brilliant idea, Airyhead." He slings his arm over my shoulders and turns me around. He's handsome in the twilight, mysterious, even.

Sarah said that Nick's girlfriend had been in love with Logan. I'm not the only one withholding part of a story.

Luckily, Dad still isn't home, which means he hasn't read my note yet, which means I'm not grounded. Yet. So I can go to dinner with Logan. Logic.

"Wait a sec." Grabbing my backpack from where I left it sitting on the pebbles, I trot down to the keeper's cottage and set it inside the door. Dashing into the bathroom I splash water on my face and hurriedly smooth on some lip balm. Then I write Dad yet another note. On the way out the door I spot a brown paper package from Mom. I rip it open—*Yes, sweaters.* A heavy teal-green wool turtleneck, and a lighter, loosely knit pale-pink mohair cloud of a thing with a ballerina neckline. Yanking off my hoodie, I tug the sea-green sweater over my head. And remember the letter, up in my room.

For a second, I wonder why I haven't opened it. But really, I know why. Know the letter will be like the others, like journal pages. Like a ship's log, but more personal: a daily account of what she sees, what she thinks. She's sent a couple of letters since I left, and now I imagine them bound in a book, a slim volume: *Observations of an Artist's Journey*. It would be a beautiful book. Powerful, like her paintings. But not nearly as warm as the sweaters. *Mom, I miss you.*

Reaching the top of the stairs, I find Logan leaning against his truck. He says, "Want to try the new restaurant in town?"

"Sure, what kind of food is it?" But I don't really care what kind of food it is. I'm still thinking of my mom, and of Lilah now.

Then Logan jostles me, says, "Raw, baby." And I feel my mood lighten.

"Do I even want to know what that means?"

"I don't know, Rush, do you?"

SUSHI

The drive to town is a blink—probably because we've been talking about music. Here by the harbor, the speed limit drops, and Logan slows, looking past me to the long wooden docks stretching away into the water, their ends floating far out—where the sea and sky merge to become a single dark entity.

"Beat matching, scratching—" With what appears to be some effort, he brings his attention back to the conversation. He's been ranting without heat about DJing. "Nothing but smoke and mirrors. It's the track selection. That's what draws the crowds."

"The crowds. As in, the girls at school."

He laughs.

I laugh. "Logan, the radio station at school doesn't even have—"

"Cutting, spinbacks—don't need it. A good playlist, some nice fades—"

"That station consists of one CD player and a couple of iPods! You can't even do the things you're talking about there."

"Well, not technically. No."

"Not technically? You mean, not at all."

"Like I said. It's the songs—" But I'm laughing again and he breaks off. "What is it? What's so funny?" He's grinning, though. He got me riled, and he knows it. I know it.

He parks the truck, and then we're heading across the road toward the restaurant, both of us laughing now about his "mad DJ skills"—

Suddenly I stop in the middle of the street, staring at the name etched in ornate calligraphy on a piece of driftwood above the door.

Sign of the Mermaid

"What," he says. "Did you drop your lipstick?" But he looks both ways down the street, and takes my hand.

"Were you a Boy Scout, or something?" I joke back. But I grip his fingers.

Dinner hour, Sunday night, yet the restaurant is empty except for a small group over in the far corner. As we wait to be seated I read a notice near the hostess station. Sign of the Mermaid is closing next week for the season. We sit down at a table for two.

"Does this whole place just shut down at the end of September, or what?"

"Yeah, you moved to a real ghost town." Logan cups his hands around his mouth and blows. "That's the sound of the wicked Maine winter wind, in case you didn't get it. But don't worry, there'll still be some places open. Two, I think. You might want to reserve me now for Saturday nights, though; I get double-booked on winter weekends."

"Let me grab my calendar." I reach for the menu.

The hostess has seated us close to the group at the corner table, probably to make the waitress's job easier. I wish she hadn't. There are three people at the round table, two who are facing each other across the table, and one more person who's staring straight ahead—*at me*. More like, glaring. I drop my gaze to the menu.

"So what are you going to have? How about some *uni*?" Logan wiggles his fingers at me.

"Give me another minute," I say, reading the word *"uramaki"* over and over.

Peeking over the top of the menu, I watch a girl about my age whose profile is toward me skillfully lift a piece of sashimi with her chopsticks and place it in her mouth. She has perfect skin and chin-length pale-blond hair cut at a sharp angle. Tilting her head back, she lets the piece of fish slide down her white throat without chewing. Then she smirks at something the boy across the table says. He's cute, with blue eyes, freckles, and blond hair streaked by the sun. His eyes flash with light as he laughs—and I go still. He's a younger version of Bo. Maybe with a better sense of humor, I decide, continuing to watch him.

Not one to be politically correct, Logan reads the menu to me in a poorly executed Japanese accent. Intent on the group at the round table, I have no idea what I order. When the food comes, Logan sorts it out. To his credit he more than holds up his end of the conversation. Nodding and smiling, I silently promise to make it up to him. He seems fairly happy.

But the guy at the corner table—the one who hasn't taken his eyes off me—is obviously *unhappy*. His fierce scowl says as much. His hair is longer than the younger boy's, wilder and darker, but with the same bleached-out streaks that make him look as if he spends his life outdoors. He's ruggedly handsome. Now the girl says his name.

Jordan. Bo's older brother.

Carefully mixing wasabi and soy sauce in a tiny bowl decorated with a painted dragonfly, I let my hair hang forward and peer through it at the older boy. He's still staring straight at me. His dark-blue eyes, close in color to the night sky, are filled with outrage.

I decide not to look up again—to spend the rest of the meal chatting with Logan and appreciating the sushi. But as snatches of conversation drift over from the neighboring table, I find myself listening to the words as if they're background music, until—

Jordan's voice—it just . . . grabs me. That's the only way to describe what's happening. His voice sounds like Bo's, but deeper, grittier. If it were a color, it would be the very blackest blue, the color of the sky at that tipping time, when dusk bleeds into something darker. His voice becomes the center of my attention now. Even weirder: I feel like he knows that it has.

He starts talking about oceanography and atmospheric sciences, and my palms turn as clammy as one of the small rectangles of sashimi. The exact meaning of what he's saying is beyond my understanding, but the words themselves—sound like poetry.

"Stellar interiors . . . subharmonic instability . . . inertia latitude . . ." His voice is almost hypnotic, and again, I think of Bo, of the way his words spiraled into strange, seductive sounds, the way they became *more* than words, the way they became music. I remember, too, how I'd been unable to control my thoughts, my—self. But now, listening to Jordan . . . that doesn't bother me. In retrospect, the afternoon with Bo seems . . . fine. I relax about it now . . .

"Attraction zones, empty . . . must propagate . . ."

And a kind of dreaminess settles over me. A dreamy . . . desire, almost, for . . . for . . .

"Why are you joining a punk band? You want a guy with a safety pin through his—"

My attention jerks back to Logan. "Huh? Wait. *What* did you just say?"

"Kidding. Where were you just now?"

"Sorry, I—I would like to be in a band. But not a punk band."

"Yeah, I don't know," he says. "You and Mary . . . I can see it."

But suddenly it's me who's seeing—something in Logan's face. His familiarity—*he reminds me of someone*. But then Logan's expression changes—to one of concern, I think—and all I see is, well, him.

"Want to get going?" he asks.

I say yes—but then it hits me.

San Francisco. The docks. The boy in the baseball cap—Logan looks like him.

But then Logan drinks the last of the tea, scrunching up his nose and commenting on the flavor—"This tastes like perfume, don't you think, Rush? The way perfume smells?"—and I realize that I'm wrong—of course I'm wrong. He doesn't look like that guy at all. I never even really saw that boy's face.

I tell Logan the tea's jasmine. We stand up—

At the same moment the group from the corner table passes by, heading toward the door.

Jordan shoots me a savage smile, a keen-edged curve that has nothing to do with being friendly, and a vivid memory of Bo holding me in his arms hits me so hard, I bring a hand to my chest. Despite the racing nighttime waves in Jordan's eyes, I almost blurt, *Where's your brother?*

Logan angles a sharp look down at me. "You okay?"

"Yes." But I'm not okay. I feel dizzy. Ill.

The waitress, who we haven't seen since she delivered our food, finally makes her way over with the bill, and Logan gets out his wallet. My intention had been to go Dutch, but it feels like I'm recovering from some kind of bizarre occurrence, and instead of offering to split the check, I just stand there. I can't take my eyes off Jordan, and now I watch as he holds the door for his brother and sister. After he lets it fall closed behind him, an eerie stillness remains.

I don't think they even paid.

"Ready?" Logan asks quietly.

When we get to the truck, he opens the door for me. The air inside is cold. The seat is colder. He slides in and starts the engine. I turn the heater on full blast. The sound of the fan fills the cab. Logan turns, reaching across the space between us, his fingers brushing my neck as he gives the teal turtleneck a little tug.

"You're kind of early, but you've got the right idea. The entire state of Maine freezes solid in the winter." He keeps his hold on the sweater, and I wait for the joke, maybe an offer to keep me warm. But he only looks at me, his clear gray eyes full of questions.

The words that had floated over from the corner table during dinner move through my mind like shifting sand. *"They collapse into each other, in an attraction orbit."*

"Thanks for dinner," I stammer. And this time, it's me who initiates the hug.

Logan's warm, the muscles of his back are hard, his chest solid, comforting.

The feel of him is almost enough to make me forget about Jordan Summers, about the way he'd stared at me all though dinner.

But not quite.

Still, it isn't until Logan's breath stirs my hair that I realize I've held on to him just a little too long, and a little too tight, for the hug to be only a thank-you.

NIGHT

The swinging beam of the lighthouse flashes across my face—

Or, it's the bright light of the moon—

It's white, *white, white*—

"No!" I wake scuttling backward on the bed, screaming. Music's pounding in my head—

The air is cold against my chest—my pajama top. It's open in the front. Something white spins by my window—

I scream again, louder this time, because I know—

Someone was here, in my room.

The white, the wings—

"I only want to look. Only want to listen."

It wasn't a dream. Not this time. Someone was here. Someone spoke.

I wrap my arms around myself. My head feels heavy—like I've been drinking Dad's beers, or—I don't know. My hands too, as I lift them to button my top, are so very heavy.

My head is muzzy, but I know—I *know*—someone was here. Somebody said those words to me, unbuttoned my top—

What would have happened if I hadn't woken up?

Trembling, I reach down to yank the blankets from the floor and then wrap them around me as I climb out of bed and walk to the east-facing window.

But all I see is a spread of stars.

I glance at the clock. Three a.m. I run a hand over my face.

After Logan dropped me off, I retrieved my backpack from the keeper's cottage. Dad still hadn't been home. Crumpling the last note I'd left, I remembered: Dad was making dinner for Logan's folks tonight.

I was glad that Logan went home to a full house. I was just as glad mine was empty.

But I wish someone were here with me now. I consider heading down to the cottage. But the talk with Dad is already going to be epic. Adding the middle-of-the-night factor, not a good idea.

Wide awake now, I'm afraid to go back to sleep. Afraid white wings will whirl by my window—*and I'll miss them*.

These final thoughts are equally distressing—I don't understand what's happening to me. But I can't just sit here. I feel like I'm going to climb out of my skin. Scuffing into my slippers, I grab the teal turtleneck. I need to clear my head.

The bedroom door creaks as I open it, the sound echoing off the bricks of the cold tower. Padding up the stairs to the watch room, I listen for a moment to the wind as it whistles through brass porthole-shaped vents, fighting a disquieting urge to go out on the deck. It's bitter out there for sure. Instead, I climb the ladder to the glassed-in lantern room that houses the Fresnel lens.

A lighthouse using a Fresnel lens is a rarity. This lens is of the first order, which basically means it's huge, ten feet across. Sitting on the floor of the lantern room, I hug my knees tight to my chest. The prisms of the lens refract the light of the lamp, the sharp glass edges creating brilliant rainbows, all the colors missing from the nighttime world outside.

Logan was uncharacteristically quiet on the drive back to the lighthouse. At first, I thought maybe it was me, or the hug that had been something more than a hug. But then I figured it out: seeing the Summers had shaken him. And that worries me. I know depression, know how the endless loop of thinking can go around in your head like a noose circling a neck.

Watching the lens turn, I sing softly to the slow rhythm of the flashing light. Thunder rumbles as if in response, and raindrops begin to run down the glass walls . . .

Suddenly a jagged arc of lightning splinters across the sky—

The lantern room flares white, and I spring to my feet—

As the sharp edges of the prisms turn to glimmering gossamer membrane.

Heart hammering, I rub my eyes with the fingers of both hands. Cover them.

That was a dream, *a nightmare, the boy with his bending, contorting body, the silver-scaled limb—it wasn't real. Isn't real.*

And when I look again—

The sharp edges of the prisms are just that. But still I hurry down the ladder, down the stairs, and back to bed.

Covers drawn up to my chin, it seems like hours before the calm comes, before I feel myself subsiding into sleep, and as I do, the words I'd heard at dinner echo in my ears, accompanied now by dark tendrils of music . . .

The sound circles me . . .

Like black birds in flight . . .

SYMPTOMS

It's early. The room is bathed in silvered morning light.

The painted cement floor of the bedroom is icy cold beneath my feet—

Because the bathroom window is wide open.

Blanket wrapped around me, I stare. I didn't leave it open, didn't open it at all, I *know* I didn't.

The white. The window. The person in my room.

My pulse picks up. But I can't panic about this now—I need to get to school. And I don't have a ride. *Damn.* There's a slim chance Dad's still down at the house. That'll mean we'll have to talk, but still. I glance at the clock. No, he's definitely gone.

Gone. A sharp pain nearly doubles me over—

Bo. I have to see him. Have to hear his voice. I sink down on the desk chair . . .

What's wrong with me?

A few minutes later, the strange cramp subsides. But my pulse remains erratic. *This is crazy—is this what Bo's brother warned him about?*

In the shower my tears mingle with the warm spray, and I berate myself. There's nothing between Bo and me—nothing to cry over. And the pain . . . is a coincidence. It has to be.

God—how am I going to get to school? I'd told Dad not to worry, that I'd ask Mary or Logan to drive me to school this week—Logan. Hopefully he's okay. I'll find out in homeroom, but for now, *Rock Hook must have a cab company.*

I put on a pair of jeans. Unfold the shell-pink sweater. My throat tightens unexpectedly. Mom likes to buy me things, as if that makes up for being MIA. It doesn't. I wish she were here.

Yeah? And what would you tell her?

There's this guy—I don't know. I think he was in my room last night. I want him anyway.

I slip the sweater on over a camisole. A rumble of thunder rolls across the water.

Down in the cottage I start to second-guess myself, thinking maybe I should stay home, take a sick day. I feel anxious, like there's something I need, badly, but have forgotten what that something is. I look myself over in the mirror by the front door, but other than being super pale, there doesn't seem to be anything wrong. I'm dressed. I'm—fine. I head for the phone—

Then stop short, halfway down the hall.

Bo is standing in the kitchen, leaning against the counter. He cocks his head to one side.

"You look as if you've seen a ghost." Drops of rain splatter the windows.

"I thought—" I walk into the kitchen. "You told me goodbye."

"Figured you must have car troubles, or you wouldn't be driving your father's truck."

"Yes, but—" I shiver, and can't help thinking, *Stalker guy.* "Did you even knock?"

"Of course I knocked." He shrugs. "Guess I knocked pretty hard. The door just . . . opened." We stand staring at each other. Shifting colors fill his eyes, then they darken like the sky outside the windows as he brings his hands to the tops of my shoulders—

My heart rate shoots up—I have a strong urge to push him away from me, know I should, but at the same time, *I want to back him up against the counter, press myself against him*—

Suddenly he drops his hands.

Push. Pull. Both of us seem to have at least two personalities. One of mine is irresistibly attracted to Bo, the other terrified. And he acts like two people as well; he said goodbye, now he's here. He wants me—I'm sure of it—but he doesn't. And what he wants me for . . . is questionable. *He* wants *my breath.*

I offer him cereal instead. Then eggs. "Fruit?" I finally ask.

"No, thank you," he replies. "I've already eaten."

I need to know what that means, but I don't *want* to know what that means. More push-pull. Self-consciously, I nibble an apple, realizing: *I'm not hungry.* And also, *I feel better.*

"That's all you're having?"

"Oh, I eat plenty, trust me." The amount of sushi Logan and I consumed last night was criminal. Not knowing exactly why, I blush.

"I've decided I do. Obviously."

"You do . . . trust me?"

He nods. I wish I could say the same about him. Should I even take a ride from him? But even as I ask myself the question, I know I will, because—

Midthought I notice the note sitting on the counter.

Arion,

Until we have a chance to talk about the truck, and I mean face-to-face, you're grounded.

Love, Your Dad

P.S. See you got the package from your mom. Anything good? Chocolate?

"Oh," I say. "Huh." I look back to Bo. Our eyes lock. Slowly, I pick up the piece of paper and hold it gingerly between my thumb and index finger. Biting my lip, I let it drop to the floor, where it slips beneath the kitchen table. "I think . . . I didn't see that note."

"Good, because being grounded"—his lips twist—"would interfere with our plans."

"Our—plans?" A thundercrack makes me jump. The lightning strike had been nearby.

"Grab your backpack, schoolgirl, wouldn't want to be late."

I look at his light hair, his ocean eyes.

I would like to be late.

Questions crowd my mind.

But Bo has questions of his own. On the drive to school he asks about my classes, specifically, which is my favorite. I tell him it's a tie, between Music Theory and Oceanography.

The windshield wipers play a swishing backbeat for his voice. He asks about my friends.

All I can think is—*I want to touch you.* I say, "Thought you didn't like small talk."

He says, "This isn't small. Not anymore."

When we arrive at school, he turns to me and places the palm of one hand along the side of my face. Warmth spreads through me. I know I should go, but—I can't move. Or maybe I just don't want to. Slowly, he runs his thumb over my lips. Without even thinking, I open my mouth—

He jerks his hand back, looking down at his fingers as though they belong to someone else. Then he looks at me, one side of his mouth lifting. "I'll pick you up after school."

Slightly dazed, I open the door. Surrounded by straggling students taking the steps two at a time, Alyssa stands under the dripping overhang. One hand on a cocked hip, she's watching us.

Bo's smile is part smirk as his gaze flickers to Alyssa. He says, "High school." But leaves it at that.

Still feeling lightheaded, I dart into the rain.

Alyssa tells me to slow down as the late bell rings and I push through the double doors.

I don't, so she matches me, stride for stride now, as I head down the hall to homeroom. "He likes long goodbyes, huh? I expect details, and I mean *gory* details, at lunch."

"Sure, but only the gory ones." She slows, and I run on ahead of her.

Outside the rain persists, but inside me a little fire burns. Totally preoccupied, I almost forget to find out why Mary didn't come to the "study session" on Saturday. Not that I stayed.

"So what happened?" I ask her at lunch.

"Nothing, really. Kevin was complaining, saying I don't spend enough time with him, that I study too much."

"*You* study too much? Isn't he the one planning on spending the next decade in school so he can become a doctor?"

"Basically."

"And this weekend . . . he wanted to see you. On a Saturday." I start to laugh. "Leave it to Alyssa to turn that into a bad thing."

"You're kidding? She was trying to turn *that* into gossip?"

"Uh-huh." I drum my fingers on the table restlessly.

"Your cheeks are, like, hot pink, Arion. Are you feeling okay?"

"I feel great." I feel like I've had ten cups of coffee actually; sitting still isn't an option.

"Hmm. You look like you're burning up." She reaches over and touches my forehead. *"Ssss,"* she hisses, drawing her hand back. "Seriously, what's with you?"

"Well . . ." My eyes scan the cafeteria. Logan wasn't in homeroom—I haven't seen him all morning.

"He's not here today," she says.

"Logan?" She nods, and looks like she has something more to add, but I lean in, and, in a voice that sounds feverish even to me, say, "Bo's picking me up after school."

"*Ooh*, looks like I arrived just in time to hear the dirt," Alyssa coos.

Damn. That girl's everywhere. "Bobby and Pete are on the patio," I tell her. "They said they're cutting this afternoon. Have anything to do with you?" Alyssa turns toward the row of windows that looks out on the flagstone patio where students cluster under umbrellas.

"I'll be right back." She sets down her tray.

"Nice move," Mary says. "So what's going on with you and Bo?"

"*Mm*, I'm not really sure . . ."

"But, '*Mm*? Did you just say, '*Mm*,' as in, *Mm*, yummy?"

Damp air creeps up my neck as Alyssa reappears, holding the door open. "I'm going to cut with those guys. Anyone care to join us in a life of crime?"

"*Mm*," Mary says. "Let me think. *Mm* . . . no, thanks." She bursts out laughing.

"It's going up to seventy degrees today, Mary, come. You can tell Bo to meet us, Arion."

"Seventy and rainy," Mary says, looking pointedly at the windows.

Alyssa continues as if Mary hadn't spoken. "Or blow him off. Seriously, I know Bo. He's not worth it." Right. She knows him the way everyone does, which is to say, not at all. "I'm telling you," she insists. "He's a cold fish."

At this, I'm unable to control my laughter.

"Fine. Laugh. But you're not going to get anywhere with him. Mary, I'll bring a Kevin or two for you. Come on."

Mary grins but shakes her head. Alyssa tosses her hair and then lets the door drop closed behind her.

It's probably a good thing that she isn't going to be around later; she'd only be pissed to see that she's wrong. I *am* getting somewhere with Bo.

I just don't know exactly where.

TIDAL

Across the parking lot, Bo opens the passenger door of the red Wrangler. He says hello and his voice—is like a touch. The nausea I've been feeling all afternoon vanishes, and I climb into my seat, albeit a bit unsteadily.

Bo's backing up when I spot Logan. He must have come in after lunch. "Hold on, I need to talk to Logan for a sec."

Bo spins the wheel—then *accelerates*. "Sorry? You need to what?" We shoot past Logan, who's standing next to his truck, hand frozen on the door handle, his gray gaze unwavering as it meets mine.

"Didn't you hear me?" I say, voice shaking slightly. "I need to talk to Logan. I think—"

"Do you *think*," Bo muses, "that Delaine has a good memory, or a poor one?"

"I have no idea—why are you asking about Logan's memory?" My own memory seems fuzzy all of a sudden, filled with . . . white noise. *What was I just thinking about?*

"Because the faster he forgets his feelings for you, the better."

"What feelings? Just because you guys have some weird history . . . What happened between the two of you?"

"It's complicated. Delaine thinks— But hey, we don't need to talk about him, do we? How are you feeling, Arion?"

"I feel fine. And no, we don't have to talk about Logan—you're the one that brought him up."

"You're the one who was checking him out."

"Um, no—" The road forks and we head west. "Wait—are we going to Seal Cove?" Bo nods. My face heats with embarrassment at the memory of my splashdown and the almost kiss. I begin to protest. Then I think of the way someone had held me down, under the water, and how I don't really know for certain that it hadn't been Bo. "Actually—"

But then our eyes meet, and there's nothing for it. I have to go with him.

"Fine. As long as I don't have to take another rules-and-regs test."

"No rules, no regulations." His lips twitch. Then his jaw tenses. "Yesterday, at Cliff House, did the things I told you frighten you?"

The things you told me, like the fact that you can take my life? "Not really," I say quickly.

"Why don't I believe you?"

"Because I'm a bad liar?" He laughs. I say, "But I was a bit . . . overwhelmed."

"Yes, well, so was I." His hands tighten on the steering wheel.

"You told me you couldn't be alone with me."

"Right. I did say that. And yet, here we are."

Moments later the drizzle stops and the sun comes out. When we arrive at Seal Cove, Bo comes around and opens my door. We make our way down to the waterline.

"I'm sure you know plenty of guys who'd like to be alone with you," he says.

Unintentionally picturing Logan's ghost eyes, I don't answer, crouching to pick up a pink pebble still wet from the water.

As we begin to walk, I reply, "No, I don't think so. Hey, let me ask you a question."

"As long as my answers don't have to be any more truthful than yours." I laugh, my question forgotten, as he hands me a white clamshell edged with purple. I place the pebble in the shell, where it sits like a pearl. Beside us, Wabanaki Bay glitters in the late September sun.

We reach the rocks at the end of the beach. Bo's light hair blows across his ocean eyes.

"We're not so different, you know," he says quietly. The water whispers, *Shh . . .*

"Right." *If we weren't so different, I'd kiss you now.* I take a seat on the sand instead.

"Homo sum, humani nihil a me alienum puto." He pronounces the words easily.

"The inscription on the plaque at the library," I say in response. "Means?"

"Means, 'I consider nothing that is human alien to me.' Above all, Arion, I'm a man."

My hands, which, seemingly of their own accord have been squeezing and releasing small hills of sand, are suddenly between his, and it's as if the two of us, touching, complete some kind of circuit. A current runs through me, plunging beneath my skin, to my blood. His gaze sharpens, and he draws me onto his lap. My knees press into the sand on either side of his hips, and unable to stop myself, I slide my arms up around his neck, lifting my lips—

With a swift movement he brings one hand behind my head, tucks my face beneath his chin. Then he wraps his arms around me, and when he stands up, he takes me with him.

Swaying on my feet, I breathe in the salt and pine scent of him, wanting in part to run, knowing, somehow, that I can't. Sound pours over me like water: The whispered sound that comes from a seashell when you hold it to your ear—sent through a Marshall stack. A hundred songs, a thousand; the music vibrates inside me. Like a wave, it draws me under, tosses me over— Until I understand. *The irresistible pull of him is the tug of the tides, the power of the sea.*

And music. I can feel *what music sounds like.*

Then slowly, the music begins to fade—but his pull remains. He keeps one arm around my waist, as if to steady me. With his free hand, he yanks his shirt over his head and tosses it on the sand. The muscles of his arms and chest look smooth and strong; I don't even try to stop myself—I slide my hands up over his chest, reaching for his face, turning it down toward me—

"No!" Releasing me, he backs away, moving so suddenly he inadvertently steps into the water. He doesn't seem to notice. "It's not that simple."

My legs feel as if they can barely hold me. "But—" I take a step toward him.

"There's more." The waves slap around his knees. "You saw the paintings that belong to my father—my family *commissioned* those paintings, and hundreds like them, a very long time ago. Red herrings.

"Part man, part monster, who *wouldn't* blame the creatures in those paintings for lost ships, lost lives? It was never part of the plan to have mermaids morph into pretty playthings for children—Hans Christian Andersen was a dreamer. Our kind, we're the stuff of nightmares."

Slowly, *immense white-feathered wings begin to spread from behind his back.* Haunting melodies mingle with the sound of the waves as the wings emerge, stretching alongside his body, extending several feet above his head. The edges of the feathers pulse with subtle movement, like the silent swaying of sea anemones, and once again, it seems that music rolls off of him. When I gasp at Bo's beauty, the muscles along his jawline tighten and he scowls.

But he doesn't frighten me now. He draws me. The ocean is the same. I'm no longer afraid of it, only enchanted. The water's temperature doesn't even register as I take a step into the sea, a step toward Bo. *An angel. Mom's right. They exist.*

"No. Not an angel."

But I have no idea how Bo can be objecting to what I've just said—I didn't say it out loud. I also have no idea how *I* heard *him*, because he didn't speak—and yet he did. But his lips didn't move.

And they don't move now, as he says, *"Although perhaps angels were our origin. The confusion was common enough. 'The Angel of Death.' People used to scream those words, people who saw my ancestors . . . But nobody wants to believe angels are killers. So men made up their monsters. Sea monsters, they called us. Sea serpents, even. People aren't particular when they're half mad with fear. Mermen. Mermaids. So much easier to blame a beautiful woman; who can stop a beautiful girl?*

"Men see what they want to see. Survivors spread stories. We let them. We made them.

"And so Sirens vanished from the minds of men. Today it's the weather, malfunctioning equipment, modern-day pirates."

The waves leap at our thighs, soaking the legs of our jeans. I stare at Bo's wings, at his face. His lips remain still, his voice a whisper in my mind, as he says, *"Not an angel, Arion. A murderer."*

I fight to keep my voice steady, but then I figure out that, like Bo, I don't need to use it.

The water is acting as a conduit for us.

"You're not a murderer." My thoughts move magically from my mind to his.

"Not today."

"Not ever."

"Maybe that's part of why I want you so much. To tell me lies like that. So human."

He brings his hands to my waist, then slides them to my hips, holding me so tightly it hurts.

My gaze leaves his ocean eyes, taking in the angles of his face, the hollow at his throat, the corded muscles of his arms. I don't care what he is or isn't, don't care about anything except eliminating the space between us. I press myself against him, grasping his upper arms—

Eyes locked on one another's lips, our silent struggle takes us out of the water. His wings loom over me like the cliffs above the beach, their unearthly beauty stark against a sky that's turned to navy without me noticing. I know I should be scared; I also know—he must be wrong.

"Self-defense, maybe," I say, my breath coming fast. "Maybe you could kill someone if your life were being threatened, but wouldn't we all? If we possessed the skill and the strength and our lives were at stake? Anyone would kill, to live."

"Anyone would kill to live. My point exactly." He straightens, starts pulling away—

But even as he tries to step back, I cling to his hips, my brain sluggish with wanting. Everything is a tangle. My body's desire twisting my thoughts. What I *see* clashes with what he's said. Then there's the music of him.

"Arion, you *need* to let go." His chin is lifted with the effort of restraint. With a hushed gust of wind—his wings vanish.

"No—" Surprise shows on his face as I grab his arm and spin him around—running my hand over his shoulder blades. *Smooth skin.* "No, you can't keep doing this to me. We can't have this—tug-of-war. I only want to *kiss* you, is that so horrible?" It's humiliating, to say these things, but I can't seem to stop myself. Again, I run my hand over his back, now his chest.

His laugh is derisive. "*Only* a kiss? You're right, you're not a good liar." He brings two fingers to my neck, to the pulse there. Presses. His fingers are hot, yet a chill runs through me. His other hand moves to my lower back, a gentle pressure. "Do you even understand what my Song does?"

"It lures. You use it to lure your—prey." The word "prey" fades to nothing.

But my fear doesn't chase away the want—although a sort of paralysis creeps through me now as he bends his head, the side of his face touching mine, his mouth near my ear.

"It works well, doesn't it?" He whispers the words, and I can barely hear them above the sound of the ocean, but I don't doubt their meaning, and all at once, I understand his intent.

"Wait—"

He brushes his lips along my cheekbone, his next words soft as shadows. "That was the idea. But it seems you can't." His laugh is dark. "Love comes and goes, with humans. Ebbing, flowing . . . an uneven, tidal thing. Love, for mortal men and women, is a beautiful lie, a broken promise. A wave that rolls up on the sand—then falls back to the sea."

Love. My paralysis is complete. Hearing him say that single word scares me more than anything he's said, or done, so far. Because I agree: love is a lie, a ghost of a ghost.

"But my love isn't like that, I assure you. It won't recede. It will *flood* you. Drown you."

Love. Are we in love, then? Is that what this is?

"On the other hand, if you were my *mark*—"

Smooth as water, he slides his hand behind my neck—

CHOICE

Fear and desire collide in me as he draws me to him, his eyes becoming whirlpools of night just before his mouth comes down hotly on mine—

But before I can even taste him, he tears his lips away—pushing hard against my shoulders, so that I stumble and fall to the sand.

He looks down at me, his chest rising and falling fast—his face pale except for a spot of color burning on each cheek. "What the hell am I doing?"

"What *are* you doing?" I jump to my feet. "Why did you make me feel like your—" I search for a word, refusing to say *prey*. *Mark? Is that what he said?*

"Because you need to know the difference! Between love, and *what we do*. But I didn't mean—"

"What *did* you mean? *What do you want?*" I practically shout.

"What do *I* want? I wanted only to show you. Teach you. Then someday, soon, maybe—" His tone turns bitter. "But *you*. You wanted—I almost lost control! Happy?"

"Oh, so I should be happy? Happy my heart nearly broke through my rib cage? Happy you paralyzed me with—" With want, with need.

Were you going to kiss me? I want to shout, *Were you going to* kill *me?* I look at the water. Look back at him. Can't speak.

Running his hands through his hair, he says, "I thought you wanted to know me."

"Yes, but that's not *who you are*, it's just something you can *do*."

"No. It's who I am." We stare at each other.

"I need to go," I say shortly.

"I can see that." We begin to walk. Bo's voice is low, angry sounding. "You know, despite your eagerness for—me, you're not ready to hear more."

"Oh please! *Teach* me. Just don't scare the hell out of me." *Or make me want you until it hurts.* "What about the breath? Where do you get it?" *From who?*

He slows then, angling his gaze down at me, his eyes making me think of a glowing pendant I'd seen in a dusty display case buried in the back of one of the old fishing shacks near the harbor that had evolved—or perhaps devolved—into shops. I'd wondered what the gorgeous green-and-gold necklace was made of, and the shopkeeper, whose skewed smile somehow seemed as dark and dirty as the rickety row of buildings, told me it was dichroic glass. The piece fascinated me, and even as I backed away from the counter, I pressed him to explain how it had been made. "Layer upon layer of metal oxides attached to the surface"—the man started around the counter—"see how the colors shift?" But to me it was his eyes that were shifting as he came toward me—the necklace outstretched like an offering, which I refused—the same way Bo's are shifting now.

And just this one look makes a cry catch in my throat, some wild yearning trapped behind my lips. A strange tone rings in my ears, and suddenly any questions I have are completely eclipsed by a chasm of ache for him that opens within me. *I need this to end—I'll die if it ends.*

"It's like I don't have a choice!" I blurt, furious now. "Like I *have* to be with you, or, or—" I drop my gaze to the sand, the only source of light left on the darkened beach.

"Arion." His voice is silk smooth as he says my name, yet somehow sharp. The way a knife can be so honed, you don't feel the initial cut when it slices you.

He cups my chin now, lifting my face until I'm forced to look him in the eye.

In a whisper, he says my name again. Sings it. "Arion." Then he asks, "Is having a choice really so important?"

I don't need to be told, the question is rhetorical.

INQUISITION

Dad is in front of the TV when I get home, watching some show about boats. For a minute, it seems like he's forgotten all about the "face-to-face" talk he wanted to have, and I'm relieved. My head is leaden—my pulse, like a caged thing. How can I talk to anyone?

But then he says, "There's steak and salad," and heads into the kitchen. So I do too.

The aftershocks of the strange afternoon still rocking though me, I get out a plate and some silverware. Dad takes a beer from the fridge.

"Well? Let's hear it. What happened to the truck?" He sits down at the table.

"I—borrowed it."

"So I gathered."

"I went to the museum," I say, taking the steak and salad out of the fridge. "That old house, the Wayside. Coming home, I'm not exactly sure, but . . . I think a stone hit the window."

"Did you fall asleep?" He gives me a hard look. He knows I'm leaving something out.

"Um, maybe?" I grimace. "I'm okay, though," I add, hoping that might be enough.

"Apparently. Where've you been? Didn't you get my note?"

Where have I been? To heaven. To hell. Is that love?

"I was with Bo. We went to Seal Cove after school." I sit down.

"After school." Dad runs a hand over his face. "That was a while ago. Bo Summers?"

I nod.

"But last night you were out with—?"

"Logan." My cheeks grow warm.

"That's what I heard. Sounds like it's not a very good time to get grounded."

"Not really."

"You know, the truck isn't for joyriding. You're going to have to pay for that window."

"I said I would."

"Yes, you did." He laces his fingers together, rests his hands on the table.

"Dad, I'm sorry about the truck. I shouldn't have taken it. But do you think you can just forgive me? I'll pay for the window, and, well, maybe, can I be grounded some other time?"

"Some other time."

"Right."

"And what 'other time' did you have in mind?"

"Um . . . I haven't really thought that through yet. Maybe, sometime soon?"

"Sometime soon as in, when you're not dating two guys?"

"Dad!"

Guess he figures that little jibe is punishment enough, or maybe he's just glad I'm not hurt, or that I finally have a social life. He takes a sip of beer. "Sometime soon. Guess we can make that work. Now tell me, what happened to the note I left for you this morning?"

"Oh. Did you leave a note? For me?" Lying to him is impossible.

He squeezes the bridge of his nose. Then he gives me another hard look. "Okay. You're officially not grounded. But you owe me one. And tell me where you need to go. I'll give you a ride. Hopefully, the Cherokee will be fixed soon, or, I don't know. I'll look around. I'll take you to school tomorrow, though, all right?"

"Sure, okay. Great. Thanks. A lot. And sorry about the truck, really, I'm sorry."

"You can stop being sorry. It's fixed. I'll send you the bill."

Dad gets up and leaves the kitchen, presumably going back to his boat show.

"Logan phoned," he hollers a moment later from the living room.

"Oh. Okay. Thanks."

He pokes his head around the doorframe. "Heard you two tried the new sushi place."

"Uh-huh, we did." I try to give my voice the kind of tone a parent reading to a child gives the final words of a bedtime story: *The End.*

Dad mumbles something about teenagers and then retreats across the hall.

INTERVENTION

Tuesday. Wednesday. Thursday. I don't hear from Bo. And I'm glad. I am.

I'm also sick. Literally. Friday, I stay home with a fever.

But I'm sick in some other way too—because I can't stop thinking about him. Specifically, I can't stop thinking of the split-second crush of his lips against mine. There was something true about it, something more real than his fantastical wings.

He'd talked about love. Told me his secrets. *Why hasn't he called?*

On the weekend, I lie in bed, burning up, tossing and turning, waving away Dad's good intentions. I can't stop touching the shell that sits on my bedside table. I pick it up. Put it down. Marvel at its royal-purple edges. Wonder what I did with the pink pearl of a pebble I'd placed in its smooth white center just after Bo gave it to me. I swear I put both in the pocket of my jeans.

It's only after I throw up for the second time on Saturday night that I think of Lilah. The way I'm hunched over the toilet—it suddenly reminds me of her, hunched over the Moleskine.

I am waiting.

Not hearing from Bo acts as a trigger, and I feel the bite of the black-eyed dog that Nick Drake sang about so beautifully. But I fight it—I do. I listen to music. Finish my homework.

I'm almost afraid of what might come out if I pick up my guitar, so I open a book instead.

But none of my favorite characters have anything on me. No great novel, no trashy romance, no story I've ever read has prepared me for feelings like these. My heart feels squeezed—my gut, raw. I can pretend I'm not thinking of Bo—but that's all it is. Pretending.

And Logan? He's on it—on me. Looking suspiciously at me on Monday when I manage to keep down a little food and make it back to school. Offering me a ride on Tuesday and again on Wednesday, joking and trying his best to cheer me up on Thursday.

Finally, Friday, he's in my face. "I don't get it," he says as I stare unseeingly out the cafeteria windows. "Last week you looked like you won a jackpot or something, but did you share the money? No." He waves a fork. "Fine. Keep the cash. But quit hiding in the library at lunch. Mary and I both know you're freaking out about something, so just tell us what it is."

Mary's sitting with us at the table, being careful not to comment. This week has been complete torture, and I appreciate her silence hugely. Dad gave me a ride every day, and that was hard, but it was easier than going with her or Logan. I've been afraid to talk to either one of them about what was—or wasn't—going on between Bo and me, worried that I'd start crying, or begin babbling about Bo's voice, or worse, his wings.

Logan's going off again: "So today, Miss Rush, Mary and I decided we should perform a little family intervention."

"He means *friendly* intervention. As in, we're you're friends."

"Whatever. You need to talk to us." Logan reaches across the table—and with a gentleness that surprises me, brings a finger beneath my chin, lifting it until I look at him.

If there's a jackpot anywhere, his smile is it, but below his pale eyes, his skin is smudged with shadows, and one cheekbone wears a plum-colored bruise. The idea of someone hitting him makes my stomach tighten—I want to know what happened, who did this to him. But I don't want to encourage any more questions. I jerk away from his touch.

Mary takes a bite of her burger, appearing nonchalant, but as she puts it down, her hands aren't quite steady. And it's this, Mary's trembling, that makes me realize how selfish I'm being. She watched Logan plunge into the depths of despair after Nick died. I don't want her to worry about me too. Same goes for Logan. It's not fair.

"It's—" A sudden pain pulses at my temples and I wince. "Bo."

"I knew it!" Logan slaps a palm down hard on the tabletop. "I told you, he—man, I'd like to get that guy in a headlock. What did he do?"

"Logan, take it easy," Mary says. She looks past him to where her Kevin's walking toward us with a full tray. The other two Kevins are right behind him.

"Mary's right, Logan. You don't have to—" The pain comes again.

"Yeah, I do! Like I'm gonna watch you walk down a dark alley and not say anything? Tell me, what did he do? Did he—"

"He didn't *do* anything." My head aches. I want to lie down. "It's what he didn't do."

Logan looks genuinely puzzled, but Mary—despite the cacophony of the Kevins as they sit down around us with a clatter of trays—gets it. She squeezes my thigh under the table.

The arrival of the Kevins means the end of our lunch period. Mary kisses Kevin and gathers her things.

"Ready?" she asks me.

My headache is slowly subsiding, but my pulse is fluttering fitfully. Still, I nod, then for good measure—yank Logan's hair.

"What?"

"Walk with us?"

He blows out a breath. "Sure."

On the way to class I tell the two of them about the club I came across. "You know about it?"

Mary shakes her head. Logan says, "Never heard of it. Must be new."

"Actually, it's old. It used to be called Pine Lodge. Then it was nothing, closed. The new owners are from New York. I looked it up online. Two Portland bands are playing this weekend, and a couple national acts are booked for next month. Wrist, and . . . Sugarcoat, I think. And Favorite Way to Die."

"Favorite Way to Die? Really? They're pretty hardcore." Logan purses his lips. Then he says, "My brother was into them." The three of us walk in silence for a minute or two.

"Sunday's open mic night," I say. "I—I think I'm feeling better, you know? I think I want to go. It's random draw, but if you get picked, they let you play a short set, not just one tune—which really only gives you time to suck. Not that a set can't be a train wreck, but at least you have time to redeem yourself."

"Ah. So that's why we haven't heard you play."

"*Pff.* What are you talking about?"

"Hey, I'm not going to say it if you aren't. Don't want to give it any power, right?"

"Give what any power?" Mary asks.

Logan mouths the words: *Stage fright.*

"I do not have stage fright." *I have real things to be afraid of.* "And what do you know about performance anxiety, hmm?"

"Not a thing, Rush. Come over today. I'll show you just how little I know about that—"

"Logan plays drums," Mary says, elbowing him in the ribs.

"Played," he corrects, tapping out a quick rhythm pattern on her shoulder.

"You're a drummer? How come you never told me? Although, it makes total sense."

"Really. And why's that?"

"Duh," Mary says. "She knows you love music—"

"Actually, I was referring to the fact that he likes to hit things."

"You kill me, Rush. Shoot me the link, will you? You need a ride, or just a roadie?" He slants a salacious look down at me. "Or a groupie?"

"All of the above," I surprise myself by saying.

Logan grabs me around the waist.

Mary rolls her eyes. "You two. When's it gonna happen? Look, I'm taking Arion early, so she can scope the place out." She jabs a finger at Logan. "You—get to carry her stuff."

CLUBBING

"Does this place have food?" Logan asks as we stand outside the club.

"Don't know," I say, shifting my guitar case from one hand to the other.

"Just wondering if I'm going to be eating my dinner or drinking it."

I look Logan over. He's tall, maybe he won't get carded, but Mary and I will. Luckily, we both have fake IDs.

"Man of many talents," Logan said with a shrug as he gave them to us earlier.

He opens the door and the three of us step into a dark, crowded entryway. Immediately, my ears start ringing, but the song thudding against my chest makes me grin.

"One of your favorites, huh?" Logan asks, eyeing my hips, which have started swaying slightly all on their own. I nod happily.

There's a knot of people in front of us arguing with a guy who's standing with his arms crossed. He's wearing the coolest shirt—twining lines of color, like a curling road map—and is obviously the bouncer, because now he tells the group that the club is filled to capacity.

One of the boys argues that they've driven from Portland. "C'mon! You gotta let us in—"

The bouncer takes a step closer to the boy.

The group leaves.

About to tell Mary and Logan that we don't have a chance, that we should go too, my eyes snag on the crowd beyond the bouncer. Waitresses wearing identical short puffed black skirts with black tights are everywhere. Most of them have dark hair. Chestnut brown. Inky black. But no matter the color, the style is the same: every girl has her hair piled up in a beehive. But weirder than that—

"What the heck," Mary says, following my gaze. "Would you call those, like, fur *accessories*?" Every waitress is wearing bits of fur: fur collars, fur cuffs, fur *anklets*. All of it is a rich-brown color—it might be mink, but I don't know. It looks real, though. Then there are the waiters, just a few, dressed all in black, and sporting tall turbans, or top hats. One waiter is wearing a toque. "He could be the chef," Mary says, like she's hoping such a good-looking guy has an excuse to wear such a bizarre-looking hat.

More people arrive, squeezing in behind us, and Logan says something to the bouncer, who, I realize now, isn't wearing a shirt at all, but is bare from the waist up, his skin covered with tattoos. Mr. Tattoo shakes his head.

"But we're locals," Logan says, his mouth set in an impatient line. He and Mary both turn to me and say something at the same time.

"What?" I shout over the music pouring from the club.

"He says he can't let us in."

"Why, we don't have the right clothes?" I nod toward two girls with super high beehives and fur-trimmed poodle skirts who've just appeared from behind the doorman. One of the girls is unnaturally pale and leans heavily on the other as they push past us, heading outside.

"Wasted," Mary says, looking after the girls.

But I'm the one who stumbles suddenly as the crowd shoves me from behind.

"Whoa." The bouncer catches my elbow—and I catch my breath. His tattoos—they seem to shift, writhing before my eyes. When I look up into his face, I find he's staring at me too. The entryway seems to spin as my ears fill with dark music that's definitely not coming from the speakers inside the club.

His voice too, is music, as he asks, "You here for the open mic?"

"Let them in, will you?" This voice is soft, but has an edge that cuts through the music and the noise of the crowd like a shark through water.

My stomach plunges. *Bo.*

"Friends of yours?" asks the bouncer.

"Close enough."

Mr. Tattoo grabs my hand and slaps a gold plastic band on my wrist. Blinking, I squint at the wristband. Although the bouncer has let go of my hand, I haven't quite claimed it, and it floats at the end of my arm, hovering between us.

The bouncer looks amused. Bo does not. Logan really does not, and Mary just looks as confused as I feel.

"C'mon," Logan says. "Let's go in."

But I don't move, just look back and forth between Bo and the bouncer, then down to my wrist, where letters seem to undulate across the band until finally, they come into focus.

HIVEHIVEHIVEHIVEHIVEHIVEHIVEHIVEHIVEHIVEHIVE

There are more words, but I can't quite make out what they—

Logan snatches my hand, lightly twisting my arm until a blush spreads up my neck as I read the words that had been upside down. **MINOR—No Service.** He pulls me into the throng where Bo vanishes as suddenly as he appeared. Mentally, I probe my emotions the way someone might touch a bruise to see if it still hurts. It does. And my head feels . . . cloudy. As if I'd just gained a little extra space in there but it's filled up with undesirable weather.

"Maybe you need to get one of those." Logan nods to a door on our right with a neon sign above it that reads, **TATTOOS**. "Since you suddenly seem so enamored with them. Plus, those sharp needles might wake you up enough to, you know, hop out of that rabbit hole Summers just knocked you down. How'd he know about tonight? You told him, didn't you? I should've known you would."

Watching the waitresses hurrying back and forth, I shake my head. "I didn't." They're very attentive to each customer and very . . . beautiful. In fact, everyone in the club is beautiful, and . . . vibrant. There's a buzz about the place, about the people here. Maybe this is why the club's called Hive.

A waitress passes wearing a fur choker and Logan glances at the deep V of her neckline. Mary shoves him. I refrain from rolling my eyes, continue looking around.

The walls are black, striped here and there with the same cyber yellow that trims the outside of the club. The ceiling is gold. The floor, littered with glitter and flower petals. Everything shines, including the song that plays now, a pop confection that pulses through the club, luring quite a few people onto the dance floor. There, poodle skirts and beehives give way to T-shirts and torn jeans, combat boots and piercings. Fishnets, flannel, bare chests, loaded smiles, and enough black eyeliner for everyone.

People stand three deep at the bar, a polished slab of wood that runs along one side of the room. It looks like someone has cut down one of the grand evergreens, split it, and sealed it. Despite the high-gloss finish on the bar, the whole place reeks of pine. I inhale deeply—the air smells fresh, even though there has to be a couple hundred people in this front room alone. Where did they all come from?

Opposite the bar, a stage is set for a full band. So where do they hold the open mic?

I find out when one of the fur-studded waitresses beckons us to a second room and gestures to the only table that isn't taken. Here, the stage is smaller, backed into a corner.

The room is packed with musicians; they easily outnumber the audience. The majority of them appear to be guitarists—who are probably also singers—although there are a couple of people with hand drums, and one boy who's struggling to set up a synthesizer onstage while his friend plays around with a laptop. A girl who'd been at the back of the room a minute ago talking to the guy behind the soundboard is passing a bucket around.

Logan leans back in his chair, hands linked behind his head. A poorly angled ceiling spot above the next table shines straight into his light eyes, and they glint as he studies me.

"Better put your name in the hat."

"There are so many people here," Mary says, looking around. "Are you nervous?"

"No, but—"

A burst of applause comes from behind a closed door just beyond our table. Apparently the club has a third room where a private party is going on. Now the door opens and Bo comes through, carrying four champagne glasses. His cheeks are hectic with color, and he's smiling uncharacteristically.

"Ever been here before?" Bo asks Logan as he puts down the drinks, pulls up a chair.

"That the best line you've got?"

Bo lifts a glass. "Touché." He hasn't even said hello to me, though now he nods at the guitar case and asks, "Are you going to play?" He's wearing a black T-shirt that hugs the contours of his chest, and when he speaks, the desire to put my hands on him stuns me into silence for a second.

"Hope so," I say just long enough after he asked to make the moment completely awkward. Choosing a glass, I take a sip of the slightly cloudy amber liquid, mostly so I won't reach over and touch him. The drink is delicious, tastes like honey, and melons. "What is this?"

"Hive's Honeywater," he says. "Specialty of the house."

"It's great," Mary agrees. "Thank you."

"You're welcome," Bo replies.

Logan makes a disparaging sound. "Whatever, let's get to the important shit. Why is this place such a twisted retro nightmare? What's with the hair and the hats?" He empties his glass and waves at one of the waitresses.

Marveling at the height of her hair, I unlatch the guitar case and pull out my Martin, walking my fingers through a few chord progressions and a couple of scales. Not that I can hear anything over the punk anthem that blares from the speakers now, but it feels good. At least my hands will be ready.

The waitress comes by and takes Logan's order. Glancing at Bo, he pushes some bills into her hand, then picks up the square of paper she's left on the table and passes it to me.

"What's your lucky number, Rush?"

Flipping it over, I suck in a breath. Bo's gaze turns hard.

"One."

Mary hoots. "Yes! Because, man, there's no way I want to hang out here all night."

"Drink your Honeywater," Logan says to her, raising his glass in an exaggerated imitation of Bo's earlier gesture. "It'll make you feel like you're part of the freak show."

But Hive doesn't feel like a freak show to me. With the Martin in my hands, I feel almost fine. An atmospheric song—all keyboard pads and soft vocals—floats through the speakers. The sound guy gets up onstage, adjusting cables, setting up a mic stand.

My hands are warmed up. In a minute I'll be singing. The hard part is over.

Continuing to run my fingers over the fret board, I watch Bo get up and move to the back of the room. Inside, a sharp little knife comes to rest at the top of my rib cage. The way he's acting, it's like he doesn't even know me. Like he doesn't *want* to know me. The two of us, standing together in the ocean, communicating telepathically . . . it's like it never happened.

Mary gives me a sympathetic look. I shrug. It's better this way.

The atmospheric song fades away until the only sound is the clinking of glasses and the whispering voices of waiting musicians.

Somebody closes the door to the front room of the club and the lights go down.

Two warm spots light the stage, then a low voice comes through the speakers.

"Good evening. Welcome to Hive . . ."

PLAYER

Guitar. Cable. Strap. Tuner. Drink. Capo. Pick.

Bo's leaning against the far wall back by the soundboard—staring at me.

Double-check tuning. Adjust mic stand.

Mary leans over and says something to Logan. He laughs, but keeps his eyes on me.

Ground feet. Soft knees. Lips. Breathe.

Strumming a percussive pattern on the Martin, I whisper sing into the mic—

> *"I wanted to know you, but you always had your secrets.*
>
> *Like airplanes, tall buildings, the mysteries that you kept . . ."*

I sing lies that tell truths.

> *"I wanted to have you, but you always kept your lips shut.*

Like veils, dark nighttime, the split of the skin when it's cut . . ."

Leaving the room behind I lean into the chorus, opening up, bleeding out—

"So I slept . . . I slept . . ."

Storyteller. Bottom dweller. Digging in the dirt.

Fingers. Frets. Lights. *Him.*

Ripping. Stars. Regret.

Dark hallways, tilting floors, unexpected steps, taking me down . . . down . . .

In front of everyone, in front of no one, I soar through the mansion of my voice . . .

DANCE FLOOR

"Arion, you were great!" Mary says, coming up to the side of the stage as I jump down. A smattering of applause comes from the people standing nearby, the denouement of the wild clapping and shouts of approval that followed my final song.

"Yeah? You think it went okay?" Adrenaline courses through me. I try to see past the crowd that's blocking the soundboard now.

"More than okay," she assures me. "Everybody was totally listening. They loved you."

"Six songs, not bad for an open mic," Logan says, coming up and taking my guitar. "And, hey, you're kinda hot with a six string in your hands, Rush. Buy you a drink?"

"Um—" Quickly I scan the crowd, trying to look like I'm not.

"He left," Mary whispers in my ear. "I thought he was going to melt your clothes off with that stare of his—personally, I think I'd combust if I looked into those eyes—then he just left."

Nodding to her, I cast one more glance toward the back of the room, surprised at how angry I am. *No hello. No goodbye. What the hell?*

"What do you say, Rock Star?" Logan continues as we head for the table. "Drink?"

"No. Dance."

"Really?"

"Really. Mary, will you watch my stuff?" Grabbing his hand, I drag Logan into the front room where a full band is burning down the house and the dance floor is mosh-pit packed. We merge into the crowd as the singer's voice does a backbend, then sinks to a whisper, an urgent bass line throbbing beneath it. His voice makes me think of Bo's voice, the way it seems to . . . enter me. *Why did he leave?*

Closing my eyes, I focus on the music, inviting it in, willing it to fill me so I don't have to wonder anymore, don't have to care. Imagining the music flooding my veins, I open my eyes and grin at Logan, who looks like he's feeling the music too—and the Hive's Honeywater.

The next song starts. I lift my hair up off my damp neck. Logan comes closer, putting his hands in my hair, making a ponytail for me with his fist. His own hair hangs dark around his face. His pale eyes are moonlight. A smile plays on his lips as he lets go of my hair and grasps my waist. Lifting my arms overhead I toss my head back, feeling my lips part. His hands move to my hips. Then he turns me around, pulling me against him.

Shutting my eyes again, I listen to his body talking to mine, my body talking back. It's only getting stronger, this something-happens-when-we're-in-the-same-room-together thing, this under-the-friendship-and-the-joking-we're-connected thing.

The song ends and I open my eyes, peeling away from him.

"Pull back all you want," he says. "It's not going to change the way you feel."

"We have to get back to Mary," I say a little breathlessly.

"We will in a second." He reaches for me.

"There she is—" I wave over the crowd.

"My turn to dance yet?" she shouts.

The next song starts, and I take my guitar case and backpack from her, setting them down against the side of the stage. She body-slams Logan, then grabs both my hands.

Laughing, I whirl her around—"Now you know what it feels like to be me!"

CAGE

Much later, as the three of us shamble across the parking lot, Logan announces he's driving me home.

"You've been drinking," Mary says.

Logan waves a hand dismissively. "Sugar water."

"Honeywater," Mary corrects. "And it's got alcohol in it."

"You would know." They grin at each other.

Headlights wash over us. Mary waves.

"You guys can come with," she says, as the Eatons' Prius stops alongside us and she opens the passenger door. "Dependable, fast service," she adds, waggling her eyebrows. "Roomy backseat." She climbs in and kisses Kevin in the middle of his hello.

"Yeah, I don't think so," Logan says.

Kevin waves and says something to Mary about picking up her car tomorrow. She kisses him again, then says, "And one for you—" and blows me a kiss as the Prius rolls away, red taillights and dust. Logan shakes his head and I laugh. We walk over to his truck.

"Hang on," he says. "I need to take a—"

"Spare me the details."

"Be right back." He disappears into the pines.

As soon as he does, the door of the club opens and two people stagger out, arms wound around each other.

Jordan.

The other stumbling figure is a tall, leather-clad girl with long dark hair. The two are a tangle of limbs and lips as they trip toward the edge of the woods on the far side of the parking lot where Jordan pins the girl against a tree.

She clenches the material of his shirt, pulling him closer, her hands disappearing between the two of them. But then she cries out—and Jordan rocks slightly, as if he's been pushed. Her muffled cry comes again, and I start toward them.

Suddenly he pulls the girl away from the towering pine, his body bent over hers, kissing her hard. She kicks—her feet scuffing the sandy ground—as he pulls her around the side of the tree.

"Hey!" I shout, breaking into a run.

I'm rounding the tree when a roar of music echoes through the evergreens and an immense set of wings bursts through the back of Jordan's shirt—

Stunned, I stop short as he wraps the wings around the girl, enclosing her in a cage of sleek feathers the color of snow.

Her screams are barely audible now, but my voice is plenty loud. "Jordan—stop!"

One white wing whips back as he half turns. He's taller than Bo I realize now, more muscular. Excitement gleams in his eyes like stars in a night sky. Before I have time to hate him for it, my attention rivets on the girl, who's gasping for breath.

"What's wrong with her—what did you do to her? She needs help!"

But Jordan doesn't help. He remains motionless for a moment, one wing aside—so I can see. Then he seals her panting mouth with his, his body shuddering with sensation. The girl struggles, legs scissoring—

I scream—

Her head drops back—and he lets her slip from the circle of his arms. Her body hits the carpet of pine needles beneath the tree with a soft thud.

Jordan wipes his mouth. "Too quick. Guess I was hungry."

To me the girl's struggle lasted forever. This moment, too, stretches out—as I stare down at her white face, her pale, swollen lips—time becoming an elongated thing.

But Jordan's smile is whip fast. "What do you think I should do? Get her to water?"

I gape at him. A million years later I say, "Water? She's dead."

"Well, technically, yeah. But I still have a few minutes. I could probably help her—"

"Help her, then!" The possibility seems to wake me, and I crouch next to the girl.

"Jordan, please, you have to—"

Swiftly he lifts the girl to her useless feet.

Then he says, "Nah."

And yanks her head to one side.

My horror magnifies the sound of her neck snapping, making it loud as a gunshot.

"Just in case," he says. Then he lets the girl drop, and gives her a shove with his foot, rolling her farther into the woods that ring the lot. "We'll let the morning crew find her."

"Morning crew?" I stare at him, my hands clenching and unclenching. Inept fists hanging at the ends of my arms. I don't dare hit him, though I want to, so badly.

"What are you worried about? She's a runaway. Or maybe you're worried about me, is that it? Don't be. Jacques is an old buddy of mine—he knows the drill. His club in New York is much bigger than this one."

"His club. In New York. Are you saying . . . there are Sirens in New York City?"

"Disposal's a much bigger issue down there. Although, a big city has its advantages." With a rush of wind, Jordan's wings vanish and he stands with his savage smile, his shirt hanging around him in tatters. "But let's talk about you, Arion Rush. What are *you* doing here?"

"I—I—"

Jordan grabs my hand and pulls me farther into the trees. His eyes shine in the dark like some kind of jungle cat, but his voice as he says my name again—*"Arion Rush"*—is so soft. There's no growl at all. And for a second, I think I'm mistaken—*have* to be wrong—about what I've seen.

But then he speaks again.

"So, has my brother found a way to have sex with you yet? A way to take 'just a little' of your breath?" Jordan's laugh is mirthless. "Not only is his 'experiment' ridiculous, but, really, who has that kind of patience? Fuck 'em and suck 'em, I say."

God, he's going to kill me.

"But you didn't—you didn't—" My tongue trips as I stall for time.

"Didn't fuck her? Please, in a parking lot? You surprise me. Such a public place. Although—" Jordan breaks off, rubbing the golden stubble along his jawline as if considering some kind of dilemma. "I did kill her here, didn't I? That was tactless."

Abruptly he pulls me up against him. "But I haven't done anything to *you* yet."

"Please!"

"Please?"

"Please don't!"

He mimics me, then says, "You're Bo's toy. If I kill you, he won't get his questions answered. And you know how that feels, don't you? I've heard you're a very curious girl, that you ask all kinds of questions.

"But you're going to forget your questions now, at least the ones you have about me. About this night. About this place." He grips my upper arms, bends his face close to mine. I feel his lips brush my ear as his music winds around me, a snaking melody that makes my skin ripple with pleasure. My mind begins to muddy, like the tidal waters of the bay where they bump up against the edge of the woods.

"Where's my brother, Arion?" Jordan whispers. "Where's Bo?"

Bo. Something wordless and heavy drops into the deep water hole, the abandoned wishing well my stomach has become. *Splashhh . . .* the heavy thing knocks against my insides.

Jordan's voice grows sharp. "He did bring you here—sick bastard that he is—didn't he?"

"I brought her."

Logan appears from between the blue shadows of the trees. "And I'm taking her home." Glaring at Jordan—who has released me with a soft sound of surprise—he holds out one hand.

Slowly, I take it, looking back and forth between the two boys. Wondering—

Why in the world are the three of us standing out here in the woods?

FIRE DRILL

When I wake up, my head is hazy. An emotional hangover, that's what it feels like. Between the trauma of seeing Jordan—I can't remember *why* it had been so horrible to see him, but it had—the uncomfortable ride home with Logan—me, insisting it wasn't Bo's brother who'd upset me, him insisting it was—and, of course, being truly upset about Bo, I almost decide to stay in bed.

Mary *does* stay in bed, which is why I miss homeroom, and my first class.

Last night, she said she'd pick me up for school. When I got home, I told Dad.

Ensconced in the living room at one end of the couch, newspapers spread out around him, he looked at me over the top of his reading glasses. I was sure he was going to comment on the time—midnight—or worse, my condition—blurry. That was how I felt at the end of the night. Not drunk. Not even tipsy. Just—like my head was filled with clouds.

But he only said, "Glad you found a place to play. Do I get to come hear you next time?"

"Um—" I have no idea what I said then, but I'm fairly certain I followed it with something about sleep.

I don't even remember climbing the stairs.

Now, thankfully, this dragging day is coming to a close. School is nearly over, and we're on the way to our last class.

Mary starts to say something about Hive, about how weird the club is, when a loud ringing obliterates her words. Fire drill.

Crowds of students propel us down the hall toward the front of the school, where we become separated. As I'm swept out of the building and onto the steps, I see Bo in the parking lot, standing next to the blue Mercedes, scanning the swell of faces, watching students spill down the stairs, across the driveway, and onto the front lawn.

God, I can feel *him from here. Feel the pull of him. I* have *to talk to him.*

While I'm trying to figure out how to get to Bo, Logan appears beside me and follows my gaze.

"What the hell is Summers doing here?"

The fire alarm blares deafeningly, and suddenly, after days of keeping my feelings in check, I lose it, rounding on Logan. "What *is* it, Logan? What do you have against him?"

"You mean besides the fact that he's messing with your head? Besides the fact that he shows up at your gig, then hardly talks to you, just fucks you with his eyes?" Exiting students flow past Logan like a river around a rock. The bell continues its incessant clanging.

I stand on tiptoe, trying to get a better look at Bo, but a fresh surge of students coming out of the building blocks my view. Logan yanks on my sleeve, says something I can't hear.

I jerk my arm away—finally catching Bo's eye. He lifts a hand, but is he waving me over? Waving goodbye? Throngs of students surround me like an unsettled sea.

My ears ring. The bell rings. Logan grabs my hand, pulls me down the steps and across the driveway. I catch a glimpse of Bo's frowning face through the crowd.

"Logan, let me go!"

He releases me immediately. "Just tell me what's going on with you and Summers—have you slept with him?"

"*What?* Logan—" Craning my neck, I see Bo open the passenger door of the car. He bends down, speaking to whoever's inside. Then he scans the crowd once more—before climbing in and closing the door.

"Guess that's my answer," Logan jeers. "You can't take your eyes off the guy."

The shrill ringing ceases abruptly, and the principal appears at the front doors along with the superintendent. I see Mary, and trot toward her. Logan follows me. The superintendent begins speaking through a megaphone, gesturing to the students, who scurry to clean up their scraggly lines.

Fire trucks come racing down Hook Avenue and swerve into the driveway. An ambulance is next, followed by the sheriff and two police cars, blue lights spinning.

The Mercedes drives away.

"Your boyfriend probably saw the cops and thought he was finally gonna get busted."

"What's that supposed to mean? And *what* is your problem?" I snap, unable to hear myself think over the wailing emergency vehicles.

"*My problem?* You're into Summers, and I'm the one with a problem? I don't think so." Logan looks away, as if searching for someone to complain to. "Why don't they turn off the damn sirens?" he mutters. I nearly groan at the irony.

The lights stop flashing and the screams of the rescue vehicles peter out, but as soon as they do, the fire alarm begins ringing again. Students laugh, sitting down in the sun, stretching out on the grass. Logan shakes his head at me.

"You want me to say I'm the one with the problem, Logan? Fine. I have a problem, lots of problems, whatever. I *meant*, what is *your* problem with Bo? Why do you hate him?" Lowering my voice, I say, "You can't possibly think, that just because—"

"You want me to tell you why I hate him? 'Cause I didn't think you wanted to know."

I stare at him. "Why wouldn't I want to know?"

He shrugs. "You haven't listened to a word I've said about the guy so far."

"What do you mean?" I blink, still angry, now puzzled.

"Oh, c'mon! I've— Okay, how about this. Did you ever ask him about the *Lucky*?"

My stomach drops. "I told you, I learned about that boat from my dad. He asked me not to talk about it. He said he didn't want me to fuel any rumors." But ever since the bonfire I've wondered how Logan knew about the *Lucky*. Wanting only to forget the doomed boat and the fate of its four passengers, I've never asked. Now, thinking maybe I can turn the tide of the argument in a different direction, any direction to give Logan a chance to cool down, I do ask.

"How'd you hear about the *Lucky* anyway?"

"Old police radio."

"Like ours?"

"I don't know. Maybe. I've never seen yours." He lets his eyes travel down my body.

"You're funny. Tell me about the radio."

"I got it after Nick—I got it last year. I have it rigged, set on the Coast Guard's digital classified information output channel."

"But—you can't get that signal. *We* can't even get that signal."

Logan looks off across the lawn.

"Wow, that's seriously illegal, National Security type stuff. How did you—hold it—*hacking*?"

"What, didn't know I could speak geek?" Logan's lips lift on one side. "Everybody's got a secret. No one at the bonfire believed me—thanks for not sticking up for me, by the way—not that I care. What pisses me off is that the mayor, the Coast Guard, your dad even, they're keeping a lid on the whole thing."

I cringe, feeling guilty—and confused. "Why? To protect tourism in Rock Hook?"

"To protect the Summers."

"What does the *Lucky* have to do with them?"

"Another disappearing act. Summers Cove, Devil's Claw. Same difference. It all belongs to them." His voice grows hard. "I told you to stay away from Summers, as nicely as I could."

"But *why*?"

"I told you! Something's not right with him, with that whole family. I swear, I—" Logan's chest heaves. "They—" He bows his head.

"They what?" I try to draw on my anger, as if it might provide some sort of support, something to keep the panic buzzing like a swarm of bees in my belly from stinging me to death. Out of the corner of my eye I see people watching us. I don't care. The fire alarm continues to peal relentlessly. "They *what*, Logan? They—are interesting? They—are *different*?" Logan can't possibly know that Bo is a Siren, so what *does* he know? Why does he hate Bo and his family so much? "What is it, Logan? Honestly, you can't possibly believe—"

"They killed Beth."

"No—" Lurching forward, I clap a hand over his mouth. The fire alarm finally stops ringing. Someone says something about a lover's quarrel. The bell for last period rings, instantly followed by the bell signaling dismissal. *"Fastest class ever!"* one boy shouts. Dropping my hand, I step closer to Logan, my trembling body nearly against his. "That's. Not. Possible."

He stares at me. I stare back. In a second we're engaged in a ridiculous, childish staring contest. The small group watching us gets tired of waiting to see what we'll do next and wanders away. Briefly

I wonder if they expected us to come to blows. Logan looks pissed enough. But he pulled me down the stairs—he said what he said. I'm angry too.

"Don't let Summers' stunt at Seal Cove fool you. Just because he 'saved' you, doesn't mean he didn't kill Beth and fuck up my brother. He—his family—they did something to Nick, something bad. So bad Nick felt like he couldn't come home."

My hands are shaking, in part because I have my own fears about Bo. But he's a Siren, not a monster—although I feel sure somehow that I saw his brother do something monstrous. Only, that's ridiculous. Other than being subjected to Jordan's chilly gaze at Sign of the Mermaid, I haven't seen him do anything.

Poor Logan—his brother's dead. He can't accept that. He has to fight off his black-eyed dog somehow, so he blames Bo and his family for Nick's death—and for Beth's—because the two drowned at the Summers' beach.

"Logan, I know what you're saying isn't—likely, but if you'll just tell me *why* you think Bo and his family were somehow involved in—in what happened to Nick and Beth, I'm sure I can—"

"You can what? Try to make me believe like everyone else that Beth's body just 'washed away'? That my brother is dead, and his body washed away too?" He speaks slowly now, as if my IQ has dropped. "Arion. The Summers said they found my brother. And Beth. That they found their bodies, *saw* them, floating, in front of *their house*, and then . . ." He glowers at me.

"Then what?"

"They lost them. How do you lose a friggin' body? But the bigger question? Is why they killed her."

"But they didn't! Why would they?"

"Why would they?" Logan repeats. His laugh is a corkscrew, a curling thing with sharp edges. "Maybe 'cause she saw them break my brother, break him so badly he couldn't even let me know where he was going, why he was leaving—"

"Logan! Please. You have to stop. Your brother . . . is dead. The Summers didn't—"

"You're in love with the guy, Rush. What the hell do you know? You're just like everyone else around here now. Telling me I'm in denial. Drinking the Kool-Aid. The Summers and their celebrity star power—go ahead, lap it up."

Feeling as if he's delivered a blow to my body, I watch, unmoving, as he sprints away across the lawn.

PEARL

"See you finally got a true taste of Logan's temper," Mary says, coming up behind me.

"Is that what that was?" Barely holding back tears, I slip into Mary's hug. "I thought maybe it was one of his multiple personalities."

"Yeah, we call that one Hothead; only, don't say it to his face, he's likely to get the wrong idea." I laugh through the tears I can't keep in any longer, and she gives me a squeeze. "Are you okay? Do you need a ride?"

"No, and yes." I swallow a sob. "Come inside with me to get my stuff?"

On the drive out to the lighthouse, I ask Mary about what Logan said.

"Nick and Beth fell from the jetty, that's what the Summers told the police. Bo's younger brother, Cord, found their bodies. He saw them floating in the water, but couldn't get to them.

"Logan didn't—doesn't—believe that Cord was alone. He says Bo and his older brother were there, maybe even their dad. They're all such good surfers, Logan doesn't believe that they couldn't swim out, paddle out, whatever, and at least get Beth's body. Logan thinks that means they must not have wanted to, and that was because they'd killed her, and if anyone saw her body, they'd know it. He's convinced of that.

"He doesn't believe his brother's body was even in the water. He thinks the Summers . . . hurt Nick. Maybe for trespassing, or—who knows." Mary looks away from the road for a second, her gaze sliding sideways. If it were anyone else, I might think they were holding back. But then she continues, and I only feel bad that I've harbored the brief suspicion.

"Later, there was a rumor, that the Summers saw Nick and Beth alive, struggling in the waves, and tried to save them but couldn't. Of course Logan doesn't believe that. Whether or not it's true . . . their bodies were never recovered."

"But, do you mean, maybe the Summers *saw them drown*?"

"Maybe. Or maybe just Cord. Or maybe they were dead already, that's what the Summers said, that's what the cops said. One thing's for sure, though, Logan blames the Summers for Nick's death. 'Disappearance,' he used to say. He used to talk about it all the time. He told me once that he thought Nick was alive. He—" Mary breaks off, and again, I have the feeling there's something she isn't saying, something important, but she only adds, "His parents yanked him out of school for a while around that time."

All at once she sucks in a breath.

"What is it?" I ask in alarm. But then I see what it is. The Mercedes. It's parked in the drive of the lighthouse, Bo and his older brother standing on opposite sides of it, arguing. I'm thankful Mary's the one who gave me a lift and not Logan—not that I would have taken one from him today.

Her eyes veer quickly away from the two boys. "Give me a buzz tonight if you want."

"Thanks. You're the best." I hug her, hard, then hop out of the car—

My boots root to the spot where I land.

"Five minutes, bro, *five*."

Jordan's voice is a heavy cashmere blanket of sound. I don't even hear Mary's car drive away. He looks at me and my knees turn to water. In the shadow of the lighthouse, his dusky-blue eyes are almost black, deep and bottomless. *A drowning pool.*

Bo strides toward me. "Come on." His voice is a quiet command.

His brother laughs as we walk away; it's a laugh edged with knowing.

We head around the side of the lighthouse, but when we get to the front and I try to open the door, my hands are shaking so badly Bo has to take the key. We step into the cool darkness of the hallway. Automatically I walk toward the second door.

"No," he says. I turn to him, my back against the inner door. "There's no time." He lays the palm of his hand along the side of my face. "I'm sorry I haven't seen you since—that day. And I'm sorry, about last night." He looks at my lips, presses his own together.

The feeling of connection, the heat from his hand— But I'm so angry. *Why hadn't he gotten in touch with me? And what the hell was last night about?*

There's another thought, deep down inside me, that's nothing at all like those two:

Tell him to go. And buried beneath that one, yet another: *Make him stay.*

"When I saw you sing last night, when I heard your voice through the mic, filling the room, filling me . . . I—look, I have to go away. And I don't have time to explain everything."

His voice is mesmerizing; the effect it has on me, undeniable. Still, I try to take a step back, wanting to be the one who walks away this time. His sea-green gaze sharpens as I shift, but my back is up against the door—there's nowhere to go. He steps closer to me, until only a thin inch of air floats between us.

Anger. Fear. Desire. Confusion. They tangle in me under his intense scrutiny. "Don't use your Siren tricks on me," I say, as coolly as I can. But my voice comes out breathy, the ache for him sneaking between my lips. "Why? Why didn't you talk to me at the club?" The question doesn't sound accusatory, the way I'd meant it to. It sounds like a plea. I hate myself.

"I *couldn't*. But after last night, I realized there's no way to fight my feelings. I knew I needed to see you, needed to talk to you. *Need* to talk to you. I came to the school but—security."

"Security?" I ask blankly. His words, his energy—the very air itself—everything that's somehow suspended between us pulses with persuasive rhythm. I can't think.

"Right. I couldn't get in, so . . ." His smile is both rueful and wicked.

"You couldn't get in, so . . . Wait. Did you pull the *fire alarm*? You're joking, right? Have you ever heard of a telephone?"

"Arion, I have to go, but I wanted to say I'm sorry, things have been kind of crazy—"

"You don't know what crazy is." I've been nothing short of obsessed with him.

"Maybe not. I'm sure there are lots of things I don't know. But I do know, I can't go away without giving you this."

His hands slide behind my neck. "Hold still."

Beneath my feet, the earth drops away—

Then something cool is touching my throat and I bring my hand up. My fingers touch a chain, a pendant. A pearl.

"I found it, diving. Had the necklace made. For you." His hands move to my waist—

Something surges inside me, the tide, going out fast, taking everything with it. I reach for him at the same moment he pulls me close and his lips come down hard on my mouth—then he jerks back, his breathing jagged. Pulling away a little, he looks down at me, his eyes dark behind half-lowered lids, thick gold lashes.

He moves slower now, his hands sliding lower, then tightening, his thumbs on my hip bones, fingers splayed out over my jeans, along the sides of my hips, each finger burning. Longing spikes inside me as he leans into me—the rhythmic pulsing that had been between us a second ago sweeping through my body as we kiss, our tongues sliding together.

Still, we aren't close enough.

Slipping my hands behind his neck, I stretch up on tiptoe, inhaling, smelling the sun on his skin as his smooth hair falls across my face. His body touches mine everywhere and the dark space behind my closed eyes expands—until there are mountains inside me, and valleys. Canyons that cut deep. But I want more—want him closer.

Pressing against him, I feel his music in my veins. Splotches of color spin in the darkness—

But all at once I become dizzy, need . . . air. Still he kisses me, deeper.

I try to pull away—he holds me tighter, his mouth moving on mine. Black water closes over me—I can't breathe. I push against his chest—but he's too strong.

My own chest grows tight, and I hear a far-off sound, like a muffled sob.

It comes from me.

He staggers back— "Arion! I'm sorry!"

Adrenaline races through my system as I strain to fill my lungs, my breath coming in short, desperate inhalations. Tears fill my eyes. He's backing away.

"No—" I choke out. Still struggling for breath, I reach for him—

"This, *me*, this is exactly what I was afraid of. I could have—"

"But you didn't." Grabbing hold of him, I try to breathe normally, will my heart to beat with a regular pattern. The fear begins to recede, leaving a strange certainty in its wake.

"But I could have—"

"No." Crossing his lips with a finger, I wrap my free arm around him. "No, you couldn't have, *you won't ever hurt me*." Am I making a statement? Issuing a command? I don't know. All I know is I can never,

ever allow those words to be a question. There can *be* no question, for either of us. No excuse to turn back.

He takes my hands, keeping me at arm's length now. "But I could. Not on purpose, but I could hurt you. Only minutes ago, I was out of control. The sensation, your fragrance as I breathed you in— These last few days, the thought of *this*, this is why I stayed away." He releases my hands, eyes the door to the outside. "I wanted to forget about you." One step back, two. His voice drops low. "But I couldn't. And after last night—I know I need to stay away from you, but—" And then he's back against me, his arms encircling me, his face, buried in my hair. "I can't."

"And I don't want you to stay away! At first, I didn't think I could handle . . . you. But now, the only thing I *can't* handle is being without you." Even at the thought, my stomach twists.

"But you'll have to," he whispers. "For a week, maybe two. That's part of why I needed to talk to you, to see you. I couldn't leave without letting you know how I feel." He pulls away.

"Where are you going?" I ask, head spinning.

The blare of a car horn makes me jump. Bo says, "There's something else I need to tell you. You heard about the boat from Portland, right?"

The chill that clings to the granite walls seems to find its way into my bones. I nod.

"From your dad—I figured as much. So you know that someone sunk that boat?"

"Yes," I whisper.

"My siblings and I have some thoughts about what happened, and we know some people, other Sirens, who might be able to give us more information. We're going to see them. We'll see our father as well."

Other Sirens. Another burst of sound reaches us as we stand in the dim hallway, an annoyingly long blast, as if the driver is literally lying on the horn.

Bo grins. "Jordie." Even abbreviated, the name makes me cringe. Bo cocks his head, but only says again, "I have to go." Taking my face in his hands he kisses my eyelids, my cheeks, looks regretfully at my mouth. He says something about things being complicated, that I should be careful, but I can't concentrate. He kisses my forehead—

Then he's gone.

My heart's beating fast. My fingers flutter to the necklace—and I look down.

The chain is silver, the pearl—is the same size as that pink pebble that went missing, the one that sat so perfectly in the center of the shell Bo gave me, as if the two things were made for each other. Of course a pearl, while smooth and round like a pebble, is not a pebble, is far more precious than any pebble. And *this* pearl, it isn't pink at all. Isn't even white. It's black. Dark and shiny as an eight ball.

TORN

Stupidly, Tuesday night during dinner with Dad, I let slip that Logan and I had a fight.

"I can see how a conversation about his brother might upset him."

"Me too." I wish the fishing tournament Dad's going to watch would start. I don't want to think about Logan, or feel guilty that I'm seeing his—enemy. Imaginary enemy. Mistaken enemy. *A case of mistaken enemy. Could be a song there.*

"If you want to talk, sweetie . . ." Dad gives me an encouraging dad smile. Nice, but we both know it's not going to happen, and I'm certainly not going to sit and watch people fish.

Later on, I'm at my desk, not studying, but thinking: If I phone Mary, we'll talk about Logan. If I phone Logan . . . I'll just want things to be the way they were before.

Buzzing comes from the bottom of my backpack. My cell? Rifling through the pack, I grab it, having a hard time believing that it's even ringing up here.

"Finally."

"Alyssa?"

"I've tried you a million times. I suppose you're going to say that your reception is even worse out there in no man's land than it is on the rest of this godforsaken peninsula?"

"It is. What's up?"

"This is Rock Hook, not New York—so, nothing's up. Why weren't you at the party?"

"What party?"

"At the Elbow last night." The Elbow is a muddy L-shaped beach not far from school where a patch of woods meets Wabanaki Bay. "Logan was there."

"Didn't know about it." *And who parties on a Monday?*

"Oh, sorry, thought you did. Hell, I thought *I* told you about it. Oh well. Next time. Hey, I heard you guys had a big blowout yesterday. You and Logan. Did you kiss and make up yet?"

I almost hang up, but then, maybe because I can't see her snarky smile, or maybe because I just can't hold everything in anymore, I tell her about the argument—certain parts. Of course the mention of Bo, how he'd been looking for me, is what she pounces on.

"Well, duh, that's it. Logan's jealous. Not that you and Summers are going anywhere."

"Hmm." I picture Bo's hands on my hips. "I don't know about Logan being jealous, but I wish I could help him. He's been through a lot."

"What are you, a camp counselor? Come on, you know what he wants from you."

"He's just a friend, Alyssa."

"A hot one. Why don't you get over yourself, admit you feel the same way he does?"

"Maybe because I don't? And maybe because you're exaggerating, about how he feels."

"Oh please. The way you guys look at each other?"

"Hey, just because you fall in love every other day, like with Bonfire Boy . . ."

A snort of laughter crackles in my ear. "Bonfire Boy was just for fun. You know, fun? Logan was totally sulking at the party, by the way. Probably because you weren't there."

"Doubt it, he's pretty mad at me right now."

Her voice grows quiet. "He beat the shit out of some kid from the mainland last night."

"He—he did? At that party? He wasn't in school today—is he all right?" I picture the two of us, arguing out on the lawn, the sun on his face. The bruise on his cheek had barely faded since Friday when I first saw it. I'd noticed it at the club too, how dark it was still. I'd wanted to touch it, to trace it with my fingers, as if that would somehow make it better. But even asking about it would make whatever it is we have between us more complicated. I know this, intuitively. And I know it because one truth is a ladder to another. And lies? They're like links in a chain. What happened last night? Is there another bruise on his face now? On his body? Or is it on the inside, where he thinks no one can see it.

"He's okay. But I thought you'd want to know. It kind of sucked. Seeing him bleed."

"I bet," I say softly. *Oh, Logan. Does that really make things better for you?*

"Maybe you ought to bring him a blankie or something." The curl of her smile is audible. For a second, she'd been sincere. But it's like, kindness, for whatever reason, is just too hard for her. And this, Alyssa pushing me toward Logan and his pain, is too hard for me. Why's she doing it? *He's a friend,* I want to insist again. But who am I trying to convince?

A sigh of impatience escapes me.

"Alyssa? You're breaking up—" I hit "End" and set the phone down.

But I can't stop thinking of Logan.

I pull out my guitar.

BREATHE

The week goes by in a blur.

It rains and gets cooler.

The ringing in my ears gets louder, and every night, I have The Nightmare.

It's becoming more terrifying—and more real.

The dream is always the same, and always different. Last night the sand and dirt wasn't a path at all, it was the parking lot at Hive, and the boy with wings—who had no twisting scaled appendage at this point—kept disappearing. Each time he did, Jordan Summers took his place. He leaned over me as I lay prone in the parking lot, the sandy grit of the ground scratching my back where my shirt had ridden up, and his wild wet hair dripped seawater on my face. I know it was seawater, because when I woke up, I smelled it. Which sounds crazy. But is true.

What gets less real is my friendship with Logan. He avoids me now, so I avoid him, not an easy trick, especially during homeroom.

Mary is trying to stay neutral, although one afternoon we hang out after school and watch *The Thing Called Love*. This time, the movie seems different. The music feels less important, the story, more. Also, I think I understand now, how the main character could fall for two guys who are so different from each other.

Though it makes me kind of edgy, I take long walks on the beach, sometimes running along the shoreline until my legs ache. Up on the gallery deck, I watch birds through the binoculars. And once, feeling like an idiot, I searched the sky for white wings.

I worry that Bo might change his mind, might stay away. My body buzzes at the thought of seeing him—or not seeing him. It's hard to study, hard to eat. And then, the severe pain I experienced when I thought I'd never see him again—returns.

Recovering from a particularly bad spasm, I lie on the bed and contemplate the stacks of books piled on the bedside table, the desk, the floor. For the first time, I notice that nearly all the books I own are love stories, little more than variations on *Romeo and Juliet*. Does anyone else find it bizarre that the most famous love story of all time is a tragedy?

"*Lips, O you, the doors of breath . . .*" I whisper the line. It holds new meaning for me now, and makes me shudder.

Mary finds me throwing up in a bathroom stall at school one morning.

"No," I say, before she can ask. "I'm not."

Friday night, after lighting a candle and getting out my guitar, I open my notebook. Reading through some pages—stream of consciousness stuff about a rock and a river—I mess around with a few chords and am totally surprised by what comes out. No river. No rocks.

"When I'm with you I can feel the heat.

A thousand suns are beating on the street where I've been walking.

I don't care if I burn both my feet.

Put your lips up to my ear, just keep talking."

Pouring my feelings about him onto paper, I try different chords and melodies, until the song reveals itself, reveals *me*.

"What I want, your hands on me,

It's the only thing I can feel . . ."

A cry comes up through my body, a series of sliding notes leading to the chorus.

"You breathe me in . . . I breathe you in . . ."

Sometimes, you write the song.
But sometimes, the song writes you.

FOREVER

Finally, Sunday morning as I stand on the deck of the lighthouse looking toward Summers Cove, I see a figure headed for the sunlit water. Energy shoots through me, then dies away. The boy isn't Bo. One of his brothers? As the boy prepares to catch a wave, I notice someone swimming near him, but a second later my attention is riveted on the surfer. He rides the big waves more like a skateboarder on a half-pipe than a surfer on the sea.

And the waves are definitely *big*. They're at least as high as my head over there, higher, while the waves below on Crescent Beach are only knee high. *Weird.*

A song pops into my head, a manic drum and bass groove slamming up against a caffeinated zigzag of a melody, perfect accompaniment for the surfer boy's wild ride. My fingers tap the binoculars to the beat.

"Good, isn't he?" Nearly dropping the binoculars, I whirl to find Bo leaning against the doorframe. "Thought you weren't afraid of me?" He joins me at the railing.

"Bet I could scare you too, if I snuck up on you like that."

"But you couldn't." He twirls a lock of my hair around his finger.

"Couldn't sneak up on you? Why not?" The nausea that has become ever-present while Bo's been gone suddenly lifts—like seasickness, when you step onto land.

"I'd hear you. Siren senses are sharp. Keener than . . . animal senses." He lets go of my hair, takes a step back. "We need to talk."

"Okay . . . How was your trip? Where did you go? Did you find out—anything?"

Bo doesn't answer, just looks out at the ocean with a frown, as if puzzled. Then he looks up. "Air currents," he says quietly.

"Air currents?" When he doesn't elaborate, I say, "Fine. Keep yourself cloaked in mystery."

"Cloaked in mystery? Is that what I am?" He crooks his elbow and brings his forearm toward his face, narrowing his eyes as he peers over the top.

"Sorry, the Prince of Darkness doesn't do it for me."

He drops the stance. "And what would?"

The wind shifts, lifts our hair around our faces.

"Arion, being away from you isn't an option for me now. I love you. I *need* to be with you."

In an instant I'm in his arms, lifting my lips—

"No." He laces his fingers in my hair, pulls my head back, his eyes on mine. "Don't you understand? We can't. Not yet. Not until . . . you're like me."

"Like you? How can I be like you? You can't mean—"

"Arion, *I could kill you*, so easily. I don't want to start anything before you're ready, but even a kiss, one that's too long—I could lose control. If you love me—But maybe you don't."

I realize I've been holding my breath. Bo notices too. His lips twist.

Words spill out of me. "I know I want to be with you." *That I have to be. That I feel sick when we're not together.*

"I see. Well, maybe the rest of this conversation should wait after all. But then everything else will have to wait too." His voice has turned hard. "I don't want to kill you with a kiss."

"Stop, okay? No more talk about kisses that can kill." I try to smile. "Deal?"

He *does* smile then, and it's wicked. "Don't you know you're not supposed to make deals with supernatural beings?" He takes my hand, pulls me down onto the deck. "If you want to take chances, maybe I should let you. Maybe I should take some too." But he lets go of my hand then, and looks away.

I study his profile as he sits with his back against the tower. *Like him.* Is he really thinking of *making* me into a Siren?

Although it's unseasonably warm, I shiver—then I lean back against the bricks too, glad for the sun-warmed feel of them through my sweater.

"So you missed me," Bo says after a long moment.

We're not even looking at each other, but I feel the pull of him. I'm desperate for the distance between us to disappear, but after what he's implied . . . I keep my tone noncommittal.

"Did I? Did your keen Siren senses pick up on that?" I recall the pain, the nausea. It is not, I'm sure, the usual way of missing. In fact, I know it's not, because I miss my sister every day.

"Just a logical guess."

There's a slightly arrogant curve to his lips.

"A logical guess—do you like guessing games?" Eagerly I turn toward him. Maybe confiding in him will lighten the mood. Bring us closer in a different way.

And so I tell him—tell him what I haven't told Logan or Mary, even though I've talked to them both about Lilah.

"I think my sister met someone here. I want to find him."

"Your sister. But—"

"It was before the accident. She fell in love with someone from Rock Hook. I need to know who."

Bo bows his head, maybe trying to hide the smile that plays on his lips now.

"What? What's so funny?"

"No, it's—not funny. Sorry, I just—I'm not an expert in this kind of thing. You must know that by now." He looks back out to the ocean. "Jordan laughs at me. Asks what kind of love this is, if I'm willing to risk your life." He turns to me, fixing me with his blue-green gaze. "But you've risked your life before, haven't you?"

"What are you talking about?"

"The day I met you. Your plunge, from the cliff."

A *swish, swishing* cuts the air above our heads as several ravens appear out of nowhere, their pointed wings angling as they change direction, then change again, the feathers of their long tails reminding me of . . . something. Forcing myself to concentrate, I try to remember my hike up the trail that day. The walk had energized me, but I'd also been thinking of Lilah, been upset.

"You think I jumped? That's ridiculous!" *But did I consider it, just for a second?*

Bo doesn't appear to be listening. He's studying the painted bricks of the tower, the swath of black cutting across the field of white that creates the dark spiral band and renders the lighthouse more distinct at a distance. Finally he says, "Were you really careless enough to slip?"

"No, of course not. I didn't slip." It's only as I say the words that I know for sure they're true. But then—

"Arion, that day, I caught you in my arms. Just as you believed. I didn't think, I just—acted. The fall would have killed you otherwise. But since then I've wondered: Why were you there, so close to the edge?

"I believe you, if you say you didn't jump. And I'm pretty sure you're right that, even though you were wearing those red boots?" A wry smile appears on his lips. "You didn't slip.

"I think," he says, taking my hands between his, "you were pushed."

NEW BLOOD

"What? That's impossible, no one was there!" I yank my hands from his grasp, leap to my feet.

"Are you sure?" He stands too.

"Of course I'm sure. Besides, I would have felt—"

But I *had* felt something, the lightest touch on my cheek, a faint caress, just before I fell.

Years ago, getting ready for bed on a winter night, I discovered one of my earrings was missing. Thinking back over the day, I remembered the tiniest tinkling sound, metal hitting ceramic, a noise that hadn't registered at the time. Going into the bathroom, I crouched down by the sink. The tiny gold hoop lay on the floor.

The silken touch hadn't registered either, *not like the image of the wings.*

"I saw—wings." My throat closes around the last word.

"Wings?"

"Circling. High in the sky, by the cliff top that day."

"Why didn't you tell me? I can't believe you didn't tell me!"

I see them in my mind's eye now, giant and birdlike, similar to Bo's angelic wings.

Maybe even the same.

"I didn't know what they were! And when I saw yours—"

"You thought it was *me*! You thought I'd 'dropped out of the sky'—I remember when you said that, days later, on the beach. For a moment I thought you'd discovered—but you hadn't! You hadn't figured out anything."

Bo's anger isn't directed at me, but that doesn't make me feel any better. I've made a mistake, obviously, a bad one. I just don't quite understand it yet.

"I'll never forget that afternoon. Jordan and I were down by the water—"

Bo breaks off, giving me a quizzical look as I shudder at Jordan's name. But I can't explain it, my revulsion for Bo's brother. I shake my head. *It's nothing.*

"Fine. Anyway. We were about to go into town. I was distracted. I didn't want to go. I'd been listening to you. A lot."

"You've said that before, about listening to me—"

"I told Jordan we should hang, go surfing. He gave me a hard time but finally said he'd wait while I went for a swim. I stripped down to my trunks, in a hurry, like I *knew*.

"I was in the water when I heard you—saw you—falling, I couldn't believe it. My wings burst from my back and I kicked— We met in the sky. I grabbed you. But when I touched you—I lost control. We crashed into the waves."

I remember it now. His wings, saturated with seawater, firm, but slippery, like wet satin, surrounding me.

"I've been an idiot. I should have known all along. Instead, I was blind, *deaf* to everything but *you*! Maybe if I'd known you'd seen the wings—but even with the disappearance of those kids from out of town, I didn't think to connect the *Lucky* to you."

"To *me*? Why would you connect that boat to me?"

"Arion, don't you see? Whoever punched those holes in the bottom of that boat, whoever killed those kids—*their murderer*—pushed you from the edge of the cliff."

"No, that's not—No! That doesn't make sense—"

"It does. I should have listened to you more closely, not to you, to your *words*. Tell me again, what happened at Seal Cove?"

Not to me, to my words? "Mary told me I went over the side of the boat on purpose, but I don't remember that. I *do* remember strong arms, dragging me under, but I thought—it all happened so fast, the water was frothy, and white, seeing was impossible, and then you were there, and the arms were yours, carrying me."

"And the night on Smith Street, with the truck?"

"I saw a blur of white, the wings. I couldn't tell you! I thought you'd say I was crazy."

"Damn. It's like whoever it is . . . they're after *you*. And yet they haven't—*Why?*" He looks out at the ocean. "This changes things."

"What things?"

"Two kayakers, a man and a woman. They disappeared yesterday. We found them this morning."

"Found them where?"

"Their bodies, I should say. On the beach. In front of our house."

"In front of your *house*? Their *bodies*? They were—dead?"

"If we'd been there, this wouldn't have happened. Someone *knew* we wouldn't be there, wouldn't be able to help them, not this time."

The back of my neck prickles. Logan's accusations echo in my ears.

"Even if their families hadn't told the police and the reporters from the *Rock Hook Herald* that the two were experienced boaters, their equipment made it obvious." Bo gives a dry laugh. "The *Herald*. Can't wait to see what they have to say this time." He continues on before I have a chance to ask him what he means by this sarcastic comment. "There's no way two skilled kayakers could have gotten in trouble yesterday. It was like a summer day. Like today. Their deaths were no accident. And . . . someone took their breath."

"Someone took—?" I stare at Bo.

He stares back. "Their breath."

Goosebumps spring up along my arms. Looking at me with his oceanic eyes, he seems more unreal than ever. Suddenly, it feels like I don't know him. And really, I don't. I only know I want to be near him, more than anything. But how much of that is me—what *I* want—and how much is his manipulative magic?

"H-how can you be sure that the boys from the *Lucky* were murdered? How do you know they didn't drown, that the kayakers didn't drown?" Unconsciously I cling to the black balustrade. "And what about me, why do you think someone *pushed me* from the cliff?"

Seal Cove, and Smith Street, Bo was right there, he was there when I fell from Rock Hook Cliff. Bo watches as I fight with myself.

"Do you really think I had something to do with all of those things, Arion? Because that's what you're *supposed* to believe. That's exactly *why* the killer left the *Lucky* at Devil's Claw, left the bodies of the kayakers along with their pristine boats at Summers Cove. And you won't be the only one so easily convinced." He eyes me speculatively. "Jordan will love this."

Trying to ignore the way my body tenses up at the mention of Bo's brother, I ask, "How could you tell their breath was—taken?"

"We examined the bodies, Jordan and I, before we phoned the police."

"But, what do the police think? Will there be—autopsies?" I try not to picture a scene from one of those TV crime shows, bodies on tables in cold rooms surrounded by sharp surgical instruments.

"It doesn't matter. Jordan made it look like a drowning. A double drowning, that's what the *Herald* will report. Same with TV Twelve."

"But you said the kayaks were pristine. If they're in perfect condition—"

"We took care of that too."

I shudder. "Did you know the kayakers? Were they—friends?"

"I don't have any 'friends,' Arion, how can I?" He begins to pace.

I want to ask him how this can be possible, how he can have *no friends at all.* There are *so many* things I want to ask him—not just about friends, but about his family, his life. I want to know how it *feels* to be a Siren. Want to *insist* on hearing the details, hearing how he—survives.

But I can't ask. Because so many of my questions are eclipsed by the pull of him, and I have to admit—by the fear I feel too, the worry that I'll cross one of the invisible lines he's drawn, the boundaries he enforces with a sharp look, and somehow, with his silence. And, of course, there is his voice. Just thinking about the sound of his voice . . .

I shake my head as if to clear it, managing, at last, to ask the obvious question.

"So you think Sirens did this? You told me there were other Sirens, but I thought somehow you meant in some other ocean, or—"

"In this ocean, in *all* the oceans! Sirens, some like us, some who are different than us, and not so . . . compassionate." His gaze drops to my lips.

"But then—you just said you don't have any friends?"

"Yes, well, I meant *human* friends. You . . . are the only one. Of course my family and I have friends. We also, apparently, have enemies.

"Arion, someone is setting us up."

SCENT

"I've got to go."

"Wait—I'm coming with you."

Bo pauses, but only for a moment. I follow him through the watch room. He doesn't slow his descent as we pass my room and I run inside, briefly rummaging through the closet before grabbing a jean jacket with turquoise buttons, one of Mom's creations. All at once hot tears well in my eyes. Mom. Dad. Do they really think living here is going to fix things between them? Throwing the jacket back, I grab a hoodie, still not sure why I even want another layer on such a warm day. Maybe it's because, despite the warmth, my skin's crawling with goosebumps.

We head down the steps that lead to the beach. Just as we pass the front door of the keeper's house, it opens— Dad walks out. His mouth makes the shape of an *O*.

Bo's voice becomes velvet. "Good morning, Captain Rush."

"Bo Summers." The two shake hands and Dad returns Bo's smile—what choice does he have? But his eyes don't quite meet Bo's. "Haven't seen you since—Arion's spill." Dad looks over at me. "You've got some color there. Looks good. You two been out walking?"

"Actually, we're just about to go for a walk. I'm taking Arion to Summers Cove."

Dad stills for a second, then he sort of squints up at Bo. "Your dad back yet?"

"Not yet." The sound of the surf seems unnaturally loud. A knowing look crosses Bo's face, and his lips twist slightly. "But my brothers are home. And my sister."

Nodding, Dad looks away. "Speaking of your dad, I was in town the other day at that library of his. Beautiful building. Ari loves that place. She's there—all the time." Realization creeps into his voice. "Bet you spend a lot of time there, given that your dad got it going." He sounds almost accusatory, as if he's just discovered Bo and I have shacked up together or something. His grip tightens on his coffee cup.

"I do." Bo gives Dad one of his Siren smiles. My father's grip on the mug loosens and his expression softens. "Nice to see you, sir," Bo says solemnly. "I think we'll get going now."

"All right . . . but come for dinner soon. Arion, invite him."

"Sure, Dad. See you later." Bo and I continue down to the beach.

"So, do you pull those little Siren stunts all the time?" I ask. *Do you pull them on me?*

But Bo's gazing out at the ocean . . .

He must have had girlfriends; what were they like? Compared to Bo, the boys at school all seem so one-dimensional. Logan is the only standout.

Logan. I can't leave things between us the way they are, can't take one more day where we ignore each other. Tomorrow is Monday. I'll phone him tonight. The conversation isn't going to be an easy one. I sigh.

Bo's head whips around—

Quickly I look away, pretending to study the organic jetsam strewn along the tidelines. Will the sound of a sigh always set him off? How about a simple intake of breath? Shivering, I wriggle my toes in the sand. Most of the region's shoreline consists of strips of granite, hard edges that allow the land to meet the ocean fearlessly. I need to be fearless too.

"Bo, how did you know I'd been near the north end of the peninsula that night?"

A minute goes by, maybe more. Time enough for me to decide that the slightly russet hue of the waves looks like a tinge of blood upon the water.

"You're going to think it's weird," Bo finally says. He scowls. "I smelled it."

"You smelled . . . what?"

"The coves, the tidewater that washes along the peninsula—everything has its own unique scent. I smelled the bay on you, the northern end. Siren senses are sharp, keener than—" The rosy color along the tops of his cheekbones darkens.

"Bo." I stop walking. *You're not an animal,* I want to say.

He stops too. "I don't know why I didn't pick up *his* scent. Didn't *hear him*. I knew something wasn't right. That night on Smith Street . . . I just don't know how he's managed to stay hidden, unless . . ." Bo glances at me.

"Hear *him*?" I try to imagine that the wings I'd seen high in the sky above the cliff, the blur of white on Smith Street, belonged to anyone but Bo. It's impossible.

Until it hits me, like a wall of water.

His brothers have wings. So does his sister.

Jordan had looked daggers at me all through dinner at Sign of the Mermaid. He'd been a threatening presence at the lighthouse that day. And at Hive—

But I barely remember seeing him at Hive, and just thinking about it?

Makes my head throb.

SUMMERS COVE

The jetty is like the spine of some petrified sea monster, and after slipping on a patch of apple-green seaweed, I tighten my death grip on Bo's hand.

Then, finally, we're at his house—houses, actually. Three shingled cottages.

"Took you guys long enough." Somehow these reproachful words, which greet us as the door of the largest cottage swings open, sound like a familiar pop song. A flash of blue eyes and a tangle of blond hair accompany the words, but vanish as quickly as they appeared, the voice becoming a burst of sound inside the house. "They're here!"

Whitewashed walls and a cathedral ceiling give the living room an airy feel, and a row of small windows set in the wall above the larger picture window overlooking the beach lets in lots of light. At the back of the long room a wrought-iron spiral staircase—an architectural echo of the lighthouse stairs—looks like it leads to a large loft area. The sound of the surf comes in through the open windows. An image of the house at Devil's Claw passes through my mind like a shadow.

Bo's sister holds out a hand that's cooler than his, but still unnaturally warm. Even so, I shiver slightly as I clasp it, remembering the first time I saw her, the curve of her white throat.

"I'm Mia," she says, her voice crisp as a stiff sea breeze. "It appears my brother's known you for some time but has been too rude to introduce us. Would you like a drink? Iced tea? Something stronger? Of course—there's always water." Her opaque green eyes seem to brighten as she says this, a flare of sun on the sea.

But the sunlit surface hides all kinds of dark things, and her dig at me doesn't go unnoticed. How does she know, I wonder, that I'm afraid of the ocean?

"Thanks, but I'm fine."

"Did you meet Cord? Or didn't he stand still long enough for a proper introduction?"

Cord had been the streak of light at the door when we'd arrived, and now I recognize him from the restaurant. He looks about fifteen. A sprinkle of freckles runs across his nose.

"You're from San Francisco, right? And you surf? Ever ride those gnarly waves under the bridge?"

"Um—no. And I—I haven't been surfing for a while."

"Huh. Bummer. You'll have to go with us sometime."

A look of annoyance crosses Bo's face.

"Ah—maybe."

Cord's hand is warm too, and almost comforting. But now there's movement at the rear of the room, and he silently releases me.

The hair on the back of my neck stands up as Bo's older brother steps forward.

"It's not like we've never met," Jordan says, voice low.

"R-right. You were at the lighthouse, and—" I gasp as he takes my hand.

At the sound, his dark brows draw down, and his nearly black eyes swirl with indigo, becoming whirlpools of dusk. The heat from his hand feels as if it might scorch my skin, and a jagged melody fills my ears. Inexplicably, I take a step closer to him.

Swiftly, Bo snatches my hand from where it lies limp in Jordan's palm, and with a quick movement spins me away from his brother, drawing me down onto a white sofa. My face flames and Jordan laughs quietly, the sound somehow suggestive.

Everyone else takes a seat now on the low, modern furniture that's spread throughout the living room. Mia passes a tray of drinks. This time I take an iced tea. Cord sets down a platter of fruit on the table in front of the couch where Bo and I sit, then flows down to the floor by my feet, folding his long legs beneath him. Mia sits in a cushioned chair across from us, and Jordan sits across from us as well, on a straight-backed chair, slightly removed from the group.

"Got your Call. What's up?" Jordan stares at me as he asks Bo this question.

"I know who it is. That boat—the *Lucky*—and the kayakers, I know who did it."

"You think it's whoever's behind that messed up stuff that happened near Madrid?" Cord asks. "The two freighters that went missing then turned up with their crews massacred—"

"Cord. We have a guest." Mia manages to sound simultaneously sarcastic and bored.

"Sure, okay, but why's anyone killing kayakers around here? It's not like Rock Hook is some jackpot at the end of a rainbow. Too isolated. Why not hit up Portland?"

"They could have followed the *Lucky* up from there," Jordan says. Then he scowls. "Bo. Remind me why this girl is here?" He jerks his chin toward me.

Bo ignores the question, leaning forward. "One person is behind this—possible, or not?"

Jordan's slow drawl snakes over my skin. "Anything's possible, bro, least that's what you're bent on proving with *her*, isn't it?"

"Shut up, Jordie. I'm serious. We've been looking for a reason for these kills—the college-bound kids, the kayakers. We've been asking, *why here?* So—how about revenge?"

Jordan lets out a whoop of laughter. "You think it's Nick Delaine, don't you?"

My fingers fly to my mouth. *Nick Delaine? Nick Delaine is dead!*

"Think about it. That couple was killed, then left here, on our beach. The *Lucky* was chained to the rocks at Devil's Claw, our land. We don't know what happened to the four boys, true, but we've been looking for a specific reason. Nick Delaine *has* a specific reason."

"You mean Logan," I correct, "*Logan* Delaine. Nick Delaine is dead. He drowned here, didn't he? And Logan thinks you had something to do with it, right? So you think *Logan* wants revenge, but Logan couldn't have had anything to do with that boat or those kayakers—"

"We're not saying he did," Bo interrupts, effectively cutting me off. "Arion. There are some things you don't know. About Nick."

"And some things she shouldn't know," Jordan practically growls. "I told you, brother of mine, this is not a smart idea. Human girls? Only good for *one thing*."

"Shut the hell up, Jordie," Bo says.

Mia sighs. "He might *believe* he has a reason to come after us; that is, if he's actually—"

"Yeah, but no," Cord says. "He would've needed help, just to survive. Although, just 'cause no one *we* know has seen him or heard him doesn't mean he hasn't hooked up with someone off the radar."

"Sorry," Mia says. "On his own, with help, I have trouble believing Nick's even alive."

My mind whirls. Logan said Nick's body was never found, so technically, he *could* be alive. *Alive.* The word vibrates inside me. Almost unthinkingly, I reach for the platter of fruit, bite into a slice of apple—

And nearly choke as the conversation comes together for me. *Nick Delaine is a Siren.*

"You want a glass of water, girl?" Cord asks.

Water. The last thing I want. Still coughing, I shake my head. *How—how can Logan's brother be a Siren?*

"There's something else," Bo says. "Arion's fall was no accident. Somebody pushed her. Somebody with wings."

A hush comes over the room.

"They were like the wings of an angel," I manage to rasp. "I mean, I know they weren't, but—" *But seeing an angel now wouldn't even make me blink.*

"She didn't tell me until today," Bo adds.

"Because she thought—it was *you.*" Jordan's low chuckle floats through the room.

"Shut it, J. Someone pulled her under at Seal Cove too. I was an idiot. Didn't believe—"

"But I didn't see any wings at Seal Cove," I object.

"Shallow water," Cord says. "Anything else you can tell us?"

"Someone tried to run me off Smith Street. I heard humming. Music. But all I could think about—was Bo. His voice. And the water; it was like—the water was pulling me." *I sound crazy.*

But Mia nods. Then she actually laughs, the sound bell-like.

"She almost drove into the ocean," Bo says, shooting a dark look at Mia. "I thought she'd fallen asleep at the wheel. I didn't see anything unusual, didn't *hear* anything, definitely not another Siren. It's impossible, but my head has been filled with *Arion's Song.*" He turns to me, seeming both angry and anguished. "It's like—you're filling the airwaves. Your Song, it's in my head. Unless I really concentrate, I can't *hear*!"

Mia laughs again—obviously she doesn't share my confusion, or Bo's frustration. "A Song can be the beginning of a great romance." She gives me a sidelong glance that suggests I know all about this, or that maybe she does.

"Romance?" Jordan tilts his chair back. "C'mon, Mia, get your head out of the clouds—or the gutter, as the case may be. Bo's just been getting in the way of someone else's good time. Tough to figure out whose, though; any Siren would enjoy killing this girl."

His chair legs hit the floor with a *crack*.

"Hell, I almost sucked her dry myself the other night."

RADIO ARION

"What?" My voice bites into the air, a harsh note compared to the voices of the Sirens.

"You want me to say it again?"

"No!" In one or two sentences Jordan has managed to do what Bo couldn't. He's convinced me.

Someone is trying to kill me.

A dark flower of fear blooms in the pit of my stomach. "Bo—"

But Bo holds up a hand as if to silence me. "Well?" He glares at Jordan.

"No problem, brother. I hear her loud and clear." Jordan leans back in his chair.

"Jordie, you'd better not be fooling around—"

"Oh, you'd know if I was doing that," Jordan drawls.

Cord looks wary. "Guys, what's going on?"

"Jordie. I. Swear." Bo's steel tone turns me cold. "And what the hell are you talking about, 'the other night'?"

Mia has gone absolutely still. "Careful, Bo," she warns.

"Dude, don't take the bait," Cord pleads.

Bo ignores them. Glares at Jordan. "Explain."

Jordan salutes him. "Just yanking your chain. Wouldn't touch your little plaything." Jordan runs a long-fingered hand through his hair, gives me a sharp smile. "But she does have a lovely Song. So . . . beautiful." His eyes darken, turning to coal, yet I imagine embers from a well-stoked fire. His words sing in my ears, and part of me wants to get up, go to him—

Bo jumps up—

"Just joking, bro, *joking*." Jordan lifts his hands in surrender, but he's grinning. "Remember, *you're* the one who wanted me to do it." Cord looks at him skeptically. "It's true. When Bo and Arion got here today, and you all were meetin' and greetin', he said, 'Try to tune her in, Jordie.' Didn't even have to try, Bo, she's broadcasting like a radio station, I kid you not."

Bo grimaces and, *can I be any more confused?*

"I told you, I heard her at the restaurant. She was with your buddy, Logan Delaine. I don't know if I'm hearing exactly what *you're* hearing; I mean, obviously you have some special feelings for this girl." A disdainful glance in my direction says he doesn't know why. "But if you're right, and it's Nick, and he's hearing *half* of what I'm hearing? He's gonna want her. Bad. If he gets his hands on her? He'll kill her."

The sound of breaking waves comes in through the open door of the cottage. Jordan stands abruptly. "I've gotta get out of here." He heads outside.

Mia stands too, and holds out her hand for my glass, empty but for the ice at the bottom. Cord follows Jordan outside.

"What was that about?" I ask Bo as he resumes his seat. "And why's he so angry?" I keep my voice down, but I want to shout. I'm angry too, and feel somehow . . . exposed.

Bo sits back. Folds his arms. "Logan, huh?"

"We just went out to eat. It was no big deal."

"Hmm. Yeah, well. Sorry for the thing with Jordan. I asked him to listen. To test my theory. I think Nick hears you."

"Listening, hearing—would you *please* tell me what you're talking about?"

"Music," Mia says, sitting back down. "You. Bo hears you. I do too."

"Mia—why the hell didn't you say anything?"

She shrugs. "You didn't ask."

Bo shakes his head, looks at her like he can't believe what he's seeing.

I say, "Hello?"

"Existing channels of communication," Bo says shortly. "There are lots of them. Humans ignore most of them. As far as *hearing* you, I—well, Jordie and I—decided to do a little experiment. I would have told you beforehand, but you might have altered your Signals. Not on purpose, but—"

"My Signals?"

"We all emit energy. We also send Signals. Some people are aware they're Transmitting. Most aren't. Some Signals are strong, others weak. There are an infinite number of arrangements and possibilities. An infinite number of Songs."

"So you think I'm . . . Transmitting. Kind of like what you showed me on the beach? But you know how to control your output, whereas I don't. Most people don't, most people *can't*. Most *people* don't have a Song."

"The Song of the Siren," Mia says. "Our very best bait."

"Right, but I'm not a Siren, I'm just—me."

"Yes. You—your Song is the most compelling I've ever heard. And it *feels* like it's meant for me alone, a language only I can understand. The fact that you're a musician, a singer, only makes the experience more powerful." Bo's expression clouds. "Your Song. That's why I didn't hear Nick."

"So you really think the guy's alive." Mia sounds doubtful. "And that he hears her Song too."

"He may even believe Arion's Calling him, the way she's been Calling me. The way he—has been Calling her."

"You make it sound like some kind of bizarre love triangle." Jordan has silently returned, his backlit form filling the doorway. I can't see his expression. "But Calls are for killing. A Siren Calls. Someone comes. Someone dies."

"Dude, be cool," Cord protests, slipping by Jordan and resuming his seat on the floor.

Jordan strides in and sits down. I shiver. It's like some line between us has been crossed. Some boundary. Or maybe it's more like—he's taken something from me.

"So? What exactly did you hear?" I ask him boldly, as if I could take it back. My tone is too arrogant and my voice is shaking, but I'm proud that I've managed to get the question out.

Until I wish I hadn't.

Jordan leans forward in his chair, forearms on his thighs, hands clasped together, and all I can think is that he's trying to control himself. He looks down at the floor, his unruly hair hanging around his face, concealing it. Watching him, my fear and frustration find their way out of me in the form of an involuntary sigh.

"I wish," he says, "you wouldn't do that."

"Jordan chose you for a mark," Bo quickly explains. "You're a focus for him now."

I stand up. "I should go." *I'm a freak. A human girl isn't supposed to have a Song.*

"You should," Jordan says.

"You shouldn't," Cord argues. "She shouldn't have to go, J. You need to get her off your radar, and the only way you're going to do that is to be around her. Build your tolerance. You need to armor up."

"*You* need to armor up, puppy boy," Jordan says irritably, "and grab your best blade."

But Jordan Summers is right—I *should* go. Because I *am* human, and maybe that means I'm a . . . temptation, for all of them. I don't know. I don't know enough!

You know they need the breath of living creatures. You know plenty. You know—

Cord springs to his feet, and I recoil—but he only reaches for my hand. His grip is solid, and so warm. It's like he knew what I was thinking, how I was feeling. And now, standing next to him—I feel better. That's the thing about them, about the Sirens. You feel . . . how they want you to feel. You can struggle against it, and sometimes that works. But other times . . .

He smiles at me. "Come on. You need some sun."

We head outside to the beach. To my surprise, Jordan follows. He and Mia sit in a pair of Adirondack chairs in front of the cottage while Cord and I walk closer to the water's edge. Bo is right behind us. He takes a seat on the sand and I sit next to him, holding my knees tight to my chest. Cord wades into the water.

"The Music between Arion and Bo is strong," I overhear Mia say to Jordan. "If Nick's here, if he's listening to her, do you think he's heard what's between them?"

"Yeah, he'll see Bo as competition. An enemy. Or I should say, even more of an enemy."

As quietly as I can, I take a deep breath of salty air. "Bo, is Nick really—"

"A Siren. Yes." Bo draws a series of circles in the sand.

"But if he's a Siren, and he's Calling me so he can kill me—"

"You think he would have done it by now?" Bo shakes his head. "He's playing with you, with all of us. This is a game to him. It's called revenge. If he'd caught you, at Seal Cove, say—"

But I don't want to hear the rest. "Bo, what does my Song sound like?"

"Your Song?" Gently, he knocks me back onto the sand.

"Stop—your sister, and—" I try to wriggle away from him, but he holds me down.

"Trust me, you're better off with chaperones."

"Is my brother harassing you?" Cord flops onto the sand on the other side of me.

"Definitely." I sit up, brushing sand off my arms, out of my hair, with trembling fingers.

"I'd never." Bo drops onto his back, covering his eyes with a forearm.

"Yeah, right," Cord says. He turns to me. "I confess, I was kind of against it at first: Bo, with a human."

"He's not 'with her,' Cord," Jordan says, face tilted toward the sun. "Bo's a scientist, like Dad. He's just—"

"Shut up, Jordie," Bo orders from his prone position.

Jordan laughs, but then falls silent. I'm relieved. I don't understand his implications—and I don't want to.

I don't want to think about the bizarre role I've been playing in Nick Delaine's life (afterlife?) either.

But I do need to figure out a way—to tell Logan that his brother is alive.

CUTTING EDGE

The wind blows against the night sky squares of the windows, shivering the glass before dying suddenly.

Sitting up in bed I stare into the darkness. A great gust of wind; is that what woke me? Something's woken me—a clattering noise.

Or—had I dreamed it? What about Bo? Had I dreamed our stilted conversations? Dreamed the kisses that had been somehow more than kisses, but also less?

We'd sat on the bed and he'd told me, *"You shouldn't be alone."*

I'd told him, *"Stay, then."*

Now I whisper into the blackness, "Bo?"

"Hmm?" He's across the room, as dreamlike in the darkness as the wind I still can't be sure wracked the tower a moment ago. As I turn on the bedside lamp, he surreptitiously slides something into the side pocket of his surf trunks.

"What's that?" I blink in the amber light.

For a moment he's a statue, hand hovering over hip. The pocket there looks about wide enough to hold a pen, two pens maybe, side by side, although it's twice as long as any pen. I've never noticed the narrow pocket before, or if I have, I probably just assumed the stitching along the side panels was for reinforcement, decoration.

"That," Bo says, coming to life and laying the jeans he must have just taken off over the back of the armchair, "is a knife."

"A knife? Why are you carrying a knife?"

"I always carry a knife."

Getting up I join him by the east-facing window. "And this escaped my attention, how?"

"I don't know." He brings his hands to my waist, reaching his thumbs down until they press against my hip bones. "Possibly your attention's been on something other than my attire."

Sensation radiates out from my naval. Still, I manage to say, "I wouldn't classify a knife as attire, more like an accessory. Can I see it?"

Bo drops his hands from my hips and slides the long, narrow knife out of his pocket.

Before we left Summers Cove, Jordan had been kind enough to inform me that Sirens don't always take the breath of their prey through the mouth. The conversation was so hideous I can't even remember how it started. But I remember how it ended.

"Usually it's a simple slice, right between the ribs, but sometimes, we go straight in through the windpipe." He'd slapped his thigh for emphasis, the smack of his hand making me jump. I have a fuzzy memory that while he'd been talking, I'd promised myself to stop seeing Bo, to forget about the Sirens. But just the thought of not seeing Bo made me cringe with pain. Cord had seen me flinch. A short while later, he'd offered me a cup of tea, which I accepted gratefully. He'd hummed as he prepared it, as he handed it to me. The pain receded.

"I've never used this knife," Bo says, gesturing toward it. "But—"

"Why? Because people—girls like me—are just so willing to—"

"Don't be an idiot. You need to understand—"

"I don't want to understand! I want—" *I want you to go.* And I do, for so many reasons. But it feels like the blade I hold in my hand is twisting in my gut. My words stick in my throat, whirl in my mind. Now a salient tone rings in my head—*what am I forgetting?*

"Careful." Bo takes the knife from me, lays it down on the desk. "It's sharp." He draws me to him, runs a hand back through my hair. The knife gleams in the dim light.

It's not as if I haven't imagined him taking someone's breath. But the knife adds a new dimension. I hadn't really believed it before—that he'd killed anyone. But the knife makes it real somehow. And now I wonder: *How can I possibly be with you?*

But again, I hear the arresting tone, almost painful, but so beautiful, and it—moves me, and I find that, no, I don't really believe it now either. Don't believe that Bo's killed anyone. That he ever would—of course he wouldn't. Of course he *couldn't.* Plus he's just told me—he's never used the knife.

Still, I struggle to speak. "Please," I mumble against his chest. "Get rid of it."

He continues stroking my hair for a moment, then pulls back from me slightly. "Ari, you need protection from Nick, and in order for me to give you that protection—" He breaks off abruptly. "I'm not used to this—to having to explain myself."

He eyes me thoughtfully. "Although, it's what you humans do, isn't it? Compromise. Bend. Try not to—break. You share everything, when you're . . . in love." He brings his thumbs to the hollow at the base of my throat, his fingertips to the sides of my neck. "I'm sorry," he says, running his fingers over the sensitive skin. "About the knife."

Then he kisses my neck, and I shiver with pleasure. But my eyes are on the windows. The wind seeps in at their sills, and I imagine it carries Signals, Calls, and Transmissions. Things I'll never truly understand. Unless . . . Bo said it was possible—for me to become a Siren. The thought makes my stomach roil momentarily, but then Bo begins to unbutton my shirt, his kisses trailing lower . . .

Gently he presses me back toward the bed, murmuring in my ear now—

"No." I flatten the palm of one hand against his chest. "I don't want—"

"Yes," he whisper sings. *"You do."* The glow from the bedside lamp turns the fringe of his lashes to platinum, his eyes to transparent blue-green seas. His Song is insistent. I begin to respond to it. To him. "Tell me now," he says, as we near the bed, "what you want."

"I want—you," I whisper haltingly.

"Are you sure?" He speaks slowly now, and my thoughts slow too.

"I'm . . . sure." And I am, even as I find myself standing on the edge of a sensual precipice as dangerous as any cliff. When he pushes me—I spiral down, into a black abyss of beauty, listening to the sound of his voice. His voice . . . is starting to change me . . .

HOMEROOM

Fingers of flesh-toned dawn creep along the horizon, creating a line of light between a sky and sea that are the same blue black. Climbing groggily out of bed, I cross the room and gaze out at the flat Atlantic, watching as the day slowly becomes the color of smoke.

A thin body of translucent fog drifts over the water, a stretching sky-size ghost. I feel similarly haunted. I'm just not sure by what.

When the sun peers out briefly from behind the gray screen of the sky, it wakes the waves, their whitecaps silvery in the pewter light. But I still feel half-asleep . . .

What's wrong with me?

Dad is almost always gone in the morning before I make it down to the cottage—so I'm surprised to find him in the kitchen. The memory of Bo saying he'd be back to take me to school is a blurry one, but I can't stop thinking of him. My obsession has reached its peak.

I am waiting.

The phrase surfaces in the sea of my thoughts, a diver showing his masked face as he comes up for air. But before I can imagine why

I'm thinking about the words in Lilah's little black book, I'm back to thinking about Bo.

Which is why I barely notice that Dad is just staring out the window, coffee cup clutched in one hand.

"Your mom phoned. She and Lilah are coming to visit. They'll be here next Monday."

"I was just thinking of Lilah!" *Was I?* "Did you just say she's coming here *Monday*?"

He repeats himself, and this time, his words slice through the haze in my head.

"That is so great! But—why didn't you tell me?"

"I'm telling you. They're coming a week from today."

"Okaaay . . . what's wrong?"

He stands. "Nothing's wrong. Gotta get to work, that's all. I'm late." He drains his cup and puts it in the sink. "Need a ride?" He kisses the top of my head and starts out of the room.

"Actually, I do." Because I need to figure out what's going on with him.

But—I don't have Bo's number, something that strikes me as hilarious as soon as I realize it. I'll leave him a note, on the front door. Explain later. I can't believe Mom's coming. Is it possible she misses Dad? Misses me?

"Dad," I shout as I search the cupboards for a breakfast bar. "We have to take them to the new sushi place! It's the only restaurant in town hip enough for Mom. Oh, wait—they might be closed. Maybe there's some place decent on the mainland? How long are they staying?"

"Not sure," he hollers back. "Hurry up, sweetie." The front door shuts.

Mom's letter didn't say anything about a visit. She mostly wrote about a new piece she's working on. The letter read like a page from a diary, like I thought it would. Like all her letters, it made me feel closer to her. And also farther away. That's a thing Mom does: she shares something about herself, giving you an intimate view of her interior life. Which seems generous, until you realize it's *only* a view. You can't get inside. You can't share that life with her. Can't make art with her, or join the conversation, because it's not a conversation, it's a monologue. It's really not so different, being away from Mom. We're not any farther apart than we were before.

In any case, she's coming, and I can't wait to see her. *Why isn't Dad more excited?*

I don't find out.

For the entire ride to school, all he talks about is boats. I can't get a word in, let alone a question.

Trying to beat the bell, I vault up the front steps and down the hall. Wet raincoats hang over the backs of chairs, and homeroom smells musky and dank. The temperature outside has dropped, so the heat is on for the first time this year, making the air thick and stuffy. The teal turtleneck is too warm, and I stand to take it off. Logan stares at me from the back of the room.

"Delaine's going to start growling any minute," Mary whispers as she slides into her seat.

"What?" *Delaine. Nick.* The image of an ocean-eyed Siren whirls through my mind.

"Hello? I was kidding." Mary looks uneasy. "Are you all right?"

"Fine, I just—forgot. I was going to get in touch with Logan. To try to patch things up."

The second bell rings.

"Well, it looks like our fearless leader is late." Mary eyes me expectantly.

The desk next to Logan's is empty. As I approach, he looks up at me, then yanks out the chair. I hesitate, startled as always by his pale eyes. Today the light gray makes me think of sharkskin. Finally, I ruffle his shaggy hair—which is getting long—and take a seat. "Real hazard you've got going on there."

"What are you talking about?" he asks in a monotone.

"Your hair? Soon it'll be tangling in those foot-long lashes of yours." Fluttering my eyelashes, I bring two locks of hair up around my eyes to demonstrate the dangers.

Logan slouches back in his seat and looks at me appraisingly. I'd worn a short-sleeved shirt under my sweater, and now, following his gaze down to my arms, I realize that although the classroom is almost hot, my skin is covered with goosebumps.

"You'd better put your sweater back on, unless, did you come over here to ask me to keep you warm? Oh, wait—you have Summers for that now. So what do you want from me? You want to make up? Be *friends*?"

He leans across his desk, and I remember the night we sat close together out on the cool deck of the lighthouse. How we'd danced at Hive.

The bruise on his cheek has faded, but there's a half-healed cut on the smooth ridge just under his right eyebrow that wasn't there before. I don't think—just reach up and touch it.

"Don't."

I draw my hand back. "I—I heard you got in a fight. At the Elbow."

"So?"

"Logan—" My lips are dry, and I press them together now, resisting the urge to lick them. He glances at my mouth. I try to relax. A long moment passes, and just as I'm about to speak—not that I have any idea what I'm going to say—he reaches out and touches me with one gentle finger—just beneath my chin. Then places his lips, whisper light, on mine.

Every line I've drawn in the sand between us washes away.

After what seems like forever—but is probably a matter of seconds—Logan leans back in his chair. His eyes gleam with something like triumph. His broad shoulders are relaxed as he tips his chair back now, basking in some invisible sun.

I become aware of the voices of other students, buzzing like bees. Legs shaking, I stand.

The line of shadow along his jaw becomes more pronounced as he suddenly pales. "Is that what you came over to say? Nothing?"

My mind reels. Slowly, I shake my head.

"Have you asked Summers? About any of it? You remember what I told you, don't you?"

"Yes," I say softly, trying to get over the surprise of my body betraying me. *Touch me,* it seems to murmur as I look down at Logan. My fingertips pulse. But am I really surprised? Logan has been like a sunny day for me, nearly *every* day since I started going to school here. But what's a sunny day, or a month of sunny days, compared to the sun itself?

"Yes," I say more firmly. "I'll never forget what you said." I take a deep breath. "But I still don't believe it. There are things about Bo, about his family, that you don't understand."

"No—*you* don't understand."

"Logan." *Your brother is alive!* I want to shout, but, of course, I can't. I can be his friend, though, like he's been mine. "Logan, I miss you."

He holds my gaze. "I'm surprised you let yourself admit that."

"What's that supposed to mean?" I say angrily. "Look, I'm sorry we—disagreed, that we still disagree. But friends disagree, Logan, and you're my *friend.*" But I can't keep from bringing my fingertips to my lips, and tears of confusion burn at the back of my eyes.

He looks away from me then, but most of the other people in the room are looking *at* me, at us. We've drawn everyone's attention. Mary stands up and beckons—just as our homeroom teacher walks in drenched and disheveled. The bell signals the end of homeroom, and students leap to their feet, practically trampling the dripping man.

Logan gets up without looking at me, and leaves. Slowly, I make my way over to Mary.

"We *so* need some girrrl time," she says, putting her arms around me. "We'll talk at lunch." She walks with me to the girls' room, where I wipe my tears and blow my nose. Then we head to English and open our books to *A Comedy of Errors*. More Shakespeare. The rhythm of the poetry is soothing, but unfortunately, I don't see anything funny about the story.

PASSAGE

"I told you, my dad gave me a ride. I'm sorry, I didn't think it would be such a big deal."

The weather at Summers Cove is miraculously clear. Bo's mood is no match. He picked me up after school, and although he barely commented when I told him my mother and sister were coming, he asked me a hundred times why I hadn't been home this morning.

Hard to believe, that's not what's bothering me.

"Bo, about last night." I remember sitting on the bed with him, remember him telling me I shouldn't be alone, and then—nothing. "Did I fall asleep on you? I mean, I must have—"

The questions catch in my throat as he pulls me down onto a blanket he's spread on the sand.

"Last night," he says slowly, as if trying to recall it himself. We're both lying on our sides now with very little space between us. "I think—" He narrows his eyes, looking at me through a fringe of sunlit lashes, then reaches around me, bringing his hand to my lower back, drawing my hips against his. "You may have been trying to find out if I have a fish tail."

I start to laugh, then stop as the pressure of his hand increases and I feel his hip bones through our jeans, feel his hard thighs. Blood pounding in my ears, I glance down. A strip of golden skin shows between the hem of his T-shirt and his leather belt. Sunlight glints off the brass buckle, and, definitely, a boy's body lies beneath it. Maybe that's why when he twines his arms around me and pulls the blanket over us—I don't protest.

But all at once he shifts so that he's on top of me—his legs straddling my hips. A dark line of music seems to bind my hands to my sides as something flashes in his eyes—

Something *predatory*.

"Wait—"

But he doesn't. His body presses down harder on mine, his mouth covering my mouth, his tongue swiftly parting my lips—

"Hey, you guys look like a giant sushi roll!"

The blanket unfurls, nearly dumping me onto the sand as Bo quickly draws back from me and sits up. "Cord. I thought you and J and Mia were out."

"We were." Cord grins. "And now—we're back."

Bo swipes angrily at Cord's calves. With a shaky laugh, I sit up too.

"Easy there—let's not shed any blood in front of the girlfriend." Cord dances away from Bo's grasping hands. "Love to hang with you two, but—" He flashes the universal surfer dude sign. "Gotta go rip it!" He bounds off.

I bite my lip, not sure how worried I should be about what just happened.

Bo tosses a pebble at the sea.

"He seems . . . caffeinated," I say. Then softly, I ask, "Are you okay?"

Bo lets out a sort of strangled laugh. "Am I okay? Sure. I almost—but sure, I'm okay." He runs his hands over his face. Adjusts his shirt. Then in one flowing movement, he stands up and tugs me to my feet. "You want to tell Jordan he was right, or should I?"

And as if Bo's conjured him—Jordan is strolling toward us. I feel my face grow hot.

But all he says is, "Let's talk," then gestures for us to join him down by the water.

"Last summer," he begins, as we sit down just out of reach of the waves, "—not the one that just ended, I mean the one before—Nick Delaine was here."

Did they plan this? Because they must know, that even though Jordan convinced me yesterday that someone is trying to kill me, I'm having a hard time believing it's my best friend's brother, my best friend's *dead* brother.

Bo says, "Crescent Beach has never been a big hangout, because the light station hasn't been occupied since one of its towers was lost—and half the cottage destroyed—in the mid-1700s. But once the Maine Historic Registry made the peninsula their pet project and got the bright idea for a national seashore; about a year ago April, we started seeing kids over there."

A year ago April. Lilah had been on Rock Hook at the end of June. Had she and Dad visited the lighthouse? Probably. But they couldn't have stayed there—it wasn't ready.

"We didn't worry about it," Jordan says. "Our jetty pretty much says 'Keep Out.'"

"As far as locals," Bo says, "we always figured the best thing to do to protect our privacy is to satisfy their curiosity. So every summer, we have a lobster bake."

"The whole town comes. Our family has a reputation for being slightly—eccentric, so of course everybody wants to get a good look." Jordan's smile is brutal.

Eccentric. Is that the best guess the residents of Rock Hook can come up with?

"A few days before the party, Nick and his girlfriend, Beth Anderson, found their way to our beach. They probably walked over from Crescent Beach. Maybe he was showing her where the party was going to be, or—we don't know. What we *do* know is that Cord heard someone shouting." Jordan looks at Cord, who's just thrown himself down on the sand next to us.

"I was inside," Cord says, as if on cue. "Taking a break from surfing. I looked out the front door. A guy and a girl were up on the jetty. It seemed like he was trying to help her off the rocks, but then he grabbed her shoulders, started—hassling her. I wasn't sure if I should get involved.

"Then he pushed her down. Flipped her onto her back. She screamed, and he yelled something like, *Is this what you wanted from him? Is this what you think he's got?* Then he—got on top of her. Started kissing her. Then he hit her.

"I ran outside. He stood up—but didn't see me. She tried to get up too, but he hit her again. She tumbled down the rocks to the water. He just—watched.

"I ran toward the water, toward the spot where she went under. He saw me and tried to get down off the jetty, but he fell—same place she did. I—I couldn't help them both.

"She wasn't conscious when I carried her out—I took too long. Her hair was hanging down. There was blood everywhere. Then our father was there, Bo and Jordan right behind him. Our father took the girl from me. Bo and Jordan went in after the guy."

Jordan shrugs. "He was barely breathing, which I figured was a good thing. But then I realized it would be pretty uncool if he died here. The questions. The attention. We stupidly thought, if we saved the guy, he'd be grateful. We could spin it however we needed to."

"But the only way to keep him alive," Bo says, "was to Deepen him."

"Deepen him," I echo. Vaguely I become aware that Bo is watching me intently.

"I told the police I saw them both dead in the water," Cord says. "I had to say—I saw their bodies but couldn't get to them."

Suddenly I'm on the grass in front of the high school, listening to Logan. "*They found their bodies—then they lost them.*" A shudder runs through me. Everybody sees it.

"It was a two-man job, trying to turn that bastard." Jordan appears to be entertained by the memory. "But the guy was broken to begin with, so it didn't *quite* click. Of course, I had zero experience. That couldn't have helped."

"You'd never Deepened anyone?" Too late, I bring my hand to my mouth.

"No. Once I heard a Song that attracted me for more than just . . . the obvious reasons. But it disappeared. She disappeared." Jordan hits the sand with the heel of his hand. "I lost her. I never even had a chance to begin the Deepening."

Bo nudges Cord. "Is J saying there's a girl out there for him?"

Cord grins and I feel a certain relief. "Yeah," he says. "I don't know about that—"

"You two really want to start?" Jordan growls.

"How exactly does Deepening work?" I quickly ask.

"Or not work," Bo says darkly.

"Bo," Cord says, "something about that dude was off from the start. That's why things didn't go right. Man, it's gotta suck to be Beth, living with the memories of that guy."

"Um, excuse me?" I wave a hand through the salt air. "*Living* with the memories?"

"Beth lives in India, with friends of ours," Bo explains. "Pretty great seeing her the other day, wasn't it?" he says to his brothers. They nod in agreement.

Seeing my confusion, Bo says, "That trip I took. Jordie, Cord, Mia—we all went to India. Our friends there helped us map out some . . . unexplained Siren activity." He scowls. "Nick's activity."

But I'm not thinking about Nick anymore. I'm thinking about Beth. Beth Anderson, a girl who used to live on Rock Hook, like I do now. A girl who went to Rock Hook High just like I do. Beth Anderson, an ordinary girl, who, everybody thinks, drowned. But she didn't die.

Our father took the girl. Our father. Not dad. Nothing so intimate. *Our father.*

I look over at Cord and he smiles, but in my head I hear the rest of it. I hear what happened next, and can't smile back.

Our father took the girl—and made her a Siren.

BIRDS

Somehow Cord convinces me to stay for dinner. I try not to think about what, exactly, that might be like as I phone Dad to let him know I won't be home to eat.

Dad says fine, tells me I won't miss much. He's just having eggs and toast tonight. This makes me hesitate. The breakfast-for-dinner thing, that's what we eat in my family when we're not feeling well. Briefly, I wonder what's wrong, but my ears are so full of Siren Songs I don't get around to asking.

Sitting at the farm table in the Summers' kitchen I *do* ask what's wrong. With Nick Delaine.

"Deepening is complicated, and"—Bo glances at Jordan—"it wouldn't be in anyone's best interest to explain the entire process to you. But in Nick's case—"

"Or any part of the process," Jordan says gruffly.

"Come on, J—it's okay," Bo says.

"Why is it okay? You going to Deepen her?"

"Whether I do or not, it won't hurt for her to hear—"

"Oh, it'll hurt. Or didn't you get to that part yet?" He gives a short laugh and turns to me. "Before you talk my brother into anything, you should know, the birth of a Siren's wings isn't pretty. Skin rips. Bones break. There's a *lot* of blood. You up for that?"

"Jordan, what the hell?" Bo snaps.

"You guys!" Cord shouts.

I shrink back in my seat. "I never said I wanted to be Deepened."

"Yeah, well, it won't be up to y—"

"Jordie." Mia holds up a hand. She appeared at the table a minute ago and now she locks eyes with Jordan. "It's easy to understand why Arion wants to know about Nick." After a moment she turns to me. "Deepening *can* be done safely. Whether it's what you want . . ." She shrugs. "The process takes time, when it's done right. And there can be complications. But it worked fine for Beth. Nick, well, he didn't complete his Deepening. At least, not with us." Her eyes flick to Bo.

"Jordan took the last of Nick's breath. Obviously, it had to be replaced. The job fell to me." Bo's tone turns bitter. "Apparently, I was too generous." Bo shakes his head. "I'll never forget the way he looked at his body as it began to engage. He was horrified. So angry—J and I couldn't hold him, not even with our father's help. He disappeared into the sea. None of us thought he'd survive."

I look sideways at Jordan. *He took the last of Nick Delaine's breath.* Is that why he's so awful? Or does he choose to be? Choice. *What is it about choice?*

"Did he really accuse you guys of being witches?" Blue waves dance in Cord's eyes.

"Enough." Jordan stands up. "We can't take this kind of risk, not with everything that's going on. What if some idiot gets his hands on Mortal Girl here? I'm not talking about a Siren; I'm talking about TV Twelve, or a cop from Portland." He turns to go.

"Jordie—" Bo grips his brother's forearm. The two stare at each other for a long minute. Finally, Jordan shakes off Bo's hand. He straightens his chair. Sits back down.

Silence falls over the room. Bo stabs at a slice of seared tuna that's lying on his plate.

"Cord and I caught it this morning," Mia told me when I'd complimented her on the tender pink fish. Thankfully, dinner consisted primarily of tuna and two types of seaweed salad.

I tried to visualize her under the waves, traveling with lightning speed . . . actually, the lightning analogy isn't accurate. Sirens aren't quite that fast. They travel at the speed of sound.

"Seven hundred and seventy miles per hour," Cord had been happy to explain earlier. "A few hundred miles per hour *faster* than an airplane."

Which meant it had taken the Summers one average American workday to reach India.

Swimming.

"Even Beth hasn't picked up Nick's Signals," Mia says now. "And, obviously, he hasn't heard her. Her precautions have paid off. But I wonder. Do you guys think Arion's Song brought Nick out of hiding?" Mia glances at Bo. "Is it possible he's . . . as enamored with her Song as you are? Or is this a vendetta, like you said?"

"There's something else," I say quietly. "Beth was in love with my friend Logan."

"So that's what Nick was freaking about!" Cord exclaims. "His brother. Oh man."

"Your *friend*. Right," Bo says. "That's how *you* think of Logan. But what does he think? Actually—you don't need to answer that. I've seen the way he looks at you."

"Logan *is* my friend. He likes to goof around, though, so maybe, if Nick is 'listening,' he might have gotten the idea, like you did, that Logan has feelings for me."

I don't say anything about my feelings for Logan.

"And if Logan does have a thing for you"—Cord looks at Bo apologetically—"and Nick is still pissed because Beth was into his brother, you're saying Nick might want to punish Logan as well. Maybe by hurting you." My face grows hot, but I nod.

"Bottom line," Jordan says. "If Nick kills Arion, he hurts Bo. He hurts his brother. Bonus: he gets Arion's breath. One, two, *three* birds, one stone. Convenient, bro, your girl is the stone as well as a bird."

Swiftly, Bo turns on Jordan—but Jordan only stares him down coolly.

Cord says, "Anything that inspires Nick is fuel for a friggin' hot fire. The more we know the better. Nick's murdering people and trying to make it look like we're responsible. He's trying to expose us. We're *all* birds, J."

"Personally, I can't wait to fuck the guy up," Jordan says. "What's the plan?"

"First off, we have to protect Arion," Cord says. "She can't possibly defend herself against a Siren."

"Right, so she definitely shouldn't be dating one," Jordan mutters.

Abruptly, I get up and begin clearing the table. Debating about whether or not they should tell their father about the kayakers, Cord, Mia, and Bo drift into the living room.

Their father. What else have they told him? Have they told him about me?

What's he like? The famous Professor Summers. Is he like Bo? Like Cord? Or is he more like Jordan?

Our father took the girl.

Jordan. He's lagged behind the others, and I can't resist asking, "What do you have against me?"

"Everything," Jordan says through slightly clenched teeth. "I don't want my brother to become a killer."

"Little late for that, isn't it?" I retort, then nearly drop a plate because my hands are shaking.

Jordan's sharp smile shows up. "Let me rephrase that. I don't want my brother shitting where he sleeps. Where *I* sleep."

"*Excuse* me?"

"We have too many suspicious eyes on us already. We've got to keep the peninsula clean. If my brother decides to make a meal of you here on Rock Hook—"

"Hold on. You're saying—Bo's never killed anyone here. But—"

"Why, you got a death wish? 'Cause I'd be happy to help you with that. Only thing stopping me is the fact that you're Bo's latest experiment with the 'real world'—the mortal world. An experiment which will fail, by the way, because sooner or later?"

Jordan lets his words dangle in the air like bait.

I take it. "What?"

"He's gonna go for that sweet breath you're so damn careless with." Jordan's eyes glitter. "And on that day, pretty Arion bird? I'll envy him."

POEM

Yesterday the school was buzzing with the news of the two kayakers, and today is no different. The words "Summers Cove" echo in the halls. It doesn't help me that Mary is absent.

Way less important, but still a problem, is the paper for O'Keefe's class. At lunchtime I sit in the school library staring at a blank Word document but have to admit: James Joyce's *A Portrait of the Artist as a Young Man* has lost me.

Searching for inspiration, I open the book to a page I dog-eared days ago.

"He closed his eyes, surrendering himself to her, body and mind, conscious of nothing in the world but the dark pressure of her softly parting lips. They pressed upon his brain as upon his lips as though they were the vehicle of a vague speech . . ."

The passage makes me think of Bo's . . . effect on me.

It also makes me think of Logan. I shut the book. *What's wrong with me?*

I'm putting the book in my backpack when the Moleskine slips out and falls to the floor.

Rifling through the pages, I stop at the second entry.

The string of complaints—the first entry—that's a hundred percent Lilah. The bitching. The boredom. It's her, the way she was. And the phrase that fills nearly all the rest of the pages in the little black book, well, I have an idea about that. The way Lilah wrote it over and over is unnerving, certainly, but if taken literally, is at least comprehensible: she was waiting for someone. Maybe I'll never know who that someone was, but, okay, I get it. Even the tiny scrawl, the inked insistence, is my sister. I can feel her ever-present impatience, feel her anger at being kept waiting.

But the second entry—that's the hardest for me to read. Because it's there that I find a Lilah I don't know.

Bare and broken open

we were both, when interrupted.

I would kill the man who did it

if it would bring us back together.

Wait by water, all you said

the words are branded in my head

and in between my shaking legs

How can I stand

this separation.

PORTRAIT

Stooped in front of my locker just after dismissal, Lilah's words rolling songlike through my head, I startle as someone behind me says—

"No one's going to be able to protect your friends this time."

Logan. "What are you talking about?" I ask, looking up at him.

"Oh, c'mon! You heard about the couple that drowned at Summers Cove—you think it's going to be like it was with the *Lucky*? The story's already all over the Internet. TV Twelve ran a feature last night. The major networks are gonna pick it up."

Slowly, I stand. "Hey, did you ever stop to think that maybe the mayor, the Coast Guard, even my dad, were trying to protect *you*, not the Summers, when they kept the story of the *Lucky* under the radar? Did you ever think that maybe people in this town care about your family, and all the other folks who were hurt by—your brother's death?" *A death that didn't happen.*

"Maybe no one wanted to rub salt in your wounds by splashing the story of four missing boys all over the place." Willing myself to continue saying things I only half believe, I go on. "The *Lucky* was found near the Summers' second home, true, but keeping the story away from the media wasn't about protecting them; it was about protecting you, from memories, from pain.

"I know you have to—live through those memories again now, because of this, this whole thing, that poor couple who drowned, but . . ."

Logan stands very still. His eyes are the color of clouds on a day when rain threatens, but never quite falls. "Nice try, Arion. Tell me what you found out."

"I—I mean it, Logan. What I just said. It's true." Trying to hold my ground, I'm pretty sure my eyes are begging. Begging him to stop trying to figure things out, begging him to understand something he never can, begging him to forgive me.

But his eyes hold no such look and they pierce me along with his words. "At least this time, they found the bodies."

"The waters around here are dangerous," I stammer, looking away.

"Yeah, well, you would know."

"That was a low blow."

"I'm not talking about your phobia, or your sister. I'm talking about Seal Cove, Airyhead, the way Summers set you up to think he was some kind of hero."

Ignoring what he said about Bo is easy, but the nickname cuts me; I want things to be the way they were before. It hurts me too because there's truth in it now. Lately there are times when it feels like a veil's been drawn over my brain, like I don't know my own mind. Still, I have enough clarity to know what I have to do.

"Logan," I say softly. "Please. You're being—paranoid. About Bo, and his family, about what happened to your brother." Carefully, I close the locker.

He steps toward me—I back up quickly against the cool metal.

"Whoa, what do you think I'm gonna do?" He reaches down and holds up one of my trembling hands. "You're afraid. Not of me? I'd never hurt you. Are you afraid of him, of Summers? Because you should be, and I think you know it. And I think, you know perfectly well I'm not being paranoid. C'mon, Arion, tell me what's going on. What else do you know?"

Down the hall a student shouts and I jump. *How can I tell him?* A minute ticks by.

"I don't know anything," I finally say.

He spins away—

"Wait." He turns back. "W-what was your brother like? I hardly know anything about him." *And I'm having a hard time believing everything I've heard.*

Logan gives me a quizzical look, then sighs and leans back against the row of lockers. "He was . . . Well, I think I told you, he liked to fight. But, hey, you'll appreciate this. He liked music. He worked the raves down in Portland. He's the one who got me going down there."

"Raves? Do you still go?"

"Once in a while. Lot of fights these days, though, at the warehouses on the waterfront, especially." He rolls one of his shoulders, reaches up and massages it.

"Ah. Another place to collect your cuts and bruises?"

"Don't know what you're talking about."

"Fine, be that way. So your brother was a DJ?"

"Nah. Bouncer. Too young for the clubs, but the promoters used him at the warehouses." Logan gives a snort of laughter. "He wanted to be a DJ, when we were like, thirteen, fourteen. He had a bunch of gear. First gig he had was in the basement of Saint Cecilia's, in Portland. We were visiting our abuela—"

"Your what?"

"Our Grams. *¿Qué pasa? ¿No hablas español?*"

"What's with the bilingual boys around here?" I mutter.

"Hey, if you're talking about Summers, the only language he speaks is bullshit."

"Right, well, I'm having a hard time picturing you in a church, speaking of bullshit."

"Not me, my brother. Nick was . . . religious. We lived with our abuela for a while. She taught us how to pray. Took us to Mass on Sundays. Nick got into it. Communion, confession—all that Catholic crap. Think the idea of sin was the one he liked best. But the spiritual connection . . . that was real for him. Until he figured out he wasn't gonna get an answer."

"An answer to what?"

"To anything. But especially to why our mom—whatever."

"Why your mom, what?"

"Why she left."

"But I met your mom. Anita. She looks just like—"

"Me. I know. Or, I look like her. But she's not my mom. She's my aunt, my mom's sister. Now you know the whole soap opera. Nick hated our mom for leaving. I didn't. Dad can be a jerk. I get why she left; I knew she wasn't leaving me. We keep in touch. We're close. But Nick, he never forgave her. Never forgave our dad. So Dad used to pound on him. Fun stuff, huh?"

"Is that why he liked to fight, because he was pissed at your mom and dad?"

"That was one excuse. You enjoy what you're good at, right?" Logan runs a hand over the back of his neck. "Then again he was good at everything. School. Sports. He was good with girls, but not good *to* them, you know? He was mean. They liked him anyway. Loved him."

"Same way they love you?"

"Back it up, Rush, you need a couch for this, don't you? And some letters after your name? I'll settle for the couch, though, long as it'll fit two. What do you say, pencil me in for nap time?"

I roll my eyes. "Definitely didn't mean to get so sidetracked."

"By my charm, I'm sure. You want to know about Nick? He was an asshole, okay? But I feel like that's not cool to say, 'cause he's not around.

He was my best friend, but the truth is, he was a dick. Probably still is, wherever the hell he's at." Suddenly Logan closes the space between us, grabs the hem of my shirt. "Why do you want to know so much about him?"

"What the—no reason!" I try to pull away, but he grips the material, twists it.

"You swear?"

"I—swear."

Logan ducks his head and I feel his breath, warm against my neck, as he whispers, "You can't lie for shit, you know that, right?" He leans into me, his body pressing along the length of mine. "Not about anything."

I stand there for a moment, mind spinning, my body responding to the crush of his. Betraying me. Then I tear my shirt from his grasp—

"Wait." With a metallic clang, his hands slap the lockers on either side of me.

"Why should I?" I push at the cage of his arms.

"Please."

The way he says that one word, with such . . . desperation, makes me go still.

Slowly he lowers one hand. His face is inches from mine. Eyes watchful, he reaches into his back pocket, pulling out a wallet. Flicking it open, he nods toward the edge of a piece of paper that sticks out just slightly.

As if what he wants to show me is in his gray gaze rather than in the wallet, neither of us breaks eye contact as I take the paper.

Finally, though, after hesitantly unfolding it, I look down at the half page of blue-lined paper and see that someone else has done this very thing many times. The paper is deeply creased. It is also translucent along one side, as if something has been spilled on it, as if, at some point, it's been wet.

EVIDENCE

LOGAN, SOMETHING HORRIBLE

COVE.

DON'T BELIEVE THE

CAN'T CONTROL

The word "control" spills jerkily down the page, as if the writer truly had none.

Most of the words in the brief note are illegible. The capital *N* signed at the bottom is not. It's clear. Strong.

"What is this?" I whisper.

"I think you know." We stare at each other.

"Did you show it to anyone?"

"I showed it to everyone—I mean, obviously, not everyone. My parents. The police."

"You showed it to Mary." He nods. "What did the police say?"

"They said shit. They said it was someone's idea of a joke."

"But couldn't they—couldn't they test it or something? Trace it, or—"

"They did test it. And they found DNA. A small amount. They said it wasn't Nick's. They said—it was mine."

"Of course it was," I say. "You touched it, you had to! But that doesn't mean—" But what exactly would it mean, if Logan could prove Nick had written the note? Even if the note is real, how can I possibly side with him about this? "Where did you get it?" I ask, stalling for time, trying to figure out what to say, what to do.

"My room. Found it on my desk one night. It was late. I'd been out. My father and Anita had gone to Portland for the weekend. One of my notebooks was lying open. Water was all over the place, like he'd just—" Logan breaks off, too upset to continue, but it doesn't matter, because I know exactly what he was going to say.

Water was all over the place—

Like he'd just come from the sea.

"When? When was this?"

"A couple days after he disappeared."

Over a year ago. It's not fair that he doesn't know the truth. I need to tell him.

But I don't get a chance to say anything—because Logan does.

"Your boyfriend's here." He plucks the paper from my fingers and steps back from me.

Bo stands at the end of the hall, watching us. All at once I feel weightless. Clearly, this time, Bo hasn't let school security stand in his way.

"Love note? Autograph? What is it you need so badly from Arion, Delaine?"

Logan carefully folds the scrap of paper, taking his time tucking it into his wallet, taking twice as long to replace the wallet in his pocket. "Just some answers." He squints down the hall at Bo. "To a test. So don't give her a hard time." To me he says, "Maybe we can study later."

"Maybe not."

Logan's light eyes ice over.

But I keep going. It's the best thing, for all of us. "Because those answers you have? They're not right. You should toss that sheet out."

Turning, I walk toward Bo. It feels like . . . I'm walking away from myself.

USING

"You know Delaine's just using you, right?" Bo says once we're in the Jeep.

"*Using* me? For what?"

"To find out about me, about my family. Jordan's caught him on our property more than once—he's convinced we were involved with Nick's death."

"And he's right," I say angrily. "And he's got proof. A note, one that Nick wrote."

"Ah." Bo tries and fails to repress a smile. "What does it say?"

"It doesn't say Logan's using me, that's for sure."

"Arion, I'm sorry, but you need to understand—"

"A real apology doesn't have any other words attached to it."

"Fine. Forget what I said, but know this: a note's not proof of anything. Logan could've written it himself. If it's real, it supports what we already know. Nick's alive. Unfortunately, your buddy Logan's alive as well. And it looks like, sooner or later, he's going to be a problem."

"So what are you going to do—turn *him* into a Siren too?"

Bo laughs. “He should be so lucky. No, I just need him to forget his suspicions, and to forget you, while he’s at it. Your ‘friendship’ with him needs to end. In fact, consider it over.”

“You can’t make that kind of choice for me!”

“Actually, I can.” We careen down the drive to Summers Cove. When we get to the bottom, Bo slams the gearshift into park.

And just like that, he’s the only friend I need . . .

WAVE

Down on the beach a steel sky hangs over a silver sea. Bo's Siren Song rings in my ears.

Fingering my lips, I watch as he strips down to his trunks and dives into the water. A moment later, the waves grow monstrous.

"C'mon, Bo, send us another!" Cord's words carry over the water from where he floats on a surfboard out beyond the breakers. Letting his pop song of a voice wash over me, I try to justify Bo's behavior. My skin feels seared where he touched me.

Close to tears, I mutter, "If only—"

Jordan drops down on the sand beside me. "If only what?"

I open my mouth to speak, but the slippery eel of a thought—something about Bo—slides off to some dark corner of my mind. I shake my head, struggling to pursue it.

Jordan studies me for a moment, then looks away.

"If only Nick and Beth hadn't climbed the jetty," I blurt.

"He still would have hurt her," Jordan says, watching the waves. "He's a Delaine."

Burning to defend Logan, defend his family, I shiver instead at the sound of Jordan's voice, and search the horizon for Bo. Finally I spot him, just his torso visible above the waterline—I know now, no glittering fish tale lies below it. The source of Bo's support is his legs. Kicking, treading water—pedaling, that's the Siren term. He can stay afloat forever. Now he windmills his arms through the waves, creating a perfect curl for Mia and her pink surfboard.

Jordan had been doing the same thing for Cord last Sunday, when I'd watched from the deck of the lighthouse. He'd been the swimmer in the water. I hadn't known then, about their wave-making game, how they take turns playing Poseidon.

Vaguely, I remember a story by Kafka, about Poseidon doing paperwork. I can't imagine the Summers anyplace but here, but if what Logan said is true, then the media—

As if Jordan is reading my mind, he says, "Mortal Girl, I know you've got a thing for Logan, but his brother—he may be more dangerous than we thought."

"Same way Bo's more dangerous than *I* thought?" I spit out before I can stop myself.

Jordan's atramentous eyes regard me steadily.

Then suddenly he lunges at me—

I scream as he jerks me to my feet—

"I heard him!" Dripping wet, Mia appears beside us. "Bo's right. It's Nick."

Bo races up behind her. "Mia, are you sure—" He breaks off and glares at Jordan.

"Don't be a presumptive bastard," Jordan says in response to Bo's narrowed eyes. "I heard him too. He's close." He releases me, examining the ocean Mia and Bo abandoned with such speed.

"Nick's in the Cove!" Cord bounds up from the water. "His Signal's cranking."

How can Nick be here? How can this be real?

Holding my breath as if that'll protect me, I start making deals with God. *Please, let me see Mom and Dad again. Please let me see Lilah.* Bo and Jordan failed to hold Nick before, even with the help of their father—how do they expect to stop him now that he's bent on revenge?

Nick—can he really be a Siren?

And Logan, how could I have just walked away from him?

God, are you still there? Because there's this boy, with eyes like a cloudy day. His smile might blind you momentarily, but please, I need you to let him know—

I love him.

The ground seems to dip under my feet. A nonexistent wind stirs the water violently and the ocean—

Begins drawing away from the beach.

Jordan shouts something, and Bo leaps in front of me, his bare back dripping seawater. Shoulders squared, he looks ready to fight—

Only there's no one to fight. Instead there's a massive wave forming off the beach, a wave twenty times the size of any I've ever seen.

Silently, I start to cry, and for a second, it looks as if everything is underwater. I stare at the towering wave looming impossibly high over a newly visible flat of soaking sand dotted with suffocating fish and scuttling crabs. *Lilah, I'm sorry. I should have been on that boat.*

Jordan and Mia and Cord move as one toward the receding sea—

Just as a great roaring detonates in my ears, the thunder of smashing waves—

No—it's *music.* Cascades of strings, great claps of percussion—

Bo's wings.

"Get Arion away from—" Cord's voice disappears in a gust of wind, and then—

We're in the air.

"Wrap your arms around my neck—tighter!" Bo commands. His legs are already around my legs. His arms cross my back, pulling me closer until our bodies touch in every possible place. One of his hands slides quickly to the back of my neck, jerking my face roughly against the hollow of his collarbone, and I feel his body, hard everywhere, as the tug of the tides washes through me.

Light, dark, light, dark, the shadows of his wings fall around us as we speed through the sky. Squeezing my eyes closed, I press my face into his neck, trying to catch my breath but succeeding only in emitting a ragged sound between a cry and a moan. Suddenly I don't have to try to hold on—my body clings to Bo of its own accord. He sings to me now, his lips near my ear. Maybe he's trying to reassure me, but the sound only makes me ache, makes me forget anything else exists besides his skin, and his Song.

"Okay," he says now, "okay." And somehow we've landed, and we're standing by the lighthouse, and he's trying to peel me away from him. But I grip his shoulders, won't allow him to disentangle himself, lifting my lips— Gently but firmly he pulls my arms from around him, sliding my leg down—the one still wrapped around his own—little by little, until both my feet are on the ground and there's an inch of space between us. The inch alone makes me groan in frustration.

"I need you—" I protest almost incoherently, swaying toward him love drunk—not even, drunk with lust—and pleading, wanting to lick his skin, sink my teeth into one of his bare shoulders.

"I know what you think you need." He crosses my lips with an index finger. "Rising is—intimate, can lead to intimate things."

"Rising," I repeat, stumbling slightly as he steps back from me.

He takes my elbow, steadying me. "Yes. I had to. And I may have to again. I need to get you away from here, until this is over."

"But it's over, isn't it? Your brothers, Mia, they'll . . . they'll make him leave." But even as I say the words, I know neither thing is true.

Nick Delaine is as tenacious as he is terrible, and as Bo's Siren spell begins to fade, I want to shout, *What about the serpentine tail?* But I'm thinking crazy. That image—it's from my dreams. Nervous laughter bubbles out of me.

"Arion. Stop. You need to pack. I'll go back, get the car."

"The car?"

"Yes. I'm going to take you away from here, away from him. We need to go."

"But I can't just go! And where? Where would we go?"

"Anywhere! Anywhere but here."

We stare at each other, and I imagine what it would be like, running away with him. How long is he talking about? A night? A lifetime? What about my family? What about—

Logan.

"I can't," I say frantically. "My mother is coming, my sister—"

"Arion, be reasonable, let me take you away from here, just until—"

"Could you leave *your* family now? Knowing that Nick Delaine is *here*?"

"He's been here," Bo counters. "Maybe longer than we thought. We need to go."

"No! And don't make me. This one thing—I need to choose. Please."

He scowls and swings away from me, walking across the pebbles to the windblown grasses at the edge of the bluff. I follow.

"Bo—"

"Ari. Nick Delaine has mutated, or—something. He's learned . . . Neptune knows what. That rogue wave he formed? That's not something a single Siren can do. And yet he did it.

"Jordan and Mia, and Cord—the three of them will handle this. They'll push the water back, protect the cottages, but only because they'll work together.

"Nick . . . seems to be on his own. He must have struggled to survive . . . You'd think being alive would be enough for him!"

Bo shouts this last handful of words at the sea. Then his voice grows quiet. "But being alive isn't enough." He turns around, looks down at me. "Is it. Not enough for any of us."

All at once the wind tears over the bluffs, lifting our hair, shivering my skin.

But it doesn't bring any answers with it, and I don't know what's enough—for Bo, or for me, or for Nick Delaine.

BLINDFOLD

Out of the sea and onto the sand steps the Siren, the winged man. Yes, I know what he is now. I know what he wants. His skin is seawater. His eyes are swords.

Silently this time, the wings appear. Not white but oil-slick black.

This time, everything is different. I step toward him. He steps toward me: *Step, stop. Step; stop.* The rhythm of a bride—walking down the aisle.

My breastbone is nearly against his—I thought he was taller than this. Then I realize, it's because of me: I'm on tiptoe, straining upward, not wanting to wait for his kiss.

Now I am predator, he is prey.

His wings wrap around me, a black hole pulling me in, drawing me down. He tips his face, and I slide my hands behind his neck, clasp him tighter. Start to drown.

Through the silken night of his feathers, a brilliant light flares and I see forever—

Until his wings close tighter, create a coffin of obsidian.

But just before the onyx blindfold takes my sight completely, and buries me in the raven grave of him, I see the man I love standing on the path—

And know he'll never reach me, because—because he is a killer, like the man who holds me now. And then they are one, but I am one with them. I am a Siren. A murderer. A monster.

I become water. The darkness is total. And the music . . . *the music . . .*

The melody is jagged, chaotic. A screaming electric guitar, smashed at the end of a set—

And then I'm screaming—

Into a bright morning bedroom, my bedroom, though the vivid image of the Siren still trespasses. I sit up and pull my knees in close to my chest. Wrap my arms around them. Streaks of darkness cross my vision—his jet-black feathers.

I finally told Bo about the series of strangely similar dreams. I also told him how I thought someone had been in my room—even though part of me still believed that the *someone* had been him. I'm ashamed, that I suspected him. But I couldn't help it.

He denied it, of course. *"There was never a time I was in your room that you didn't want me there."* Then he went detective on me, asking lots of questions. Uncomfortable, embarrassed—I didn't bring up the topic again.

But this nightmare is worse than embarrassing. It's humiliating.

The creature that's haunted my sleep for so many nights—

Has become *desirable.*

My skin prickles, and I imagine . . . he somehow crawls beneath it.

CONTROL

Bo not only took me to school in the morning, he parked and walked me to the building.

As he predicted, his brothers and Mia drove back the massive wave. They also told Bo, when he stopped home earlier—after apparently spending the night patrolling the grounds below the lighthouse, something that I found simultaneously romantic and unnerving—that Nick Delaine had vanished. Against Mia's wishes, Jordan spent the night searching the coves along the coast. He found no trace of Nick.

Sick with nerves, I spent most of the day in the nurse's office. Now, in the matchbox of a room where Lilah will sleep, I open the window—starting as the sea air blows in with a *whoosh*. Childishly, I pretend that when Mom gets here, she'll magically make everything better.

But Bo and his siblings have come up with a plan of their own to fix things, and Bo told me that, since I refused to leave Rock Hook, they'd make it safe for me stay.

During dinner, I find myself telling Dad that I'll be spending the weekend with Mia.

"How's the *zuppa di pesce*?" he asks. But I can almost hear him thinking, *Weekend slumber party, that's a teenage girl thing, right?*

"It's really good." He looks pointedly at my bowl. It's full. "Guess I'm excited."

Definitely, I can't eat. But at least I don't need to be concerned about Dad. Over dinner he decides to take advantage of the fact that I'll be away this weekend and go to Bangor a couple days early to see friends. Surrounded by people, he'll be safe.

"I'll be in town when their flight arrives. Won't have that long drive two days in a row."

There's been no change in Lilah's condition. Six weeks from now we'll fly to California for her procedure. As for Mom, it doesn't matter to me anymore that I don't have the relationship I want with her. I just want *her here*. And whatever issues she and Dad have? They've become unimportant as well. They don't involve surgery. They don't involve Sirens.

And how much more can they argue?

"If you'd had a real job instead of being captain of a fishing fleet, charter boats, party boats—is that really what you planned to do with your life? And now, you've ruined Delilah's." Mom hadn't been able to stop. She'd needed someone to blame.

In part she was right, Dad *hadn't* intended to work on those kinds of boats. He'd planned on adventure, sailing the world. But Mom herself had changed all that. She'd wanted Dad in one place, and that place was San Francisco, where *she* wanted to be.

Yes, they discussed splitting up, but instead, my parents are going to try again. The move, the possibility of a new life, Lilah's upcoming operation. These things have given them hope.

Hope. That muscle is strong in me now. No longer atrophied or in need of exercise, hope seems to bounce in my chest. Unfortunately, it has company. Fear. And uncertainty.

"Are you psyched?" I ask, forcing myself to make conversation.

"Sure am." But Dad seems distracted as he finishes his food. Also, he burned the garlic bread—very unlike him. Maybe he's nervous about seeing Mom. That last letter she sent hadn't told me anything new, but I have no idea what she's said to him.

Tossing the burnt bread out seems to wake Dad up. "Bo going to be around this weekend?"

"I'm not really sure." Keeping my eyes on the sink, I run hot water for the pots.

Dad clears his throat, and I glance up. He's giving me one of his dad looks.

"Hey, there are *three* houses at Summers Cove, and Dad? I'm going to be with *Mia*."

Bad liars always sound defensive.

We aren't even staying at the cottages. We'll be at Cliff House, because, supposedly, it's safer. But no way will Dad let me go out there.

To ease his mind, I begin telling him about Mia, tossing around words like, "girl talk," "shopping," and "hair," in the same way he seasons his soup, which is liberally, until his worries are forgotten. Sadly, I can't forget my own.

"We don't want to broadcast this all over the seven seas," Cord told Bo.

He'd meant—one of them needed to speak with their father, face-to-face.

I'm not the only one who needs protection, and tonight Cord will go back to India, believing that the only way to keep Beth safe is to personally tell her as well: Nick Delaine is alive and out for vengeance. Now more than ever, she needs to remain in hiding.

"Neptune knows how," Cord said, "but Nick's honed the Deep Skills. He must have. He has to be behind the arc of violence we've mapped, because that arc ends here. Nick is the only Siren we know of with a reason to come to Rock Hook. It totally makes sense that he's trying to exact revenge by creating a series of unanswered questions that will expose us to the world."

"Unanswered questions" was Cord's tactful way of saying missing boys and dead bodies.

Now, bringing the cold air in with him, Bo appears at my bedroom door. He's just come from saying goodbye to Cord, who'll leave late tonight.

"Less boat traffic," Bo explains. "Less air traffic. Less chance of being seen in his Full Expression." The bed sighs as he sits down beside me.

"You didn't worry about anyone seeing you in your . . . Full Expression"—my face grows hot—"when you flew me to the lighthouse." *And your Siren spell made me want to—*

"Some risks are worth taking," Bo replies, his gaze level.

"What about the risk Cord's taking, swimming to Goa alone?"

Bo reaches for my iPod, starts scrolling. "He'll be safe. We don't know *exactly* where Nick is, but Mia picked up his Signal. Finally. It's faint, but she heard it. He's definitely in this part of the world. J and Mia are going to swim the length of the coast, see if they can get a bead on his location. If they do, we'll confront him together. Meanwhile, say hi to your bodyguard."

"Is that a step up or down from lifeguard?"

Bo doesn't answer, just sets the iPod down and lifts my left hand, examining the calluses on my fingertips. "You know," he says after a moment, "it'll be the four of us at Cliff House."

I jerk my hand away—

"Don't worry, Jordie won't be around much. When he is, just—don't listen to him." With a shrug, Bo holds up my earbuds. "If things get weird, put these in."

"Beeswax, yeah? And what if I *want* to listen? You going to tie me up?"

"Sure thing, Odysseus, you *and* your red boots. On second thought, that might make things too easy for Jordie when he—"

"Shut up!"

"Okay, but seriously, he's my *brother*. He's a good guy. And despite any revelations you may have had? So am I. Now, your job's not too tough. I'll take you to Cliff House tomorrow after school. You'll stay inside. Out of sight. Cord will be back Monday, at the latest. Our father will probably be with him. By then . . ." We sit looking at each other. The plan is simple: Two hunters. One babysitter. Switch. In the end, when they catch Nick, it'll be three against one.

"What will you . . . do to him?"

"Arion." Bo's voice is dark now, black on black, like a shadow at night. He touches my face. I lie down on the bed . . .

"But—" I protest weakly. "He's like you."

"We'll take his breath," says the shadow voice. "It's the only way—"

His lips graze my neck.

"To kill a Siren."

I'm lost in his Song . . .

TRUST

"I don't want you alone for a second."

Bo is actually walking me *in* to the school—or, trying to. But the front doors make a bottleneck, and we're unexpectedly stuck in the crowd on the front steps. More than a few girls—and a couple of guys—glance at Bo. At his face, or his form, at his light hair shimmering in the morning sun. Some people turn away after a quick look, moving off as if pursued. Others are rooted, unable to leave Bo's orbit. None of them can meet his eyes.

"I won't be alone. There are at least twenty people in each of my classes."

"What about in between? The hallways. Bathrooms."

"Fine, I'll tell Mary when I have to pee." Bo's brows draw down. "Sorry, I know it's not funny. But the halls are crowded. Plus, Mary and I usually walk to class together, except gym."

"Do you have gym outside?"

"On a day like this, definitely."

"Then you need to play sick, go to the nurse."

"I can't, I did that yesterday." Only I hadn't been playing. "The PE teacher warned me about missing any more—crap."

Bo follows my gaze. "Nice boots."

"I'll have to borrow Mary's sneakers. I can't miss gym."

"What about Delaine?"

"What about him?"

"Ask him to walk you. When you go outside."

"But you said—"

"Forget what I said. I've been thinking about your ardent admirer. If Nick sees you with Logan, his attention might be torn. That might mean extra time. I'll be close by, so if—"

"Do you really think Nick Delaine will come *here*?"

"I don't know, but if he does, Logan might act as a distraction, even a deterrent, and—"

Bo breaks off, his expression becoming unreadable.

"And what?"

"And he'll do anything for you. Trust me on that."

Trust. The word seems to waver.

"Just get him to walk you, Arion."

It may be a little late for that now that I've lied to his face and acted like a total bitch.

Bo narrows his eyes. "What is it?"

"Nothing. I'll talk to him. That was the bell for the end of homeroom. I've got to go."

Only going isn't so easy. Something's nagging me, some thought I've tucked away in a corner of my mind, a dark corner, where the wriggly-as-eel thoughts about Bo have recently taken up residence. But finally, after exchanging a look with Bo—a kiss would be impossible—I start down the hall, leaving him behind.

As I walk away, I feel his eyes on my back. It's reassuring, but also . . . also . . .

Another eel thought slip-slides away before I can catch it.

Continuing down the hall, I become aware that I feel slightly nauseous.

The lovesickness. It's getting worse. It kicks in right away now, as soon as I leave Bo's side. The Siren sickness. I'll never be able to leave him now. Not ever.

BODYGUARD

Logan emerges from the classroom with a girl who's obviously crushing on him. She keeps touching his arm as she talks, and now she brings her lips to his ear, as if sharing a secret.

Secrets. *I have to tell him, tell him everything.*

"Surprise, surprise," Logan says when he sees me. He stops walking and makes a show of saying goodbye to the girl, whispering in her ear like she'd done with him. But when she runs a hand through his hair, he jerks his head away in annoyance, waggling his fingers in farewell. "What's up, Rush?"

"Have you forgiven me?"

"You mean for lying to me? Or for telling me my brother's note is bullshit?"

Briefly, I close my eyes. This was a very bad idea.

He taps the pointy tip of my red cowboy boot with the blunt toe of his black motorcycle boot. "Where's your master?"

Keeping my eyes on our boots, I say, "What, did you get a motorcycle or something?"

"Why, you wanna ride? That why you're lurking outside my class?"

"Something like that." I kick lightly at one of his boots.

"Our *disagreements* aside, Rush, you totally ignored me today in homeroom."

"Yes, well, I was late. I was there for like, half a minute."

And the last time I talked to you in homeroom, you kissed me—then walked off the set.

Our eyes lock and he grins. He's thinking of the kiss, he has to be.

"You know what?" I start to turn away. "Never mind."

"Wait, what's going on?" He pulls me into an empty classroom.

"Nothing. I have to go."

"There it is again, sweet nothing. And where do you have to go in such a hurry?"

"Hello? Class? Why, what are you going to do, cut next period? I can't just do that."

"Why not? Boyfriend breathing down your neck? Why, yes, as a matter of fact, he is. Okay, then, bye-bye, see you around." He turns away, about to step into the hall.

"Logan."

He turns back. "Hmm?"

"Will you—will you walk me to the gym?"

"Since when do you need an escort to PE?"

Wordlessly, I look at him. Stare, although I know I shouldn't. His long eyelashes cast shadows on his cheekbones as he looks down at me. Now the full bow of his mouth curves into a smile. "Rush." He shakes his head. "Why do you fight it?"

"Hey, I'm not the fighter," I manage to say, dropping my gaze to his bandaged hand. "Who was on the receiving end?"

"No one you know. Listen—"

"Come on, what happened? Tell me."

"Yeah, no, it's just a scratch—"

"Are you okay?" My voice gives something away I didn't even know I had. One of Logan's dark brows lifts slightly. He heard it too.

"Arion." With his other hand he touches my forehead—the space between my eyebrows. The tight scowl I hadn't known I was wearing relaxes and my shoulders soften. Logan's fighting makes me sick with worry, but now that he's touched me, something besides worry buzzes through me.

"We have some crazy chemistry," he says softly, running his fingers down my arm. "You can't deny it. Even with the Silver Surfer acting like he owns you—"

"Stop, okay? Nobody owns me." But my voice falters. His lips twitch. I narrow my eyes. "Delaine, what the hell are you trying to do?"

"Me? Nothing. Well, maybe something. A little something. 'Course it doesn't feel little, it feels big. Heavy. I'm like that guy, what's his name? You know, the guy who pushes the boulder up the hill, and it keeps rolling down, and he's got to keep hauling it back up, forever?"

"Sisyphus," I say drily.

"Right. I'm Sisyphus. And you're the boulder. I get you to the top of the hill, but you won't look at the view—"

"That's ridiculous! There's no view in that story. The view—"

"Is everything. But you won't see it. The truth, I mean. You just . . . roll away from it."

But he's laughing now, and I start laughing too. And suddenly it's all so—Logan. So familiar, the mix of sulking and laughter, anger and . . . that thing he does to me.

"Come on, Logan, I've got gym. But seriously, we have to talk, okay? I can't argue with you, we can't have these fights, it's crazy." *I have to tell him, he deserves to know.*

"Stupid crazy. Total waste. But okay. We're talking." He leans against the doorframe.

"I mean," I give him a pointed look, "we need to *talk*."

"What, we're not talking? Sounds like we're talking." He reaches out—lays a finger across my lips. "That—is not talking. Not. Talking. Look—now I'm not talking either."

Automatically my gaze moves to his mouth, his full lower lip. My stomach goes into a spin as I take in the unshaven shadow along his jaw, his cheekbones, and finally, his light eyes with their impossibly long lashes. My lips pulse beneath the gentle pressure of his finger—

I slap his hand away. "You're a jerk."

"Oh, come on," he says, laughing, grabbing my arm as I whirl to go. "A jerk?"

"That's what I said." I yank my arm back.

"Yeah, well, I'd like to hear what else you have to say. So, okay, let's talk. I mean, let's *plan a time* to talk. That's what you want, right? Such a girl thing," he scoffs. *"Let's talk,"* he adds in a mincing tone.

"I can see why someone hit you."

"No one hit me. Although if you want to take a shot—"

"You'd probably like it."

"That's a distinct possibility."

I roll my eyes and move toward the door. He moves at the same time and we collide. He chuckles. The sound I make is closer to a growl. I dodge around him.

"So when are we going to have our girl talk?" he asks as he follows me down the hall.

"Why don't you phone me tonight?"

"Tonight? Not soon enough. How about we meet up on the front steps after school?"

"What, you don't have a phone? Oh, I remember now—you don't know how to use it."

"Man, I've really rubbed off on you. You used to be such a nice girl."

"Still am." The smile I give him is saccharine.

"Yeah, you are. Now if you could just get rid of the boyfriend—hey, why are you suddenly allowed to hang out with me?"

"I was never *not* allowed to hang out with you." I glance down the empty hall. We're both going to be late.

"Whatever, he's got you on a tight leash."

"*He* wants us to be friends."

"Summers *wants* us to be friends? That—does not make sense. Why?"

"He knows you make me happy, that you're my—friend." *God, could I tell a bigger lie?*

"The guy is even weirder than I thought."

"He's not so bad, you know."

"Yeah? Tell me about him." And for a second, I think maybe Bo's right, that maybe Logan wants to find out more about the Summers, through me. But the thought is barely complete before Logan adds, "Tell me something real."

Real, like Logan.

Unfortunately, it's the unreal aspect of Bo that Logan wants to know about, he just doesn't realize it.

"Logan, there's . . . nothing I can tell you about Bo that you don't already know."

We stop and I look up at him, willing him to accept what I'm saying without questioning me further, needing it to be enough. Because how can I tell him—*you're right, the Summers had something to do with Nick's disappearance. They made Nick immortal, and he wants to destroy them for that. But they were only trying to* help *your brother, even after he tried to murder his girlfriend, Beth, the girl who loved you.*

"What I know is that you need to stop seeing him. Whatever happened—or didn't happen—to Nick, that's not what I'm talking about right now. The hold Bo has on you, I saw it in action the other day. It's sick. I'm saying this as your friend. You've gotta get away from him."

And hearing Logan say it, I know it's true. But his words are an answer that only brings more questions. Questions like, *how?* And, *when?* And, *why—why can't I be with someone I want to be with so badly?* But I know why. And Logan's right. I have to let him go.

Only, when I open my mouth to say *I know*, what comes out is "I can't."

"Ah. The cage of can't. You *can't*? Or you *won't*? Is there a reason you can't?"

Logan's gaze is penetrating, but he'll never be able to guess my secrets. He only knows I'm holding something back. And after another moment, when he realizes I'm not going to say anything else, he recognizes I'm offering something too. His pale eyes search my face, and I guess he finds what he wants there, because he decides to take the atonement, incomplete as it is for him. It's a compromise, but love always is. No one knows that better than me.

"I'll call you," he says.

"When?"

He sighs and shakes his head a little, looking away. "As soon as I can."

We've been standing in front of the open doors to the cafeteria, and now he says, "Hey, is this close enough?" The track and playing fields are visible through the windows on the other side of the sea of tables. My class is already out there.

I force a smile. "What's your hurry? Thought you were going to cut, Big Talker."

"Are you kidding? Kenninger'd kill me, even if he is the Existentialism teacher. Thanks for making me late, by the way."

"Anytime. And yes, this is close enough."

TRIO

Logan jogs off and I start into the cafeteria, then remember: Mary's sneakers.

Two long hallways and one wrong turn later I arrive at the art room. Quietly, I slip in the door and make my way over to her.

"Hey! Cutting gym so you can be with me every second of the school day?"

"You sound like Logan. Actually, I need to borrow your sneakers."

"Fine. Use me for my shoes." She jots down the combination to her locker. "They're really comfortable—don't let the smell put you off."

"Thanks for the warning."

After swinging by her locker, I make my way back to the cafeteria, planning on cutting through. But as soon as I enter the lunchroom, I hear a single leaping note from a violin arc through the air—and I jerk to halt.

Then, as if I've surprised the music, instead of the other way around, it simply stops.

I start across the cafeteria—

The sound of shimmering strings fills the room. Violin. Viola. Cello. The piece is a trio, the instruments so drenched in effects—they swell and bloom into something grander sounding. The music is dark, and lovely, but also—somehow violent.

The composition cuts off abruptly, leaving a foreboding echo reverberating in the air. Then the final vibrations are completely obliterated as jangly guitar chords burst through the speakers.

"Carry me, across the threshold, push me down the rabbit hole for tea."

Curious to see who's responsible for the bizarre playlist and why they're DJing for an empty cafeteria, I start walking toward the radio station's picture window.

"Smiling while our lips and teeth grow cold, we will walk a plank into the sea."

On the other side of the glass Alyssa sits in a swivel chair behind a desk covered in CDs.

Behind her—stands Bo.

"And, so the story goes. I try to fix it . . ."

He's facing me but looking down at Alyssa. Now she passes a disc over her shoulder.

He steps forward to take it—

She laughs and yanks it back.

Bo scowls in frustration and steps closer to her, reaching again for the CD—

Quick as a cobra, she spins around in the chair. Standing practically in the same moment, she brings the full length of her body against Bo's, lifting her face to his—

"Then you give me your lips to kiss . . ."

Surprise darkens Bo's expression—a cloud crossing the sun. He takes a step backward but she moves with him, dropping the CD, grasping his hips.

He brings his hands to her shoulders, as if to push her away—

But as he moves, so does she, sliding her hands up his body, twining her arms around him. She closes her eyes—

Which means she misses the horrified look spreading over Bo's face.

She's a big girl, and now her arms tighten around his torso. Then she reaches up with one hand—her fingers twisting among the golden strands of his hair. Her mouth, red with lipstick, is mere inches from his.

Bo looks at her lips—

And on his face, anger takes the place of horror—then turns to desire.

My knees stop working, and I sink to the floor. I have to help her. But I can't move, like a nightmare, where you can't run. Transfixed, I kneel on the cafeteria tiles.

"You say, 'I love you' . . ."

Love.

Bo.

"No!" I scream. *"No!"* And then my body is a bullet.

I spring to my feet, fists pounding the window. Hitting it so hard I'm sure the glass will shatter. But the window remains intact, my fists, my screams bouncing off like so many raindrops, ineffectual thunder. What are the alternatives? Even as I continue to pound on the glass, I'm frantically considering. Even if I run, by the time I make it through the cafeteria doors and around the corner to the entrance of the radio station, it will be too late. It's *already* too late. I scream out—

"Alyssa!"

Maybe it's the sound of her name, or maybe the sound of my fists thudding against glass that finally reaches her—

Or maybe she's just realizing—she's made a terrible mistake. Because suddenly she's wide-eyed with panic, twisting her body, trying to turn her head—

But Bo holds her firmly, his mouth battened on hers.

Then all at once he looks up—away from the face of his prey. The aureate rings around his pupils appear to ignite with shock. With obvious effort, he pushes Alyssa away—

Released from his hold, she stumbles backward. Her eyes seem to clutch at me—

Then she falls—arms sliding across the desk, sending CDs everywhere. She crashes to the floor.

Time stops.

In a sort of slow motion, I look at Bo, his eyes blazing in his pale face. I want to run to him. Run away. My heart splits in two, and I look down at Alyssa—

She's dead.

Staring in disbelief, I try to move. Can't.

Bo looks at Alyssa too now, then at me. His voice comes from the other side of the glass, as if from underwater—

"She's breathing!"

My eyes fill with tears. "You *wish*!"

As if the two words have released me, I bolt around the corner and through the door of the radio station—Bo is gone. I crouch next to Alyssa's prone body—

She *is* breathing!

But as I stare at her ashen face, her blue-tinged lips, trying to figure out how to help her—

Her body begins to convulse.

Racing to the main office I burst through the door. "Call nine-one-one!"

The secretary who basically runs the school looks at me as if I've gone insane.

"What's wrong? Are you hurt?" She eyes me skeptically, one of those people who doesn't believe there's trouble unless there's blood.

"No! It's Alyssa—Alyssa Saffer. Sh-she's in the radio station!"

"That girl's been into one thing or another since the day she got here from New York City." The secretary cocks her head to one side. "You two get in a fight?"

Lunging toward her desk, I grab the phone. Punch 9-1-1.

"The high school, send an ambulance! She can't breathe, she's convulsing—"

"We're sending someone now. Please stay on the line." The woman on the phone seems to be from the same slow-moving world as the office secretary. "State your name, please."

"Arion Rush."

"Tell me what happened please, Miss Rush. Who's having trouble breathing?"

But all of a sudden it's me—I can barely breathe myself.

"Hello? Miss? Can you tell me what happened?" The voice on the phone seems to bend, slowing and warping, becoming unintelligible as the questions continue. "Can. You. Tell. Me."

No! No, I can't tell anyone!

Or, maybe I can.

My boyfriend's a Siren. He dropped me off at school today. Guess he couldn't handle it.

But it's me, *I* can't handle it, can't handle any of this.

"An accident." My voice is a whisper now. "Hurry."

The receiver lands on the desk with a *thunk*. The secretary is at the office door now, the principal right behind her. I follow them into the hall—

Then turn the other way, and start running, running . . .

An ambulance passes me. A police car. A van from TV Twelve.

I don't stop running until I get to the harbor. Luckily, Dad is there. I tell him I'm sick—

Then throw up on Mary's sneakers.

AEGIS

"You have to come to Cliff House," Mia insists. "It's the only way to keep you safe."

"Oh, really? And how are you planning on keeping all the other people in Rock Hook safe? Did your brother tell you what he did?"

After bringing me home, Dad reluctantly left for Bangor. When Mia showed up, I was down in the keeper's cottage sitting in front of the picture window staring at the sea, watching the waves churn up tangles of seaweed and toss them along the shore. Emerald and titian, olive and black—the colors tumble in the broken waves.

"This isn't about Bo. It's about your safety."

"Right, because a bunch of Sirens should definitely be able to help me with that. And since when do you care?"

"Band," she says calmly.

"What?"

"*Band* of Sirens. Look, I know you're freaking about Bo. But you shouldn't be alone. We know Nick is—"

"You're all so desperate to convince me Nick's alive, that he wants to kill me. But why should I even believe you? How do I know—" *You're not lying and the killer isn't one of you?*

Close to tears, I break off, unable to think straight, not about this. Is it Mia, is she spinning out some silent Siren Song? Some Signal? *Or am I still under Bo's spell?*

"Arion, come with me. Like we planned. Forgive Bo." She shrugs. "Couples fight."

"This wasn't a fight, this was your brother almost killing someone!"

"But he didn't. He didn't kill anyone. Calm down! We've been through this with Jordan. Bo will be okay. We'll help him. The rest of it . . . is normal. Lovers argue. Get jealous."

"Wait a minute, *Bo* will be okay? What about Alyssa? And do you really think Bo's not here right now because *I'm jealous*?"

"There's a northeaster on the way. You'll be stuck here."

"Good. Fine. I want to be stuck." I lift my chin. *And I want to know why you're here and he's not.*

God, how can I even want *to see him?*

But Emily Dickinson explained how, in one of her letters. We read it in English class:

"The heart wants what it wants."

After biting down hard on my lip for a second so I won't cry, I tell Mia to go.

She gives me a thin smile. Says, "I tried." And leaves.

Dad warned me about the weather. I wish I'd gone with him. But I feel painfully tethered to Rock Hook. I continue to bite back tears, abandoning the cottage now.

The wind slams the door at my back.

LIGHTS OUT

Taking the steps two at a time, I reach the drive and hurry across the pebbles.

A burst of jagged music, a whirl of motion—

My scream cuts the air—

Jordan uncurls from a crouch and makes his way to standing, his white wings vanishing impossibly beneath smooth shoulder blades. His midnight gaze slants down at me. My hands fly to my chest—

"Is that where you keep it? Is that where your *humanness* lives, the 'essence' Bo covets, even more than your breath?"

Jordan's voice circles around me, the tug of it so hard I think it might pull me apart. I imagine him searching through the pieces until he finds what he wants.

"Heard Bo got hungry. Guess whoever he hit up didn't have a voice like yours to distract him." Jordan's lips push into a sort of pout, as if considering something. But he merely says, "Whoa—did you see that avalanche?" and saunters over to the edge of the bluff. He raises his voice above the wind, and its beauty covers me like a blanket as he shouts over his shoulder, "It's going to be an epic storm. Oh man—check those perfect barrels, it's reeling out there."

For a moment all I can do is follow his gaze, watching the waves tear at each other. The surf conditions don't look good to me; the curls look like claws. Look like they'd crush anyone who tried to catch them.

In the boldest tone I can summon I say, "Why are you here, Jordan?"

He turns and looks at me. I wait for his sharp smile, but it doesn't come. Maybe he's still trying to figure out what his brother sees in me. Or maybe he's just seeing a meal.

"You should have gone with Mia." His eyes are black now, abysmal.

"You—should leave."

But he doesn't. He cocks his head, as if he's listening. "I'm not sure where Bo is right now, but he'd want you protected. Come with me to Cliff House."

"Why, so you can guard me from someone who's supposedly more horrible than he is?" But even as I say the words, to my dismay, I walk toward Jordan.

His percussive laugh is a dismissive thing. "You know, I ought to just put you out of your misery. But I told Cord I'd behave." His brows pull together. "Mia's Calling. I have to go." He rakes me with one last look. "Sure I can't change your mind? Of course, I could if I wanted to. But hell, as far as I'm concerned, Bo's better off without you. Have fun with Nick when he comes. And he *will* come." In a stunningly fast whirl of white, he transforms, leaping from the edge of the windswept bluff and into the salt air.

I've never seen Bo turn the same miracle, not really. The times I've been with him when he's Risen, I've been too close to truly see him. I've been in his arms.

I want to be there now. But I'm finally starting to understand. Wanting Bo is a lie.

A smattering of raindrops hits my face. Jordan is a speck in the sky. And there's something else—something not in the sky, something missing from the sky.

The flash of the lighthouse beam.

Hurrying inside, I climb the steps of the tower then scale the ladder to the lantern room. Sure enough, the light is dead. But it isn't the bulb, sitting like a sooty jewel in the crown of the prismatic lens. The electricity is out.

There might be boaters who need the bright beacon this afternoon. *Why hasn't the emergency generator kicked on?*

But maybe this isn't an emergency—maybe it just feels like one to me. My own personal emergency.

The moon is going to be full tonight, but even a Hunter's Moon won't be enough to help a boat in trouble, and it'll make the high tide even higher. A Blood Moon—the other name for a full October moon—that doesn't sound like it can help anyone either.

Now, in my bedroom, I stand in the center of the floor, feeling unmoored. Like the space is too big. The chances of a signal are zero, but I dig out my cell anyway.

There are messages, lots of them. Text bubbles stretch down the screen.

SARAH HISANO: Alyssa's at Maine Medical!

BOBBY FARLEY: Holyshit

SARAH HISANO: They flew her from emergency center on mainland she's not waking up

BOBBY FARLEY: Sheila coma?

SARAH HISANO: Yes coma

PETER HILL: Heard from my dad she has something weird

SARAH HISANO: Hypoxia

MARY GARRAHY: HYPOXEMIA

BOBBY FARLEY: Wtf is that

KEVIN EATON: Official name: high altitude pulmonary edema.

MARY GARRAHY: It's serious. Oxygen deprivation can cause brain damage.

PETER HILL: `Doesn't make sense rock hook is at sea level`

SARAH HISANO: `So? Sea level?`

KEVIN EATON: `She passed out at school. How did she wind up with something like altitude sickness?`

Mr. Premed is super smart. His question . . . could create a lot more questions.

Impatiently, I text Mary—

`I need to talk to you.`

But the text doesn't go through, and besides, the group message is an hour old. I need to go back down to the keeper's house, see if the electricity's working, call Mary from there.

And say what?

I close my eyes.

"She's not really a flirt," Mary told me one day on the patio at school as we watched Alyssa wriggling on some senior boy's lap. She said Alyssa barely knew him.

"O-kay," I said as Alyssa and the boy stood up and exchanged a hip-grinding kiss. "So, then, do you Mainers have a special word for what she's doing?"

"*I* don't use words like that," Mary said in mock shock. But then her expression became solemn. "I worry about her. I don't get it. Why so *many* guys?"

I hadn't replied. Hadn't really cared what Alyssa did, or why.

But now she's in a hospital in Portland.

Not only do I care, I'm the only one who knows what really happened to her.

DISSENT

I sit motionless on the edge of my bed.

Alyssa. What had she seen in Bo's eyes? Had she felt the tidal pull of him the way I do? Had she been *lured*? Have I?

In my mind, I see them, his body curving over hers, the two of them fitted to each other.

Humming softly, I try to push the sickening pictures away. And fail.

Bo . . .

The promise of light on the water, the yearning I feel when the late-afternoon sun slants through my bedroom window. When warm spring air blows gently on my skin.

That's not sickness. That's possibility. That's—Bo.

Please don't be true, please don't be true . . . The words become an endless loop. But I can't make a deal with God on this one, because it *is* true. The boy I'm in love with is . . . inhuman.

Of course I'd known. But there's "knowing," and there's *knowing.*

Had Bo *known* what it would be like to suck the breath from Alyssa's body?

I realize I believe he had.

Jumping up, I begin to pace—

The door swings open—

Bo and I stare at each other.

His hair is wild, his beautiful, otherworldly face haunted. Hunted. My immediate thought is, *Shouldn't he look healthier after nearly sucking the life out of someone?*

He takes a step toward me—

I take a step back.

"I see," he says.

"I—I didn't hear you. On the stairs."

"Of course not." He looks at me strangely.

No, of course not. He never makes a sound on the stairs, always seems to float just above them. His watery walk has fascinated me from the second I saw him. But right now? He seems more fire than water.

"Where have you been?" I blurt. "What are you going to do? The police, they were on their way to the school when I left."

"School." His laugh is a footnote. "What a weird place. I didn't mean to hang around. I just wanted to check out the radio station. And then . . ." His eyes are caliginous whirlpools. He turns and closes the door. Legs trembling, I sink down on the desk chair.

Bo purses his lips, glances at the bed. Normally we would both be on it.

"The police won't be a problem." He sits down in the armchair across from me. "They wouldn't recognize a clue to this kind of . . . crime if they found one. And that girl—"

"Alyssa." The fact that he doesn't know her name disgusts me.

"Alyssa." He shakes his head. "She won't remember. At least, I'm pretty sure she won't. If she does, she'll be scared. Confused. She'll think she's crazy. So she'll make something up."

"Confused like me? Do you think I'll make something up? Some excuse to forgive you?"

"Arion, I'm so sorry." He looks at me intently, as if he's listening to something.

I know he is. He's listening to the parts of me that no one else can hear. *But can he hear how afraid I am? Why I am talking about forgiveness? He tried to kill someone!*

Tears well in my eyes, which is understandable, unlike the words that burst from my lips now. "Why her? Why not me?"

"What the—how can you ask that?"

"She threw herself at you, I saw it, but *you*— Was her 'essence' so irresistible?"

Bo shakes his head, his expression baffled.

"It wasn't her 'sweet cloud of life,' then? Her 'honey mist'—isn't that how you described the breath to me once? *My* breath? You couldn't resist her body." Before I can say more, I walk to the window, press my forehead to the cool glass. I know perfectly well what I saw today. He didn't want her body. But the truth—I can't seem to hold it in my head. He almost killed Alyssa. And yet, I—I—

Can feel only *jealousy*.

He stands now and comes over to me, puts his hand on my shoulder—

The floodgates open. The current runs between us, a racing, pulsing thing. I desperately want to touch him too, want to kiss him.

But I shout, "Don't touch me!" and jerk out of his reach. I do this, when what I really want to do is throw myself at him, like Alyssa had.

This crazy desire to be with him, even after what he's done, and the misplaced jealousy—

Suddenly I understand.

"Your Siren Song—turn it off! Make it stop!"

"Arion, no, please. I didn't want to do it!"

"You didn't want to do what, kiss her? Feel her body against yours?" Crossing quickly to the door, not knowing where I'm going, I do know I'm being idiotic. Maybe if Bo were someone else, another boy, a *human* boy, these accusations would fit. But I know that what Bo did wasn't about lust—it was about *hunger*. *Need.* Only, again—it's like I can't keep that idea in my head, can only feel the sharp pangs of jealousy.

I burst into tears, trying to focus on reality. *I saw what he did!*

What he did. The slippery eel thought of it slithers to the far reaches of my mind.

It could be me next time. The idea lands hard inside me, then lifts off again—vanishing.

"You wanted her, you can't tell me you didn't, I saw the whole thing!" I bring my fingers to my lips, as if I could touch my words, as if, even after I've said them, I can catch them, mold and shape them into what I really want to say. *You nearly killed her!*

And then, finally, Bo's music quiets. His voice, too, is deadly quiet, as he asks me, "What is it that you want to say so badly, Arion?"

I feel his Siren spell slipping off of me, sliding over my skin almost, as if it's nothing but water, and I'm stepping out of a pool.

Before I speak, I will him to disappear, to leave and never come back. Then I take a breath. He doesn't flinch.

"If I hadn't stopped you—you would have *killed* her." But even as I regain control over my voice, my words, I lose it.

And that's when I say it.

"You're an animal."

The words ring out against the white walls. Time skids to a standstill.

Bo's eyes brighten.

The tears won't fall, though. Sirens. They can't cry.

He lifts his chin.

"Fine. I would have killed her. Is that what you want to hear? You stopped me, and I'm glad. I'm *grateful.* But yes, I would have killed her. And I would have enjoyed it."

I gasp. He looks at my mouth.

Then he gazes into my eyes, and for a split second, there's this moment, I can almost see it, something glimmering at the edge of my vision, something waiting, offstage, a moment of clarity, in which we can still step toward each other and save what we have—

But what we have isn't real.

For a heartbeat, as if remnants of his Siren Song still linger in me, I want him anyway.

And that sickens me—I'm sick.

"You knew, Ari." His voice is shaking. "You've always known. *I told you what I am.*"

"You told me, but—" What is *knowing*? Is there a brain in your gut? Because that's where I feel this, the truth of it.

"Like I said, I would have enjoyed killing her, would've been into it. Killing you—would bring me even more pleasure. Does that make you feel better?"

A choking sound escapes my lips. The ephemeral moment where anything can possibly be fixed between us, ever, evaporates.

"I'm not who you thought I was, am I?" His voice drops lower. "But you're right, you *are* confused. Lines are crossing for you. Music, friendship, sex . . . and what you know of Sirens. But *if you were a Siren*, you'd understand."

He walks toward me. *"If you were a Siren."* The words peal with warning.

"No!" I explode. But it isn't just the idea that he wants to Deepen me, that he thinks he can make that choice for me—against my will—that he can *take* my other choices *away*—

There is also this: fear. I feel it fully now. Finally.

"If you were a Siren."

The words echo in my head, as if the inside of my skull is a cavernous room. And other words reverberate as well—

"Music, friendship, sex." And I hear his music now, ramping up again. Feel the pull of him, through my fear.

And I want to grab him—want to kiss him. Want to lie down on the bed, let his pull take me like a riptide. I want his tongue in my mouth—want to fill myself with him, feel him in the dark void that's already forming at the thought of losing him, a chasm that's already beginning to split me in two. My body trembles with energy I can't control, but instead of crying out, *I* do *understand, I love you more than anything, I want you, don't ever leave,* I fight the feelings, and scream, "Get out! Get out, get *out*!" and start to shove him toward the door before his Song can overtake me.

"Wait! Arion, listen—" A burst of music seems to emanate from him, permeating me—

"No! That's not fair! I *won't* listen! To your music *or* your threats! Just *go*!"

I watch my hands on his chest, my fists, pushing, pushing, pushing him away—

His ocean eyes fill with sharp light. "Is this really what you want?"

"Yes! And *you* want something else! *Someone* else! *Get out!*"

I'm wrong, and I know it. He doesn't want Alyssa, *not that way*. But does it matter? Even with the river of induced jealousy coursing through me, even with Bo's Song in my ears—

I know he would have killed her if I hadn't been there. Know it in my gut, in my heart.

We're done.

I squeeze my eyes closed—and my throat burns, wears itself raw as I shriek, *"Get out,"* over and over again, even after he's gone.

RISING TIDE

A great clap of thunder shakes the sky, and I spin toward the windows—then back toward the door—fighting an almost physical compulsion to run down the stairs after Bo. My heart lurches in my chest as I grasp the doorframe— I feel sick. Dizzy, like I'm seasick. I feel heartbroken—because I'm lovesick.

Love. Sick.

I struggle against the pull of him, but I can't help it, I climb the stairs of the tower as quickly as I can. When I get to the watch room, I grab the binoculars from the floor. *I just need to see him one more time. Then I'll be done.* Imagining I'll see him striding away from the lighthouse, or heading toward the water or Summers Cove, I step outside onto the gallery deck—

The wind snatches the door from my hands, slamming it back against the bricks, and I throw an arm up against a brilliant burst of light—Maybe the storm won't last, maybe it will all blow over. But then my eyes adjust to the brightness. No, it's the sunlight that won't last. I've been fooled by a hole in the clouds. A menacing bruise of a cloudbank is moving in from the horizon—

"Arion!"

My name floats high on the wind. Even as rain splashes my face, my heart lifts.

Bo! How could I ever have told him to leave?

No. I had *to tell him to leave.*

"Arion!"

Wet hair plasters my face and my neck. Tangled with wind—his voice is hypnotic as ever.

"Arion, please!" The Call comes again, and again, like a chorus. Beautiful, sensual, words on the wind. *Where is he?* My limbs feel languid and strange. My skin grows warmer until I feel liquid, a part of the rain. I just want to *see* him. His voice . . . it's so dreamy, and dark—and different. *Oh, Bo . . .*

"Arion, help! Down here! I need help!"

Not possible, he'd never— Stumbling, I lift the binoculars up—

"Logan!" The name bursts from my lips, waking me, as if from a dream.

Logan Delaine is dangling off the side of a sport fishing boat tied to the seawall!

The boat tosses wildly in the waves—at any moment, it could be smashed to bits.

Pushing off the railing, I run for the door. The wind holds it fast. Heaving my weight backward, I haul the door open and race across the watch room.

Hurtling down the stairs, I try to make sense of what's happening. It should have been impossible to hear Logan's voice above the storm—and I can't imagine why he's down there.

Logan, what the hell are you doing? You idiot—get out of the water! Whose boat is that, where'd you get it? And Logan, your voice—

It feels like I've never heard it before.

GEMINI

Knives of rain stab at my face as I dive down the steps to the beach. Racing across the sand, I vault up onto the breakwater, tearing along the concrete path that tops the black granite boulders.

"Logan!" Black sheets of rain pound the roiling sea. The fishing boat spins in the water.

The full moon won't rise until tonight, but already it pulls on the Atlantic. Monstrous waves lash at the seawall. Dodging under the rail at the end of the path, I navigate the uneven tops of the rocks, crouching down, crawling now, leaning into the wind as I work my way toward the boat. A wave breaks on the rocks in front of me, spraying water five feet into the air, nearly toppling me off the wall. Another wave hits, soaking me—

Logan is no longer visible.

Panic explodes in my gut as if someone's landed a kick there. I scream out his name—

The wind throws it back in my face. *Where is he?* Was he forced from the boat by the waves?

A giant breaker roars up over the rocks—for a second I'm blinded by a wall of water. The wind tears at my clothes as I make my way to my feet, trying to get a better view of the boat.

How is he keeping it tied to the seawall? The Coast Guard—why didn't I phone them?

A curling wave breaks over me, knocking me to my knees. Briny water burns my throat as a mouthful goes down. I gag, fighting the water like a drowning person.

A snarling wave pushes the boat closer— *Luck!* The wall isn't much higher than the deck; I just need to jump out, clear the rocks along the side. The next wave brings the boat nearer still. I take a deep breath—

And jump.

Landing on the slick deck of the fishing boat, I run to the far side where I last saw Logan, shouting his name uselessly into the wind—

Then I hear it. *The humming.* With a sound like a Doppler shift, ominous music fills my ears—*the ethereal songs of my nightmares.*

I cry out as the aural hallucinations vibrate inside me somehow, as real as the rain that pelts my skin. Fantastically orchestrated melodies, spectral harmonies familiar only from the dreams that have recently become so vivid—

I cry out once more as I see him.

And for a moment, the raindrops stall in midair. The ocean, impossibly, stills.

His face is as familiar as the music.

As familiar as the first time I saw it.

Moving as smoothly as a shadow, he emerges from the ocean, lifting himself halfway up the side of the boat with muscled arms, his dark skin dripping seawater.

Logan.

But—*not Logan.*

Hanging off the boat, the lower half of his body submerged in the rough sea, is a boy with the same face, the same dark brows and shadowed jawline, and now, spreading slowly across that face, the same wide white smile.

This boy is almost unbearably beautiful, but he is not Logan. He is not my friend, my sulking, laughing Logan, with the rainy-day eyes. At the realization, I gasp for breath—

But there's none to be had. There's only water where the air should be—

And I can barely choke out his name.

SIREN

"Nick."

"Arion." His tone is casual, his voice—*sublime.*

It's as if the stars have fallen from the sky. Fallen and found a home, in him.

His grin grows but doesn't reach his silvery eyes.

We stare at each other as the storm slaps the sea.

"So nice to finally meet you face-to-face," he says. His eyes glint with dark humor. "Join me in the drink?"

With one hand, he reaches for me—

And then—I'm in the sea.

His hands circling my waist, he holds me above the waterline. But even with most of my torso out of the water, the waves crash mercilessly against me.

They seem to roll off Nick as if his dark, gleaming skin repels them.

Moving his hands to my hips now, he lifts me slightly higher, the tips of his thumbs pressing low on my pelvis, and to my horror, I find that *nothing* about him repels *me*.

I close my eyes, or rather, they simply shut—

I don't have the will to keep them open. Don't have a will at all.

His music is profound—a work of art that will endure forever. At the same time, it's a forgotten song, the music of antediluvian rituals. There's the rhythm now: *Step, stop. Step; stop.*

He draws me closer, until my body is against his—

And I don't care if I live or die—as long as I can be with him now.

He, too, is halfway out of the water, floating effortlessly in the whirling waves. Projected onto the inside of my eyelids is the image of his torso. Broad shoulders, a flat stomach with muscles that ripple like waves on a quieter day.

In my mind's eye I stare at his hip bones, then look slightly lower. No shimmering scales, and yet—

He is the man from my nightmares.

"I thought you were Logan," I mumble, a blissful fog filling my mind. "You look just like him—how?" My voice doesn't stand a chance against the wind, but still he answers—

"Twins."

Even with my eyes closed, I know he's smiling. I hear the curl of it.

Feeling the pull of him now, I'm more than ready. *I am waiting.*

And just like that—I know. It's him. The details—they don't matter. Nothing matters.

I am waiting. And he is waiting.

I turn my head—

He places his full lips on mine. Quick as a flash of light, the thought of Bo crosses my mind—

Then burns away under the kiss of the Siren.

Our bodies snake together, curve and crevice, neck and arm, waist and hands—hands . . .

He draws back—

That only makes me want him more.

But suddenly he laughs, and my eyes fly open to see him lifting his face to the black sky.

"Your breath *is* sweet, intoxicating, even, but this is far too easy. Where is he? Your ever-present hero." Nick's sterling eyes skim the surface of the sea. Scan the sky.

The heat of his body clashes with the cold of the sea. Will I die burning in his arms? Or will the well-earned hypothermia finally claim me?

I don't care, but through a nebula of lust I wonder, *Bo, will I ever see you again?*

Nick's head jerks down and his eyes burn into mine. "You're Calling him!"

The words seem to echo out over the water, reverberating inside me, and something in the tone of his voice—or maybe the words themselves—break the Siren's spell—

Nick Delaine is holding me—Nick Delaine is a killer!

"I don't know what you mean," I sputter. Bitter anger crawls up my throat like bile. Of course I want to live! *Have* to live.

"You do know. Go ahead! Draw him here, and I'll kill you both!" With a sound like the highest tide thundering in, immense white wings emerge on either side of his torso, branching above us. The water turns to turbulent froth as he kicks—

And lifts me into the air.

He sweeps me through the sky, holding me tightly along the length of his body, his low laugh filling my ears. In an instant we're at the top of the lighthouse where he sets me down roughly on the wet deck and I slip, nearly fall. As I regain my footing, I instinctively press my back against the white bricks of the tower. He watches me with mercury eyes as my gaze darts to the door that leads inside. The storm rages around us.

My gaze slips to his hips. His legs, where they emerge from a frayed pair of shorts strewn with sand and bits of kelp, are powerful looking—

There's no trace of the snakelike appendage from my nightmares.

"Not as pretty as a Summers boy, but maybe I know better what you want." He steps closer, his hands moving to the top of his shorts, his voice hissing beneath the sound of the storm. *"Something serpentine."*

"You're horrible—crude!" But I haven't forgotten the most recent dream, the humiliating craving. It makes partial sense. My subconscious had kept the truth from me, the dark chimerical being who visited my dreams looked like Logan. He looked like Logan *but was Nick*. Nick—*he'd been in my room*. And the wings, they'd been his—

"Crude? You're about to *die*, and you're worried about manners? Oh, Miss Arion, I've been *so* polite, gone *so* slowly. I could have had you on the cliff, or at Seal Cove. Or Smith Street—you were practically home. I could've taken you the rest of the way. *I still can.*"

"No!" My heart thuds against my ribs.

The Siren comes closer. "How does the expression go? Whatever doesn't kill you makes you—?" His low voice is an invasive vine, coiling, twining inside me. I can't speak. "Arion, don't *be* like that, play along."

"Stronger," I manage to stutter. "Whatever doesn't kill you makes you stronger."

He clicks his tongue. "That's not it at all." It seems as if his cinereous eyes might start a fire. "The expression," he says, his lips near my ear, "is whatever doesn't kill you, *makes you scream*."

A branch-like bolt of lightning electrifies the sky. He laughs. "It's the screams, *during* the screams, that's when a victim's breath is sweetest. I love the screams of women—they're so delicious. But men have a greater lung capacity, so sometimes I prefer them. Men, women, boys, girls—I like to *make* them scream, or"—he tilts his head to one side—"simply *knock* the wind out of them."

He shrugs. "I enjoy dropping people from high places. When they hit the water, or the ground, out comes the breath—in a big whoosh." He smiles—Logan's smile—and fingers a lock of my hair. His dark hair is a tangle of wild tendrils, mossy seaweed twisted among the long strands. "Like a seagull dropping a clam on a jetty. You must have seen gulls dropping shells on that seawall of yours?" He looks down past the edge of the platform, then brings his mouth close to mine. *"Smash,"* he whispers. I feel his breath on my lips.

"Do you like watching the gulls, Arion? I used to enjoy watching the birds on the beach by my house, I used to enjoy lots of things—*when I was human*." His last words seethe with anger, hatred. It's obvious he hates himself, hates his "condition," but most of all *he hates the Summers*, and finally, I truly understand why. *They did this to him.*

"What do *you* enjoy, Arion? Besides cockteasing my brother?" Shock must have shown on my face. "Oh, I know all about you and my twin. But do you know about Logan and *my* girlfriend? My brother's a charmer, but be warned, he'll break your heart."

My entire body is quivering with fear, but I can't help being fascinated by the number of misunderstandings that have taken place. Does Nick Delaine really think Logan is to blame for Beth falling in love with him? Does he truly believe Bo and his family are responsible for *killing him*? *They saved his life!* I start to shake my head. He misreads me.

"No, you can't tell me differently; I've been listening to you for weeks and weeks. So I know what *you* want. And girls love my brother, same way they loved me.

"But Summers seems to think *he* has your heart." Nick places a hand on my chest, working his fingers into the loose weave of the wet wool, already stretched far beyond its original shape. "Bo Summers. That voice. But Bo's holding back, isn't he? He has to. My brother, he'd give you everything. I know him. But it's understandable, why you're—*torn*." He yanks the sweater until the neckline plunges. Slowly, he trails his fingers up to the hollow of my throat.

His hands are intelligent looking, beautiful, like his face. Logan's face. Logan's hands. He brings his hands to my shoulders now—squeezes, releases—*an expression of indecision?* Hope soars inside me.

Then he tugs on the silver chain, lifts the pearl. A strange smile crosses his lips.

"Seems you've recently decided on Bo, but you may change your mind. The two of them really are so different from each other." He stares at me. "But you're so very different yourself, Arion. Where did you get your Siren Song?"

His metallic gaze moves to my mouth. My hope blows away on the wind.

"You intrigue me," he says. "When I pushed you from the cliff, were you considering suicide? Hmm? Because you went over the edge so *very* easily—just the touch of a feather, one soft feather of mine." He brings his wings forward, crossing his arms, running his fingers through the tips of the lustrous feathers. "Just one, against your cheek, a whisper of something silky, and over you went."

"You—" But I bring my trembling voice up short, because suddenly, Nick's eyes actually seem to *see* me, and I can see him, the man inside a monster—the boy.

"Your singing was so sweet as you took your little nature walk, then stood atop the cliff looking, and looking . . . but when you fell, *nothing*. I've never seen anything like it, not in this entire long year I've spent in *hell!*" His eyes seem to catch fire now, burning white hot—and just like that, the man is gone, and there's only the monster. He puts his hands around my neck.

"No scream," he hisses. "No cry." He shakes his head. "Very disappointing. Then your boyfriend leapt up out of the sea, like some damned dolphin. Of course he wasn't your boyfriend yet, was he? He took his time there, and you *know* why. He was afraid of what he'd *do* to you. Same thing I'd like to do." His fingers tighten and he scowls. "I had no idea he was nearby that day. You've twisted my Siren senses more than once, Arion Rush.

"You—you and Bo. You should both thank me, don't you think? I played matchmaker—*and now you both have so much more to lose!*

Without my little nudge, your paths might never have crossed. Or maybe they would have. He was listening to you, wasn't he? Oh, right—that's why he didn't hear *me* for so long!" He pushes me away.

I fall—then manage to right myself. But even in my panic, I recognize the truth. Because of me, Bo had been distracted. He didn't pick up Nick's Signal until it was too late, until the boys from the *Lucky* were gone, until the kayakers' dead bodies were left posed like puppets on the Summers' property.

My teeth rattle like the bones I'll become. Or will they be smashed in the fall this time? Clearly, Nick intends to drop me from the gallery deck.

"Fortunately for me, your boyfriend's busy today. So we can try again."

"Not without a fight." I clutch my wet sweater to my soaking skin.

"That sounds fun—but slightly unrealistic." He gives a short laugh. Logan's laugh, when something isn't funny. "I want you to try a little harder this time. Just give yourself over, the way you do when you sing, when you play your guitar. Don't look so surprised. The air current is sweet outside your window. I like to float, and *watch*. So what do you think the big secret is, about music? Can it save your soul? A soul," he muses. "Do you think I still have one of those?"

He doesn't wait for an answer. "I'll stay close this time, my lips on yours . . . all the way down." He runs his thumb across my mouth, and his voice grows rough. "A little practice? So we do it right this time." Then his lips are on mine. My efforts to push him away are nothing. He simply leans in—the weight of his body crushing me against the wet wall. His tongue slips between my lips—

Instantly I feel *the pressure*. A painful sucking, starting in my throat, becoming a terrifying tightness in my chest. I try to kick, move my arms—but Nick has me pinned to the bricks. My eyelids flutter shut.

My heart is racing, my mind searching—

But there's no answer. Pinpoints of light dart in the dark behind my lowered lids . . .

He jerks his mouth away—sagging against me, his hands still gripping my hips. I gasp for breath.

"How does he do it? How does Summers stop—and leave you with your life?"

My splotchy vision clears and I meet his eyes, the crashing waves of silver and black—

Suddenly he grabs my wrist. "I'm going to take you now—*are you ready?*"

And, as if I'm as light as one of the feathers from the wings he caressed so sensually, he lifts me high above his head—

And throws me to the wind.

And this time as I fall, I do what he wants.

I scream.

BLACK SEA

A heartbeat later, Nick's body slams into mine—

He clamps onto me, viselike.

His wings move faster as he takes control of the rate at which we fall, his arms and legs bars of a cage that surrounds me. We slow slightly—

And he covers my mouth with his.

Squeezing my lips closed, I try to turn my head— But he holds me with one arm, bringing his fingers to my mouth, prying it open, shoving his tongue in. *Pressure.*

It feels like my lungs will explode—or collapse.

Earlier Nick mentioned hell. Now I'm sharing it with him.

My mind splits off . . . I'm singing in the church choir, dragging palm fronds down the aisle. Sparse a cappella melodies mingle with the medieval harmonies . . . *All the singing I've done . . . won't give me the extra breath I need to live through this.*

Each day we breathe about twenty-five thousand times, maybe thirty thousand . . . *the sucking sensation, it hurts.* My thoughts start to stumble over one another as my brain becomes deprived of oxygen. *Breaths come in pairs . . . except for the first breath, and the last.*

But what's another breath or two? The fall is sure to kill me.

I close my eyes. *The last thing I see will* not *be Nick Delaine with his maniacal eyes shining like the moon—the moon, spinning out of orbit.* Instead I picture Bo's face, marveling for one last time how his eyes hold the sun at their centers . . . the sun, surrounded by water, the deep greens and blues of the sea . . . the sea . . . is black.

BREAKWATER

Half in, half out of the stormy Atlantic, I cling to the breakwater. Waves crash against my back. Desperately trying to catch my breath, I clutch at the crevices of the wet black boulders, the rain stinging my face. On my right hang the remnants of an old lobster trap. To my left is a crab trap, a disintegrating fish head tied at the center.

That's why he left me alive—I'm bait. Bait for Bo.

Killing me isn't enough. It never has been, or I'd be dead by now. Jordan was right, I'm one of the birds. But more importantly to Nick, more horribly, I am the stone.

Bo. I told him to leave, and I meant it. I can't be with him—not anymore. But I also can't help hoping he doesn't fall for Nick's trap. I don't want him to die, no matter what he's done, and I have no doubt that Nick intends to kill him.

With an intense effort, I haul myself up—one rock, then another, clinging, climbing. Partway out of the water, now all the way out, I will myself to crawl up the side of the soaking seawall. It feels as if I'm dragging my body behind me, that I'm somehow a foot or two in front of myself, looking back on a burden, this body, so numb it no longer seems like my own.

Nick's body is half man, half angel. His mind belongs to a beast. *Where is he?*

My arms tremble—I can hardly feel my feet. But I continue to climb, the sharp edges of the rocks slicing my hands. Even though I can't see it in the rain, the path that runs along the top of the breakwater can't be far above me now. Uttering a string of obscenities plus a prayer, I stagger to my feet. My ribs feel bruised—or broken. Every breath jabs like a knife.

The path is an inch out of reach now, the rail just above it.

Flinging my arms up—

I grasp at the air. My palms slap down hard on the wet granite as I fall—my left ankle catching between two rocks. For a second, I give up, one leg bent beneath me, the other trapped.

Leaning my forehead against the granite, I don't know which is colder, my skin or the unyielding stone. Then the wind screams—and I yank my leg free with a cry of my own.

Scanning the sky for Nick, I assess the jagged gash in my calf just above the edge of my boot. The cut is bleeding heavily. Struggling to stand, I put my weight on the leg and yelp—but finally, reach the top.

Flash. In the dark of the day, the beam of the lighthouse cuts through the clouds. But how is that possible when—

No, the light comes from the end of the seawall—*Bo!*

The storm mimics midnight. Silhouetted against the black sky, Bo looks luminous. His back is to me, his great wings extended as he battles the Cimmerian creature who Called to me so convincingly, and in so many ways.

But it's *my* Song—my swan song—that's lured Bo here today, just like Nick planned.

And knowing that, I can't run. Bo's saved me more than once from this same monster—in return, I suspected him, feared him, and doubted his love. Even now his stunning Song fills my ears, my very veins. Maybe Jordan is right about this too—maybe I've reached the point where I can't live without Bo's Song. Or maybe I love him. Despite what he is, despite that we're over. No matter the reason, *I have* to do *something*.

Can I distract Nick? He said my Song had thrown off his Siren senses before.

Planting my feet, I stare into his sterling eyes, willing my own eyes to blaze. Adrenaline fills me and I open my mouth, screaming into the wind—

"Stop!" My voice tears through the air—

Then dissolves into sky, into clouds so thick they look like roiling smoke.

My gift, my Song, is nothing compared to the hatred of Nick Delaine, whose eyes flash like a blade now as they lock onto mine. And this time, instead of feeling his gravitational pull drawing me toward him, the invisible will of his terrible Siren Song *pushes me back*.

Sliding toward the edge of the seawall, I lean forward, trying to resist—

He and Bo continue their combat, two strange angels. Wings moving at odd angles, sharp, misguided scissors. Their Songs sound as if they've been orchestrated by the sea and the soaking sky, a merciless sky, that continues to dump rain so cold it feels like ice, on a sea so unpredictably wild, it serves as a mirror for this unforgiving Siren *who will not stop until he kills one of the only boys who could be like a brother to him*. It's true; who else can understand Nick at this point? Logan wouldn't recognize him as his brother if he saw him now.

If only Nick had waited, if only he'd let the Summers save him—save him completely. If only he hadn't fled from the one family he can ever really belong to. But in his fury he bolted, only to return in order to destroy Bo's life, and mine, which will in turn wreck the lives of our families. I can't let it happen.

"Nick!" I shout.

"Ari!" Bo's voice trails over his shoulder. "Get back!"

But I can't move. Is it Nick's spell? Or am I simply too saturated with seawater and despair?

Nick's mouth curls at one corner. His Song sings under my skin.

My faith begins to fail. How can we win against Nick Delaine? I've looked into his eyes—I'm looking now. The annihilating rage is there. He's a murderer.

Sheets of rain lash my face, but it isn't the pain that makes me cry.

This is how we'll die.

A bolt of lightning cracks the sky, and a peal of thunder rolls across the water. Then, for a split second, there's a lull in the storm.

"Nick, *please*." The words slip through my lips, two notes of an unwritten hymn.

Amid the chaos of their terrible dance, Nick's black-ice eyes keep me captive. But he says nothing. And when Bo risks a quick glance over his shoulder at me— Nick slams a fist into his face.

Blood gushing from his lip, Bo stumbles—

With both hands, Nick grabs his head. Slams it to the stone beneath their feet.

"Bo!" I strain against the invisible bonds. "Please! Nick! Please don't hurt him!"

Nick's gaze holds steady, flares bright—

Then, amazingly, the current between us shifts. The forceful energy pushing against me doesn't stop completely, but it lightens, like the ocean at a time when the tide is neither ebbing nor flowing but slack, about to turn.

He's changing his mind. He's going to let us go! I suddenly wonder—if we'd met before, when Nick had been human, when he'd been Logan's twin—*Would we have been friends?*

But Nick laughs now. Swings again at Bo—

Who's on his feet, and this time dodges Nick's flying fist, springing at the silver-eyed Siren—*a flashing blade in one hand.* His other hand is a fist that connects with Nick's jaw—

Bo thrusts the knife—

And misses.

Nick doesn't waste time. He grabs Bo's outthrust arm, twisting it up—forcing Bo to his knees and the knife from his hand—

The weapon spins through the air then clatters on the granite, jouncing, tumbling, and finally catching in a crevice midway between us. Then Nick is on his knees as well, bending Bo backward, sealing Bo's lips with his own—

"No!" I scream.

Bo's hands fly to Nick's throat—then both boys are prone. They roll over and over as I leap toward them—

But Nick pins Bo beneath him, and all at once they go still. I scream again.

Bo's hands drop from around Nick's neck—

His legs go limp.

Even as I shout, *"No, no, no!"* other words—my own words to Bo—ring in my head: *"Maybe you could kill someone if your life were being threatened, but wouldn't we all? If we possessed the skill and the strength and our lives were at stake? Anyone would kill, to live."*

My life *is* being threatened—I can't deny it, and as Bo's Song vanishes like morning mist over the sea, I feel as if *I* might disappear as well, might die from the loss of it, of him, if Nick doesn't kill me first. *Bo!* But I can't help Bo—I can only save myself. My strength is nothing compared to Nick Delaine's, and I don't have the skill—

But I have a knife. It shines at my feet.

And all at once, I remember. I've seen it before. Held it. Begged Bo not to carry it.

But that was in another life. Lightning glints off the blade now, off the slim handle slick with rain. And as Nick comes reeling toward me drunk with Bo's breath, I swiftly scoop it up.

He laughs when he sees me holding the weapon. "This was never your fight. And besides"—his full lips push into a pout—"I don't want to ruin my dessert." He laughs again, Logan's grin on his face, his head tipping back—

Which is why he doesn't see the blade coming.

And if a wall of water hadn't slapped my back, maybe I wouldn't have moved at that very moment, but I did move—I'm moving now, propelled by the Atlantic, and wondering—*wondering* in this split second that stretches into an endless eternity—*where to aim the knife.*

But then in my mind's eye I see Jordan's hand coming down on his thigh—hear the *smack* of it, loud as a gunshot in my memory's remix—and I know. The windpipe.

Surely to slice it will take Nick's breath more quickly even than a Siren's kiss.

FREEDIVERS

The hand that knocks me from the seawall is bloody—Nick's hand.

My forward momentum sank the knife deep into his throat—

But he still had some momentum of his own.

My shoulder strikes rock. My back—slaps water. Then the sea—

Swallows me.

My heart thrums in my chest. Swim *up*, swim *up*, swim *up*—

But the water is frigid, and I'm exhausted.

Too *late,* too *late*— My pulse beats a frantic rhythm, as I sink . . .

Into darkness . . .

Until I'm back in San Francisco, with Lilah, the bright turquoise of the public pool surrounding us. Diving in the deep end, wearing underwater smiles. She makes it to the bottom first, like always.

We swim one lap together, two— Lilah pulls ahead—always ahead—and vanishes.

Now my body is a submarine, lost on maneuvers. My heart is a butterfly, caught in the net of my body. My heart . . . is a rhythmic tattoo, fading . . .

The blackness behind my closed eyes becomes an infinite space. I gaze into the inky darkness . . . find a theater stage, velvet curtains drawn open to reveal a black screen.

Pictures appear. Lilah, Mom, Dad . . .

Images form faster now, flickering on the screen . . . more family, and friends. Mary, and Logan. *I'm so sorry, Logan.* Further back now, steep streets, in our old neighborhood, blue skies and boats, Mom and Dad, holding hands, running on the black sand of Stinson Beach.

Beach—sand. Ocean—*water.*

Please, let it be quick.

But my body falls slowly, drifting through watery twilight.

My hair floats around my face in a dark cloud, like the tentacles of a jellyfish swirling around itself. My tears are the sea . . .

The curtain closes now. Darkness descends . . .

Nighttime, time for sleep . . .

Only suddenly, I feel heat, and a petal-soft scalding touch—the *sun*—on my mouth.

I try to open my eyes—

No longer know how.

I'm dreaming. No, dying.

The sun presses against my mouth more urgently now, until my lips part, and warmth surges through me, springtime entering me. A breeze from a hot summer day swells my lungs with sweetness, fills them with air impossibly fragrant with grass, sea spray, and flowers. I breathe in rosemary and sage—the desert, after rain. I inhale deeply—feeling a sort of shock that I can, but it's a buffered, far-off feeling, surreal as the scent of sun-warmed pine needles and August evenings.

Breathe. I hear the word in my head, and open my eyes.

He surges away from me, and I follow, mesmerized by his beauty, by the tiny beads of water covering his body, catching what little light there is. His wings have transformed, have become like the undulating fins of a fish. Nearly translucent, they shine with a subtle rainbow of iridescence and sway with each movement of the current. Above us, the storm may still be raging, but down here, the water is calm. Peaceful.

Will my wings look like his?

Like him, I'm able to breathe underwater. When he spins toward me, possibly to make sure I'm following, his hair drags across his face, rippling like seaweed. I mouth, *How?*

But even as I ask, I realize—we're connected. There's no need to articulate my questions by forming words with my lips; words aren't necessary—the water is once again our conduit.

I'm confused, though, by the darkness of his thoughts, by my inability to comprehend them all, by so much—static.

But he holds out a hand to me—and this I understand. Staring at his diaphanous appendages, his animal beauty, I take it.

Through the hair that drapes his face, his eyes are two dark mirrors reflecting the sea. A sea that is such a dark green at this depth, it appears almost black.

And yet it teems with life. Schools of fish glide by—scaled bodies smooth and supple. I imagine swimming off . . . marvel at his torso instead, as he tugs me along behind him now, my attention torn between the strange world around me and his graceful, nearly naked form. His shoulders look broader, stronger, than ever.

But— *Oh!* A strangled cry issues from my lips along with a stream of bubbles. My lungs feel tight, a horrid sensation. A sharp pain causes me to bring my hands to my rib cage. I squeeze my eyes closed.

He tightens his grip on my hand, and we begin to ascend faster, pausing every few feet so he can blow his honeyed breath into my mouth. But the sharp pains continue. *Diver's disease? The bends?* In the back of my mind, I hear Jordan Summers' words. *"I lost her. I never even had a chance to begin the Deepening."* Then I remember another scrap of the same conversation:

"How exactly does Deepening work?"

"Or not work." Bo's words.

He pulls me faster through the darkness.

He sent the first sweet breath into my lungs, and my senses exploded, expanded, but now, in the reverse, they begin to shut down, a lotus flower, closing at dusk. I open my eyes, but my vision fails. Then, I can't hear, can't hear anything except my heartbeat, loud and slowing in my ears.

Until there is nothing . . .

Except his hand . . .

Holding mine . . .

Then even the sensation of his touch is gone, and all that remains is a futile feeling, that the vast body of water washing over me is winning, and that I've lost.

That he—has lost me.

BLINK; FLASH

Cloth slides over my skin.

Not water, cloth.

Cotton sheets, on a bed.

"Arion?"

Mia's voice. More sharp-edged than I remember. *Broken.*

Slowly, I blink my eyes open.

The light in the room is bright—too bright.

"The silver apples of the moon, the golden apples of the sun."

I close my eyes.

KILLER

"... Neptune knows if she'll ..."

Voices. My senses wing around my body, checking like an anxious parent. Hands? Okay. Spine? Fine. Throat. Raw. I try to speak—my eyes snap open.

Mia stands next to the bed gazing down at me, her eyes like the winter sea.

"Lilah—" My voice is a dry rasp, and in my gut—a strange hollowness. "Is she here?"

"She's at the lighthouse with your mother. They know you're with us."

"I've got to go—"

"The storm delayed their flight—it's Tuesday. Their plane didn't get to Bangor until yesterday afternoon. I left your father a message last night. I told him you fell asleep over here, while you were waiting for them to return."

I am waiting.

I try to sit up—

Pain fires through my chest.

Mia pushes me back on the pillows. "It's too soon," she says shortly. She's holding something else back besides me.

"The seawall." Pain shoots through my limbs. "Bo. He heard my Call. He came—"

"Nick Delaine got his last wish, then, didn't he?"

Not quite. Because as beaten as Bo looked on the breakwater, he survived.

But I just nod, staring past Mia at the floor-to-ceiling bookshelves on the far side of the room. They're overflowing with CDs. But besides the shelves and the bed I'm lying in, the space is empty. It's like whoever lives here hasn't unpacked yet, or is about to leave. Still it's a deeply welcoming space. Late-afternoon sun fills even the corners with glowing amber.

I'm in Bo's room, in his bed. I feel my whole body relax.

But then my stomach twists.

We're safe—because I killed Nick Delaine.

Black water closes over my head.

DRUG

Music can be a seductive thing. *Sexy.*

Music can fill a need. *Addictive.*

Music can be a mind-numbing, soul-numbing, heart-numbing drug. *Anesthetic.*

An hour? A day? A week? In my dreams, I hear singing. Hear Sirens.

When I wake, Mia is once again standing over me.

"How are you feeling?"

"I'm fine," I lie. It hurts to breathe; plus, a flood of questions is threatening to drown me.

She simply nods, Bo's nod. I'm about to ask where he is, when she says, "Really?"

Apparently coming close to death hasn't made me a better liar.

Then she begins to sing, and reality becomes a flickering thing . . .

Time is fluid . . . Time is stuck. But then I wake again, and think—*There is no time. I have to get home.*

"Wait." This time it's Cord. His face is so pale the smattering of freckles across his nose stands out in sharp relief. "This won't hurt a bit." While singing what he tells me is an ancient Welsh melody, he puts thirty-three stitches in my calf. I don't feel even one of them. In fact—I don't feel anything.

As he watches me hobble into the living room, the side of his mouth lifts in a wobbly grin.

"Now I have an excuse," I say, testing my weight on the wounded leg. "For why I didn't run home right away. My folks will easily believe I did this on the jetty between our beaches."

"Lying like a Siren. C'mon. I'll drive you."

"You're not old enough to drive," I scoff. "Where's Bo?"

Cord blinks. Then all at once his face crumples.

"What's wrong?" I grab his arm. "Cord, where's Bo?"

"He's—gone."

At the same moment Cord chokes out these words, a tall man strides through the front door of the cottage. He has to be Professor Summers. His eyes are the same blue green as Bo's—except they lack the flare of gold and instead gleam with the cold fire of phosphorescence.

He studies me with a detached air, and the edges of my vision seem to darken.

"What do you mean, *gone*?" I manage to rasp out.

Jordan appears in the doorway behind his father. Backlit by the afternoon light reflecting off the ocean, he's nothing but a dark silhouette. He must have just come from the water; droplets cling to his skin, the sun hitting them so they shine, highlighting his broad shoulders—

Shoulders broader, stronger, than Bo's.

The shoulders I'd been looking at as I was pulled to safety.

"No!" I cry out. "No! *Bo* came to me under the waves. Bo—blew magic into my mouth!" Frantic now, I look around the room. Bo's family watches me with their Siren eyes. I jab a finger toward Mia. "You—you were singing! And Cord. How can you sing, if, if—"

"How can we not?" she answers coolly.

It can't be true. *It can't be true, it can't be true, it can't be true!*

But the Sirens aren't lying. Not this time. Bo hadn't lost me. I'd lost him. And it was Jordan, with his dark eyes, his wild hair washing across his face, who had saved my life, not Bo. I'd just been too disoriented to realize it.

"I—I want to see him. I want to see Bo! I don't believe he's dead. I want to see his body!"

"You can't," Mia snaps. "The sea took it."

THRESHOLD

Cord follows me outside where I sink onto the sand, staring with disbelief at the sea, hating it.

He says, "My Song, Mia's—they'll hold for a while. You'll be okay. But you'd better let me take you home. Your folks have probably been worrying about you. They know you're here, but still."

Too shocked to speak, I only look up at him. He extends his hand, and finally, I take it.

But my parents aren't worried, not about me.

"Hello?" I holler as I come through the front door. There's a wheelchair in the hall.

"We're in here," Dad answers softly from the bedroom at the back of the cottage.

Lilah is lying in his bed, sleeping, her raven hair strewn across the pillows. My parents are sitting on chairs they've brought in from the kitchen and—there's something wrong with Dad's face. His mouth looks—small, his eyes nearly lost in the swollen folds of skin that surround them. Mom's eyes are like a wall of bluestone.

"What is it?" I ask. "What happened?" My parents look at each other. "Tell me!"

"*Shh,* Arion. Nothing happened. I mean, not here. It's—" Mom breaks off. Bending down to hug her, I take a closer look at Lilah. It doesn't look like there's anything wrong with her. Of course I know there is. But I don't know everything apparently.

"Sweetie." Dad takes my hand. "Lilah . . . isn't going to have the procedure next month."

"What? Why not?" I yank my hand away, bring it to my stomach.

"When your mom phoned and said she was coming for a visit and bringing Lilah, she . . . told me a few things. None of them good." He wipes at his eyes.

"What things?" He *had* been sick, *heartsick*. "What *things*? Just tell me! Mom?"

"Arion." Mom closes her eyes. "We're going to lose Delilah."

"What? No! What are you talking about?"

"Ari, your mom's trying to tell you, we're going to have to say goodbye to her."

"To Lilah? Why?" My attention ricochets back and forth between my parents. *"Why?"*

"About ten days ago Lilah had an MRI," Dad says. "She'd been, well . . ." Dad looks questioningly at Mom.

"Behaving differently," Mom says. There's a choppiness to her voice. "She—she was still . . . in her own world much of the time, but . . . she was acting differently."

"Acting differently how? What was she doing?"

"It doesn't matter, Arion. I decided she should get another scan. I—I wasn't so sure that the surgery was the best idea anymore and—your dad was here. I just went ahead. Scheduled the MRI. It showed some blood clots. In her brain. There's nothing they can do. The clots are . . . precarious. Any type of procedure, even something exploratory . . . could kill her."

Mom looks like she wants to hit something. Then her shoulders slump. "They said discovering the clots was like finding a . . . a series of land mines. She has a few months, maybe less. She's going to die, Ari."

"But—" MRI results? Some technician reading an MRI? That's all it took, after all this time? "They *have* to operate. Then she'll come back, from wherever she is. She can't *die*! They're wrong!" My shoulder slams into the doorframe as I spin around and run from the room.

Out in the living room, I dial Summers Cove, then wonder why. Why am I calling? *Bo's dead. And Lilah—this can't be happening.* I still have the receiver pressed to my ear when Jordan bursts through the door, his eyes pools of night. Dressed only in jeans, he has a T-shirt clutched in one hand. He grabs the phone out of my hand and tosses it on the table, pulling me outside.

"What is it? Your Signals, they're spiking. Cord's Song, Mia's, they should have—"

His obvious concern floors me, but I don't give a damn about any Songs. "It's my sister. She, she—" I tell him everything, can't stop the flood of words. When I'm finished, the only sound is my jagged breathing, strangely syncopated with the wash of the waves hitting the seawall. It's that sound—the sound of the ocean entwined with my breathing—that makes me think of Bo, that makes me suddenly ask Jordan, "Why are you here? Why don't you hate me?"

"I do." A searing melody invades my head, Nine Inch Nails in every sense, pinning me in place. "You must know by now I'd like nothing better than to empty you." Abruptly the music stops. "But I loved my brother, and he would have wanted—forget it. You have another question. Ask it."

But I hesitate. It's as if one of the cold waves has made its way up from the sea and is trickling down my back.

"How—how can I ask you now, ask any of you, for anything?"

"Ask," he demands. His voice is a nighttime seaway, tempting me to travel to a dangerous place.

"Will you? Will you do it? Will you Deepen her?"

"Not me," Jordan says quickly. "My father."

"What do we do first?"

"First, *you* tell her. Everything. Everything you know about Sirens, the little you know about Deepening, as much as she can stand to hear—"

"She won't understand. Not a word."

Something gleams in the depths of his eyes. "Don't expect her to be as enthusiastic about the idea as you are."

"You don't get it! It's her mind. She won't understand, she can't—"

"Arion." The wild sea of his gaze impossibly comes to stillness, and holds mine. "Words are limited. They're—containers, incomplete by themselves. Since your sister's accident, have you ever really known what she can and cannot understand?"

UNDERTAKING

The next day, Jordan's handsome face is free of its usual scowl as he carries Lilah to the top of the lighthouse. The rest of us trail behind them in a silent, snaking line—Cord, Mia, and Professor Summers; my mother, my father, me—all of us spreading out as we wind our way up the spiral stairs, until each of us is alone with our thoughts.

One by one, we emerge from the watch room, stepping out onto the deck and into the waning light of a blood-red sunset, the wind hitting our faces, lifting our hair. Everyone gravitates to the rail, to the view, to the ever-unfamiliar sea. It feels like someone should say something meaningful. Like we should throw something over the edge. Rice. Flowers. Ashes.

The ocean. If it attracts me like this—me, who has a love-hate relationship with the sea—what does it do to the Sirens? Spread at our feet, a relatively thin railing of wrought iron between us, does it Call to them like some roiling Romeo? And what about Lilah? What is she feeling? I wish I knew.

To an outsider, it might look as if she's had too much to drink, the way she stares at Jordan, eyes wide as the sky. The way Jordan supports her so carefully. The aura of instant intimacy that surrounds them, even as he sets her on her feet—a stranger couldn't be faulted for thinking a few drinks have played a part; after all, it's cocktail hour.

But this is far from a party, and none of us are strangers, not anymore. Bo is dead, and now, as we arrive back at the keeper's cottage, the sky losing its light, early evening pressing in on us, the talk is of nothing less than Lilah's life.

Jordan leans against the mantle looking down at Lilah, who doesn't appear to register his presence at this point, and is gazing into the fire. Still, for some reason I imagine them connecting, becoming a pair. *Breaths come in pairs . . . except for the first breath, and the last.*

My head is a mess of emotions. I take a deep breath—Cord waggles his eyebrows. Part of his indefatigable efforts to make me feel better, this comic intimation only makes me want to cry. And if not for the almost inaudible susurrations of Song that he and Mia breathe into my ear at every possible opportunity, that's probably what I'd be doing instead of passing a tray of sliced salmon and crackers to Mom.

Mom, whose current state of calm seems almost pharmaceutical in nature, is sitting with Dad and Professor Summers. He's telling my parents that Bo is out with friends. That he's sorry he can't be here.

The necessary secretiveness of Sirens won't allow the Summers to tell anyone that Bo is dead, at least not yet, and before I left the Cove yesterday, they'd started to explain just what they will say. But I'd excused myself and gone back to Bo's room, burying my face in his pillow.

Lilah's gaze shifts from the fire to the windows, and something about her eyes—some subtle change—convinces me: she actually sees what's out there.

"Look," I whisper to Cord as he hands me the tray of hors d'oeuvres that no one has touched. "She sees the ocean, she *sees* it. It's so ironic, it's like the only thing she can really grasp about her surroundings is the sea."

"She seemed to grasp Jordie pretty well when he carried her up to the top of the tower."

"That's not funny."

"I didn't say it was," Cord replies with a seriousness I didn't know he possessed. "I take it you didn't tell her yet. About Deepening, about us."

"No, I didn't. I'm grateful, *so* grateful. It's just, what's the point of telling her a bunch of stuff she's not going to understand? Plus, it's not like she can respond, or say anything back."

But Cord isn't listening. His attention is on Lilah. Now it shifts to Jordan.

The two boys exchange a look I can't decipher, their Siren eyes swirling. I shift my weight. Will Lilah's eyes become even more beautiful? Show every imaginable shade of blue and green? I imagine my parents staring at her heightened beauty with disbelief. But then again, they probably *won't* stare, at least, not into her eyes.

"Arion, may I speak with you?" I follow Professor Summers outside. "I've discussed the arrangements with your parents. Of course we can't tell them everything; revealing our true nature for instance would most likely be counterproductive. It appears as if they may need a little more time to adjust to the idea of me treating your sister. I can't say that I blame them. They're desperate, but I'm a scientist, not a doctor. However, based on what I've discerned of Lilah's condition, time is not on our side. I'm leaning toward being slightly more persuasive."

He's going to Siren Song my parents. I nod. "Whatever it takes."

The professor returns my nod. "It's paramount that we leave as soon as possible. I suggest we go tomorrow evening. Our absence won't arouse suspicion; the Institute knows that extended travel is necessary for me, in order to make new discoveries and acquire new plants and animals for our collection, for my studies."

My face grows hot. *Is that what Lilah is to him, a new specimen?* The only person he's Deepened—that I know of—is Beth. Is Lilah just an experiment to him?

"I understand," I say, swallowing hard.

The professor glances away, then back to me, as if he's growing impatient. "Your sister will be safe with us," he assures me.

Us. My heart constricts. The definition of the word is so changed now, so horribly altered.

"I've told your parents that Lilah will be spending some time at a rehabilitation center that uses—alternative therapies."

"Mom loves any kind of therapy," I say. "You'll get zero objections from her."

"Good. I'll choose one of our centers where the communication is known to be sketchy, on the Indian Ocean." He looks up, as if he might find further inspiration in the sky. Fitting.

"Dad will definitely think that's a good idea. He'll wish he was going himself."

The professor nods again. "We'll be in touch—but not often. We'll return in June—"

"*June?* But that's—"

"Yes. It's a significant amount of time." He glances at the door of the cottage. "I've got to get back to the Cove. I'll phone your parents tonight. Why don't you come over in the morning? We'll be able to speak more freely and—"

"Say our goodbyes. Yes. Thank you."

And before the professor can say anything else, I duck into the house—

And sit by my sister.

MONSTER

But it isn't until that night, after dinner, that I try to talk to her. Slipping into her room, I sit down on the edge of the bed.

Lilah's lying in the grainy late-evening light, so silent, so still—but her eyes are open, so I know she's not sleeping.

I push her bangs back from her forehead. "Lilah. There are . . . things I need to tell you."

Of course, she doesn't answer.

I chew the inside of my cheek. *Why am I doing this? She won't understand. She can't.*

"You're going to live, Lilah, you know that, right?" Maybe it's my imagination, but for a second it seems like . . . but no. There's no change in her expression.

"Lilah, I don't know if you can understand, but in case you can . . . Professor Summers, the man who was here today? Well, he and his family, they're . . . they're something called Sirens." The words are choking me; I have to keep clearing my throat, trying to find the right ones. "Sirens are . . . these amazing beings. They can fly, and swim underwater—they can *breathe* underwater. And they can *sing* like you wouldn't believe. And you, not only are you going to live, and be . . . healed, but you're going to be a *Siren*, like Jordan, and Mia and Cord." A sob catches in my throat. "Like Bo. He was their brother. He—he was killed. There was—there was someone named Nick. He—"

Light flickers in her eyes—then it's gone. A time-lapse playback of a day, the sun traveling across the sky, leaving evening in its wake.

"Lilah?"

Nothing.

Then suddenly—her raven brows draw down.

"Lilah!" Spinning around I slide to the floor and kneel next to the bed, my face close to hers. "Can you *understand* me?"

She focuses on me, just for a second, and then, as if an invisible hand has yanked her hair—she turns her face away, squeezing her eyes shut. A single tear slides down her cheek.

Nearly capsized by a wave of emotion, I grab her arms, hanging on like I'm a little kid again, and I want her attention.

"You understand what I'm saying, don't you? How long? How long have you—"

She laughs, but it's a horrible, vacant sound, as if her throat is full of ghosts.

Then she turns toward me— But her eyes are empty. They don't see me.

"No!" I cry out. "Please! Come back!" I lean over her—but Lilah is gone.

Is she in pain?

She's always been in pain, I realize, *inside.* She was in pain long before the accident—the revelation comes hard and fast, like a blow. I just don't know *why*. All I know is that, sometimes, she'd tried to make me feel her pain too.

But right now, that doesn't matter. I just want her back.

"Mom!" I shout. "Mom, you need to come in here!"

"Stop."

The sound is a dry scraping in her throat, *but it is her voice*. "Oh my God, Lilah—"

"What. The hell. Are you saying?"

"Oh my God, you're *talking*, you can talk! And your eyes—" Her eyes are no longer blank. They're sharp. Focused. And filled with hate.

"Of course. I can. You idiot."

"Wha—" I break off, staring at her.

"I just. Don't. Want to. I don't need to. We don't use words."

"We—what? Lilah, let me get Mom—"

"Shut up. She knows." Lilah sits up.

"She—she knows? She knows you can speak? What did you mean, 'We don't use—'"

"As if you could understand."

"Understand what?"

"When he comes, I'm going with him this time, for real. Fuck the haze that fills my head half the time. Fuck the blood clots. And I'm not stupid—I know what he did was awful. Leaving me, and . . . and the other things. But he needs to . . . do things sometimes, certain things. I don't care, I *understand*. He's above everything. What he did—it doesn't matter."

I desperately want to know who *he* is, but I try to follow her line of thought instead, hoping maybe it'll keep her with me. I speak very carefully, very softly now.

"And what did he do, Lilah?"

She continues in a sort of dazed state, and I'm so afraid she'll just stop and slip away. I crouch silently next to the bed.

"He and Tommy—I thought they were playing. They didn't know each other, but I thought, okay, it's a guy thing. We'd taken the boat for a lark—it was his idea. He talked them into it. And so, they were having fun. Roughing each other up. Whatever."

Tommy Burns. One of the fishermen the police think stole the boat that Lilah was on—the boat that was smashed to bits, destroying any evidence of what happened that night.

"But then they disappeared. They were gone for so long—I finally went to find them. They were down below. Tommy was—passed out." She stops and looks into some invisible distance. "Or maybe Tommy was sleeping. Anyway, he said, *'Do we need him?'* And I . . . I just said . . . no. I said: *'I only need you.'* Then he asked if I was sure. He was smiling. His smile, it's so beautiful . . ."

She's drifting, and I recognize the look on her face. It's like she's back in San Francisco, staring out the window at the bay. I squeeze my hands into fists until my nails dig into my palms.

Eventually she continues, voice dreamy. "He leaned over Tommy then—he moved so slowly, but fast too. It was like, one minute he was whispering in Tommy's ear, and the next—he was standing beside me again. And Tommy . . . his eyes were open, like, he wasn't passed out anymore. That's when I thought that maybe . . . But he looked okay, you know? Lying on his back, face turned to one side, like he was . . . thinking, and just wanted us to go." She shrugs. "So we went. We went back up without him. The waves were getting bigger by the second—it was wild. Exhilarating! But then . . ." Lilah's head cocks a little to one side like she's puzzled. "He grabbed Jack."

Jack Sims. Tommy Burns. Two fishermen—guys in their twenties—who grew up together, who worked for Dad. Who, almost without a doubt, died that night. And whose bodies were never recovered.

"He—he kissed him. He *kissed* Jack.

"It took me a minute, but then I was like, okay. Okay, Jack's kind of cute. I was thinking, the three of us. Thinking, that's what he wanted. But the timing—it kind of sucked." Her laugh is one quick jerk of a saw blade through metal. "The storm was on us. And suddenly—

"Jack was gone. It was . . . a wave. A wave washed him overboard."

It's like she's just deciding this, just now deciding that a wave washed Jack Sims over the side of the boat, and watching her decide—as if she has some control over what happened, even now, some power—I can't stop myself. "*Who?* Who, Lilah?"

But I already know the answer. I've known since he pulled me from the boat that bobbed so dangerously against the breakwater. The boy in the baseball cap, the one I saw but didn't see. Nick.

The way Logan seemed so familiar when I met him. And the night we went out to eat—I had that flash of recognition. But it faded fast, and I let it. Unless—

How far reaching is a Siren's spell? How long lasting?

Lilah goes on now, like she hasn't heard my question.

"And then it was just us. Finally. I wanted him *so* badly. Like when we met. And he wanted me. He said nothing would interrupt us this time, no one.

"But then everything was hurting. I was—sick, I guess. My throat, my chest, there was—such pain. Pressure. Then—blackness."

Horrified, I clutch her arms, shaking my head, unable to speak—

"That's right. Saying nothing is easier, isn't it?" Her gaze turns sharp again, hard. "*Aquaphobia.* Was that your way of trying to show your support?" She laughs, a wild, high-pitched sound. "Along with your sympathetic looks, and the *pathetic* hair brushing—as if we were *like that*! All you ever were was *in my way*! God, I was so glad when you left San Francisco. I could finally breathe."

I try to shout for Mom. Nothing comes out.

"I told you, you can shut up, she *knows*. Obviously when I found out they were going to *drill* into my *head* and fuck with my brain I had to break my silence. But I told her: she was the only one, the *only* person I'd talk to. 'Selective mutism'—Mom loves to play therapist, you know that. I figured if that's what she wanted to call it . . ." She purses her lips for a second. "She didn't tell, but she wouldn't leave me alone either. Constantly in my room, *wasting* my time with her questions. I didn't tell her about him, of course. I knew she wouldn't get it. She doesn't know what love is. Mom." The word is a snarl. "She started lying to me. Telling me I was 'unresponsive' for hours at a time. She'd come talk to me in the evening. Tell me she'd tried for half the day to get me to say something, to 'acknowledge' her, but that I only stared out the window. Well, duh, I had to watch for him, didn't I? Had to be ready when he came. God.

"She said that some mornings she came to wake me up and I wouldn't 'wake'—that's how she described it. I didn't believe her. Then the scan—but she lied about that too. She said I needed to have it done, that *we* did, because another MRI would show that there was nothing wrong with me. She said—" Lilah sits a little straighter, almost like she's listening to something.

"She said?"

Lilah jerks to life. "She said shit. She told me a bunch of lies. And then the goddamn doctors with this blood clot thing—and now you, with your, *what? Sirens?*" She's already shaken me off, and now she rubs her arms as if my embrace has caused her pain.

"It's true." Tears run down my face. "Everything I said is true, and the guy you met—"

"True?" Her wild laughter scurries around the room. "Then I guess that means you'd let your imaginary *monster* friends turn me into one of them. I'd rather die, thanks."

"They're not monsters! Not at all! Although . . ." My sobs hiccup to a stop.

"Although what?" Hatred burns in her eyes, and I realize—she's always hated me. Like she just told me. *I was in her way.*

But there's pain too, right alongside the hatred. It bruises her, softens her, and all at once she looks so young. Her pain must be worse now. Unbearable.

I know what it's like, to want one of them.

"Lilah, the guy you met—"

But suddenly I stop.

Lilah. She can talk. She can think.

And Mom. *Mom knows.*

My veins begin to fill with ice—thin ice that creaks and groans, and starts to crack.

"Although *what*?" she repeats, unaware of the tectonic shift occurring inside me.

"Although they have some strange dietary habits," I say coldly. Something corrosive is seeping into my gut, taking the place of pity. I bite my tongue so it doesn't come up—the coppery taste of blood fills my mouth. Still, I can't hold back.

"So, you think you'll see him again?"

"I know I will, and if I'm going to die from a bunch of 'land mines' in my head? It'll be in his arms."

"No. It won't. He's dead, Lilah. Nick Delaine is dead."

Her mouth opens—closes. But she doesn't ask me how I know his name, or anything else. She only says, "Then I want to die too."

"Well, you're not going to."

"Why? Because I'm going to become a *Siren*? That guy Jordan is a total freak, by the way. Acted like he *knew* me."

"Nobody knows you," I say from some hollow place inside.

"I won't stay in this world without Nick."

I look at her then, knowing just how crazy my sister is. Is it because of Nick, because of what he did to her? Or was it the accident, the shock of it?

Or has Lilah always been—off? I think of the things she's done to me over the years. The way she nearly broke my arm on the playground. How she let her boyfriend "practice" on me—that's how she defended him later, as if there was any defense for what he'd done, for what she'd told him to do.

I shrug now. And I say, "I guess it's up to you."

"Not entirely," Mom says, appearing in the bedroom doorway.

Dad is right behind her.

BACKBONE

"You heard her," Mom said to Dad. "His name is Nick. The boy that—did this to her."

Mom's words turned us to stone—that's what it was like. Like we were stone statues in that claustrophobic closet of a room.

Then Lilah's eyes became slits—she looked like she wanted to kill Mom.

And Dad, bewildered, said, "A boy? How could a boy—" He broke off then, but I heard the rest of his thoughts like he was still speaking: *Cici, what are you saying? A boat did this to her, not a boy. You've told me that over and over. This is my fault.*

He'd had little more than a week to try to assimilate the idea that his daughter was dying. Mom had told him about the blood clots when she phoned. But she hadn't told him that Lilah had been talking to her for nearly *three months*.

Maybe she thought Lilah would tell him herself.

But Lilah didn't tell Dad anything, because less than a minute after he showed up in her room, she was gone again. She simply closed her eyes. I watched my father watching her, watching the rise and fall of her chest. Making sure she was alive. Then he started crying.

Mom steered him to the living room. I floated after them like some small phantom ship.

Dad stopped crying after a while, and they began talking. I listened to them go around in circles. That's when I learned that Lilah has been talking for three months. "Or . . . longer maybe," Mom said. "Now that I think about it."

"You mean you weren't *thinking* about it before? Is that what you're saying? Did you *think* of me? Of telling me? Did you *think* I might want to talk to her? To you? To the doctors?"

Then he asked, "Was she—was she speaking before Ari and I left?"

And my mom whispered, "Yes."

Dad's face—it hurt me to see it. I drifted away into the kitchen. They didn't notice.

"But then you were gone," I heard my mom say. "You were here, and I was there, with her. I was there *for* her. I started rethinking the implant procedure even before I found out."

"Great; thinking *and* rethinking. Thinking enough for both of us, huh, Nancy?"

I didn't have to be in the room with them to know that at that point, my mom had a deep V between her eyebrows. She doesn't like anyone calling her by her real name, but when Dad does it? That's when you know: the argument has turned into a fight. But since big blow-outs aren't Dad's style, he shuts down. It may seem like he's throwing a gauntlet—"Nancy" instead of "Cici"—but he's really just slamming the door in her face. He always walks away at this point. And then it's The Silent Storm. The Storm lasts a day sometimes. Or a week. Maybe it's always been there, some violent weather system undermining their marriage. Eroding it.

But it was because of the silence—that's how I knew, how I *know*, Dad never made the connection. If he had, he would have said something, right then and there, would have attached the name "Nick" to Nick Delaine. But he didn't, and why would he? The accident took place in San Francisco. And as far as Dad knows, Lilah never even met Nick Delaine. He died before she had the chance.

Dad. He can't be mad at Lilah. She's obviously sick.

But Mom isn't sick—she's just a liar. She lied to Dad. And she lied to me.

In the morning I walk down the beach to Summers Cove. The tide is out, leaving a cold expanse of sand behind, wet and unwelcoming. The wind is from the south, blowing in my face. The sky is gunmetal gray.

Cord comes outside to meet me, and I tell him about Lilah and Nick. Tell him about what Lilah called "the haze" in her head.

"It's possible he had her in the first stage of Deepening. The storm, the wreck—he was interrupted. But how he even—"

"She met him here. She must have." I allow Cord to lead me into the house. "Can you—will she be okay?"

Thankfully Mom and Dad hadn't heard the whole conversation, hadn't heard the word *Siren*. But even if they had heard, they wouldn't have had a clue. So the Summers' secret is still safe.

I *know* I should feel sorry for Lilah, and I *do*. But I'm her sister. She could have talked to me. Then again, she hated me. Hates me. And I . . .

I have a hard pebble of pain in my chest.

Cord still hasn't answered my question. He ushers me into the kitchen, pulling out a chair at the table, motioning for me to sit. Now he begins to hum softly . . .

"Mom should have told us . . . Maybe . . . maybe I could have done something . . ." My eyes close as I let his Song inside. There's a sort of trust growing between the two of us.

I wish—I'd trusted Bo.

"You did do something," Cord whisper sings in my ear. "And now *we're* going to do something. My father is. It's gonna work out."

Cord's voice fades—the same way my questions fade—as one by one, the other members of the Summers family drift into the room.

Soon they're sitting at the kitchen table, talking about the upcoming trip to India, and the northeaster. But to me, the storm was a lifetime ago. The revelation that Lilah is still essentially herself, that she's lied to me this entire time—on top of losing Bo—has leveled me. The voices of the Sirens are the only thing keeping me going now.

Even Professor Summers' arctic tone gives me a strange sort of comfort.

"We have several agreements in this family, agreements that, apparently, Bo chose to ignore. And you—" He turns on Jordan. "Your 'method' of delivering Arion to safety—you could have started something unstoppable."

"But I didn't," Jordan responds, his tone as frigid as his father's. "And what I did do—I did it for Bo."

"Regardless. *Relationships* with humans are—"

"What about you—you and our mother?" Cord protests. "It's because of you that Bo—"

"Are you saying I'm a hypocrite?"

Their mother—I wonder if she would think it was wise for Cord to challenge his father this way; Professor Summers seems like an unforgiving man. I try to imagine what his wife must have been like. Bo's mom. I asked about her more than once. Bo always said he'd tell me her story when I was ready to hear it.

"Not yet. Not until . . . you're like me."

But I'll never be like him now. Like he was.

Lilah will.

I try to find some solace in the idea of Lilah becoming a Siren as Professor Summers continues to berate Cord. She'll be able to see what Bo saw, beneath the waves. *She'll fly on angel's wings. She'll never cry tears again.*

The thoughts are cold comfort, like the professor's voice. He'll Deepen her. Bo's father. That he'll be the one is somewhat reassuring. It also makes my skin crawl.

"Lilah will need all the information we can give her in order to adjust to her new—situation," Professor Summers says, as if reading my thoughts. It's eerie how intuitive they all are. "The legacy will be different, of course. She will not be a Siren by natural birth . . ." The professor trails off. Maybe he's thinking of Bo. Or maybe he's trying to figure out *exactly* what's on my mind.

But how can he? I'm trying desperately to hide my true feelings now.

My heart hammers. *My sister. She'll always, always be in danger.*

And not just because the seas are home to other Sirens.

After Mia left the keeper's cottage at the start of the storm, she went to Summers Cove. When she arrived, she found a crowd of people at the top of the drive. Logan was correct, the media was far from satisfied with the coverage of the drowned kayakers, and not only was TV Twelve waiting on Smith Street along with reporters from the *Rock Hook Herald*, but there were vans from several major networks as well, plus journalists from Portland.

The most surprising member of the party, and possibly the ringleader of the media blitz, was a man named Troy Grayson, a detective from New York City who's somehow connected to the case of the missing boys who rented the *Lucky*.

Mia hadn't *meant* to Call Jordan, drag him into the fray, but she'd panicked, and her Signals had spiked. Jordan landed on the bluffs above the farthest cottage, and kept close to the woods. He'd been cautious, listening for Nick. When he'd finally approached the top of the drive, he'd been just as surprised as Mia to find a media circus poised to invade the Summers' privacy.

The reporters were spilling down toward the three cottages by the time Bo arrived. They nearly saw him in his Full Expression—the Summers' worst nightmare. Apparently after we'd argued, he'd Risen, with the idea of leaving the area. But after traveling only a short distance, he returned. At that point he, Jordan, and Mia were effectively caged on their own land.

Mia told me that when Bo heard my Call, "He went wild, he would have done anything. He didn't care who saw him. Luckily Jordan and I were able to garner the attention of the group by throwing the papers a few red herrings. We offered to show the TV crews where we'd found the kayakers and managed to get everyone to walk south on the beach. Bo was able to slip away."

And slip away he had. Bo was dead, gone forever. I see him again now, fighting with Nick on the seawall. Nick Delaine. He devastated us all.

Snatches of Song wash over me as the Sirens bathe themselves in a continual hum of sound. Jordan's low voice reverberates against my breastbone.

How could I have chosen this life for Lilah? But there'd been no other choice, and I can't let the Summers see my fear now. They're being generous, saving my sister.

And actually, the life of a Siren might suit Lilah just fine. After all, they are practically professional liars. Not that I've told any of them except Cord what I learned last night. It's too much of a betrayal to share, and they'll find out for themselves soon enough. She called them monsters, but she . . .

"She won't want to come back," I say, mostly to myself. Then I blurt, "And what about you? How can you come home in June, any of you, how can you come back at all? The national seashore will be opening in July—tourists will be all over the place, on the beach, in the woods, here, at the Cove—and even when summer is over, how will you—"

"Think the northeaster may have created a solution to your pet peeve, Girlina." A streak of green flashes through Cord's eyes as he shoots a look at Jordan, who, to my shock, grins.

"Things will work out," Mia says bluntly. Her pale-blond hair has never looked so icy.

But they aren't working out. Your brother is dead.

"How?" I reply. "How will you even know what's going on here? You'll be in some undisclosed location, teaching Lilah how to be a Siren—" I suppress a shudder. There might be danger lying ahead for Lilah, but danger is better than death.

"I—I'm sorry," I say. "Professor Summers, thank you. Cord, Mia . . . Jordan." *Bo.* "Thank you for doing this."

Mia's mouth quirks—she's detected my mixed emotions. *After all, she's only human,* I can almost hear her thinking.

Tears prick the corners of my eyes. I will them to stop. I've had enough salt water for a lifetime.

In retrospect, it's easy to see that what Dr. Harrison told me was true. After Lilah's accident, I suffered from depression. It had been an inky curtain, draping me in darkness, causing me to lose interest in everything I loved. Then I started concentrating on playing guitar, and writing songs. The writing opened doors inside of me. I can't let those doors close. Bo is gone, and that means despite the twisting cramp in my gut, I need to focus on keeping the black-eyed dog at bay.

I. Will. Not. Cry.

Thanking the Summers again, I start toward the door. If all goes well, they'll pick up Lilah sometime tonight, so, I'll see them again. But this is my real goodbye.

Hurrying now, wanting to get away, I hike across the sand, and in a moment, stand beside the giant jetty that divides what's really one long, sandy strip into two. It hadn't been a stretch to convince my folks. This was where I'd fallen.

The cut in my calf throbs as I picture Bo at the water's edge, where I first saw him.

My heart hurts too, as I struggle over the prehistoric backbone of boulders, the wall that hid the Summers from so many people, but not from Nick Delaine, and not from me.

FALL

At school, Alyssa stops me in the hall, giving the teal turtleneck a quick once-over.

"Is that new?" I shake my head. "But you look different," she insists.

Staring pointedly at her slutty black cat Halloween costume, I raise an eyebrow.

She rolls her eyes. "Fine. Don't talk to me." She starts to walk away, when one of her feet skids out from under her and she stumbles. Haltingly, she turns to me.

It's like watching a moonrise over the water, the way the fear and confusion slowly fill her face, her skin paling, then blanching further.

She glances furtively down the hall. "What—what was he trying to *do* to me?" she whispers. Her voice is a tracery, barely there. Then she jerks like a puppet whose strings have been pulled—and stares straight ahead.

Maine Medical hadn't known what to make of Alyssa's symptoms. The story she told on Monday when she came back to school after being out for nearly three weeks was that she'd been dieting and had fainted. But will she stick to that story? *How much does she remember?*

Now she rolls her eyes again. It's almost like a tic. "Fine. Don't talk to me," she repeats. Then she walks away.

Stunned, I stand still for a second. Then I think, *Such a good idea.* How about—

I don't talk to anyone?

I've already been lying low, eating lunch in the library. How hard can it be to keep on hiding? Just look at the Summers. They hide in plain sight.

Mary calls. Logan calls. Even Pete and Bobby call. But their efforts to get in touch with me . . . feel like intrusions. Everyday voices carrying across airwaves—how can that possibly matter? There is no call I want to answer, no call I *need* to answer.

There is no call I can't resist.

There is no Call . . . at all.

Dad gets an answering machine for the cottage.

I smash my cell.

It never worked here anyway.

Nothing works.

PACIFIC TIME

Mom is in San Francisco. Again. Why is she always leaving? Pointless to ask, because I don't believe anything she says now.

And actually, I know why she's out there; I know all her beats. Why she's out there—*Art*—and why she's not here—*Your father.* She had, I remember now, told me these were the reasons she was going. This time. I just hadn't listened. But Dad's rattling reminds me.

"Mom's going to be out in California for a while," he says, searching through the pots and pans as if he's misplaced something, giving me time to digest what he's said.

But I already knew she was planning on staying at the old house for a while, the house that, conveniently—coincidentally?—hasn't sold.

"Arion, your father and I . . ."

Your father. Like some new, identifying hashtag, she'd thrown it around for a few days before she left. Every time she talked to me, as a matter of fact. *Your father.* Like he belongs to me now, like maybe I'm even the one who's responsible for his behavior, responsible for him. Like she's washed her hands of him. And maybe she has.

"I know," I say now, watching him search the cupboards. I hate seeing him like this, disoriented in his own kitchen, where he's usually king. "It's okay, Dad."

"I didn't say it wasn't, it's just—of course it's *okay*, I just . . . wanted you to know."

To know what? That she's going to be away for a while? Or that—

She's not coming back.

I instantly dismiss the thought. Even she wouldn't be that heartless.

My father is looking out the window now, looking toward Summers Cove.

"Dad?"

He startles. And then he startles me, by saying, "Why don't we go out for dinner, Water Dog? How's that sushi place?"

Jordan Summers' staring eyes—it's almost like they're in front of me. Like he is.

I say, "Closed for the season. How about we go over to the mainland?"

My father, who loves to cook—who *never* goes to restaurants *because* he loves to cook and because he's a *great* cook—jumps at the idea. It makes my heart sink just a little, even though I'd been the one to suggest it.

He smiles, but his face still has that slightly baffled look, like he's woken up in someone else's life. I feel kind of like that too, although not for the same reasons, and it pisses me off that Mom has done this to him, that she's unavailable when he needs her most.

Lying to the rest of the world, maybe that makes sense, but lying to Dad and me? I can't forgive that.

But. She and Lilah are family. And I still love them. I just . . .

Hate them too.

I. Will. Not. Cry.

In fact, I almost laughed when, the day before she left, Mom said, "I'm concerned about your reaction to your breakup with Bo." My parents, the kids at school, everyone believes we broke up, that Bo went to India with his family. It'll be easy enough to say he's decided to stay there.

In her infinite wisdom, Mom insisted I see a therapist for what she deems my "unhealthy unwillingness to emote." At each session, I set myself on repeat.

Shrink: *"How do you feel about that?"*

Me: *"Sometimes it's pain. Sometimes it's hollow. Never the same. Are we finished for today?" Because I'd rather curl up with a book.*

And I do. I read constantly.

"The heart wants what it wants—or else it does not care."

Emily Dickinson, right again. Funny how I never noticed that second part until now.

The paper I wrote for O'Keefe's class wound up changing too. I used the end for the beginning, and the beginning . . . I just scrapped it. Beginnings don't always matter. Sometimes they're just a place to start. And way back when I started O'Keefe's assignment, I never would have chosen isolation as a theme. But there it was. In Hardy's *The Return of the Native* and Joyce's *A Portrait of the Artist as a Young Man.* Isolation. And now? My paper makes perfect sense.

Sometimes I miss Dr. Harrison just a little—Mom would love that. But I'm pretty sure he'd at least get that I'm quoting song lyrics. The new therapist, with her rote questions, she's just dialing it in. And even if she asked the *right* questions? Even if she *listened* to my answers? I wouldn't be able to confide in her. Because how can I tell anyone the truth, about anything? Plus, how do I explain to a therapist that I don't need to talk about my feelings?

Along with my mantra, the music keeps them in check, the MP3s I receive as email attachments, nearly every day, from Cord, sometimes from Mia.

The emails tell me that Lilah is "adjusting."

The music . . . soothes me. Keeps me numb.

WASTEPAPER BASKET

Until one day, I stop listening.

It's not easy at first. At first there are fevers, and chills. There's nausea and vomiting so bad I need pills. Motion sickness medicine, that's what I take. Because whenever I move, I throw up.

I remember how Lilah sat still for days, staring unseeingly at the Golden Gate Bridge. I know now it wasn't the bridge that she watched, but the water below it—*I am waiting.*

Now I'm the one waiting. But just to get better.

Lilah didn't fight it—her Siren sickness. Her lovesickness. But I do.

I fight it with music, and writing. Day after day, I write page after page.

The stuff is crap: bad poetry and songs that collapse under the weight of sentimentality.

But what doesn't end up in the wastepaper basket? Gets me through Thanksgiving.

And the less I listen to the Siren Songs, the more my love for Bo starts to seem like . . . something other than love, just like I suspected at the end.

But I wonder some days, without his Song in my ears now, what we actually had—because it *had* been something—a singular, stellar something—that I wouldn't wish on anyone.

Unbelievably, some days I miss him. He'd been a beautiful boy—who wasn't a boy.

So I think of him sometimes, but I don't cry. Refuse to cry.

Why should I? When all I've lost is an illusion.

FLOOD

But then it comes. Comes out of nowhere.

Comes out of me.

I'm in the bathroom, brushing my teeth when it happens.

I brush, I rinse. I pour the remainder of the water from the glass I've been using down the drain, watching the miniature whirlpool as if hypnotized. Then I set the glass back on the sink.

The glass. It's such an innocuous thing.

Until I notice that it's empty. And suddenly I think—*I'm empty too.*

And now, although I don't remember leaving the bathroom, I'm in the bedroom, standing at the east-facing window and looking down through a night so clear, the stars appear pointed. Sharp. The wind is picking up, and I watch the black ocean rock wildly, spiky waves reaching toward the stygian sky.

The way the spires of water smash themselves against the shoreline suddenly strikes me as suicidal. I turn away.

Two hot tears squeeze themselves out of my eyes, then two more. Soon, tear after tear is rolling down my cheeks, and great, heaving sobs wrack my body. Another minute and I'm crying so hard my chest is hitching, my breath coming in wet gasps.

I'm finally, finally crying for Bo. Not for our relationship—for him. I'm crying about his death. About his life.

The life my sister will have.

She'd fought like a demon when they tried to take her.

Until Jordan started singing.

He sings to her a lot, that's what Cord writes in his emails. It helps, he tells me. Some.

I cry for her too, now.

And maybe she doesn't deserve my tears. Maybe Bo doesn't. But I can't help it.

I'm not empty—I'm full. Overflowing.

Lastly, I cry for me, because I killed my best friend's brother, and no one can ever know.

And for one hectic second—my heart hurts for Logan. But then I picture Nick smashing Bo's head against granite. Imagine Nick leaning over me while I slept, unprotected, in my bed.

I put my hands over my eyes, trying to block out the worst, but the awful images, the cutting memories, remind me:

Nick hadn't been Logan's brother, not anymore.

And that keeps me from crying for Logan. *But does it absolve me?*

Sobbing, I stumble over to the bed, climbing on as if it's a life raft, as if it can save me.

But it's too late. Turning my face to the pillow, I let the tears take me—and I go under.

It's finally happening. I'm drowning.

PORTAL

Winter. In Maine.

It's not too much of a trick to avoid people.

Sure, there's school. But there are snow days, and vacation days, mental health days, and of course sick days—though I'm way over the allotted number of those.

But at least I'm not sick anymore. It's amazing how clear my head is.

On the calendar, it's still the end of autumn. But outside it's cold and bleak and a million shades of gray now that the leaves are off the trees.

"Stop making excuses," Mary said on the phone earlier today.

"I'm not making excuses."

"Hermit. Recluse."

"Try, musician. Writer."

Mary and I talk nearly every day on the phone. She was upset that she hadn't gotten to meet my sister, but I explained that Lilah wasn't here for long. I felt guilty lying to Mary, telling her that Lilah's surgery was "canceled" and that for now, she's staying out in California.

"She's living in a hospital facility that specializes in advanced neurological research," I said. And I wondered at the way the lies came so easily.

"Wow," she said softly. "I'm sorry to hear that. I really do wish I'd met her."

"Well . . . you will. When she visits again. Sometime. She's going to be okay. Eventually."

That's when Mary started talking about Kevin's uncle. "He's a neurologist."

"Oh. Uh—" I'd scrambled for the right thing to say. "Well, don't talk to Kevin too much about this, okay, Mary? It's . . . you know, family stuff. Private. In fact, I don't really want to talk about it anymore. It's kind of depressing."

Mary said she totally understood. Then she asked, "Did you let Logan in on all of this?"

"Uh, no. But you can. That'd be great actually." *One less lie to tell.* "Only, just the basic facts, okay?"

"The basic facts," she said, "are all I know. Your sister's surgery was canceled. She's back in California. Your mom is too, I guess?"

"My mom is too, that's right." My mom. Back and forth she goes, between here and California. But Lilah has nothing to do with it.

Once in a while Mary stops by, or we meet at the library.

Sometimes I imagine I see Bo in the stacks. And then I tell Mary, I need to go.

My inbox is crowded with unread emails from the Summers that I downloaded the last time I was at the library. I select them all now and move them to a folder containing the rest of the unopened emails from India. It's almost easy at this point, not to listen—

A message pops up in my chat window.

IM with Jordan Summers <JordanSummers@mac.com> Today 1:00 p.m.

```
Why don't you answer your email?
Skype. Today. w/ your sister. 11:30
p.m., our time. That's NOW.
```

I jab at the keyboard— This Internet connection . . . I hit the keys again—

Skype opens.

Oh—

Her eyes are the same brilliant blue, only now there are traces of green, tendrils of mossy color swaying in the depths of her irises. Instantly, I feel myself being pulled toward watery reaches, toward a distant realm, a faraway world.

"Arion? I hear your Internet sucks—sucks, ha! Hey, are you there? Can you see me? There you are! You're crying." She laughs. "Why?"

I close my eyes, feeling for the shoreline. *Lilah. A Siren.* I touch my cheeks. She's right—of course she is. My face is wet with tears.

Opening my eyes, I drink in the sight of her standing there in a white summer dress. I have a million questions—

But suddenly she flings her arms wide—spins in a circle. Her raven hair—streaked with silver now, beams of moonlight—flies wildly around her face.

I gape, watching her twirl in a sparsely furnished room with high ceilings and saffron walls. The Summers' house in India.

"Well?" she cries out, stopping abruptly. Her voice fills the room, and now—I hear *her music*. As if pulled, I move closer to the screen. "Well?" she repeats. "How do I look? God, you're so close to the screen—your face looks like a balloon!"

"You—you look beautiful." I blink rapidly. "How are you?"

"I'm *great*!" She wraps her arms around herself in a passionate self-embrace, then she writhes in a suggestive manner that's so—crude, it's alarming.

Suddenly the lower part of her torso glints with metallic scales, her legs twist, elongating into a serpent's tail—

I shove my chair back—

The illusion fades. She's once again a beautiful girl in a diaphanous white dress standing in a large, nearly empty room with golden walls.

My hands begin to shake.

She lowers her voice, and again, I hear her Song, as she asks, "What's wrong?"

"It's—nothing. I've—missed you." *You lied to me.*

Like smoke at a crowded party that you can't avoid inhaling, her Song begins to seep inside me. I want to cover my ears, but I know it won't help.

She grins, curves her arms overhead, and performs a simple plié. Then, to my shock, she leaps several feet into the air. Like, four feet. *Siren skills?*

"Ari, this second life . . . it's so much better than the first."

She looks as if she's ready to leap again, when all at once her body seems to *spill*—like water—as she drops to the floor in a crouch.

"Sirens approaching," she says in a stage whisper, her eyes wide in mock alarm. She laughs, and like before, the sound simultaneously thrills me and sets me on edge.

I have the sensation of being in a tunnel. "Lilah—"

At the sound of her name, Lilah's head cocks to one side. The colors in her eyes swirl and shift—then her gaze falls to my lips. She looks at them wonderingly, and I have the feeling that she hasn't actually seen me until just this moment, hasn't heard me. She purses her own lips and taps them with an index finger, as if considering something. Then she springs up from the floor—

In the same moment, Jordan Summers appears in the open doorway behind her, shirtless and dripping wet.

"Little Mortal Girl," he says. Droplets of water run down his muscled arms.

"Hi." I avert my gaze, but not before I see Lilah reach over and pluck a strand of seaweed from Jordan's forearm. And just that—the intimacy of the small gesture—tells me what's between them. My stomach surges.

"Okay, you can start the party now." Cord nearly knocks Jordan over as he bounds into the room. Lilah spins around and begins talking to him a million miles a minute.

She's like a more potent, manic version of herself. The way she'd been before the accident—times ten. Maybe times a hundred.

Jordan steps close to the screen, and finally, I meet his eyes. See the glittering spread of a dark sea. The color of the ocean—it's just a reflection of the sky. But it's also affected by what lies beneath. Even half a world away, I feel the pull of him.

"She's a new Siren," Jordan says in a low voice. "When she comes home, be careful."

"She's my sister," I say shortly. "I don't think I need to be careful."

His midnight eyes hold mine. "Oh, but you do. She takes what she wants."

I don't blink. "She always has."

Lilah snaps to attention. "Are you two talking about me?"

Jordan's expression shuts like a door.

Cord says, "Uh-oh."

Lilah shoots him a black look, then turns back toward the screen, toward me.

But I'm still looking at Jordan. And I'm thinking—only not thinking. I'm remembering. But not well. *That night, that night at Hive . . .*

What is it about Jordan and that night? About Jordan and that club? Jordan and that—girl.

There'd been a girl.

Slither. The thought slides away.

But it leaves something behind. Some residue. Like oil on water. Something that reminds me: *there are more of them.*

"In this ocean, in all *the oceans! Sirens, some like us, some who are different than us, and not so . . . compassionate."*

How many, Bo? Is there a whole hidden world around me?

"We've discussed it, you know."

I nearly jump. The screen in front of me seems to brighten, the resolution becoming crisper. Lilah's skin, it's so . . . luminous.

"Discussed—discussed what?"

"You," she says.

Confused, I watch in fascinated disgust as her long pianist fingers creep up Jordan's arm to his bare shoulder until her hand fits to it, cups it in a way that's more than possessive, that's almost—greedy. As if her hand alone can swallow him whole. Her bright eyes move like the sea on a windy day, rocking and hypnotic. Unbalanced.

"You say you don't want to be a Siren," she scoffs. "Yet you were in love with Bo."

"No. I wasn't. I—thought I was." I glance uneasily at Jordan. His brother lost his life saving mine. This isn't a conversation I want to have in front of him.

"Really. Well, *I'm* your sister. You definitely love me."

"Yes. Of course I do."

"*So?* Am I supposed to live *forever* without you?" Lilah's face darkens.

"No—I mean, yes. I mean—I missed you so much, Lilah. When the doctors said you were going to die—this was the only way! I couldn't let you die."

I stop, aware that her eyes are once more focused on my lips. Then they flick up—meeting mine. My stomach turns to acid as I see the ocean inside her, murky and roiling with something unspeakable. She's Lilah—but she isn't.

"You took my notebook."

"I—"

"I want it back."

"You can have it. It's here. You're right. I took it. I'm sorry, I just—"

"You just couldn't help being a nosy little bitch. Send it to me," she snaps.

It's like a black hole has opened at my feet, and she's pushed me to the edge of it.

I don't say anything. I think Jordan is maybe trying to tell me something, that maybe Cord is looking embarrassed, or, or—but I don't know. I feel like . . . I don't know anything. Like she's reduced me. And in a way, I want that. Not to be diminished by her, but to erase myself. I consider the hole. Consider allowing myself to drop into it. To plummet into black nothingness.

But then her voice—it's like a balm. Her abrupt mood shift is truly terrifying, but her voice . . .

"You'll love it," she says silkily. "I mean the singing, come on! What's not to love?" Her beauty is magnified as she leans toward the screen and begins humming a song from our childhood, a duet we sang together for years. I remember the teachers now, the music lessons, and Lilah, always the best at everything. Except for singing. I'd outshone her there. No secret.

But now her voice is more beautiful than mine can ever be, and she sounds like *she* has a secret—one I want to know. I'm that little girl again, the one she *let* tag along. My resolve begins to weaken. Why had I come to the conclusion that being a Siren is hell? Is horror?

Lilah's voice is an orchestral instrument of beauty. Harp strings vibrate through my body. Woodwinds caress my soul. *Lilah.* She's always enthralled me. Had me under her thumb, under her spell.

But I can break that spell now. *Have* to break it—

Quickly, I hit two keys.

Command-Q.

Skype quits—

Break the connection.

SISTERS

Breathing hard, I stare at the desktop, images flooding my mind.

Nick Delaine, the serpentine tail of my nightmares . . .

With a ding, a new message appears in the bubble of the chat window.

> IM with Jordan Summers <JordanSummers@mac.com> Today 1:15 p.m.

Only it isn't Jordan.

> Knock, knock! Ari, it can be me and you again, the way we were. San Francisco? We can go back—we can do anything!

I can almost see her, raising her arms—hear the ripping sound as her wings tear through the back of the filmy summer dress. Glorious white-feathered limbs seem to surround me as I picture her. My sister. Not my sister. A Siren. A liar.

It'll be awesome! The breath alone is worth it—Ahhhhhh . . .

The groan of pleasure that unfurls in the window implies ecstatic remembrance.

So she's done it. She's *killed.* I hadn't thought, hadn't expected . . .

The messages come faster now. I shrink back from the screen.

You've GOT to do it!

Although it does seem strangely incestuous, for me to Deepen you.

So you can choose ☺

Will it be the cutie—Cord? Please not Mia—she's such a bitch.

We'll truly share everything if Julian does it. That would be nice, wouldn't it? Nice isn't my favorite word, but you've always liked it.

Or Jordie! Of course! Oh yes! I'm asking him now. He's saying no. He's so humorless.

But don't worry, Arion, I'll convince him. He's definitely the best—and hottest—answer.

And speaking of answering, what the hell? Why aren't you writing back?

My new cell rings from the bottom of my backpack. *Where did she even get the number?*

Pick up!

Think of the endless games we can play. Just like when we were little.

Follow the Leader ☺ You were always *so* good at Follow the Leader.

Nothing has to change!

Not now.

Not *ever*.

It could be me and you again. *Us*, like we used to be. The Rush Sisters.

Really, it already is!

Be home soon, little sis!

VISITOR

The black-and-white-striped tower blocks the worst of the wind today, and the afternoon sun hits the gallery deck at just the right angle, heating the iron. It may be the shortest day of the year, but the rays of the sun appear to be at their longest, golden fingers reaching across the sky.

"Hey," Logan says from the doorway to the watch room. "Can I sit down?"

Somehow his unannounced appearance doesn't surprise me, but that he's asked if he can sit shows how much things have changed between us. As does the fact that he doesn't sit too close when he finally lowers himself onto the blanket where I'm soaking up the sun.

I've been avoiding him. He knows it.

He thinks it's because of Bo. It isn't.

His eyes rove over my face. "You're looking good, Rush, not quite so pale. Well, still pale. But you've lost that ghostly pallor you've been sporting for a while. Thought for a minute there you were going goth girl on me, Sarah style. Guess you finally decided to start breathing again?"

"Something like that," I say, shuddering slightly at the reference.

"Great. Now you just have to start hanging out. Rejoin civilized society."

"Does this count as hanging out? Wait—that would imply you're civilized, and we both know *that's* not the case."

"Ooh, you've gotten quite sharp, I'm not sure I can keep up."

"Don't try, I had a good teacher."

"Anything else you want to learn besides how to be a wiseass?" He arches one eyebrow suggestively. Then he says, "Be nice to me, it's my birthday."

"Happy Birthday." I punch him in the arm. Then we grin at each other like lunatics.

"Miss you," he says.

"Miss you too."

"Cool." Logan leans back against the bricks of the tower, clearly relieved but not about to make a big deal of it. He probably recognized the black-eyed dog lurking around me the last couple months. Not that he'd really been close enough to see it. I'd made sure of that.

I thought maybe Logan would come on strong after—but he didn't. I felt him watching me in class, but he'd probably say he was watching *out* for me, just like Mary was.

"If I'd known it was your birthday I would have—"

Known it was Nick's birthday too. Oh God. Logan.

"You would have what? Baked me a cake? Didn't know you could cook. I gotta say, I can't see you in the kitchen."

"Ah—yeah, neither can I."

"So then . . . what were you going to say?"

"I was going to say . . . that I would have gotten you a book. One of those old pocket paperback novels, like the kind you always carry around, something you probably do because girls find it endearing. A boy with a book, you know?"

"I do not know. Endearing, huh? Your feelings are showing, Rush."

"I have no feelings." I manage to say this with a straight face and am rewarded with a burst of laughter from Logan.

"How do you know they're novels?" he asks. "How do you know they're not, like, astrophysics texts?"

"They're probably self-help books. If they're not, they should be."

"Such a pretty girl. Too bad she's so mean."

"Yeah, well, don't take this the wrong way, but you look good too." I pretend to examine him with a critical eye. "No scrapes and bruises."

"Yeah, but maybe you should check me over, you know?" He starts to slide his jacket off. His leather jacket, which doesn't look warm enough to begin with. I'm wearing a down coat. "Because no one's been keeping an eye on me since you retired to your ivory tower here—"

"Okay, okay—keep your clothes on. It's December."

"Is that the *only* reason you want me to keep my clothes on? Because—"

"Yes! I mean, no! Come on, put your jacket on! It's *winter*."

"Yeah, now it is. But you've been holed up here since—well—for a while."

The conversation stalls. We lean our heads back. Look up at the sky.

"What about the raves in Portland?" I say finally. "Where the fights break out. Have you—"

"Trying to quit. Bought a punching bag. Playing drums again. Just think, you'd already know all this late-breaking news if you ever hung out. Seriously, hibernating up here—"

"I am not hibernating. I'm—working. On music."

"Huh. You're working on music."

"I am."

"And I'm working on music."

"So you say. Practicing drums again."

"Kind of a cool coincidence, don't you think? That we're both musicians, that we have that in common?"

"Hmm . . . I guess. Especially since, you know, we don't have anything else in common."

Now he punches me in the arm. But lightly. "Let's jam sometime."

"Maybe."

"Come on, Rush. You've got a guitar. And I know you can sing."

I've been trying to match his tone, but as soon as he brings up singing, all I can think of is the real reason I've been isolating myself up here. "I'll let you know," I say, and look away.

"Hey, I'm sorry," Logan says, "about you and Bo." I glance at him. He grins. "Okay, not really," he says. "But I am sorry you've been hurting. Obviously you haven't wanted to talk, but if you change your mind . . ." He bows his head a little, his hair falling around his face, the smell of his minty shampoo reminding me of another life. "At your service."

"Yeah, no. I'm—" A mountain—an entire mountain range—fills my throat. "I'm good."

"O-kay . . . if you say so."

"I say so."

I just wish I could say more. But how can I? How can I tell him his brother was alive, just like he'd thought, but that now he's dead, for real, gone forever. Like Bo.

Bo. He's gone forever from this place . . . But not from my thoughts. And neither has Nick, who's left me with one last question.

"Logan?"

"Yeah?"

"Well . . . I don't mean to, you know, bring it up, but . . ."

"It's up. Go for it, Airyhead."

"No, it's nothing, I just—how come you never told me Nick was your twin?"

Logan is instantly alert. He doesn't move a muscle, but something in his eyes—a sudden silvery light there—reveals the change, a change that, along with the sterling gleam, reminds me—for one or two pulsing seconds—of his brother.

"Nick," he says, and I realize that he's echoing me, repeating what I've said in order to draw my attention to it. I've called Nick by his name, as if I know him. As if he's familiar to me. I didn't say, "your brother," which is what I should have said, which is what I *would* have said—before. Before I knew Nick.

My breathing becomes shallow as Logan continues to study me: my face, my eyes. He's looking for clues. He's suspicious. He has every right to be.

But. Nothing I can tell him will make things better.

I set my jaw, determined to remain silent.

Until the light in his eyes dims, and I'm reminded—as I so often am when I look into Logan's eyes—of clouds, and rainy days.

"Logan, I'm so sorry!" My voice breaks a little. "I'm sorry, I knew I shouldn't have brought it up. I—I don't even know why I was thinking of him."

But this last line? It's a throwaway. It's me scrambling to make things better but slipping up instead. It's me lying. Because I do know why I was thinking of Nick. It's because I always think of him—not always, but every day. I think of all of them every day. Every time I catch a movement out of the corner of my eye—a seagull soaring through my peripheral vision, a pine bough bending in the wind—I think of Nick, and of Bo, and of Jordan. I think of my sister. I think of all the Sirens every day, and I worry, and I *wait*.

Maybe Logan senses how upset I am, not that he knows all the reasons, because now, although he doesn't quite release me from his suspicious gaze, he runs a hand along his jaw, along the blue shadow of stubble there, and says, "It's okay. I guess I figured you knew."

"You—you figured I knew what?"

My heart thumps almost painfully. Logan narrows his eyes just a little.

But all he says is, "I figured you knew that we were twins. Everyone—" He shrugs. "Everyone around here does."

My heart slows. I want to apologize again, to say something, anything, to make up for my stupidity.

I'm never going to bring up his brother again, ever. Nick Delaine is dead, and he needs to stay that way. He needs to be dead to me. And especially to Logan.

Who stretches now—like he wants to literally reach outside this moment, reach for something different, maybe even just a different conversation.

And then he does.

"Don't know if you saw this or not." He digs a crumpled piece of newspaper out of one of his pants pockets and offers it to me. "Came out today. Thought you might find it interesting."

"Thanks." I scan the headline. Interesting doesn't begin to cover it.

The Rock Hook Herald, Thursday, December 22

Rock Hook National Seashore Opening Delayed

By James Tabir

The superstorm of October 10 was a turning point in local history for Rock Hook Harbor residents. Due to record-breaking high tides at the time of the storm, the waters of Wabanaki Bay rose to unprecedented levels, destroying the land bridge that supported the narrow causeway connecting Rock Hook Peninsula to the mainland.

National disaster funds, still being allocated since the storm, continue to meet residents' immediate

> needs and provided financing for the fleet of motorboats and water taxis that currently serve as a means for locals to cross the bay and attend to business concerns on the mainland.
>
> Emergency funding continues to flow into Rock Hook Harbor's downtown area and marina. However, the latest word from Washington is that monies will not be made available to assist with the opening of the new national park slated for this July.
>
> Mayor Chase Waller—who has rejected bids for a bridge to span the bay, stating that they are simply too expensive—is in final negotiations with Overwave Ferry and held a press conference yesterday in Bangor, where he told reporters, "I don't have time for broken promises. If Washington wants to hold back funds and delay the opening of Rock Hook National Seashore indefinitely, that means losing local jobs and income for the island—"

The island.

This part of the story isn't news to me, of course, but the fact that Rock Hook Peninsula is actually an island now still amazes me, even nearly three months after its transformation.

Cord had been right. My pet peeve has been taken care of—in a big way—and for the present, the wild land surrounding the lighthouse will remain what it's always been: the coast of Maine's best-kept secret.

In my mind I give a nod to Neptune, which makes me think of Bo . . . Lilah is part of his family now, or maybe they're part of ours. Either way—the thought makes me nervous.

Logan and I talk about the article, then run out of words. The silence feels awkward. I need to change that, need to reach out to him, the way he reached out to me, by coming over.

"Hang on, I've got to get something."

When I return, Logan's lying on his back. He grabs at my ankle—then, seeing I have my guitar, quickly sits up. "You're going to play for me?"

Nodding, I sit down cross-legged and start moving my fingers over the frets, warming up my cold hands. Then I begin to play a chord progression that found me late one night, and start to sing . . .

"It's a little push-pull,

It's a battle of our wills.

You will want and want more,

Like water washing on the shore."

To my surprise, Logan starts to hum, his voice slightly husky, harmonizing with the second verse. Next comes the chorus. He goes still.

"It felt like we were making love,

It felt like you were in my blood,

Like there was something we both understood . . .

And oh, how I wish, that we could stay like this. First kiss . . ."

"That," Logan says when I finish, "is a great song."

"Really? I mean, you think so?"

"Yeah." After biting his lip for a moment, he says, "You wrote that for him, didn't you."

I shut my eyes. The sound of the surf down below is surprisingly soft. "I did. I wrote it for him, but . . ." Eyes still closed, I form a series of chords with my left hand, the fingertips of my right hand plucking the strings almost anxiously. I let myself explore a little longer, until finally, my left hand finds a chord I don't recognize.

Resting the palm of my right hand flat on the strings, I damp the echo of the unknown chord, and open my eyes.

"I wrote it for him. But I played it for you."

"I'm glad," Logan says, in the same gentle voice he used a minute ago when he was singing with me. "Play it again, will you?"

So I play "1st Kiss" again, and this time, the wind takes my words—scattering them out over the shining sea . . .

When I finish, we both sit back against the bricks of the lighthouse. The silence isn't awkward now. It's an invisible connective tissue between us, the same way the music was just a moment ago. The music . . . maybe you never really know who you're writing it for.

BLUE HOUR

The blue hour comes and goes while Logan and I lie daydreaming on the deck.

It's like the conversation has been keeping us warm, but now we're finally talked out, and I'm starting to feel the cold.

"I'm hungry," I say, rolling onto my side.

"And what, may I ask"—he rolls onto his side too now, facing me, his hand brushing my hand—"are you hungry for?"

"Delaine, where do you get your material?"

"My beautiful mind." He props himself on an elbow and leans over me, grinning.

"Well, maybe you and your beautiful mind would like to stay for dinner? Dinner, as in, you know, something with actual calories. Don't worry, my dad's home. He'll cook."

Logan laughs and stands up, then reaches down and pulls me to my feet. But once I'm standing he doesn't release me, and we both just stay, close together, grinning at each other.

One Saturday morning when I was a little kid, Dad asked if I wanted to go to the hardware store with him, something we'd done together on weekends for as long as I could remember. For the first time ever, I said, "No thanks." For whatever reason, I wanted to stay home.

Dad smiled and turned to go, saying, "Okay, see you soon. Love you."

"Love you more," I sang out.

"Not possible," he said. "Love runs downhill."

At the time, I hadn't known what he meant, and for years, I pictured love as this thing that goes running around, making people kiss, maybe giving out chocolate hearts on Valentine's Day. I used to imagine it, running up and down the hills of our San Francisco neighborhood, the ones that, despite Mom's warnings, I ran up and down too, full tilt.

When I was bigger, I started jogging on those same super steep streets. Whenever I ran up a hill, I went for it. But on the way down, afraid of hitting the bottom of one of those precipitous slopes running flat out—and maybe winding up in the middle of an intersection, or with a popped kneecap—I always held back.

Now, looking into Logan's eyes, I remember that feeling, of running full tilt.

Logan. He's a mere mortal, but he has his own extraordinary Song. And I want to hear it. Surely he wouldn't blame me for keeping a handful of secrets—secrets that aren't mine to tell?

Keeping a couple of secrets can hardly be considered holding back. And doesn't he have some of his own?

Besides, what's the point of telling him everything now?

I become aware that the thumb and index finger of my right hand have found the pearl on its sterling chain, that I'm rolling it between them. I let the black pearl go—

Just as Logan reaches for my hand.

His fingers are warm as they interlace with mine. Warm, not hot. Not scalding. Not—dangerous. *I could kiss him,* I think. *I could kiss him right now.* He'd kiss me back; I know he would.

We wouldn't have to stop.

My stomach dips—

And I contemplate the possibility that, maybe, I'm ready to join him—Logan, and the thing called love—running downhill. But I need to be sure. Because Logan is definitely a no-stops kind of guy.

"Good thing I came over, huh?"

"I guess," I say lightly.

He laughs. "Rush. You're so full of it." Then he turns away, leaning on the railing while I fold up the blanket. I took my guitar back inside quite a while ago, took it down to my room. Now I imagine taking Logan down there too. He's never been in my bedroom. Again, I picture kissing him—

Suddenly his shoulders stiffen.

"What the— Someone's up on Rock Hook Cliff." He grabs the binoculars off the deck. "Oh man—they're stepping over the fence!"

I hurry to his side. "Let me see."

Logan hands me the binoculars and I spin the wheel in a futile effort to bring the shadowy figure at the edge of the cliff into focus.

My stomach twists—

The figure jumps.

"We have to do something!" Logan shouts.

Mesmerized, I watch helplessly as the jumper appears to wrestle with the air, struggling, until finally the falling figure's head is pointing down, moving fast toward the sea.

A brilliant flash of white cuts the sky—

Enormous wings burst from the back of the falling body.

I scream, stumbling away from the railing, tripping over nothing—

Logan catches me, holds me close with one arm as he takes the binoculars and raises them to his eyes—

"You've got to see this!"

He shoves the binoculars back into my hands, and I look—

The wings appear to have extended to their full span, sweeping the figure high into the sky. I can just discern a pair of shadowy arms, reaching toward the heavens.

Then once more the figure changes direction, easily now, diving headfirst toward the water.

With the wings folded tightly back, the body becomes a blade, slicing through the dark waves—

Before disappearing into the deep.

ACKNOWLEDGMENTS

I'd like to thank:

Danielle Burby, my incredible agent. Arion may not know who she writes for, but I do. Josh Getzler and everyone at HSG Agency. Miriam Juskowicz for making my dreams come true. Robin Benjamin for brilliant editing. Swear you have a photographic memory! Kim Cowser and Katie Kurtzman for always-available-no-question-is-too-small support. See you at the shrine of Saint Stevie! Courtney Miller, I'll see you there too. Please bring the rest of the amazing Skyscape team: Britt Rogers, Ben Smith, Jeffrey Belle, Hai-Yen Mura, and Mikyla Bruder. Michelle Hope Anderson, Karen Upson, and Jessica Gardner—Oh, the details! TY. Writer Charlotte Agell—can you believe it? See you in Maine. Writers Heather Lennon, Natalie Zaman, Tara Kelly, Suzy Ismail, Annie Silvestro, Suzanne Heyd, Jennifer Haase, Christine Brower-Cohen, Jamie Sussell Turner, Barbara Blaisdell, and Robert Burke Warren, who were all early readers of at least a portion of this book if not the entire thing multiple times over. Patti Witten for Obvious. (Better late than never!) The agents and editors I've connected with online and through SCBWI. You know who you are, and I hope you know how much you helped me grow as a writer. Thank you for your open doors and expert eyes. Sarah Davies, remember that one package? Holly McGhee, I'm so glad I met you when I did. Emma Dryden, for the editing experience that prepared me for all others, and for your kindness, intuition, and friendship. Emily Winslow Stark for encouragement, Skype chats, and laughter. I'm so glad you were with me on the roller coaster! Mary McDonald for praising my writing efforts for so long. R. Star Aufderhar for nautical research. (And for making me understand that Logan had to drive a beat-up white pickup truck.) Stacy Dahling Smith, for being the best listener I know. Life coach Magdalena Sabatino for holding the light when I couldn't. The crew at River Road Books, especially Karen Rumage, Laurie Potter, and Kim Robinson; you guys are bartenders sans alcohol. Thanks for letting me pretend I work there. Kim—thanks for the spiritual guidance. Kamil Vojnar, for allowing me to use the gorgeous piece, "Man With Angel Wings," as the face of Sirenstories. Rosanne Cash and the Redroomers. What can I say? Reunion. Now. The YA community and the other writers I've connected with on Twitter, you were there when I needed you, TY. Kripalu Center for Yoga and Health, my home away from home. Steve Meltzer for the laughs, and for reminding me more than once that Arion is a smart girl. You're a Jersey Boy now, and I'm glad. Kathy Connolly-Oliver, for the seahorse. Shasti O'Leary Soudant for the *beautiful* book covers.

Lastly and most importantly: Charles, for bringing Arion to my attention. You have magic in you, and kindness. You are the love of my life, and my continual inspiration. U R the Best. <3

When I write, I listen to music. Here is a partial list of bands that inspired me while I was working on *Shining Sea*: The xx, PJ Harvey, Jai Uttal, David Cook, Linkin Park, David Greenwood, Carter Burwell, Marcello Zarvos, Muse, PT Walkley, Ron Haney/The Churchills, the singer-songwriters and composers who contributed to sirenstories.com—especially Proofsound and Face The King—and Pete Yorn, whose music made my isolation that much more splendid.

For information on the *real* Clean Ocean Zone, please visit www.cleanoceanzone.org.